BLACK PARK

Ricki Thomas

A Wild Wolf Publication

Published by Wild Wolf Publishing in 2013
This second edition published by Wild Wolf Publishing in 2016
Copyright © 2013 Ricki Thomas

Second print.

ISBN: 978-1-907954-34-4
Also available in E-Book Format

www.wildwolfpublishing.com

Also by Ricki Thomas

Hope's Vengeance
Unlikely Killer
Bloody Mary
Holiday of the Dead (contributor)
Bonfire Night
Wild Wolf's Twisted Tails (contributor)
Rings of Death
Deadly Angels

For my children and Mum, as always, with love

Chapter 1
Black Park: September 2003

It was the final week of the school summer holiday and the Fowlers had risked the changeable weather to bring a picnic to a beautifully peaceful and popular nature reserve. They were lucky; the sun streamed through the branches of the abundant trees that surrounded the clearing, the threatening clouds long gone.

Dan and Carol relaxed, watching their three children dart from one imagined adventure to another. "Careful on that tree, Toni." Carol had reluctantly accepted over the past ten years that her first-borne was never going to be the girlie-girl she had wanted, rebuking pinks and shunning dolls to play with pretend swords and guns instead. She sighed as her words went unheeded.

"She'll be fine, love." Dan patted her hand with half-hearted reassurance before lying back to soak in the blissful warmth, closing his eyes.

Toni huffed, waiting for her mother to turn away so she could continue investigating the long-time dead yew tree. The wizened trunk was vastly bigger than her arm span, but that only made it more tempting. Using a ladder of small branches, some no bigger than twigs, and the many nicks in the bark, she hoisted herself up to sit on the first substantial branch. Her younger brother stood jealously below.

"Oh, wow, there's a hole going right inside the tree." Toni scrambled to her feet.

Carol rolled her eyes. "Don't you dare go inside, young lady."

Her warning drifted with the breeze as Toni examined the opening, intrigued by the blackness, mysterious and inviting. Keeping one eye on her mother, she inched as slowly as her enthusiasm would allow towards the hole and waited for what seemed like hours until Carol was distracted by her toddling sister. With a flash of courage mixed with fear, she let go of the branch and jumped down.

And screamed. A shrill, sickening scream.

It was the most unbelievable and intoxicating day of Toni's short life. Not only had she had her favourite tuna and cucumber sandwiches followed by jam doughnuts, all bought from a supermarket on the way, but she had found the rotting body of a human baby inside a tree. She was scared to blink in case it all disappeared and turned out to be another of her dramatic daydreams.

Three hours had passed since her frantic yelling had alerted the world to the macabre discovery, and as soon as the police had arrived, they had wrapped her in a grey blanket. She had no idea why, but realised she was being treated specially because she was the only person, bar the kind policewoman who was holding her hand, who had been given a folding chair to sit on.

Pam had asked Toni several times to repeat the order of events, scribbling notes on her small pad, and when she rephrased the question again, Toni couldn't restrain the bored sigh and impudent roll of her eyes. "I've already told you, why do you keep asking me the same things?" She turned to watch a fire engine trundling along the dirt-path towards them and her sense of awe returned. "What's that for?"

Pam surveyed the clearing, the crime-scene tape that circled the gnarled tree, white-suited forensic scientists and officers examining for evidence. The fire engine bumped alongside the emergency vehicles and stopped, and seven eager firemen hopped from the cab. "I think they need to cut off the top of the tree so they can get the body out. It wasn't a problem for you to slip through the hole, you're just a little thing, but us grown-ups won't fit."

Confusion tinged with sadness clouded Toni's face and, with childish logic, she gasped. "It's probably been there a hundred years. Why do you have to cut it down? If you want I can go back in and get little Jane, I won't mind."

8

"Jane?" Pam scribbled the name below her notes.

"That's what I've called her. I know I was shocked when I saw her, I don't think I've ever screamed so hard, but I've got used to it now."

"What makes you think the baby is a girl?"

Her hands splayed, palms up, and her tone was incredulous. "Because she's wearing a dress, of course."

Carol strode towards them. "I was wondering if you've finished with Toni yet? It's just it's gone dinner time and Maisie's fretting. She's already had three doughnuts and, well, it's not good for her."

"I want to stay and watch the firemen cut the tree. Please, Mum, I'm not hungry anyway. Please can I stay?" The fluttering eyelashes reminded Carol that her daughter did have a feminine side, despite its rare appearance. She looked to the policewoman for an answer.

"It's probably best if you go home with your mum and dad now, I can come and see you tomorrow and let you know how it all went."

Toni was beside herself. She sprung to her feet, a frustrated tantrum brewing. "But I found Jane, I want to see what happens to her. You wouldn't even know about her if it hadn't been for me. Please, I'm really interested in what's happening, in fact I'm going to be a police lady when I grow up." Carol and Pam shared an amused glance.

"Children," Carol sighed, "I suppose I don't mind if you don't." Toni's eyes shone, imploring Pam with an impish smile and praying hands.

"I can give her lift home later if you like, as long as she keeps out of trouble while she's here." Carol nodded and returned to her husband's side, where he was struggling to control hungry Maisie's flailing body in his arms. She called to her son and, relieved, they took the path towards the public car park.

Recovering the body was an arduous and lengthy task, and those waiting on the side-lines to finally meet the dead child struggled to hide their boredom as the firefighters carefully removed the colossal head of the tree, guided safely by a tree surgeon who had been brought in to help. Word had already spread about the discovery, excitable day-trippers having left the incredible scene and quickly started the rumour mill grinding.

DI Thirsk, acting head of the investigation in his superior's absence, gazed at the helicopter that circled the scene, a nosy photographer snapping away. "Can't you get rid of that thing?"

"I'll try." The constable issued the request into his radio, and Thirsk sighed, tired, hungry and eager to slip onto his recliner chair at home with a single malt. Irritable, he turned to the little girl, who clung to Pam's hand. He hated children with a passion and had no understanding of either maternal or paternal tendencies. It was clear the young constable was broody, whatever that meant, and he wondered how long it would be until he lost her to motherhood, like all the females did in the end. Well, most, anyway. "When are you getting the kid back its rightful owners?"

Pam smiled at Toni with pride. Four hours had passed since her parents had left and she had expected the youngster to be drooping by now, but Toni remained riveted and alert. She had keenly watched the events, absorbing every scrap of information she had been given. "Toni, have you had enough yet? It must be past your bedtime by now."

"Oh, please let me stay just long enough to meet Jane again. I want to see her in the light, see what she looks like properly."

Pam eyed the darkening sky, the dregs of the sun teetering, streaked with pinks and oranges, over the distant trees on the horizon. "Sweetheart," Thirsk's stomach clenched at the sugary nickname, "there's not much light left to see the body in. And it's probably going to look quite horrid, too. Really, I should be getting you home."

"Please." Toni couldn't go, not yet. She had to see Jane. She *needed* the baby firmly in her memory, despite not understanding why. She stared at the firemen, ropes firmly controlling every movement of the top half of the yew, guiding it aside to reveal its grisly contents. "They've got most of the top part of the tree off already, surely they'll be bringing Jane out any minute?"

"Half an hour, okay." Pam glanced at Thirsk. His dislike of any person below the age of twenty was legendary on the force and she knew she was pushing him. He sneered at her with distaste and strolled towards the stump, repulsion replaced with intrigue. A forensic photographer clicked every angle of the scene, documenting the moment that would seem to have never existed by the next morning. She moved aside, nodding that her work was done, and Thirsk eagerly stepped forward.

The body was tiny and in an advanced state of decomposition, probably exacerbated by the recent erratic weather, and the rotting smell was cloying. It lay in an unnatural position, bent with the head back and mouth wide. A distinctive Broderie Anglaise petticoat dress clung to the scant remains of taut, dry skin, and wispy, silken hair tufted the scalp. Thirsk felt no emotion towards the figure, it was a dead body and he had seen plenty of them, large and small. All that interested him was the cause of death, because that would determine whether they were looking for a murderer, or a confused, and possibly mentally unstable, parent who had flipped on finding their baby dead and dumped the body, probably from fear of their negligence being discovered. He glanced at the time-served pathologist who eagerly surveyed the infant. "Any thoughts, Bernard?"

"Well, judging by the size, it's probably a new born, and an educated guesstimate from the flesh that hasn't been devoured by bugs and beetles, I'd say it's roughly two to three months dead. Obviously, I've no idea of the sex, the dress could be a red herring."

Too quickly for Pam to stop her, Toni darted from the chair and scampered to the stump, throwing herself to the edge to see what she expected was a cute and cuddly baby, a beautiful doll. The reality brought bile to her mouth and immediately she retched. Thirsk pushed her aside, angry. "Get that bloody brat out of here. Get it out." Pam, close behind, grasped Toni's heaving shoulders and led her aside, where the ten-year old wrapped her skinny arms around her neck, clinging. Sobs racked her body, tears and mucous streaming. Pam hugged her tightly, desperately wishing her reaction had been faster, as the traumatic image would undoubtedly stay with the child for life. Thirsk, furious, looked on with repugnance. "Get it away from here, MacAllister. Now."

Pam took Toni's small hand in her own and led her away from the horror. "Come on, sweetheart, let's get you home."

The school term was about to begin, but that made no difference to Julia Collins. She hadn't attended since before Christmas the previous year. Her parents had received countless reminders of her truancy, gradually becoming threatening, but they neither cared, nor heeded. Julia hadn't been planned, which had been hammered into her so often, verbally and physically, that she no longer cared about her parents, her education, or herself. Social Services had been involved with the family regularly over the years, but the antagonism towards them from her parents, and her mother's insistence that Julia was loved and cared for, and was simply a drama queen, had led to their visits tailing off.

It was her thirteenth birthday, yet there were no cards or presents, no cake or party. She viewed the day as another painful reminder of how many years she had tolerated the abuse at home. But each year, as she grew from a small and trusting child to a budding woman, she understood a little more that the way she was treated was wrong. A sad figure, she scuffed aimlessly through the council estate, a familiar, solitary figure haunting the streets. Today, as every day, she felt she didn't exist.

She had stolen a pound from her mother's handbag first thing and took it to the corner shop to spend on crisps and chocolate, but the headline on the local newspaper caught her eye and she stooped to read the article. She replaced the junk food on the shelf and bought the paper, folding it under her arm. It was the last straw.

Now she had a purpose in life, and returning home wasn't part of the plan. She marched briskly to the bus stop and caught the twenty-two into town, winding her way towards the offices she had never been to. "I want to see Janet Dremill."

Janet had tried her best the previous autumn to help both Julia and her parents, but they had made it hard for her and, overworked, she had eventually given up with the family. So Julia's arrival surprised her. She took her to an empty room and offered her a drink, which the girl refused. "So why are you here, is everything okay?"

"I ain't going home again, and I'm not budging from here until you put me in a kid's home or something."

"Julia, we can't do that, it's not that simple. How about you start seeing me again, once a week, or maybe twice, if you'd like? We don't have to meet at home if you don't want to, we can meet at school or…"

"You ain't listening to me. If you send me back there I will kill myself." She lifted her sleeve and Janet gasped at the raw, scabbed cuts that had been self-inflicted. "I mean it."

Chapter 2
Ten Years Later

"Hi, I'm home." Toni slammed the door behind her and hung her cap and jacket on a hook. She breathed deeply, savouring the delicious aroma that floated through the air. "Dinner smells great, what is it?"

Carol moved the crossword to one side and checked the pan of potatoes that simmered on the hob. "Mince and mash today, with cabbage. Are you hungry?"

Toni exaggerated a shrug with a sly smile. "It's me you're talking to, of course I'm starving. As always."

"It'll be another ten minutes, but I want to have a word with you first. It's just, I was in your room earlier, you know, collecting your washing, and, well…" Her words petered out; she shouldn't have been in the room without permission.

"For god's sake, what does it take to get a bit of privacy around here?" Way past adolescence, she was too old to be throwing a wobbly, but she could feel one brewing anyway.

Carol grasped Toni's shoulder and guided her to a seat. "Don't go off on one, I didn't have to say anything."

"But you did, so?"

She laid a hand on her daughter's arm, her tanned skin contrasting with the crisp whiteness of Toni's shirt. "I saw your, well, your, er – collection. In the wardrobe."

Toni stood abruptly, the invasion into her private world intolerable. "Then you weren't looking for dirty clothes, were you? You were snooping. I've fucking had enough of this. If it isn't you, it's Leon or Maisie going through my stuff. The only person around here who has any respect for my privacy is Dad. Fuck dinner, I'm going out."

Carol grabbed her daughter, shocked by the extreme reaction. "Toni, you're going nowhere. And stop swearing, Maisie's only thirteen, she doesn't need to hear that."

Defiant, Toni glared at her mother. "Fuck you."

Usually mild-tempered and patient, Carol's cheeks burned with anger. "Toni, I'm worried about you." She hadn't meant to shout. The house fell silent as the rest of the family stopped what they were doing to listen to the altercation.

"There is nothing to worry about, and what I do in my private life is down to me. It's none of your business." She glared for a second, challenging a retort, before storming from the room.

Carol thumped the table, frustrated. "It's become an obsession; it's got to stop. For your sanity."

"Fuck you." The door slammed.

Pam MacAllister, her fourth daughter clinging to her hip, dried her free hand and rushed to the door, and was unsettled to find Toni on the doorstep, still in uniform and clearly aggravated. "Come on in, hun, I'm up to my eyes in dinner and god knows what, so you'll have to talk around me working."

Toni followed her unlikely friend through the chaotic living room, toys and clothes strewn over every surface, with three youngsters jerkily dancing to the pop songs that blared from the television. On reaching the equally disorganised kitchen, she automatically began to set the table for dinner, the house a second home for nearly ten years since she had struck up a seemingly lifelong friendship with the policewoman who had cared for her on the most pivotal day of her life. "I don't suppose you've got room for one more? I've fallen out with Mum again and can't bear the thought of going back tonight. Pam, I've got to leave home, I can't stand it any longer, I swear."

Setting the infant in a well-worn highchair, re-used and abused over the years, Pam placed several plates of varying sizes according to the age of the recipient on the cluttered side and dished out some steaming rice. "You know you're always welcome to dinner, sweetheart. Do me a favour, though, feed the baby while I do this." She ladled a tiny portion of stew onto the rice in a plastic bowl gave it to Toni, who stirred it. "So, what's happened?"

"She's been going through my room, sneaking through my wardrobe this time."

"She's a right old busybody, your mother." She winked, cheeky and knowing. "Found your toys, has she?"

Toni could see the innuendo, but it failed to raise a smile. "Don't be daft. As if."

"Kids. Colin. Dinner. Aunty Toni's joining us."

The three dancers hurtled into the room, climbing onto chairs to await their food, and Colin followed lethargically, brushing a kiss on Toni's forehead as he passed. "Again? You may as well live with us, you're here so often."

"I wish." She truly did; if only it had been a serious offer, but with four children in the poky, modern rabbit hutch, Toni understood there wasn't room. They settled at the table and Toni fed the baby to give Pam enough time to eat her meal in peace. In between scraping gravy and spit covered rice from the child's mouth and chin, Toni managed a few mouthfuls. "I mean it though, this time. I'm twenty and still sharing a bedroom with my kid sister."

"What is she now? Thirteen? Fourteen?"

"Thirteen. I'm too old for this, I need my own space."

Pam smiled at her husband. "Have you got any small flats going at the moment, Col?"

He shovelled a huge forkful through his raven beard, washing it down with a sip of water. "In fact, yes. An unusual place came in a few days ago that would suit your personality down to the ground. It's not very big, but it's clean and full of character."

"Just like Toni." Pam quipped, taking the familiar conversation light-heartedly.

Another mouthful disappeared behind the bush of black whiskers. "It's part of the old abbey, a developer recently converted the building into flats and they did a great job. They're nice places, all of them, just right for a single person, or young couples without a family. The rent's fairly reasonable too."

"How soon can I move in?" Pam laughed, but Toni's question was genuine.

Dan cleared the plates from the table and tipped the scraps into the composter. His daily task was to wash the dishes, giving Carol time to have a bath, following each tedious day in the job she detested. But tonight she followed him to the kitchen and armed herself with a tea towel. "We need to talk."

The dreaded words sent Dan into a panic, wondering what he had done wrong. He rinsed the plates, keeping his eyes down to avoid fuelling his wife's wrath.

"I'm guessing you heard Toni go off the wall earlier?" She placed the milk and margarine in the fridge, busying herself until there were clean dishes on the draining board for her to dry.

"Perhaps the whole street did. It was pretty loud."

"Yeah, well you could have stood up for me when she was effing and blinding, no mother should have to put up with that sort of language directed at them."

The realisation of his wrongdoing relaxed him, all he needed to do was listen to her moan for a while, offer some sympathy and a hug, and the rest of his evening would be free to potter in his greenhouse. "What was it all over this time?"

Carol reached past Dan and turned the tap off, and she took his hand, frowning above her spectacles. "I think you need to see something."

He followed her tentatively up the staircase, and when they reached the bedroom their daughters shared, he waited as she knocked. "Maisie, can you come out for a minute, I need to show your dad something in there. In private."

A deep huff, bored and rebellious, rang from the room, followed by a lazy shuffling, and the door opened wide. Maisie stood with a hand on her hip, head cocked to the side impudently. "I know you know I'm on the pill, but it's none of your business and the doctor gave me them because I have

17

heavy periods. Lecture me now, I'll give you three minutes, and then I can get on with what I was doing before you bothered me."

Dan and Carol's eyes met, stunned yet humoured, and he restrained a smile. He had no idea what he had been led to the room for, but he was sure a discussion about his youngest using contraception wasn't on the cards. "It's not about you, Maisie, it's about your sister. Now, please can you leave the room for a minute like I asked." Answered by an indignant glare, Carol reluctantly realised that Maisie had no intention of missing out. "For heaven's sake." She unlocked the wardrobe door using the copy of the key she had found recently, having whisked it to the key-cutter to have it duplicated before Toni returned from work. She knew she shouldn't have, but her maternal instinct had told her that Toni was hiding something. She lifted a cardboard box down and opened the flaps, taking a small, tatty scrapbook from inside. She flipped through the copious newspaper cuttings glued to the pages. "It's all about that dead baby."

Dan shook his head, relieved. "Is that all?"

Julia knocked and huddled against the wall, sheltering as best she could from the rain that pelted against the peeling paintwork of the door. It opened a crack and an unfriendly man grunted miserably. He didn't like her, she knew that, but she didn't care – she just needed her stuff. "Have you got some?"

"How much?"

Julia fiddled with the crisp note in her pocket; her income support had been paid into her account that morning. "Twenty, this time."

The door closed and she waited, her worn hoodie soaking up the downfall and clinging to her skin. A couple of minutes passed slowly, the gloominess of the threatening clouds depressing her, and finally the door creaked again. He took the money and relinquished the tiny plastic bag of cannabis. Pushing the buggy that held her sodden toddler,

Julia headed for the corner shop to buy half an ounce of tobacco and a bottle of Lambrini. She only misbehaved every other week when the money came in, but she lived for those nights. There was nothing else in her life.

Bumping the pushchair up three flights of stairs was arduous, but she had no choice as the lift had been vandalised again. Julia had been allocated the two-bedroom flat the year before, having spent a ridiculous amount of time in a bed-sit while her application for housing slowly clambered up the waiting list, and she relished having her own private space. A place where she could close the windows, shut the curtains, lock the doors. A place where she could pretend the rest of the world didn't exist. Relieved to be home, she left Antony in his seat while she rolled a joint and poured a glass of warm perry. Leaving them on the grimy worktop – a treat to look forward to once she had put the child to bed – she rustled up some value baked beans on toast for her son's dinner.

It was only five in the afternoon when she finished feeding him, but Julia couldn't wait any longer for her fortnightly indulgence, and she tucked Antony under his Thomas the Tank Engine covers, bought from the back of a lorry the previous Christmas as his main present. She barely spoke to the child, saving her breath for the odd command or instruction. She had deliberately fallen pregnant to secure a home, but that was as far as the longing for a baby had gone. She could never let herself get too close to him, the vulnerability would crucify her. "Sleep now." There was no kiss, no cuddle, no affectionate stroke of his pale cheek. She switched the lamp off and shut the door behind her. The first sip of her drink, the first lingering drag on the joint. Julia sighed with bliss and sank into her corner of the sofa.

She switched the television on, mindlessly flicking through the channels until she found a reality programme that relieved the boredom of her lonely existence once a week, and was beginning to relax when a noise came from the hall. Intrigued, she peered through and noticed an envelope on the floor. Collecting it, she returned to the sofa and tore open the flap, retrieving the page from inside. She scanned the message, once, twice, and after the third time she ran to the bathroom to be sick, retching first, then scrubbing her hands, again and again.

He had found her.

She had escaped, she had disappeared. She had covered her tracks. But he had found her.

The Lambrini and weed had never been so necessary.

"You see, that's the beauty of owning your own business; you can break the rules." Colin dangled a set of keys, a fluorescent tag indicating the flat number, from his fingers as he strode towards the arched entrance to the old monastery. The brickwork was a mottle of grey and charcoal, the ancient stone two feet thick, and monstrous gargoyles sat along the eaves keeping guard against evil spirits and trespassers. Toni gasped in awe at the unusual building, so full of character. So protective. In her heart she already knew it was hers.

Colin prodded a security code onto the keypad by the double doors and they entered the neutrally decorated foyer. He bounded up the stairs, two at a time, leaving Toni trotting to keep up. "There are seven left but…"

"Out of how many?"

"Thirteen. All one beds. But the one I want to show you is unique."

Colin and Pam were the most wonderful friends. They knew her intricately, the way her obscure mind worked and obsessed, and they treated her with the respect of an adult, yet with the care of a child. If Colin thought she was going to love the flat, she knew she would. The main staircase ended with a long, airy corridor and Toni followed her friend patiently. Once they reached the end, he led her through a small door to a slim, uncarpeted staircase that was steeper than it was long, the windowless walls shrouded in darkness.

At the top was a tiny landing, barely big enough for two people, especially when one was as broad and tall as Colin. He hunched as he fed the key into the cast iron lock, ducking in anticipation of the low entrance, and guided Toni inside. "There's no electric on, I'm afraid. I told the developer it was short-sighted, but they didn't want any more expense. Tight as anything, they are, and they're making a bob or two, but I can't deny they did a tremendous job of the apartments."

From the square hallway behind the solid oak door, treated woodworm holes confirming its authenticity as an original, there were four further doors, each painted a crisp white that was grey in the darkness. Toni opened the one to the left and a slight glow of moonlight, obscured to a haze by the dense clouds that threatened more showers, showed her everything she needed to know: she was about to leave home, and this was where she was going to live.

It didn't take long to inspect the modest flat, but the failing light showed enough of the four rooms for Toni to fall in love with it. The Gothic arched windows, intricately detailed inside and out, gave the rooms a menacing air, and the rough plaster of the newly emulsioned walls was a tasteful feature that complimented the building. "Colin, why didn't you tell me about this place earlier?"

He grinned affectionately. "You like it?"

"I absolutely adore it. It's amazing. Perfect."

"Thing is, I know you don't earn much yet, so I'm prepared to waiver the management fee for a couple of years while you get on your feet."

Toni laid a hand on his sleeve, her expression warm but firm. "I appreciate that, Colin, I really do, but I pay my own way in life, so thanks for the offer, but no thanks."

Chapter 3
Breaking Families

The atmosphere at the breakfast table was as drab as the weather. The heavy rain dashed the window, tapping and dripping incessantly, a gloomy background to start the day. It was the end of the financial month so Dan was working long hours and had left the house an hour before Carol had risen. She boiled the kettle – her appetite, as usual, scarce before noon – and nursed a strong tea at the table, hoping to see her eldest before she left for work. Five minutes before her mother was due to leave for her factory job, Toni thundered down the stairs and, desperate to clear the air, Carol was relieved.

"Mum." Her tone was frosty, reminding Carol how stubborn her first-borne could be.

"It's like that still, is it?"

Toni re-boiled the kettle, throwing a herbal teabag into a mug. "I'm moving out. I went to see a place last night and I paid a deposit."

Carol was choked and time stood still. Was her daughter's fixation with the horrifying events over a decade before really strong enough to break up their family? "You are willing to leave home because I think your obsession is unhealthy?" Incredulous. "I just don't believe this, Toni, I just don't believe you. Selfish, that's what you are."

Unconcerned, Toni dropped two pieces of bread into the toaster and removed the teabag from her mug. "I'm not interested in an argument, that's one of the reasons I'm leaving; I just want a quiet life. Some privacy."

"You're leaving because I challenged you about that ridiculous collection of newspaper cuttings you've hoarded over the years." Carol was pacing, a habit when her uncommon anger surfaced.

Toni turned and caught her mother's eye, resolute. "I'm leaving because I'm twenty years old and need a bedroom of my own, a cupboard I can lock and know will stay locked, and an atmosphere around the house that isn't like a nursery full of miserable, sulky children."

"And what's that supposed to mean?"

"You know what," Toni pushed the cancel button on the toaster and hoisted her backpack to her shoulder, "fuck breakfast, fuck this place. Fuck you. I suggest we don't talk until I've gone."

"We can talk tonight."

"No, I meant until I've taken my stuff and moved out. Don't hassle me any more, not if you want a relationship with me in the future." Toni slammed the door behind her, the sound ringing in Carol's ears. She sank onto the pine chair, head in hands, scraping her hair back in frustration. Wanting to cry, she was just too tired. Too weary.

Castle Street Police Station was an imposing building, the multi-coloured panels between the vast windows a reminder that the gaudy architecture was designed in the seventies. Toni had been working there for just under a year, having applied to join the force shortly before she had left university with her predicted above average grades. She had joined at the lowest rank, but was eager, and she was as determined as she was independent. One of the lucky few, her contracted hours were regular and overtime wasn't called for often, meaning her days were usually a comfortable routine.

She took the stairs, nodding to a couple of colleagues as she passed them. She had been an exercise junkie for as long as she could remember, rowing for a team during the summer weekends, and training in a gym several days a week. Swimming and diving were a frequent activity and she regularly hiked and hill-walked in autumn and winter. She trotted easily along the corridor that was central to the second floor and settled behind her desk in the general office, tucking her shop-bought lunch of avocado and prawn salad into the top drawer of her functionally organised desk, before switching her computer on.

Without warning, the bad day got worse as her boss sprung from nowhere. "What's this?" Andy Feldman waved an A4 booklet in her face, the commonly outraged tone of his voice snapping at the heels of her cheerfulness. Embarrassed, she felt her cheeks flush. "What the hell do you think you were doing, woman? Can't you read instructions? Are you as dumb as your hair colour suggests?"

Heads went down around the office, trying to blend into the background, and Toni struggled to find the words to pacify the red-faced bully. "Serge, I was just…"

"I was just! I was just! Stop mithering and tell me what the hell you think you were doing."

Toni knew she shouldn't but, always one to challenge a slight, she couldn't stop herself. "I was applying for promotion so I could get a guv'nor who treats me with some respect."

Silence hovered in the still air, breaths held as the team members waited for Andy to explode. His face mottled and Toni imagined steam belching from his ears, and eventually, "You've got another year minimum before you can apply to change departments and, even then," he tore the application form in half and slammed it on her desk, "I swear I'll do anything in my power to make it five. Vanessa over there," he pointed at the teenaged civilian whose face drained of colour at the mention of her name, "has a shed-load of data to input, you can help her for the rest of the day." He stormed towards his office and Toni knew it was pointless saying a word. Her boss was a lecherous arse through and through, but according to rumours, those who had reported him in the past had been sidelined for promotion thereafter; somewhere up above he had good connections.

Toni sidled over to Vanessa, who gave her a sympathetic smile. "Is he always like that?" She sounded like a kitten, high-pitched and plaintive.

Toni nodded, leaning across to see the monitor on the girl's desk. "Only with strong females, he doesn't like women with brain cells. In fact, I swear he thinks it's impossible that the 'inferior' sex can actually have them. Stupid arse."

Vanessa tinkled prettily and showed her colleague what needed to be entered onto the computer. Her innocent tone quickly became irritating, and Toni's teeth clenched as she soaked up the instructions as accurately as possible in order to return to her desk. "Yeah, yeah, I think I've got it. Let me do the next one and you can watch." Toni took the next form from the pile and tapped on the keyboard a few times. She saved the page and turned to the next form.

Timid Vanessa was impressed at how fast Toni had picked up the job that had taken her hours to master. "That's right."

"Good, just show me how to set the page up on my PC and I'll take the next file."

Julia lay in her single bed, the covers wrapped tightly around her, and tried to ignore her son's incessant wailing, eventually pulling the pillow over her head. "Just shut up, Antony, I've got a headache and you're making it worse."

"Hungry." Having rarely had the pleasure of being talked to by his mother, apart from the odd word or two, Antony's power of speech was grossly inferior for his three years. He was an unhappy child, sickly, and dreadfully lonely. Julia always ensured he was clean and neat, and that he ate sufficient calories to maintain a decent weight, regardless of the nutritional content, but there was little bonding between the two. The health visitor had raised concerns more than once, both to her superiors and to Julia herself, but her worries had, so far, been unheeded.

Antony whinged again, louder this time, and patted the blanket. "Hungry, Julia. Atony hungry."

She drew her head from under the pillow with a snarl. "It's Antony, how many times do I have to tell you, you stupid boy? Finish off your beans from last night, the plate's still on the table." He ran off and Julia shuffled up the bed, her head thudding from the bottle of Lambrini.

And then she remembered the note she had received the night before.

Hastily, she took baccy, papers and the bag of weed from the old shoebox she had stored them in, eager to obliterate the memory. Seconds later, she inhaled deeply, holding her breath, feeling the fuzziness tingling through her.

A loud rapping on the front door startled her and she hurriedly stubbed the joint out, squirting cheap body spray into the room to disguise the distinctive smell. She dragged her dressing-gown around her body, threadbare from years of use, and stumbled towards the front door. "Who is it?"

"Hello, my name is Simone Lewis, I'm a social worker…"

"Piss off."

Shocked by the rudeness, Simone stood for a moment, before continuing through the door, "Julia, I need to talk to you and I think you'd prefer that it's done privately. Can you open the door, please?"

Curled up against the pillow, knees folded into her chest, Julia puffed away at her smoke, savouring each lungful for as long as possible, willing the interfering busybody at the door to leave her alone. Eventually the shouting stopped and she relaxed.

"The only option we have is to involve the police." Grace was reluctant to take such drastic measures but in the case of little Antony Collins, it seemed the right action to take. "You know the procedure, you've done it before, haven't you?"

"Yes, remember with the Fortenski family, just after I started working here." Simone hadn't made the call personally, but she had taken enough notes to know what to do this time. "I'll give them a buzz."

"Tell them it's just a frightener for now, but we're prepared to apply for a court order if Julia Collins doesn't cooperate. I'm sure that will be enough to get her to open up and talk. Let me know how it goes."

An hour later, Simone returned to Albert Block, escorted this time by two uniformed constables, and she stood to the side while Sally Ross hammered at the door. "Julia

Collins, it's the police here, with a representative from Social Services. We need you to open the door immediately or we'll have no choice but to break it down."

Julia, annoyed at the intrusion and somewhat scared, curled tighter on the sofa, her son playing mindlessly with a box of matches in the corner. She hoped they would leave if she gave no response, but a cracking thud at the door told her that was wishful thinking. She jumped up to open the door before they could damage it further – nobody on the run-down estate wanted their security diminished. "What do you want? I ain't done nothing wrong."

Simone followed the officers into the flat, which reeked of stale tobacco and marijuana. "We've had several concerns raised about Antony's welfare, Julia, and we need to speak with you."

"Well, you're here now, get on with it." Julia slumped back onto the faded and tatty sofa, the cushion still warm, and it dawned on her that she could use their presence to her advantage.

Simone regarded the child, his complete ignorance to the evolving situation, and her heart welled with sorrow at his obvious solitude. She beckoned him over, trying to catch his eye, her face beaming a wide and friendly smile. He made no response. "There's no easy way of saying this, Julia, but we've had reports of neglect from healthcare officials, they're concerned about Antony's welfare."

She had the flat now, they couldn't chuck her out as long as she kept up with the rent, so what did it matter any more? At least he would be safe somewhere else, now she had been found. Julia's expression remained blank, but her resolve was strengthened. "If you want him, take him. I don't give a shit." Did she? She wasn't sure.

Simone was crushed for the boy, but she had seen this abhorrent attitude before. "That's not what our organisation is about, Julia. We try to keep families together, not tear them apart. We want to help you."

PC Ross glanced around, dust and filth, the sticky grime on the surfaces built over too many months – the clear evidence of illegal substances having been used recently. She knew that a small amount of weed for personal use wasn't going to be an issue unless they needed the threat of arrest to make the young woman behave, but she still took in as much information from the unkempt room as she could. "Look, I never wanted to get pregnant, it was an accident. His father pissed off when I told him and I ain't got nobody to help. I'm fucking tired of looking after him; he's bloody hard work. I'm just tired. If you don't like the way I look after him, just take him away, see if I give a shit."

Simone sat on the other end of the sofa, the sun-bleached burgundy fabric clashing with the bright green coat that complimented her dusky skin. "Have you seen your doctor recently, Julia? I wonder if you may be a little depressed, which would be completely understandable in the circumstances." She nodded, with a concerned smile.

Julia stood, dismissive and uninterested. "I don't see quacks. Do what you want with him, I don't give a shit. I'm going out."

Ross didn't like the girl and didn't care whether she was mentally sound or not, her attitude was disgusting. "You're not going anywhere, young lady. There's enough evidence of cannabis use in your flat to bring you in. Cooperate with the kind lady or I'll be nicking you."

Simone gave Ross a disapproving once-over; she knew from years of experience that threats were ineffective in situations like this. Julia Collins's apparent disaffection for her child was disturbing and there had to be a history to the story. Something had happened that was so traumatic the young woman had learned to block her emotions – it wasn't uncommon in abuse victims. Of course, the most important person in the picture was the poor, little boy in the corner who played alone, oblivious to company, to the world. His safety, security and well-being were priorities, but ripping him away from what, as far as she knew, was his only family could be counterproductive. "Julia, sit down. Calm down. I've heard what you've said and I haven't dismissed it, but before people start coming in here and ploughing up your life, why don't you talk me through things? Tell me how it's been and what has led to you feeling so hopeless now?"

Julia dropped onto her seat with a petulant grunt, no longer adolescent, but behaving like one. "I don't feel hopeless and I ain't got nothing to say. I get my social every two weeks, I buy a ten or twenty bit, a quarter of baccy and a bottle of plonk. Once every two weeks. I'm stuck in here every day with him, I ain't got no friends and no family, and I don't go out or buy new clothes. So I treat myself once a fortnight – big deal. Make what you want of it, I don't care."

Ross placed hands on hips. "An admission. Miss Lewis, should I…"

"I think Julia will be fine now. It's best we talk in private, so thank you for your help, it's much appreciated." Ross bristled, muttering, from the flat, followed by her colleague. These girls whose sole aim in life was to get pregnant, regardless of the father, just to get themselves a house and an income made her sick. She hadn't been born with a silver spoon in her mouth, nobody had pulled any strings for her, but she had applied herself at school and searched for work, and was now fully independent as a result. If she could do it, anybody could, it was that simple.

Simone waited until the footsteps outside dissipated and turned to face Julia. "I'm sorry about that, she was a little over keen, wasn't she? Now that all the drama's over, can we start again from the beginning?"

"Look, Miss whatever…"

"Mrs Lewis. Call me Simone, though, I hate formalities."

Julia sighed, disliking the visitor and subject matter, but oddly relishing the company. She didn't trust the woman who faced her, with her fake concern and insincere smile, but she couldn't stress enough how little she would care if she were to take Antony and never bring him back. It was safer that way, especially after the note. "I meant what I said. Antony would be better off with someone else. I'd never see him hurt, but I don't care about him."

"Julia, when you say these things my heart bleeds, not because I feel sorry for Antony, but because I can see that something is hurting you so deeply you don't understand it yourself."

"You don't know nothing about me." Julia tore a paper from the packet and dribbled a line of tobacco on top, deftly rolling a cigarette.

"You're right, I don't, but I'd like to."

"I don't like your sort, a bunch of tossing do-gooders who meddle with people's lives, but you never end up helping the ones who really need it."

Simone was getting the emotional reaction she was trying for. "Like who?"

"I bloody told social services over and over that my dad was hurting me and Mum, but they never took me away, never gave me a better life. They just left me there to rot until I made them listen. You're full of empty promises, you lot, a bunch of bloody jobsworths. Just take him away, it'll save us all a lot of time and trouble."

"You know as well as I do that I'm not going to do that, and I know you don't mean these words. Why don't you tell me what happened when you were young, what's made you so angry?"

"Why don't you piss off if you ain't going to take him? I ain't got nothing more to say."

"I'll come back and see you on Monday, we can talk more then."

"Don't bother. If you won't take him away, then I won't let you in."

It had been a long and tiresome day for Toni, entering seemingly endless data onto the computer, page after page, file after file. Most days after work she would take some form of exercise – the endorphins made her feel euphoric and helped her to sleep like a baby – but Fridays were lazy days. After the brewery had refurbished the décor and updated the quality and selection of food a couple of years before, the Cat and Mouse had been adopted as the station's local. The manager didn't mind, the clientele brought the money in, and profits were what spoke to him. Toni nodded to him as she walked through the side door. "Gray, how are you doing? I'll have a pint of soda water please."

He took a glass from the rack and scooped up some ice. "Not on the voddie tonight then?"

She shook her head. "I'm still in uniform, so I can't."

He chuckled, nodding towards a table. "It doesn't bother that lot in there. That's why they sit in the back room."

She shrugged. "Anyway, I've got to pick up some boxes from the supermarket so I need a clear head to drive. I'm leaving home next weekend." He passed her the drink, waiving her offer to pay.

"I've got some boxes in the storeroom if you want, could save you the journey. And they're strong."

Toni smiled. "That's really kind of you, thanks."

"I'll put them by the back door, you can take as many as you want." She took her glass to the rowdy table in the corner that her closest colleagues adopted every Friday. Sally Ross shifted her stool to one side, patting the one beside her for Toni to sit. "How's Friday been for you, Sal? Mine's been bloody awful."

Soon the two women were discussing Julia Collins and her neglected child and, astounded by what she was hearing, Toni gasped and sighed periodically. "She sounds dreadful. Some people don't deserve to be parents."

"I know. I wanted to slap her, the way she treated him."

"I hope I don't ever meet her, I'm not very good at keeping my mouth shut."

Although they had worked in the same department for six months, they'd not become friends, but this was quickly changing as they realised they viewed life from the same angle. When Sally offered to buy her a vodka, her resolve went; she was loving the company and could pick up the car and boxes the next day.

The two middle-aged men sat in The Nag's Head, supping their pints and sifting through a pile of photographs that Sean had taken through his window. His prime reason for buying his house had been the excellent view from the front room – the perfect scene was essential to him. He was a likeable man, a constant twinkle in his startlingly blue eyes and an ever-ready smile to greet whomever he passed on the street. He was passionately religious, an avid churchgoer, and had been welcomed in Moor End as a valuable member of the community.

His closest friend for twenty-seven years wasn't held in such high esteem. Jim had moved to the estate shortly after his marriage, eager to work and support his new wife, but things had soured after being made redundant when their daughter was young. The early-nineties recession had sapped the employment and morale of families throughout the country, but the poverty-stricken area was hit over and over again as businesses and factories closed their doors for the final time, unable to afford the rapidly rising costs involved. For years he traipsed to and from the Job Centre, hopeless, unemployed, and rapidly becoming unemployable as his attention to personal hygiene diminished. Jim had all but given up.

Three years after Jim had arrived at Moor End, Sean followed, purchasing a run-down semi near to Jim and his wife to refurbish on the cheap. He had loved spending time with the young family, cherishing both the mother and the child, but had remained single, despite many amorous attempts from women, young and old, all drawn to his cheerful persona. It came as no surprise to Jim when he found his best friend in bed with his wife, he had suspected their affair for a long time. But bored of his fruitless life, of Maria and her ever-decreasing interest in sex, it hadn't mattered. Sharing Maria with Sean was fine, because he had far more exciting recipients, who weren't drab and flabby, to enrich with his body. He loved Maria, she

32

cooked his meals and washed his clothes, but she had aged without grace, her hair grey and wiry, face lined heavily around the lips and eyes, and an aura of gloom surrounding her.

The affair had continued without upset to anybody, kept private to avoid damaging Sean's flawless reputation, and none of the neighbours had questioned his endless visits to Jim's home – the two men were friends.

Eighteen years had passed since Jim lost his job, and his life had declined to a haze of beer, drugs when he could, and the only hobby he had: children. More specifically young girls. And it happened that Sean shared the hobby.

Extensively involved in the community, it had been easy for Sean to integrate with young families, and as time passed his perversions went unnoticed. The neighbourhood children had nicknamed him Uncle Sean and freely taken his proffered gifts of sweets and trinkets without concern from their parents.

Nobody was keen on Jim, though. He was filthy, unkempt, and reeked of alcohol and stale ashtrays, and he barely concealed his lust for bonny girls. Mothers crossed the roads to avoid him, warning their treasured spawn to beware of the evil pervert.

Jim reached the final photo and passed them back to Sean. "Well, did you see any you like?"

"Yep, the brown haired one at the beginning."

Sean tucked the photos into his pocket. "I was hoping you'd go for that one, little cutie, isn't she?"

Jim nodded and they raised their glasses high, clinking their agreement with a smile. "Roll on Tuesday, that's what I say."

Chapter 4
Drastic Measures

Carol had been looking forward to a lazy weekend, but the factory foreman asked her at the last minute to do overtime the next day. Over forty and invisible, she often wondered where she had gone wrong in her life. She didn't come from a wealthy family – her father had been a salesman and her mother a dinner lady – but they had been hard-workers, ensuring that she and her brother never went without. She had tried hard at school, but academia was never her strong point. Dan had been her first love; she had been with him since they were fifteen, and marriage had been a natural progression.

She would have liked a career, but when the babies had come along there seemed no time – or point. Dan had procured an apprenticeship after school and slowly climbed the managerial ranks of the factory she now worked in, so money wasn't a problem. Although a good man, he was old-fashioned, expecting his wife to take care of their home, but he worked long hours so they could afford everything they needed and wanted. He was also kind, attentive and faithful. However, Carol was unfulfilled, and despaired of how rude her three children were to her, feeling they took her for granted.

And Toni was leaving home. The raw agony clutched her chest, pulsing cruelly. From the moment of her birth, the helpless baby wet from the womb and whimpering on her belly, Carol had experienced love she had not known existed. A fierce protectiveness that would have seen her give her life in an instant to protect her child. She had been twenty-one, a mere child herself, and she'd been petrified of the responsibility, but on holding the child who had shared her body for nine months, she had been smitten. Leon had followed three years later, and Maisie was a welcome surprise four years from then. When Dan had suggested she work at the factory for some pocket money, she had been sterilised, scared of another unplanned pregnancy, but the job was mundane and unfulfilling and she often wondered what might have been.

But Toni had always been special. Unique.

And Toni was leaving home.

Carol shook her head to banish the throbbing misery. She languidly stirred the stew in the pan and checked the vegetables. A key turned in the front door and she wiped her hands, straightening her hair and glasses, forcing a motherly smile she didn't feel. Dan sloped in, loosely brushing his hand on her arm in greeting. "What's for tea tonight?"

"Stew, mash, cabbage and carrots. Have you had a good day?" She didn't care so much, but, needing to discuss the altercation between herself and Toni with him, she wanted him firmly on her side. His grunt was hardly an answer. "Toni gave me some, er, news this morning."

Dan took a beer from the fridge, tugging the ring-pull. "Do you want one?"

"No." She drained the potatoes. "She's leaving home."

Wide-eyed, Dan emptied the can and took another before sitting by the table. "That's good, I wondered when she would finally fly the nest. We were married with a house and baby on the way by her age."

Carol pounded the masher into the potatoes vigorously, the restrained tension flooding out. "It's a different world nowadays. I don't think it's good that she's leaving home." Her jaw clenched, willing the threatening tears away. "And I'm worried about that Baby Jane business, I'm just…" They escaped and coursed down her cheeks, seeping along the laughter lines to her chin.

Dan was surprised at the outburst and pulled her onto his knee, wrapping her in a comforting hug as she sobbed. All cried out, he let go and held her face, removing her glasses to dab at her damp eyes with a piece of kitchen roll. "That baby was a huge emotional experience, love, and at a tender age. But it's just an interest, really. I mean, if you'd found a body, you'd naturally want to find out who it was, what happened to

35

it, wouldn't you? I know I would. Anyway, she probably wouldn't have joined the police force if it weren't for what happened, and we couldn't hope for a better profession than that for our daughter, could we?"

"But Dan, it was ten years ago. I think she should have moved on by now." Carol wiped her eyes, mindful of the potatoes cooling.

"I think she's a very balanced young lady. She's attractive, clever, kind and polite. It's time for you to set her free, let her grow into the adult who's lurking there, cut the apron strings."

She was wounded by his words and her frustration was barely disguised by gritted teeth as she dished up the dinner. "You think that's all this is, a spot of empty nest syndrome. You're only capable of black and white, you. This is grey, Dan. It's a grey area. Maybe we should have got her counselling all those years ago, nipped it in the bud, made her realise that although the discovery was gruesome she needed to file it away. Who knows, maybe they should have offered her counselling, the police, the doctors, God knows, the school."

"Oh, come on, Carol, aren't you taking this all a bit far. She's just got a keen interest in a cold case, and she was involved to a fair extent in the early days. That baby was never identified, or if it was, we've never been told. They never found the parents, the cause of death. Unsolved cases like this, conspiracy theories, UFO's even, billions of people around the world focus on them, investigate them, people who have nothing at all to do with the case. Let her enjoy her hobby, because realistically that's all it is."

Carol didn't retaliate, scared of where her exasperation would take her, and Dan wanted the whole thing packed away, sealed and labelled futile. She spooned a mound of mash onto five plates, vegetables, goulash. He remained quiet, not wanting to fuel the ashes he knew still burned.

Maisie strolled in, carefree and cocky with youth. "Alternatively, it could be just that Mum doesn't want Toni to have a mind of her own, we all know how much she loves to be in control." Neither had realised their youngest was listening. Without a word, Carol put the serving spoon on the side and wiped her hands on a tea-towel. She walked, head high, from the room and up the stairs.

Locked in the bathroom, with no witnesses to dish out snide comments, she cried.

Sally Ross had a reputation for being tough. She could kick-ass in martial arts, tackle contact sports with ease, and down pint after pint to keep up with the boys. Swearing like a trooper came naturally. She also never let a slight, no matter how small, go. Nobody messed with Sally; it wasn't worth the payback.

She had been on form all night, laughing hard, shouting rude and crude jokes, drinking like a fish. Although a mile apart in character, Toni found her hilarious, but she had depths that Sally would never reach, and compassion was one of them.

It was mid-evening and the end-of-week celebrations had become raucous for the stalwarts left behind, now the sensible few, or those with families, had gone home. Not a big drinker, two vodka tonics had made Toni giggly, her cheeks rosy and burning. Sally followed her to the toilets, setting her bag on the side to touch up her make-up, while Toni went to the loo.

"What are you up to this weekend, Toni?" She smeared red lipstick on thickly, unaware the vibrant colour was ridiculous teamed with the uniform she still wore.

"Packing my stuff, I'm moving out next week."

"Wow, exciting stuff. Whereabouts are you going? Fella involved? Nice place?"

Toni chuckled as she flushed the toilet and unbolted the door, joining her colleague at the basins to wash her hands. "It's no big deal, I've got one of those converted flats at the old abbey. It's just me, I haven't got a bloke."

Sally winked as she patted powder onto her flushed nose and cheeks. "We'll have to do something about that. Are you talking about St Martin's Place or the one across town?"

"Yeah, St Martin's."

"You want to be careful of that estate just across the road. The new flats look great, but the Rattery's a place to avoid."

"The Rattery? Is that what they're calling the Canal Estate now?"

Sally nodded knowingly and took a brush from her bag, dragging the bristles through the black bob she had untamed a couple of hours before. "That girl I told you about earlier, the one who hates her kid, that's where she lives. Honestly, I just couldn't believe it. She even admitted that she didn't want him, right in front of him, loud and proud of it."

"That's awful. I thought things like that were a fallacy." Toni was bored with the well-worn whinging – Sally had done the story to death – and she headed for the door.

Sally, repetitively drunk, wasn't finished. "The place is full of them. This one clearly didn't give two fucks about the kid and he was pretty backward, I can tell you. Doubt he had two brain cells to rub together in there. Poor little mite. It's obvious the kid's neglected. Place was a tip, stank of weed, empty booze bottle on the table, you know what I'm talking about."

"I'm pretty new to the job, I haven't experienced one like that yet." Please could they change the subject?

Sally clicked her handbag shut, dragging it to her shoulder, but she didn't move. "You're pretty naïve, even for a rookie. How do you fancy being teamed with me next week, if I can swing it, that is?"

"I guess. I doubt the Serge will have it though, he's been down on me since the day I started."

"Old Andy Pervert Pandy!" Laughing, Sally joined her by the door and Toni tugged it open. "He's only like that because he fancies you."

Carol stayed in the bathroom until the redness in her cheeks and eyes subsided, wallowing in her agony. Whatever she thought of to cheer herself up, the same elephant would roar her back down: Toni was leaving home.

Why did nobody share her concerns? Was she being hypocritical? After all, she had left home aged twenty. Maybe Dan was right and Toni's interest in Baby Jane was simply a hobby, not an obsession. Maybe Toni would blossom from leaving home.

Or maybe Carol would begin the withering and wilting into old age that was inevitable once her babies didn't need her any longer.

She unlocked the door and crept quietly to her bedroom, hoping Dan would come once he had eaten his meal. She sat on the bed, mulling over the same thoughts, the same words, that had been droning endlessly since Toni had dropped her bombshell that morning. Eventually her husband appeared, a gentle smile on his face and a belly bursting with dinner. He pushed the door to and opened his arms wide for a cuddle. "Are you okay, love?"

She nodded, throwing a soggy tissue in the direction of the bin. "Please can you have a word with Toni, make her see sense." Her voice was sweet, feminine.

"As far as I can see she is seeing sense, love. It'll do her the world of good, and probably you too."

"Me?" Was her husband blind? What part of 'bad idea' didn't he understand? "How on earth could it do me any good?"

"Because it's time you stopped doing everything for those ungrateful kids and started doing things for yourself instead. You've been a mother for years, tirelessly pandering to their every need, keeping a tidy house, making sure their clothes are clean and ironed, being a confidante, taxi, emotional support. What about you? What about something just for you?"

"Like what? There is nothing else, it's all I know now, the house, the kids. You. I'm not capable of anything else."

"How about studying? Why not go to a night school, get an exam in something or other?" She sent him a withering glare and he held his hands up in defeat. "Time's a wonderful healer, Carol. Just give it time, but don't deny Toni's freedom to soar as a grown-up just because you're too emotionally unstable to let her go."

Annoyed, he opened the door sharply, and Carol heard Maisie whisper 'go, Dad, go'. He slammed the door and something deep inside Carol snapped. Suddenly she knew what she had to do. She fingered the key to Toni's wardrobe in her pocket, patient enough to wait however long it took for the house to be empty.

Julia counted the money in her purse. It wasn't a lot, enough to buy another small pouch of tobacco and a bottle of Lambrini if they ate value baked beans and spaghetti hoops for the rest of the fortnight. But would she need to feed the boy? She was undecided. She fed his chubby arms into the sleeves of his second-hand coat and tied his cheap trainers onto his feet, and she swept him onto her hip, not prepared to bump the buggy down and up the stairs again.

Walking the short distance to the shop at the bottom of her block of flats, Julia's head was filled with a dense mist that clouded her thoughts. There were so many things to consider: the letter, the boy, social services. Her life. She'd had a twenty bit rather than a ten that week, and a quarter ounce pouch of tobacco would usually last. But that damned social worker, the police; she had chain-smoked since their visit, and now she had to spend money she couldn't afford to use the rest of the weed. She grabbed a bottle of perry and took it to the counter, shrugging her son up her hip – he was too heavy nowadays for her to carry him easily. "Twelve and a half grams of your cheapest baccy, please."

"Heard the social were making a fuss at your place this morning." Jo Bentley had never been shy in coming forward. She lived for gossip and the part-time job at the convenience store was the perfect place to hear it all – and share it. "Everything okay?"

Julia took the pouch without a word and shoved it into her pocket. With the nosy words ringing in her foggy mind, she headed for the door, pulling it wide, and as the cool evening air chilled her cheeks, she had a sudden moment of clarity. She turned back. "Everything's just fine, Jo. Everything is just fine." If they wouldn't take him away when she asked nicely, she was going to have to force their hand. Julia knew exactly what to do, and it was for Antony's own safety. For the first time in weeks a smile settled over her podgy face and she returned to her flat with a spring in her step.

"I'm going to get off home now." Toni had just finished her third vodka and her head was spinning a little, a sensation she detested. She would leave the car, its boot loaded with flat-packed boxes thanks to the landlord, and pick it up the next morning.

Sally grabbed her jacket and handbag. "Me too. What way are you going?"

"Across town."

"I'll walk with you. I catch the number twenty-nine so I'll keep you company up to the bus stop."

Toni had enjoyed Sally's sense of fun. She had been on the force a couple of years longer, but didn't appear to be ambitious; she was still a constable and seemed happy with that. Toni had heard her reputation on her first day at work and had found it hard not to judge her on the gossip, but she made a point of reserving an opinion until she had met a person properly, and from this evening's experience she was content to ignore the rumour-mill and take Sally for the bouncy, loud whirlwind that she appeared to be. They left the pub to a couple of catcalls and walked, both still uniformed, towards the canal.

"Have you ever wanted marriage and kids, Toni?"

"I might do one day. Maybe. Mind you, you have to meet a bloke first."

Sally laughed – too loud, too drunk – and Toni squirmed. "I've got a zillion men-friends I can pair you off with, don't you worry about that. At least you're not like them lot." She pointed to the grimy flats ahead, unsightly, graffiti-covered walls parading the poverty within.

Toni smiled nervously. "You really have a bee in your bonnet about unmarried mums, don't you?"

"Oh shit, yeah, I do. Half the girls I went to school with are mothers now and I'm only twenty-four."

Toni could see the point Sally was making, but motherhood wasn't as cut and dried as that. Baby Jane's mother had abandoned her, dead or alive, and she didn't doubt the poor woman had been disturbed and desperate rather than cruel. "I think the fathers have something to do with it too. Or should have."

"If you're going to open your legs, then it's up to you to make sure about contraception. An accident's no excuse, it's about taking responsibility for yourself. They make me sick, the scroungers, all of them."

Toni was shocked that someone so bigoted was allowed to serve on the police force. They crossed the footbridge over the canal, Albert Block looming, imposing and ugly, to their right. "I don't share your views."

"Oh, come on, I'm only saying what everybody else thinks, but don't have the gall to say out loud. The tax they take off my wages every week probably feeds one of those slags and her brats in there." She pointed to the 1970's architectural abomination. "Yet I'm the one who works day-in, day-out for it."

"And if you accidentally got pregnant and couldn't work, what then?" Toni didn't want the debate, Sally's opinion was too idealistic to be realistic, and she was pleased they were nearing the bus stop.

"I'd have an ab…" Sally stopped, her feet rooted to the cracked concrete, staring ahead with disbelief. "Oh my god."

Toni followed her gaze and immediately dialled emergency services. "Police, please. Someone's dangling a kid

42

over the edge of a third floor balcony in Albert Block. On Canal Estate."

Chapter 5
A Long Wait

It was the first night Simone had seen her husband for over a month. A prominent Jamaican businessman, Ian spent more time in his home country than his adopted one and Simone felt she had the best of both worlds; the life of a single, albeit faithful, woman for most of the year, and the bliss and mind-meeting of a solid marriage for the rest of it. She had been eagerly awaiting their reunion and was disappointed that the untimely call had thwarted their romance. "Can't someone on duty deal with it? I know that Monica's in tonight, and Gordon had no plans."

"She's asking for you by name."

"Who?" Simone didn't mean to be abrupt, but she couldn't contain her irritation.

The sound of rustling paper, then, "Her name's Julia Collins. She's got a son called…"

"Antony." Simone sighed, her resigned expression leading Ian to roll his eyes and sink down the bed, throwing a pillow over his head. "I know where it is. I'll be there as soon as I can." Simone moved the pillow aside to kiss her husband, his disappointment wringing her guilt, and she dragged on the clothes she had only just discarded. "I shouldn't be too long, honey. I'm sorry."

She left her pleasant home, a modest semi on the latest estate to be built on the edge of the town, within five minutes and the journey was short thanks to the clear roads. A couple of dozen people, a mixture of uniformed police and nosy neighbours, flanked the main doorway to Albert Block, and she squeezed through, showing her Social Services identification. She trudged up the stairs, her large frame and lack of fitness causing her to wheeze by the time she reached the third floor. The door to number thirty-three was open and she went to the lounge, nodding a greeting to the over-eager policewoman she recognised from earlier in the day. "I hope you're going to take that kid away now, like you should have done this morning."

Simone ignored Sally's snipe. "Has a doctor been called?"

"They refused to come out, said they don't do home visits unless it's life or death. They said to take her to A and E."

Sally and Toni were off duty and a little worse for wear, but neither wanted to miss the adventure of a young woman losing the plot, so had stayed on after calling for help. Sally had discreetly given Toni some mints to cover the smell of alcohol on her breath and, so far, nobody had detected anything. Toni had tried to talk to Julia Collins, but had met a brick wall, a stony silence, apart from insisting she would only speak to a social worker called Simone Lewis. Toni watched the scene with sympathetic eyes, a contrast to Sally's unrelenting judgement, but she too couldn't understand risking the life of your child, no matter how desperate you were to be heard.

Simone checked the toddler, who was sleepy on a constable's lap, clothed in pyjamas and wrapped in a blanket. "Julia, are you going to tell me what led to this?" She sat on the end of the sofa, her body pointed towards Julia, who was curled tightly on the other end with her sleeves pulled forward, hoodie obscuring her fleshy face. A minute passed with no response. "Julia. You told these people that you would talk to me. I'm here now, so talk."

She glared at Simone, defiant and angry, spitting and venomous. Cold. "*Now* will you take him away?"

"You know as well as I do that we have no choice now. We have no choice but to take you to hospital for a medical assessment of your mental health. Do you understand what I'm saying?"

"I might be bloody poor and a bloody waste of space, but I ain't bloody stupid, alright."

"Define stupid." Sally snorted at her joke, but the rest of the room ignored her.

"Julia, would you rather go to hospital in a police car, or I could take you, if you like. The police will stay with Antony until my colleagues find a place for him, so you don't need to worry about him. We need to get you back on your feet first."

"For heaven's sake, will you stop patronising me, you black cow? I ain't going to hospital because I don't need to, all I need is a break from him, it's for his own good. You're taking him away, then good, I'm happy. Just bloody hurry it up, I want some sleep this side of midnight."

Simone was used to racial abuse, it was an unfortunate part of her life, regardless that she had been born and bred in England, and the slight washed over her. She tagged a constable and whispered her concern that Julia Collins may misbehave if she were to drive. The officer agreed to take his car and, after a small struggle with Julia, they were on their way within minutes. Sally and Toni left the flat and headed to the bus stop they had almost reached a couple of hours before, this time sober and subdued. "Can you believe a mother being so hideous to her own kid, it makes me sick to the stomach."

Toni regarded the woman, who believed herself so perfect she was intolerant to anybody who didn't, or couldn't, live up to her high standards. She was unable to hold her tongue this time. "Have you ever had a kid, Sally?"

"No, of course not. I'm only twenty-four, for god's sake."

"Then until you become a mother, perhaps you might think about reserving your judgement to those who have, those who understand what it's all about." They had reached the bus stop, and Toni continued to walk without a goodbye, leaving her colleague stumped for words. For once.

Carol was used to Toni coming home late on Fridays, having had a drink or two with her mates, but it was nearing midnight and that was unusually late. She lay in bed, feeling stupid for fretting, after all, Toni was not only a grown woman, but a copper, so was unlikely to come to any harm. Turning on her side to face her husband, who slept peacefully without a care in the world, she felt a mixture of trepidation and victory wash over her for the hundredth time. She had been anticipating a colossal argument when Toni realised what she had done, but the later it got, the less she wanted it. Maybe she should return the box, go to sleep and forget about it. But all-seeing Maisie was in the room now. She closed her eyes tightly, willing herself to sleep, but after ten minutes she sighed, realising it was going to be a long night.

After tossing and turning for an hour, Carol held her breath when a key sounded in the lock. Toni tiptoed up the stairs and quietly into her bedroom, where she donned her pyjamas in the dark, before going to the bathroom. Carol listened to the nightly routine – hot water to wash in, cold to clean her teeth. The chain flushed, the light went out, and Toni padded to her bedroom, closing the door. Now Carol could sleep.

Julia still hadn't been seen by a psychiatrist by four in the morning, and she and Simone were exhausted and bored. A nurse had taken a summary of the problem, which she had shown to the duty doctor in the emergency department, and they had called Doctor Mathura at home. Simone had tried to make conversation a few times, but Julia was lost in her world, bitter and vengeful. Having worked ten hours straight the day before, Simone gave up; she needed sleep.

"I do love him, you know. I really do. I'm just terrified they'll take him away."

The social worker was surprised by the statement that came out of the blue. "But that's what you asked – forced – us to do. I don't understand."

"I didn't mean you. I had to do this, I couldn't stand the thought of what they might do to him. I knew he would find me one day, I always knew. That he would take Antony away. At least while you have him, I know he's safe."

"I'm not sure I'm following you, do you mean Antony's father?"

A blanket descended over Julia, grey and heavy. Her jaw tensed and the emotional glimpse at the truth behind Julia's bizarre behaviour was gone. The girl focussed on her fingers, skin peeling and scabby beside the nails, and Simone felt the chink in Julia's barrier close tightly. She folded her flowing jumper over her ample bosom, tucking in the edges, uncomfortable with the dark secrets that weighted the atmosphere, and wished she was back in the loving arms of her man.

Joyce Frobisher was a creature of habit, and seven days a week, fifty-two weeks a year, every year, her alarm would wake her at five with a rousing symphony or concerto. This morning it was Handel, and she clambered out of bed, careful not to waken her husband of forty years, who slept soundly in his own bed. Shrugging on her gown and slippers, she shushed her three dogs, pouring crunchies into their bowls, while preparing a strong, sweet mug of tea. Twenty minutes later, she had bundled the boisterous pets into the back of her car and was on her way to Black Park.

She had lived in the area all her life, from her young and carefree childhood, through marriage and childbirth, to her son leaving home to take a wife. They had owned the same modest house for the duration of their marriage, and she had recently retired, giving her more time to travel, her life's ambition after working for so many years to afford the luxury.

Black Park was stunning place to exercise her pets, a heaven on earth of natural flora bursting with busy wildlife. On the outskirts of Kendrick, it had four hundred and fifty acres of unspoiled beauty, set amongst the hubbub of traffic that filled the surrounding roads. Joyce loved it so dearly, she had stated in her will that, come her death and cremation, she wanted her ashes scattered over the thousands of bluebells that covered the ground from April on.

The park offered many differing settings, from nature walks to bridleways, to dense woodland and open fields, but her favourite place had always been the refreshingly invigorating pathway that circled the expansive lake. In summer, the water would twinkle with reflected rays, prettily contrasting with the array of mature plants that surrounded it, which, in turn, met the changeable skies that created a perfect backdrop.

The lake was striking in winter, a sheet of freezing water, rarely iced over, and framed by stark empty branches littered with abandoned nests. With fresh, new colours in springtime adding hope to the day, and autumnal oranges, reds and yellows emitting drama, its beauty was unfailing.

The breeze was biting as Joyce parked the car on the gravelled area, setting the dogs free to run ahead. They knew the lakeside well and bounded to the water's edge, leaping and yelping excitedly. Joyce took their leads, just in case, and locked the car. It would normally take about an hour at a fast pace to tread the winding and scenic route around the lake, a harmonious and rejuvenating start to the day, but with no plans bar the everyday mundane chores that had to be attended to, Joyce was unhurried, and had only strolled a third of the way in the time it would usually take her to finish the walk.

A young woman, clad in a grey tracksuit, jogged towards her and she smiled in greeting, but suddenly the woman fell, rolling on her back, clutching her ankle. Joyce trotted over, her dogs stopping, panting their concern. "Goodness, are you okay, dear?"

Toni winced with pain, embarrassed that her ungainly fall had been witnessed. "Fine, fine. I'm fine, just a twisted ankle. I'll be fine."

Joyce bent down. "Let me take a look."

Toni waved her away, wishing the woman would disappear. "Really, it's fine." Intent on standing to prove a point, she hoisted herself up, limping lamely on the injured foot with agony etched on her brow. "See, I'm fine." Joyce chuckled and Toni regarded her, curious. "What's so funny?"

49

"I'm medically trained and I can tell you right now that you're not okay. My car's back there, let me give you a lift to the hospital to get it checked out."

"No, no," she waved her hand, dismissive, "there's no need, really. I wouldn't be able to stand on it if it was broken. It's just a twisted ankle."

Joyce stood tall, an Amazonian figure who towered over Toni, and was instantly authoritative. "Yes, you would, depending on the break, and anyway, ligament injury can be far worse than a broken bone. Let me take a look."

A child obeying her teacher, Toni sat on the dusty path with old leaves cushioning her from the cold earth and removed her trainer, exposing a slightly swollen, reddening ankle. Joyce prodded and poked expertly, concentrating. "That needs a support bandage at the very least."

"I'll strap it up when I get home, it'll be fine."

She raised her eyebrow and Toni rolled her eyes dramatically. "I'm supposed to be packing today, I've got too much to do to be stuck in hospital for six hours waiting for an X-ray."

"An injury like this won't just go away because it's inconvenient." Joyce helped Toni to stand, supporting her injured side with her shoulder. "I hope you do a desk job, because I can't see you being too physical for a couple of weeks."

Toni recalled the previous day, eight solid hours of overwhelmingly tedious data entry, and sighed, annoyed. "Fuck." An awkward glance at the commanding woman and her cheeks flushed again. "Sorry, I mean oh dear. I'm sorry, Mum tells me I swear too much, it's just I'm a cop and I can't stand deskwork, my life's going to be hell now."

"Your mum's right. A policewoman, eh? I always remember being told that you know you're getting old when policemen look like they belong in school. What are you, eighteen? Nineteen?"

"Twenty." Toni leant on the lady heavily as she shuffled painfully towards the car park, followed by the dogs, who were confused by the deviation to their normal routine. "I'm Toni, by the way, Toni Fowler."

The woman stopped walking and her brow furrowed momentarily as she regarded Toni. The spell broken, she smiled and continued to lead the patient. "Pleased to meet you, I'm Joyce Frobisher."

The two women covered a few random subjects during the long hobble and found each other pleasant and rewarding company. Despite Toni's frequent assurances that her ankle didn't need medical attention, Joyce insisted that hospital was the only outcome she would settle for. Unusually, headstrong Toni felt unable to quibble with the older woman, her aura so confident and masterful.

They arrived at A and E just as the October sun broke through the clouds on the horizon. Toni's ankle throbbed so hard it felt fit to burst and, reluctantly, she had to admit Joyce had been right to drag her to the hospital. Wasting hours of the precious Saturday in a waiting room was irksome, but she had no choice – it was either now, or later under the orders of her boss. Her hand hovered over the handle, ready to open the door. "Just here will be fine, thanks."

Joyce eyed her, amused, and continued driving slowly, searching for somewhere to park. "If I drop you off here, you'll just get a cab back home without going in." She chuckled, deep and heartening. "I'll come in with you for a while. Anyway, I've nothing better to do and I'm enjoying your company. I'll give my husband a call to let him know where I am while you book in."

By the time Dr Mathura had arrived at the hospital, been briefed about his patient's condition and circumstances, and arrived in the cubicle that had housed Julia and Simone for the previous six hours, both women had fallen asleep, Julia comfortably on the trolley and Simone curled awkwardly in a wooden armchair. He put his fleshy fingers on Julia's arm and wobbled her awake. "Miss Collins, my name is Doctor Mathura. I'd like to speak to you please."

Julia grunted as the memory of the long night resurfaced, she wiped her eyes and stifled a yawn. "Mmm."

"I understand the police brought you in because you threatened to harm your child."

"I didn't threaten to harm him, I dangled him off the balcony because I wanted somebody to take him away."

"I don't think she intended to drop him." Sadly, Simone wasn't sure she believed herself.

Dr Mathura stared frostily over the top of his glasses at the social worker and she smiled lamely. Turning his back, he stepped between his patient and the woman. "Why did you put the child at risk?"

"I asked them to take him away and they wouldn't, and I don't want him around no more. I just don't want him. I can't, 'cos he ain't safe with me."

Simone had no intention of being bullied by the short, ignorant man and she rolled from the seat, standing squarely in the doctor's sight. "I think she may have a touch of depression. It's not normal."

Perplexed and annoyed, his gaze settled on the obese woman. "Tell me again who you are?"

She held out her hand amiably, with a pleasant smile. "Simone Lewis, I'm Julia's social worker."

He rebuked the gesture and remained stony faced. "In that case, would you mind leaving the room in order to give my client some privacy." Stunned and slighted, but unable to object under the circumstances, Simone took her bag from under the chair and left. Dr Mathura returned to his patient. "Miss Collins, if you were to be discharged, would you try to harm your son again?"

"I didn't try to harm him, I told you. I just wanted somebody to take him away."

"Have you ever harmed yourself?" The question was redundant; he had already spotted the numerous threadlike, pale scars that ran along her forearms where her sweatshirt sleeves were pushed up.

Julia's head felt ready to burst; she was overtired, overwhelmed, and the man wasn't listening to a word she said. He had labelled her before they had even met and was conveniently pigeon-holing her to suit his own agenda. "So what if I have? What's that got to do with asking for my son to be re-homed?"

He raised an eyebrow, pen poised on the clipboard in his hand, and whispered to no one in particular. "Re-homed like a dog." He turned to the two medical students who accompanied him. "Arrange to have her detained. I'll sort out some medication for her when I get back to my office."

"Detained?" Julia was too fatigued to understand properly, simply wanting to go home and snuggle under her duvet for the rest of the day. "What do you mean, detained?"

Dr Mathura swept through the curtain, closely followed by his assistants, and she sat, confused, her legs dangling from the trolley. She repeated the word to herself, muttering over and over, and gradually the harsh reality hit her. Panicking, she jumped down and peeped through the curtain to see a nurse approaching with a wrist tag and pen. A sudden shudder of claustrophobia ran the length of her body and she darted out, racing along the corridor, desperate to get out, to get home. "Julia. Julia Collins. Come back here."

It was so quick that Toni wasn't sure what had happened. She had been waiting at the reception desk when a woman burst through the double doors that led to the examination cubicles. A nurse followed, screaming for someone to stop the patient, and suddenly the woman was on the floor, held down by four hospital staff. Toni watched, curiously amazed, as the girl sat, swearing and cursing, and when she caught a glimpse of her face, she realised the woman was Julia Collins. Obviously she was a nutcase after all, Toni mused, wondering if she had been overly harsh on her colleague when she had abruptly ended their conversation the night before. She whispered to her companion, "I was in her flat last night, she dangled her toddler off the balcony. They brought her in to see the mental health team and took the boy into care. Looks to me like they've sectioned her."

Joyce calmly surveyed the drama that was evolving before her. The frantic, terrified girl. The brutal orderlies restraining her. The anger and apathy directed at a distressed woman who was clearly confused and petrified. She had seen some harrowing scenes over the course of her sixty-six years, especially during her successful career, but this one tugged her heartstrings and saddened her. "I don't think you should have told me that, Toni. I think that information was confidential, wasn't it?"

Shocked, Toni regarded the older woman, her brow knitted. "Maybe not, but does it matter? I mean, it's not like you're going to tell anyone. Are you?" Joyce remained expressionless and Toni wished she had never uttered a word. "Look, I don't know who you are, but I'm sorry I told you that. You're right, I was out of order."

"Just don't make the same mistake again, careless talk can cost a police officer his or her job."

Admonished, and annoyed that she had been, Toni finished registering with the receptionist, all her details, including her new address-to-be, now saved to the computer, and she hobbled to find an empty seat in the packed waiting area. A red electronic display on the main wall indicated that the average waiting time was currently four hours, and Toni was frustrated at what was becoming a wasted day, especially after her brilliant intentions on waking so early that morning. Joyce followed her to the seats and stood beside her. "I've scared you, haven't I?"

Toni lied. "No."

Joyce shrugged her bag strap comfortably over her shoulder and zipped her expensive, padded anorak securely. Tapping her nose, she smiled and the discord ebbed away from Toni, her shoulders relaxing. "I've got to get the dogs home; they can't stay in the car too long. If you like I could come back after I've settled them home, give you some company while you wait. Or I could just pick you up a magazine from the WVS shop?"

"I couldn't possibly ask…"

"Yes, you could. Which would you prefer: magazine or company?"

Toni laughed cheerfully, but in truth she was desperate for the woman to go, despite her kindness. The warning Joyce had given her felt deeply uncomfortable, and Toni couldn't understand why. Hers had been a throwaway comment, and maybe she shouldn't have said anything, but why challenge it? And somehow the challenge had sounded like a threat. Careless talk can cost a police officer his or her job? "You've got a life to get on with, if you want to get a magazine then that's really kind of you, but please don't go to any more trouble."

Joyce regarded Toni, eyes flitting over her face as she drank the strong, yet delicate, features into her memory, and her forehead briefly furrowed again, before allowing a smile back. "Toni Fowler. I know your name from somewhere, I'm just not sure where. I can't place you. I'll get you a magazine, maybe a bottle of water too, then I'll be off."

By the main doors, stunned Simone Lewis was waiting to hear the outcome for her unruly client. She watched, agitated, as Julia was led away, hands strapped behind her back, screaming and crying. Yes, the girl was clearly disturbed. Yes, she needed help, badly. But the humiliation, the heavy-handed overkill? She sighed, resigned, and headed from the hospital – a good cuddle from her Jamaican Adonis would take her mind off things.

Chapter 6
Melissa Barton

Tuesday had finally arrived and Sean sat in his front room, peeping through the slats of the blind, which conveniently sheltered his filthy hobby from the outside world. He was overwhelmed with anticipation for the plans they had made. Today, he didn't need to take photos, because he was going to have the real deal in flesh and blood soon. It was early and the school gates hadn't yet opened, but the excitement was intense.

For many years, Maria had been enough for him, then a vibrant and happy person with a wonderfully kinky flair in the bedroom, but when she had married his best friend and moved away, he'd had to find another outlet for his sexual kicks and had chosen the children who passed his flat on their way to school. A year on, he had purchased a camera to photograph the girls as they trotted by in their lacy, white socks and cute-as-a-button shoes, which gave him something physical to take to his lonely bed.

When he had followed Maria and Jim to Moor End, he had rekindled his relations with Maria, but she was no longer enough now the seed of paedophilia had been sown, and he had continued his hobby. Photos weren't enough, though, he had wanted physical contact. Nothing illegal, just talking and the occasional hug; some interaction with the girls to add depth to the photos. Aware he needed the trust of both parents and children to avoid suspicion, he had worked tirelessly for community events, and eventually the children had started calling him Uncle Sean. On coach trips to the seaside or events at the village hall, he would laughingly take snaps of chosen girls, all willing to pose openly for the cheery man. Nobody had suspected a thing.

As the years passed, whenever he had the urge, he would discreetly set the camera up on a tripod by the window, and for half an hour in the morning and afternoon, he had the perfect vantage point to view the stream of youngsters as they shot along the pavement, racing each other, shouting and whooping, carefree in their innocence. To him, it was a harmless pastime, yet he was careful to hide the equipment after each session, and took the precaution of having the rolls of film developed in other parts of the country to avoid awkward questions. The onset of the digital age in the early nineties had been a godsend, and he had wasted no time in setting up his operation on a flashy camera and personal computer.

A decade passed and his impeccable standing in the community remained untouched by scandal, but then Jim discovered the equipment he had left standing in his haste to attend an appointment. Fearing his life in tatters, he was amazed when Jim showed no judgement, only interest and intrigue. And a few days later, Jim asked to be involved, and sharing the recreation made it more thrilling. But the power of partnership also made them more daring, and when Jim's daughter had left home, leaving them both with only with Maria for their sexual needs, they had discussed escalating their seedy hobby.

They had bought a camcorder, taking video clips of pig-tailed girls in their pretty blue dresses as they ran along the street to school, instead of photographs. And on one such occasion Maria walked in on both men massaging inside their pants. She had feigned acceptance, but Jim had beaten her senseless that night, threatening death if she dared say a word, and she had kept her mouth firmly closed thereafter in self-preservation. Tolerating the knowledge that both her lovers needed titillation she was unable to give, she paid with both her health and looks, becoming weary and haggard.

As time passed, the same old, same old became stale, and neither man was sure who had thought of the idea – it had been discussed over a heavy drinking session – but they had realised their pastime could be lucrative; men – maybe women, who knew – were willing to pay good money to see such innocent photos and footage.

Learning from library books and the internet, Sean had dabbled and experimented, eventually establishing a members-only website. News of the operation was spread by restricted word of mouth in the sleazy local pub, and soon a couple of voyeurs had been willing to pay a monthly fee online to be issued with a password, which gave them access to the gallery of innocent, unsuspecting children. Jim and Sean would change the videos and photographs once a week to keep the stock fresh, and soon they were making a decent profit for very little outlay. But it still wasn't enough, their cravings had intensified, and now they wanted to touch as well as look.

Despised by most in Moor End, Jim's contribution to the activities was behind the scenes, but Sean was a different ballgame; trusted and loved, affable and kind, his suggestion of videotaping community get-togethers was welcomed without suspicion, an innocuous recording of the fun had by all. He and Jim would select the children they were tempted by, and he would film them as they played, or while he conversed, off camera, with them. Nobody suspected the innocent footage would appear later on an improper website for the stimulation of paedophiles around the world. Why would they?

The website remained under the authority radars for years, and this strengthened their belief that they were invincible. But Jim had developed a perverse crush on pretty Jenny, five and naïve, and they debated the possibility of snatching her for their warped sexual gratification. It took a month to devise a watertight plan that would avoid detection, and to find a location where they wouldn't be disturbed, and they had taken the trusting child to abuse her body, wiping her memory with Rohypnol. The carefully structured few hours had been worthwhile, although they had worried for a while that they may have overstepped the mark, that the girl might remember something and tell a trusted adult, but they eventually realised the abduction had been successful. This was the green-light to post the footage onto a concealed page on the website, charging a high price for the password, and the money had flooded in. The new riches, coupled with glorious

58

memories of the pivotal day, left them euphoric, and now they had tasted the forbidden fruit, they wanted more.

There would be no turning back. There couldn't be.

Today, it was Melissa's turn.

Inside the walls of nineteen, Princes Street in Moor End, it was business as usual for the Barton family. A hectic rush every school day, Val efficiently shepherded her children with military precision – washing, dressing, eating, hair brushing – to present them to the school in perfect condition.

Despite the bright and cloudless sky, the chilly October wind was deceptive and it whistled through the estate. Val insisted Melissa and her younger brother don their new winter coats before leaving the house and they walked briskly up the hill to the school gates, where she dropped them off with a light kiss on the forehead. Chatting and laughing with the other mothers, she loosely watched them bundle through the doors.

With a group of old school friends, Val strolled to the corner shop for a few bits and pieces, and they went back to hers for coffee. Lucky enough to take a few years from her career to be a mother and housewife, she had time on her hands and impromptu meetings between the women were commonplace.

Eventually the friends left and she pre-prepared dinner for when the children came home, the unimaginative and cheap staple of chicken nuggets and fries. The day having flown by, she wiped her hands, checked her hair in the hallway mirror and returned to the school.

Her friends were gathered again, sharing the latter parts of their day, gossiping and laughing, stressing and moaning, and soon the bell rang and children swarmed from the doors, excited to be going home after the long Tuesday. Her son ran up, cheeks pink with the exertion of the games lesson he had just had, and she asked about his day, which he related with great speed before running after a ball with his friends. Val waited, idling, watching the doors, watching the crowd on the street dissipate as everybody went back to their worlds, and a knot of unease began to unravel in her stomach. She pacified the irrational thoughts that were surfacing, sure that Melissa was simply late coming from class. But fear took over – maybe mother's instinct – and she grabbed her son, rushing towards the now-clear entrance.

A teaching assistant, who had spoken to Val before about some school matter or other, was leaving the first classroom along the corridor and she noticed the mother's concern. "Are you okay, Mrs Barton?"

"Melissa hasn't come out yet, I'm a bit worried."

"Come with me, I'll get the secretaries to put out a call." The concerned assistant led Val and her son through the corridors towards the main reception area on the other side of the school, patting Val's shoulder reassuringly. "Don't worry, she was probably held back in class or something. Maybe she misbehaved."

Val's teeth gritted, furious at the thought. "She's six years old, for God's sake. You can't hold her back at that age without me knowing."

They reached the main desk and the assistant tapped on the bell. Presently a secretary came from the office and checked the register for Melissa's class. "I didn't think she had." She looked sympathetically at Val, whose eyes were wide with fear. "She wasn't in school today. She's marked absent for both the morning and afternoon sessions."

Val's body was suddenly heavy, too heavy for her legs, and she steadied herself against the desk. She said breathlessly, "But I dropped her off myself."

The assistant guided the mother whose world was falling apart to the reception sofa and helped her to sit, and told the secretary to call the police.

Julia hadn't eaten for three days, nor had she spoken. They were the only two things in her life she had any control over during the dismal, enforced stay in Ward Twelve. Because of her 'bad behaviour', as the nurses frequently referred to it, she had been placed in an isolated room on the Saturday morning and hadn't seen anybody but medical staff since. Dr Mathura had spent a maximum of ten minutes a day with her, denying her more time as long as she refused to speak, and once the nurses had realised her intention to remain silent no matter what, they only came in when she needed either medication or food. They had asked several times whether she had relatives or friends they could notify, but she had simply hung her head, not because she was being awkward, but because she had no friends, and she wished to remain estranged from the only family she knew existed. Simone had requested to see her on both Monday and Tuesday, but was informed that Julia wasn't allowed visitors until she began to cooperate, and the staff hadn't thought to tell Julia that somebody outside her depressing and gloomy prison cared.

The three days had felt like an eternity, and she had spent the solitary time reflecting on the events of the dramatic night when she had lost control of her mind. She missed her freedom. She missed the luxury of doing what she pleased, going out when she wanted to, eating what she fancied. And she missed the telly. But not once had she missed her son, his hopeful, expectant face and his fleeting, toothy grin, because she knew she had done the right thing in having him removed from her care.

She was staring aimlessly through the window when the door opened and Dr Mathura entered, flanked by the two colleagues who had been escorting him when he first met Julia. "Do you have any plans to talk to us yet?"

She wanted support and healing, but his tone was interrogating. Julia sat on the bed, unmoving, and concentrated on gazing into the middle distance outside the window.

"We're here to help you, Julia, but we can't if you won't let us know what we're helping with." He scanned her notes briefly. "Have you found that the Diazepam has helped with your anxiety?"

She thought of her dulled senses and the overwhelming feeling that nothing really mattered, including her. Especially her. She thought of how weak she was, how her muscles tired from even the short distance to the toilet on the other side of the room. But she didn't care. Life had been dreadful. She couldn't remember a time when it hadn't been filled with fear, violence and self-loathing. Julia had no words to say.

He waited impatiently, sharing a few muttered words with his colleagues. "Julia, you have to start talking to us at some stage, the police have been asking to see you regarding the incident on the night you were brought in."

Julia glared at him intensely and unease flooded his body. "I'll only speak to Simone."

"Simone?"

She retreated swiftly to her solitary world and, with a rueful shake of his head, Dr Mathura gave up and left. Luckily for Julia, the junior psychiatric doctor who accompanied him remembered the large, coloured woman who had been with her on the night she arrived, and he was ordered to find her details for the doctor.

At the tender age of six – vulnerable, trusting and eager to please – it had been easy to abduct Melissa for their depraved pleasure. Not only would they enjoy her body in any way they saw fit, but would upload the video that evening to their sickening, exclusive gallery.

Melissa had seen no danger when she had willingly gone to Maria's house, whom she knew to be a kindly woman from the church. The idea had seemed fun at first, with the promise of cakes and biscuits instead of a monotonous day at school. It had felt naughty, and she had been prepared to keep it a secret like she'd been told to, but something about the atmosphere on her arrival made her nervous and scared.

She told Maria that she wanted to go home, that she wanted her mummy, but the woman's face had transformed from a pleasant smile to a scowl, and she had forced her to drink a glass of funny tasting blackcurrant squash.

The carefree life she had known ended at that moment, and was replaced with devastating terror when she woke in a semi-dark place, a dank odour choking her, and her head pounding, making her feel sick. She could remember the bitter drink and the following weird, fuzzy sensation, but had no recollection of arriving in the badly lit room with stark, cold walls, and two men, who wore balaclavas to conceal their identities. She longed to be in her mum's warm, protective arms, away from the growing horror.

Melissa started to cry, a whine that Jim found intolerable, and he slapped her face hard, telling her to shut up or he would hurt her again. She tried to stop, holding her breath to control the sobs, but it was too difficult. She heard Uncle Sean's voice and momentarily her heart lifted, until he said they were going to knock her out again. The men forced her to drink some more of the squash that didn't taste right and her head became hazy once more.

She awoke a while later, now in darkness, and her head thudded woozily. She lay on something soft, but underneath the floor was icy and hard. She whimpered, afraid, alone, and confused by the agony that burned intensely throughout her abdomen and between her legs. Her eyes gradually accustomed to the blackness and she made her way towards a crack of light that she assumed was an exit. She hammered on the metal with her fists, desperate to escape, screaming and scratching.

Suddenly the door opened, the bright daylight stinging her eyes, and a silhouetted figure slipped through, closing the door behind. Melissa's heart beat so fast she was scared of fainting and her breaths came hard and fast. Without words or warning, a hand grabbed her from behind, forcing her into a headlock, and the person shoved her roughly onto the floor again. She felt something damp over her face, a sweetish, chemical smell, and she struggled to breathe, her arms and legs weakening, drooping. Then she was on a gentle wave, the ebbing tide relaxing her, a warm calmness.

The call from Princes Street School had been dealt with urgently, and soon the news of a missing child reached Thirsk's ears. He knew, everybody knew, that the first few hours in a missing child case are the most imperative. If they didn't find her quickly, if she wasn't safely in the arms of an unfound friend or relation, having wandered away on an impulse, they knew they could be looking for her body. At this stage, there was little his department could do, although CCTV recordings supplied by the school were being scrutinised by two officers, in the hope they may hold the key to her disappearance and possible whereabouts.

After leaving Melissa that afternoon, Sean had taken both the camera and camcorder home, bringing them up the stairs to his rudimentary office in the third bedroom, which fronted the house.

He connected them to his laptop and began to transfer the best photos, and the video clip of Melissa's molestation, to the website, along with an enticing advert to tempt the regular viewers to part with their money in return for the latest footage. Taking his mug of warming coffee in his hands, he leant back to wait for the files to upload, but became aware of some commotion outside. He peered through the window, curious, and was shocked to see a number of police cars. Several uniformed officers, and some others, who he assumed were plain clothed detectives, appeared to be making house to house inquiries and he was nervous; maybe Melissa had remembered something and told her mother. Hurrying now, he checked the status of the uploads and was pleased to see them finished. He hastened to pack up the equipment to hide safely, just in case.

He had just dropped the camera, camcorder and laptop in the drawer of his divan bed when a knock came, and his heart began to race. He could feel his face prickling with sweat as he trotted down the stairs to answer the door, and he wiped it with his sleeve before forcing a genial smile to greet the caller. "Oh," he feigned shock, "officer, what on earth has happened?"

The policeman held out an A4 sheet displaying Melissa's pretty face, grinning mischievously, and Sean winced. "We're searching for this girl, Melissa Barton, and we wondered if you've seen her at all today?"

"Well, no, I haven't. I've seen her at the church a few times, but not today. Is something wrong?"

"She was reported missing this afternoon. If you see her, please could you let us know immediately?" The officer was already walking along the drive towards the street.

"Of course, of course." Sean closed the door and kicked the telephone table beside it with frustration. "Shit." Snatching his jacket from the hook above it, he took his keys and left the house through the back door, jogging to the end of the garden and along the alley to Jim and Maria's house a few doors away.

An hour of hushed discussion later – the disastrous cock up, the plan to dispose of the body – Sean decided the best thing he could do was offer his assistance to the growing crowd of worried people outside. He stepped from the house, concern etched on his face.

Although dinnertime came and went, hope that the girl would be found was still rife and the Moor End community were happy to stand on their doorsteps, either to feed the enquiring officers with things they had seen over the course of the day that may help to find Melissa, or to watch the unbelievable scene with both interest and apprehension.

The streets were clear of children that evening, no screaming and shouting, no merry laughter and childish chanting. But without any idea who had abducted Melissa – if that were the case – all anybody could do was pray for her safe return to the folds of her family.

Chapter 7
Julia's Controversy

Dr Mathura finally had the chance catch up with paperwork at his desk, freeing his aching feet from the new leather shoes that pinched his toes. Julia Collins's patient notes were top of the pile with a post-it note stuck to the first page, displaying the name and number of the social worker, and signed with a smiley-face. He settled comfortably in the plush chair and reluctantly picked up the phone, dialling. "Can I speak to Simone Lewis please?"

Simone was seldom at the office as she spent most of her working hours visiting the families in her care, but on this occasion the doctor was lucky. She had been hoping he would call and welcomed the invitation to meet him at the hospital, despite already clocking up an hour of unpaid overtime. She tucked her half-eaten sandwich into her bag, alongside the chocolate bars she kept for days like this, and grasped her car keys.

The traffic was dreadful, as always this time on a weekday evening, and the three-mile journey took nearly an hour. Stressed, she was relieved to find Dr Mathura's office easily. He greeted her without a trace of the rudeness he had shown her during the early hours of Saturday morning, and arranged for his secretary to prepare some hot drinks, which Simone gratefully accepted as she sat opposite him. "How has Julia been?"

"We've found it difficult to get a word from her, to be honest, she's very stubborn. Has she been on your books for long?"

"No, I met her for the first time on Friday. She wasn't very responsive with me, either. From a few of the things she's told me I have a suspicion that she was mistreated as a child, but there's been nothing definite forthcoming. I was hoping you'd be able to tell *me* more by now."

"She has a lot of anger, it's bubbling – no, raging – inside her. She's barely spoken to me or anyone else, and she hasn't been eating. In fact, she hasn't been doing anything. She just sits there, on her bed, staring out of the window. I can believe that she's had an unhappy experience, but the fact is, unless she speaks to us and gives us a chance to help, there's little we can do. I'm prepared to discharge her with a recommendation that her GP keeps an eye on her."

Simone sat straight, unable to hide her shock. "Surely not. I think she needs the intensive help and therapy she can get in here."

The statement triggered the doctor's memory as to why the intrusive know-it-all social worker had irritated him so much the first time they met. Despite studying for twelve years to qualify, and a further eighteen to reach his esteemed title, she still thought she knew his job better than he did. He stood with growing indignation. "In my role as Senior Psychiatric Consultant for this hospital, it is my belief that Julia's treatment can be effected adequately by her GP. I will prescribe some medication to control her mood imbalances, and I intend to release her to her GP's care today, as soon as the police have seen her for a statement."

Simone's jaw clenched so hard it ached and she wanted to shake some sense into the diminutive man who somehow loomed powerfully over her. "So be it, but how do we ensure she meets her doctor's appointments?"

"That's not my jurisdiction, it'll be the responsibility of Julia, her GP, and probably your services too."

The coffee was cooling on the table, untouched and forgotten. Simone hoisted herself up, her bulky frame belittling the doctor. "Can I see her?"

"Be my guest." They both knew the meeting was over and, disgusted, Simone let herself out.

In the corridor, a uniformed officer stood by a notice board, waiting to see the doctor about the same patient. He had been plucked from the ongoing search for Melissa in Moor End, reluctantly spared from the team after a call from the psychiatrist at the hospital. The secretary showed him into Dr Mathura's room.

"My patient was brought to the hospital in the early hours of Saturday morning after an incident that may have put her child in danger. I was informed that the police had been involved." He explained that he intended to release the woman from his care, but needed to know if they would be charging her for the trauma she had put her son through four nights before.

The constable checked the details he had copied from the file at the station to his notepad, a reminder of who 'she' was, and of what 'she' had done. "Do you think Julia is mentally ill?"

"I don't think she has a clinical psychological condition, no. I think she needs some kind of help, that she's had some kind of traumatic experience that has set this behaviour off, but I think a GP handing out some anti-depressants, maybe a sympathetic ear, would be far more appropriate than a ward like this."

"Do you think she would harm her child, or should I say, put her child at risk of harm, if they were to be reunited?"

"Who knows? In my personal opinion, I don't think she intended to drop him or anything drastic like that. Everybody has a breaking point and I think she reached hers."

"If we were to take this further, prosecution wise, what effect do you think it would have on her?"

"Detrimental, of course, it wouldn't do anybody any good."

"Thanks, Dr Mathura, you've been very helpful. Now, you mentioned on the phone that she'll only speak to her social worker. Have you contacted them yet?"

The psychiatrist's jaw tensed, the recollection of the terse meeting resurfacing. "She's just gone to see the girl. You must have passed outside my room."

"So she's with her now? I'll go and see Julia, if that's okay, and see if she'll make a statement while she's got company. I can't see us prosecuting, to be honest, but obviously that's not ultimately my decision."

Julia watched blankly as Simone entered, drowsy and dulled from the medication she had been forced to take, and the social worker was shocked at how oddly frail the chubby woman had become since she had last seen her. They exchanged a few words and Simone explained that Julia would be allowed to leave the hospital after she had given a statement to the police. The officer joined them shortly after and Julia agreed to speak to him alone. Simone told them she would 'get things in order' at the office before returning to take Julia back to her flat. In reality, there was nothing to get in order, apart from her fury that Julia Collins was being discharged without proper assessment and assistance, as far as she was concerned, and she was about to direct that at her boss.

As head of the department, Grace often worked into the night, but recently the departmental cutbacks had doubled their caseloads and she felt as if she never went home. She beckoned Simone into her room and closed the door behind her. "What did you want to see me for?"

"I need to discuss the Collins family with you, did you not get my text?"

Reddening, she skimmed the texts on her mobile. "Yes, I see." She read the detail and sighed. "Well, obviously you're going to be quite involved with the family from now, until things have settled down. We need to set up a CPC as soon as possible. Have you done one before?"

"Yes, quite a few times. We know who the health visitor is from the previous concerns she has informed us of, perhaps she can help us to get her doctor involved. From what I understand there are no family members or significant others. The police were with Julia when I left the hospital, and they hadn't decided whether to prosecute her or not. You're not planning to put the boy back in her care, are you?" Simone was genuinely worried for his welfare while Julia's breakdown was ongoing, and was frustrated that nobody else seemed to share her concerns.

Grace waved a manicured hand, dismissive. "Of course not, not yet, anyway. But it's got to be the natural conclusion somewhere along the line. I imagine she's regretting her actions now; the spell in Ward Twelve will have been a frightener. I bet she can't wait to be reunited with little," she glanced at her notes, "Antony."

"I'm sorry, but you're wrong. She told me in no uncertain terms that she doesn't want the boy back. She says he won't be safe in her care, although she won't reveal why."

Grace tipped her head to the side. "A problem with Antony's father, do you think?"

"She's never mentioned anyone."

"Then she's just at the end of her tether. She's a little disturbed right now, but I'm sure that, with help, this family can be reunited and left to their own devices in the long run. We've seen it so many times before: an isolated parent, usually mother, with no support from family or friends, possibly depressed and definitely living in poverty. We need to set up a plan of action, a structured strategy to furnish the girl with support and practical help. You'll be involved intensely at first, but I'm sure it won't take long before Julia Collins is back on her feet."

Simone listened to the scripted patter with disbelief, a sense of wonderment at everybody's apparent inadequacies. Why could no one see that this mother, left untreated, was a danger to her child? Did the poor little mite have to die, or be seriously injured, before anybody took her concerns seriously? The words choked her, the incredulity so intense. "Grace, with all due respect, she dangled Antony from a third floor balcony, why does nobody seem to remember that?"

"It was a one off, my love, a cry for help. She's had a few days of peace and quiet now, and I have no intention of placing the child back in her care until a support mechanism has been set in place. Every mother loves her child, she'll be an empty shell without him."

70

"Every mother?" She spoke aloud unintentionally. "I'm not so sure any more."

Grace had only recently recruited Simone, whose credentials were strong and references amazing, onto the Child and Adolescent Support Team. She had taken to the job instantly, meeting the families inherited from her predecessor, efficiently keeping on top of the extensive paperwork, blending into the department as a likeable and jolly member. Grace had had no complaints, but the trust had to be earned. Having read the notes, she felt Simone was being overdramatic in this case. She sighed. "Oh, Simone, so jaded. I've been doing this job for over twenty years, my love, I think I know what I'm doing by now, don't you?"

The patronising words slapped Simone and her cheeks flushed with irritation. "I have also been doing this job for over twenty years, and…"

"Yes, my love, but not in this country, eh? It's all different in the less developed countries, everything's different."

There were no words to follow the blatant racism and Simone sat, silenced and open mouthed. A minute passed, with Grace sitting smugly behind her desk, fingers pyramided, a condescending smile on her face. Eventually Simone left the room, speech still evading her, and returned to her desk. She would follow Grace's orders – realistically she had no choice – but she would also document her disapproval of the reckless decision, safeguard herself in case there was fallout later.

Opening a new document on her computer, she typed a summary of the situation, followed by bullet-pointed disgruntlements. She was on the second page when the call came from the hospital asking her to collect Julia, and she saved the file and closed the computer down for the night. She collected her belongings together, grateful to be leaving at last.

The traffic was light now and the journey was soon over. Simone would have preferred to drop the girl by the doors of her block of flats and set off home to her sexy husband, but she was duty bound to give Julia the support she needed.

The young mother was desperately relieved to be home and she led Simone into the silent flat, locking the door behind them. She switched on the kettle to make a cup of tea for herself and Simone, rolling a cigarette as it brewed, and brought the drinks to the living room with a packet of value biscuits, adding them to the mess on the small table. She sat in her comfortable spot on the end of the sofa, Simone following her lead at the other end, and lit the roll-up, inhaling deeply. "Do you think you'll be okay here tonight, Julia?"

"I guess so, ain't got a choice really. But I've got my own bed and my own bog, and I know that Antony is safe. Yeah, I reckon I'm going to be fine." She took another long drag, savouring the taste, the light-headedness as the nicotine swept through her.

"Do you remember what I told you about what's going to happen from here?" Simone crossed her legs, and swiftly uncrossed them, remembering instantly how uncomfortable it had become, and she made a mental note that she must start the diet soon; Ian liked her meaty, but there had to be a limit.

Julia curled into the cushions, her fleshy features and oversized head belittling her plump body. "You come round first thing tomorrow, we go to the doctor, get me stuck on some tablet or other, and then you start arranging that meeting."

"It's not just about taking a tablet every day, Julia, I think you'd do well to ask for counselling. You don't have to tell me what's happened in your past, but I think that, whatever it is, getting it off your chest to a trained professional would be really beneficial to you."

Julia's eyes flitted to the carpet and remained there, while her cheeks became pasty. She resembled a lost child. "Simone, you've stuck around today," she caught her eye, exposing trust for the first time, "and I kind of believe you don't just want to help, but that you might really help. But, I'm sorry, I ain't telling nobody what happened." Her hand clutched her chest, emotion pouring from the clenched fingers. "I really can't say. You're right, my childhood was shit. They did stuff to me that they shouldn't have, and they made me do things I didn't want to, and I saw things no kid should ever see. But I can't tell nobody."

"Why, though?"

The vulnerability was gone as she pulled herself together. "Let's just say my life wouldn't be worth living, some people would make sure of that. I can deal with things, especially now Antony's gone somewhere where they can look after him properly."

"He won't be gone forever, Julia. You're his mother, he's your responsibility."

"No, I don't want him back. Maybe one day someone's going to listen to me and realise I mean that. I really do. I don't know if I love Antony, it's too hard, but I do care enough to want him to grow up somewhere where he *is* loved, and he *is* looked after properly, with a family who have enough money to give him what he wants and needs. And keeps him safe, he needs to be safe. I can never do that, I ain't got no career, and no qualifications to get one, and benefits just don't pay enough for the basics, let alone treats and days out, and holidays. He's better off elsewhere."

Jim cracked the door open, pulling it wide when he saw Sean, face pale with the cold and his bulbous nose crimson. "Did you find out anything more?" He closed the door hastily.

"They're searching everywhere. It's getting dangerous out there. We need to finish things off, and now." Sean laid a loving hand on Maria's shoulder. "Come on, Maz, let's get this over with. Have the cops been round to yours yet?"

Jim nodded. "About an hour ago. I told them we saw nothing and they were happy with that."

"Good. Come on, Maz, let's get the car."

Sean led his friend's wife through her back door, each checking covertly to ensure they had no witnesses, and padded along the unkempt garden to the narrow path that separated them from the houses behind. They entered his house, a few doors down, from the back and he snatched his car keys from the rack by the front door. Furtively, they crossed the driveway to his car, slipping in and starting the engine. The journey to the edge of the estate was short and they were pleased to find the row of garages in darkness, with no police activity and, uncommonly, no youths hanging about, smoking and drinking. Sean left the engine running as he slipped through the low opening that was set into the overhead door, returning shortly with a tartan shopping trolley, which he heaved into the boot of the car.

As he pulled away, he turned to Maria. "Black Park again?"

She nodded. "I know a good place where it shouldn't be found for a while."

The nature reserve was in blackness when they arrived, away from streetlights, and Sean parked the car on the verge of a nearby lane, rather than risk one of the several rangers, who lived and worked on site with their families, spotting them and becoming suspicious. He lifted the trolley out and handed it to Maria, who rapidly disappeared into the depths of the heavily wooded outskirts, wheeling the trolley behind her. Sean returned to the driver's seat to wait while she disposed of Melissa's body, preferring not to escort her as he figured the less he knew, the less he could be interrogated about should their hastily made plan be rumbled.

Twenty minutes later, she wheeled the trolley towards the car and he restarted the engine, pulling away as soon as she clambered in after placing the bag in the boot. "All done?"

"Done and dusted. Let's get home."

Half an hour later, she crept through the back door of her house, only to be met with Jim's furious fist. "You stupid fucking bitch." He struck her again. "What did you fucking do that for?" And again. "If we get caught, it's your fucking fault." And again.

And again.

Sergeant Andy Feldman was buzzing with the excitement of being part of the investigation, and nearly all of his officers

74

had been deployed over the course of the evening to assist with the search for Melissa in one way or another. He had preferred the comfort of staying in the warm confines of Castle Street Police Station, with hot drinks and snacks available whenever he wanted, but the to-ing and fro-ing of his staff had kept him informed with the events outside.

He knew he had a bad reputation with the female officers, because he couldn't keep his hands and lecherous thoughts to himself. He had been married for over ten years, but any semblance of happiness had left the partnership years before. They stayed together only for their two young children. His wife was a gratingly jealous woman and he dared not eye up the competition in her company for fear of her wrath. At work it was a different matter, and the sexy uniform was a bonus. Sally Ross had been a favourite to ogle, to undress with his eyes and mind, for a couple of years now, but the new blood, Toni Fowler, had given him some exciting dreams recently. Not a man to rock the boat, he hadn't acted on his fantasies, but coming to work was a release.

He gestured to Sally and she reluctantly ended her conversation and strode over. "Serge." She would normally have been home by this time of night, but every officer had been asked to stay while the search for Melissa was ongoing.

"I'd like you to go to Moor End, there's been reports of a disturbance in Princes Street…"

"That's where the kid went missing, are they linked?"

"I don't think so, just a domestic, the usual stuff, but I don't want to take an officer from that team to visit. Anyway, there's nothing we can do about it, but just go along and do a few head bobs, offer a bit of sympathy, that kind of thing. It was a neighbour who called in, said there's been screaming and shouting from the house. She said the woman's name is Maria." He passed a slip of paper to Sally, who checked the address was legible. "Apparently it's not the first time they've had trouble, the neighbour says she's called in before, but as far as she knows, they've never pressed charges."

"Okay, Serge. I'll take Fowler with me."

"Old hop-along Cassidy over there. Are you sure her dainty little ankle can handle it?" The sneered comment didn't match the salacious glance he gave Toni, his stilled fingers resting on the paperwork recently delivered from the control room. His behaviour always followed the same pattern when he hankered after one of his staff, treating them badly as a deflection of his own guilt, and Toni had been getting the brunt of his temper for the past couple of weeks. He leered at her, cute and petite, her blonde hair neatly wrapped into a bun at the nape of her slender, kissable neck. "If you must."

Sally repeated the minimal instructions to Toni, who sighed with relief to be getting away from the desk that had homed her since the previous Friday, partly due to her injury, but mainly because Feldman enjoyed demeaning her, and they collected the keys for a pool car on their way to the parking bay. The trip across town to poverty-filled Moor End was short and uneventful, and they parked outside a tatty semi that was in a state of disrepair, the postage stamp front garden littered with rotting junk and rubbish. The front door opened a crack and Maria watched nervously as the officers stepped over the debris to greet her. Toni and Sally had attended many domestics, they happened by the dozen over the weekends when alcohol flowed and tempers ran high, but seeing the swollen, scabbing, raw bruises around the women's eyes was never easy to stomach. "What do you want?" Maria was guarded.

"We've had reports of a disturbance…"

"Forget it, everything's fine." She tried to close the door but Toni put her foot in the way, instantly regretting it as the healing injury complained.

Sally was puzzled. "What are you doing, Toni?"

"I think we should have those injuries checked out, the bruising is very severe. Is your husband in, Maria? I assume it was him who did this to you."

"Well you're wrong. I fell down the stairs." This time, Toni removed her foot just in time as she slammed the door.

"What were you doing back there? You could see she was fine."

"What I could see was an open laptop with what looked like a disturbing image of a child on the screen. I think we need backup." Sally was already summoning help on the radio by the time Toni finished speaking.

Chapter 8
A Beaten Wife

With the amount of police activity surrounding the area, still searching for the missing girl, several officers responded to Sally's request for backup within minutes, and two met her at the back of the house, while four joined Toni at the front. When their hammering and shouting brought no response from inside, they issued a warning that they would break in if they received no answer. The wooden door was rotten at the edges and the lock aged, and they gained access easily with one sharp kick. DI Steadman ran through the filthy house to the back door to let her colleagues in.

Maria sat on a sofa that had seen better days, resigned to the raid, and she appeared to be alone. The officers began to search the house. "I told you everything was fine. There ain't nothing to see, so why don't you lot just bugger off."

Toni opened the lid of the laptop, which had been moved to the side of the cluttered table. The computer had been closed down, the screen blank. "Shall I turn it on?"

Steadman, the most senior officer on the raid, moved alongside her and clicked the computer, and slowly it booted up. "Get on the internet and look up recent searches, look at recently opened programs, check the disc tray, memory cards, whatever. Find whatever it was that you saw from outside." She turned to the battered woman. "Where's your husband?"

Maria shrugged, her swollen, heavily lined lips moving grotesquely. "I dunno. Probably down the pub, I expect, like he always is. What's it got to do with you?" She glanced at the computer nervously as Toni manoeuvred the keypad mouse.

"What's his full name?"

"Oh, for heaven's sake. Jim bleeding Collins. What's this all about? I ain't done nothing and nor has he."

Sally scanned the purple and blue battered face and sneered. "Sure looks like he has to me."

Whoever had turned the laptop off had been in a hurry and hadn't had a chance to delete their final activities; an image covered the screen and Toni's stomach lurched. "Shit, there's a picture of Melissa. I think you'd better see this."

Steadman wished she hadn't, and she withheld a gasp, dragging a pair of handcuffs from her duty belt. "I've seen enough. Bag it and get it to the techies, I want to know everything that's on that machine. Maria Collins, I'm arresting you for having underage pornographic material on your computer." She fastened the handcuffs without a struggle while issuing a caution, and shoved her towards a colleague, face twisted with repulsion. "Where's Melissa, Maria? Is she alive? And where's your husband?"

"No comment."

The officer guided Maria to the door while Steadman called her boss to tell him of the revolting discovery. Heading the Child Abuse Investigation Team, DCI Thirsk now had a good reason to be involved in the action, and he left the office minutes later, having given orders to find the pub Jim Collins frequented. The Nag's Head was closest to the house, an obvious choice, and a team burst in shouting his name. Immediately, the clientele focussed on their beers, not wanting to be involved, except one, who stared wildly, a deer caught in headlights.

Surrounded, there was no point trying to run, and the officers closed on Jim, shoving his arm painfully up his back and cuffing him. When Steadman spat the standard caution at him, citing Melissa's disappearance as the reason for his arrest, the only thought that sprung to his mind was that his stupid wife had buckled under pressure and spilled the beans. At that moment, spewing his disgust at the arrest with colourful words and indignation, he hated her more than he thought possible.

As Jim was led away by two constables, Thirsk rushed over and fronted him. "Where's Melissa Barton? What have you done with her?"

"Melissa who? I ain't saying nothing without a solicitor present."

"Come on, Jim, she's six, for god's sake. It's over, you're going down for this, at least tell us where she is so we can help her."

His plea fell on deaf ears, Jim merely laughed, exposing his yellowed, gravestone teeth, and the officers hauled him to a car. Thirsk glanced at Steadman. "Come on, let's go to their house and help with the search. You lot," he scanned the remaining officers outside the pub, "question everyone in there, he might have said something that will help us find her."

Running the short distance to Jim and Maria's home, they were aware of time ticking by, that each wasted minute could mean finding a body rather than a tortured child. Thirsk had always disliked children, even as one himself, and oddly this made him perfect for his recent promotion to Detective Chief Inspector in the Child Abuse Investigation Unit, as emotion would never cloud his judgement. His initial months on the job had been productive; he was successfully ploughing through the cases with his brash manner and curt ways, and that pleased his superiors.

The house was filthy throughout, with clutter and thick dust on every surface, the un-vacuumed carpets barely visible under the piles of rubbish that littered the floor. Beer cans and empty bottles were scattered over the furnishings in the living room, alongside overflowing ashtrays, and the cloying stench was gut-wrenching. The décor was hideous, with garish beige and brown wallpaper and magnolia gloss, and years of dirty hands had left grey, greasy stains on the walls and paintwork. Officers probed every corner, removing anything that may be relevant to both a child's murder and a pornography ring.

Thirsk and Steadman tried the kitchen, appalled by the stacks of unwashed dishes, glued together with solidified food, and they tugged open cupboards and drawers, desperate to find something – anything – to indicate where Melissa could be. "Guv, there's a pot of Rohypnol Flunitrazepam capsules here, no prescription label, they could have been used to drug her."

"Bag it." He tugged at the door of the built-in larder, wincing at the stickiness of the handle. Stepping inside the dingy space, he opened a further door, which revealed a staircase leading to a cellar. "Melissa, are you down there," he shouted as he ran down the steps. But switching on the light showed a bare room, apart from a wooden chair near the back. The walls had recently been whitewashed, evident by the heavy paint fumes, and the floor swept clean.

Steadman had followed him and was as disappointed as he by Melissa's absence. "Jesus, Guv, it's like a bomb site up there, and then they've got all this neat and tidy space down here. Doesn't make sense to me."

"No." He scratched his head. "Get someone to photograph this room from every possible angle."

"That image I saw on the laptop – god, I wish I hadn't – that could have been painted white. I think. I'm not sure."

"We'll need forensics down here. I want an inch-by-inch inspection. If he's had Melissa in here, there must be something." He climbed back up the staircase, slowly now with his despondency, and called a constable to the kitchen. "Bag every glass and mug you can find, I want them tested for DNA and traces of Rohypnol." Thirsk turned to Steadman, who had reached the top of the stairs behind him. "I'm going back to the station; I've seen enough of this shithole to last me a lifetime. You come with me. It looks like the only way we're going to find Melissa is by dragging it out of that arsehole and his tart."

Jim and Maria had been taken to separate interview rooms at the station, but neither had been interviewed and they were tired. They knew why they were being detained and were worried, going over the events of the day in their minds, wondering what the police may have found to incriminate them. Jim and Sean had discussed the possibilities of being caught many a time over their pints at The Nag's Head, or at home as they watched their income soar from their improper hobby, but they had never considered Maria's involvement in

81

an investigation, and Jim knew she was a loose cannon. She must have said something to them, otherwise the police wouldn't have caught up with him so quickly, and he wished she had been included in the conversations. He resolved to stick with the story he and Sean had devised, and if Maria was going to blabber, drop them from a height, he would retaliate; he had plenty of ammunition to fire back if need be.

He sat in the small, featureless room nursing a plastic cup of icy water, which was lame compared to the drop of whisky he could be enjoying. It was going to be a long night, and he laid his head on the table, too angry with his wife to sleep, but tired all the same.

Thirsk and Steadman exited the lift on the first floor. She would normally have used the stairs but wanted to spend as much time with her boss as possible; she had been keen on him for years, not that he had noticed. PC Gamboli, who had been guarding the rooms, greeted them. "Jim has requested his solicitor, but Maria said she didn't need one."

"Right. Any idea who his brief is?"

Gamboli laughed; he knew his boss hated the weedy, insipid man. "Jason Averill."

Thirsk rolled his eyes. "Great, a night with that tosser. Can't wait."

"He should be here soon, anyway, we called him an hour ago."

Thirsk hovered by the door to Interview Room 2 and glanced through the window at the prisoner, his head in his arms on the table. "It's him, alright, if there was a book on how to spot a paedo he would be on the cover, sick bastard. Has he said anything about Melissa since he's been in?"

"No."

"Damn, I hope we're not too late for her." Thirsk glanced across the corridor, through the window of Interview Room 3, and saw that Maria's head was also laid on folded arms, her wiry salt and pepper hair dishevelled.

Steadman followed his gaze to the haggard, grey woman. "Why don't you speak to her while you're waiting?"

82

"No, it's a waste of time. I don't think she's part of Melissa's disappearance, to be honest. I'm sure she knew about the website, and she might be a craggy old witch, but the sexual cases rarely involve women. No, I'm holding out for him and I want to be here when that smarmy dickhead of a brief arrives."

Steadman chuckled a little too long, hanging on to his words. "Do you want me to talk to her?"

He shook his head and the way his grey fringe flopped across his eyes warmed her heart. "No, I want you in with me."

And it warmed a little more. "Good Cop?"

"You've got it." For a moment, Thirsk considered who should take Maria's statement. "That rookie who spotted the laptop, that was some neat observation there. Without her we wouldn't have found that bastard anywhere near as quickly. Have you any idea who she is?"

Gamboli was one of several officers at the station who had noticed Toni's charms; she was unaffectedly pretty and appealing, and heads turned wherever she went. "Toni Fowler, Guv, works in the general office."

"She should still be working, Guv, everyone's been told it's all hands on deck until Melissa is found."

"Get the control room to get her up here. She can have the excitement of Maria's company. And get her to bring another plod with her."

"I don't think she's been here that long, she's pretty inexperienced." Steadman had more interaction with the second floor than her unsociable boss.

"Then it'll give her experience, won't it? Make sure whichever plod she brings has more experience. I don't know, just sort it out. I'll deal with Maria and the whole paedo ring after the kid's found. Anyway, if Maria's not having a brief with her, then it doesn't matter if they cock it up, does it? Piss off then, Gamboli, go and sort it out."

The constable nodded and trotted up the stairs, passing Dave from the technical department on the way. Thirsk spotted him and waved. "Dave, old mate, what have you got for me?"

"It's all good so far. We can definitely link him to a child pornography website. Rob's trying to hack in to it now."

"What does that mean?"

Dave explained in basic terms, aware of Thirsk's refusal to understand anything technical. The older man scratched his head through his hair, brow knitted with confusion, and Dave wasn't sure if it were possible to describe the process in a simpler way. But Thirsk was more savvy than he made out. "If he's having to hack in, what was it that rookie saw when she switched the computer on? The website wouldn't have just popped up like that."

"No, there are two different issues here. Rob's looking into the website, but what Fowler found was one of a set of thirty-three pictures that were uploaded onto the laptop, either directly from a camera, or from a memory card or disc. We don't know which yet, because nothing was with the computer when it came in."

"And the pictures are definitely of Melissa?"

"Yes, no question about it. They were all uploaded at just gone nine in the evening, according to the file properties." He noticed Thirsk's bewilderment and shook his head. "I'll make it simple for you: someone plugged something into the laptop at nine last night and uploaded several pictures of Melissa. Whatever device it was, it didn't come in with the laptop. The guys doing the search of the house are aware of this, and are looking for it."

"See, you can do it, plain speaking isn't that difficult after all, is it?" Dave was used to ridicule and didn't bat an eyelid. "What's the content of the pictures?"

He hung his head. "Not good, they're pretty hard to look at, but the good news is that she appears to be alive."

"Then I hope it's not a case of that was then and this is now." Again, he looked through the window, despising the filthy lowlife with an obscene mind who sat behind the table, awake now with the commotion outside the room. "I don't suppose he was in any of them."

"No, whoever staged those photos made sure they weren't caught on camera. We have no idea where the assaults took place."

"Are the walls whitewashed?"

"No, plain concrete or breeze block. It's a dark room with scant furniture – wooden chair and a yellow table, a makeshift bed, if you can call it that, on the floor – and there were a number of sex aides involved."

Thirsk glared at Jim, catching his eye. "Sick fucking bastard."

Toni, her painful ankle all but forgotten with the excitement, was amazed to find herself hobbling alongside Sally Ross to sit in on her first ever interview, and equally pleased that her colleague had attended the interview rooms before. She had known when she had taken the job at Castle Street that Thirsk was still on the force, albeit in a different department, but if he recognised her, he hadn't shown it.

He was as scary as he had been ten years before when they had met after she'd discovered Baby Jane, and she was embarrassed by the slight tremble in her hands as he barked orders, specifically to the more-experienced Sally, of the information he wanted them to get from Maria. He stated that, if she mentioned Melissa specifically, or her possible whereabouts, they were to immediately terminate the interview and let him take over. He instructed them to record the proceedings so he could listen to it after he had seen Jim. They were being dropped in at the deep end, but Toni had heard his reputation for pushing his staff to the limit.

Maria sat on the uncomfortable chair, her facial wounds now cleaned and steri-stripped by the station's first-aider, and glared at the two women as they entered. "I ain't done nothing and I don't know nothing. What are you keeping me here for?"

85

"You know why you're here, Maria." Sally's tone was brusque. "Do you know where Melissa Barton is?"

"No."

Sally placed the file she had brought onto the table and opened it. "So, what led to the fight tonight, then?"

"I don't know what you're talking about." Maria's eyes hadn't wavered from Sally's, challenging and obstructive.

"Oh, come on, Maria." She tapped the top page of the folder. "I've got the documents of seven domestic disturbances here in front of me, we know Jim treats you badly. He's had a go tonight, and you're sitting here, losing sleep, while you cover his arse. Is he really worth that devotion?"

Toni was unsure where Sally was heading with her questioning, but kept quiet, ready to take notes if needed. "Well? Tell me what happened. Do you understand the implications if Melissa isn't found safely soon? We don't think you had anything to do with her abduction, but your help to find her is invaluable, we're really concerned for her. All I want from you is what happened, it might help us find her. She's just a little girl, Maria. You've got children, haven't you?"

"My Jules is dead to me, and I don't know nothing about that girl. Just like I told your lot when you came to my door."

Watching the interview on the screen in the observation room, Thirsk, still waiting for the solicitor to arrive, rolled his eyes at the inexperienced officer pussyfooting around. "For heaven's sake, toughen up, woman, it's like watching fucking paint dry."

Sally and Toni couldn't hear him, but Toni shared his view and her patience ran short. If she was acting out of turn, who cared? "What did you do to upset him? Did you find him with the kid and have a go at him, let him beat the crap out of you rather than tell us what he had done? You know that makes you an accessory, don't you?"

Maria hadn't considered that, and Thirsk was impressed at how easily the young rookie had broken the woman, who burst into tears, her craggy skin reddening as the thread veins that littered her face swelled. "I don't know anything about no girl, I swear. I fell down the stairs. Jim weren't even there, he was down the pub."

Thirsk turned to Steadman, who had joined him, also bored of waiting for Jason Averill. "What did Gamboli say her name was? The blonde one."

"Fowler, Guv, been on the force ten months tops."

"She's a natural, I reckon." Gamboli stuck his head around the door to inform them that the criminal lawyer had arrived. Groaning, Thirsk nodded for Steadman to follow him to brief Jason Averill.

Inside Interview Room 3, Sally, stunned to be the good guy for once, pacified Maria as she sobbed heartily. "Look, I know it's difficult, but whether you admit Jim hit you or not, I think he's going away for quite some time. What difference does it make now if you cover his back? You're likely to get yourself in more trouble if you're not honest, because we know that you knew about the child porn."

The sigh was drawn out as Maria, resigned, collected her thoughts, swallowing hard to stop her tears. "Okay, okay, stop bleeding nagging me." She swallowed again with an audible gulp. "He likes a drink, does my Jim, and when he gets himself tanked up he gets a bit handy with his fists, it's as simple as that. I can normally handle it, but this time was worse than normal."

Toni watched the woman as she spoke reluctantly, her nose misshapen from years of battering, her demeanour impassive and unassuming, like most of the domestic violence victims she had met in the course of her job. She felt sorry for her, but also thought the women had a responsibility to take control of their own lives. It was difficult for her to choose which side of the fence to sit on. "We have Jim in custody, Maria, and I can assure you he hasn't had enough to alcohol to stop him being interviewed, so that's all crap, really, isn't it? In fact, from the smell of you, I can tell you like a drink too. Did you provoke him?"

"You're bleeding provoking me, this is bleeding harassment. I didn't do nothing." She wiped her tears and nose with her jumper sleeve and Toni cringed. "He's always down the pub, might as well live there, for heaven's sake, all the bleeding time he spends there. Maybe he only had one drink, how would I bleeding know, but this," she pointed angrily at her puffy face, "is what happened all the same."

"So, he had been to the pub, or you assumed he had been to the pub, and he came home, angry? What happened then?" Toni loved that she was getting a response, it made her feel powerful, and confirmed to her that she had chosen the right career, for now, anyway.

"He's always coming home worse for wear. He likes a drink, I told you that."

Sally tapped the paperwork for a second time. "We had a call from a concerned neighbour just after ten, reporting screams and excessive shouting from your property. What happened to make him so angry, angry enough to do this to you?"

"I just get on his nerves, that's all. There was no reason, he just needed to let off a bit of steam."

"Did you know Melissa? I heard she's a real sweet little thing."

"She's Val's kid, that's all I know. I served my time when I was bringing my girl up so I don't have much to do with the kids around our street. First thing I knew about her being missing was when the cops started turning up outside the school. Then everything went crazy, so I just stayed inside and kept my nose out of it. I reckoned Jim was at the pub, he had been out since lunchtime after he had woken up. He got home and he was really angry about something, but I don't know what. When he's in a bad mood he likes to take it out on me, so I just went to bed, but he couldn't leave it and he dragged me out," her voice tailed off, the memory of the beating painful, "by the hair." She ran her hand, old before her years, over her steel-wool curls, wincing.

Toni threw her hands on the desk, shocking the other two women. "But you weren't in your nightclothes when we came round after the reports. So that's not quite true, is it?"

Maria snapped back to the present, affronted by the allegation, and some vigour returned to her voice. "So what. So sometimes I sleep in my clothes. Big deal. I ain't never given him a reason to thump me, I just stand there and take it. Normally he'll give me a few punches and get bored, but this time he was really angry and wouldn't let up. So forgive me if I didn't bother to get a bleeding nightie on."

"So he assaulted you for no apparent reason. Nice guy." The sarcasm was laden and Toni was astounded by how tough she was being. It was unlike her, but she was enjoying it in an odd way and it was getting results. "I mean, and pardon me if it sounds like a stupid idea, but hasn't it ever occurred to you to leave him, just leave him to wallow in his filth while you actually find a life for yourself?"

"First of all, my religion doesn't tolerate divorce, and secondly, you don't know much about bleeding wife-beaters, do you? Sitting there all prim and bleeding proper, barely out of bleeding gymslips yourself." She leant forward and glared at Toni. "They don't let you go, they hunt you down and either get you back like a prisoner, or kill you and your family, I've seen it all before. I've been with my Jim nearly thirty years, at least I know what I'm getting with him. It ain't the injuries, I'm used to them. He's not all bad, he's got a good heart." Her tirade had stopped, and so had her tears, leaving an aching silence throughout the room.

Sally took over the questioning, concerned that Toni was out of her depth. "Maria, I hear what you say about your religion, but it's a different world nowadays. Jim's going down anyway, he won't be coming back home, so where's the harm? Even if he did miraculously escape a custodial sentence, you know he'll do this again and again, he's not going to change."

"Well if he ain't coming home, there ain't no reason to divorce him, is there."

"Fair enough, but I still think you could do with someone who doesn't treat you badly by your side. We can put you in touch with people who can help. You mentioned you had a daughter earlier, that you're estranged, can you not try and resolve things with her, let her support you? If he's like this with you, I doubt she got off punch free when she was growing up."

Maria sat quietly, undecided, and Toni picked up the thread. "You knew about the child porn, you must have, the images were on the screen while you were in the room. So maybe you were too scared of Jim to challenge his filthy habit, but if you agree to help us press charges for your injuries, it will help with our investigation greatly, and maybe the fact that you were an accessory won't do you too much damage. I'm sure cooperating with us will stand in your favour."

"Plus," Sally could see Maria was being swayed, "we can find your daughter. You don't have to be alone."

"I don't know about Jules, we fell out big style and it was a long time ago. Last I heard, and that was on the grapevine, was that she had a kid herself."

"Tell me her name, Maria, we'll find her and do what we can to help."

"Julia. She was Collins, but she might be married now, for all I know." Sally and Toni exchanged a stunned glance. They knew exactly where to find Maria's daughter.

Chapter 9
A Wife Beater

Thirsk and Steadman outlined the circumstances of Jim's arrest to Jason Averill, and waited in the observation room, watching Maria's interview, while the solicitor spent some time with his client. Eventually, Averill informed Gamboli that they were ready. Thirsk and Steadman took their coffees to Interview Room 2, introducing themselves to the tape and the odious man behind the table. Jim Collins was unkempt, his clothes a mess and hygiene wanting, and Thirsk had seen hundreds of wasters like him during his thirty-four years on the force. "You've been briefed, I take it?"

Averill nodded, pointing to his A4 pad on the table, poor handwriting scribbled over the page. The folded corners and ink smudges on the paper revealed a disorganised and careless man, and Thirsk mused that he and his client fitted each other beautifully. "Are you ready to tell me where Melissa is? We need to know."

"My client informs me that he doesn't know Melissa Barton." His voice was as weedy as his attitude.

Thirsk and Steadman, tired of sitting, were leaning on the back wall, either side of the barred window, and they glanced at each other. Before Thirsk's promotion, they had worked together closely and could read one another, and situations, well without words. "Why did you beat your wife up, Jim?"

"She told you that, did she?" Jim leant back and crossed his arms, cocky, and Averill squirmed – nobody had mentioned domestic violence.

"Actually, she did, but she didn't need to – it's written all over her face. Pardon the pun. Did she find you with Melissa and you beat her to shut her up?"

"Fuck off. She fell over in the shower. She's a clumsy bitch when she drinks too much and she's always on the pop nowadays. Bloody alcoholic, that woman."

"We found images on your laptop of Melissa Barton being abused, and the girl is still missing. How did you get those images, Jim? Was it you who took them? Where is she?"

"I ain't got no laptop, I'm one of those techno-whatevers, I don't know how to use them. The wife bought it, thought she would try and be a bit clever, stupid cow, and then she got hooked on that bloody Facebook thing. If there's anything on that thing it didn't come from me."

Thirsk let out a snort, incredulous. "It's hardly the type of thing a woman would be looking at, Jim, be realistic. I may look it, but I'm not dumb."

"She ain't your normal woman." His lips twisted with disdain.

"You, Jim, *you* have obscene photos of a girl who's been abducted on your computer, it's all…"

"No." Jim sneered and the image of his yellow, plaque-covered teeth firmly lodged, uninvited, in Thirsk's memory. "You know that somebody has put them on that computer, that doesn't mean it's me. Try the wife like I told you."

"The school the girl was snatched from is across the road from your house. Quite a coincidence, don't you think? What did you do before you went to the pub yesterday, eh? A little fumble with a terrified girl, maybe?"

"Inspector Thirsk, I…" Averill half stood.

"Shut up. Where is she? Where is Melissa?"

"If some kid's gone missing and got herself hurt, it ain't got nothing to do with me." His dismissal was cold and emotionless, eyes empty, which irked Thirsk, who was proud of his own ability to build a protective wall between himself and reality. "I was in bed until gone midday, the wife will tell you that, and I went straight to the pub when I got up." Thirsk wanted to add 'without washing' – the room was thick with the man's stale body odour and halitosis – but knew it would be unproductive. "You dickheads picked me up from there. So I had nothing to do with some little tart skipping school, and nothing to do with anything on a computer."

"Inspector Thirsk, you don't actually have anything on my client at all. The computer's not his, he doesn't know the missing girl, he has an alibi..."

Thirsk glared at Averill, who shrank, and returned his scorn to Jim. "In your dreams, Jim, stop wasting my time, it's getting wearing now. What is it, Jim? You were down the pub? Those idiots down there are so pissed and drugged all the time, they wouldn't be able to tell what day it was, let alone whether you were there all day or not. They're hardly credible witnesses, are they?"

"Smacker don't get drunk, and he'll tell you."

Thirsk sighed, patronising, and shook his head lightly. "And Smacker is who?"

"The landlord, that's his name." Jim smugly lounged back in his chair, an ankle on his knee, and placed his hands behind his head. A foul stench emanated from his armpits and Steadman discreetly turned her head, fingers covering her nose and mouth.

Thirsk nodded to his colleague who, reading his mind, left the room to find someone to take the landlord's statement. "Maria's pressing charges, you know." He doubted it was true, but he needed to knock Jim's confidence.

Averill was angry that he knew nothing about the violence. He had spoken to the detectives and his client individually, and neither side had mentioned it. However, because Jim had been arrested for a completely different matter, the police were not compelled to have told him and he had to withhold his objection.

Beside him, keenly noticed by Thirsk, Jim's arrogance had wavered. His brash position remained, killing the once fresh air with his stench, but it was bravado, the peacock tail of a disconcerted man. "Nah, she wouldn't do that."

"Right across the hall, Jim, she's in a room right across the hall. I have two officers taking the statement as we speak. I bet she's not going to lie and tell me you don't use that computer. There isn't a person on this planet who doesn't know something about computers." Such a hypocrite; he could switch his PC on and type the password, but after that he was clueless. He sat back, drumming his fingers on the arm of the chair.

"I don't know how to use the bloody thing, I told you." He gestured to the door. "So she's giving you the old 'I'm so mistreated and such a victim' crap. Fine, she's a fucking attention seeker, my Maria, but she'll drop the charges when she sees sense, I'll make sure she does. Don't be taken in by her stupid little voice and fluttering eyelashes, that woman's not as innocent as she makes out. I took a few pops at her, she'd annoyed me. I was tired and she was nagging me. So what? She needs to be kept in her place, that bloody woman, trust me."

"I think we can safely agree that I will never trust you, Jim. I haven't met your wife yet, so any little-girl act she may have put on hasn't reached me. The photos on your computer, where did they come from? Did you get them off the internet? Or did you take them? I think we both know the answer to that, don't you?"

Jim smiled, relaxing, as he realised that they had nothing solid on him when it came to Melissa. A few bruises on his wife's face, but nothing to link him to the girl's disappearance. All he had to do was keep denying any knowledge and he was sure he would be back in the pub in by the end of the day. "I don't know nothing about them. I told you, I don't use that thing, I ain't got no idea when it comes to computers and all that crap. I'm a technophobe." He grinned with pride for having remembered the word he had been searching for, and the spittle on his stained teeth glistened in the harsh light.

The interview had produced nothing except to cement Thirsk's immediate and intense dislike of the man, but he was confident Jim was lying. Steadman returned to the room and her boss was relieved with her impeccable timing. He nodded to the door and terminated the interview, and as he left the room, he breathed deeply, filling his lungs with the fresh, untainted air. Averill gathered his notes together and rushed after the detectives without bidding the prisoner goodbye, and he grasped Steadman's elbow. "Why didn't you tell me about the domestic abuse? Don't you think that was a little unethical?"

Thirsk and Steadman caught each other's eyes, the corners of their mouths twitching. "I'm sorry, Jase, did it make things difficult? I just felt it was irrelevant to the case we're investigating. Don't you agree, Guv?" The disgruntled solicitor strode away, muttering under his breath, and they chuckled.

In the interview room opposite, the two constables were wrapping up their interview with Maria Collins, and Thirsk leant on the wall to wait for them. "You may as well get off home to bed, Steadman, you look exhausted."

She sagged her shoulders elaborately to display her weariness. "You got me, Guv, I'm bushed. See you tomorrow. Well, later today."

She headed down the stairs, just as Toni and Sally stepped out of Interview Room 3. Thirsk closed the door behind them and whispered needlessly. "Did you get anything?"

"Not much, but," Sally passed him the DVD of the interview, "watch this if you want."

"Thanks, girls. I'm sure you did well in there."

"Should we let her go home?"

He checked his watch, it was after one in the morning. "No, let me see this first, but you two get on home, I'll make sure you get paid overtime for this. Go on, get out of here."

"But what about finding Melissa?"

"We won't find her overnight, not unless one of these two lowlifes admits where she is."

The two tired newbies trudged towards the stairs, and, as an afterthought, Toni turned back. "By the way, did you know that it's their daughter who hung the toddler over the balcony the other night?"

His eyes widened. "You're kidding me? Didn't they section her?"

Toni shrugged. "I think so." She remembered the scene in the hospital – Julia's capture by the nurses, the authoritative

Joyce Frobisher – and for the first time in an hour felt her injured ankle tweak.

"Interesting. Do me a favour, girls, go and see her tomorrow, get an idea of what it was like growing up with those two scumbags." He spotted the shared, worried expressions on their faces and sighed. "It's okay, I'll clear it with Sergeant Feldman, he'll be fine."

Simone had been reluctant to leave Julia, spending several hours talking with her, making mugs of tea, and listening to her experiences at hospital. She had concluded that Julia was good at saying a lot without actually telling her anything, and she still had no inkling about the girl's childhood. She hoped that the more time she spent with her, the more the girl would trust her, and she was sure it would all tumble out when Julia was ready. Simone checked her watch and was shocked to see midnight was long gone. She tugged her cardigan around her ample bosom and clutched her bag. "I really must go, Julia, it's so late. I'll be round tomorrow to help you organise a doctor's appointment."

Julia was grateful Simone was leaving, desperate to go to bed and put the past four days behind her, but as they stood, a jingly tune began to play. Julia rummaged through the mess on the table for her mobile, holding a finger up to Simone. " I'll be with you in a sec." She held the phone to her ear. "Hello." Julia listened for a moment and her eyes widened with worry. "But they came to see me earlier, this copper, at the hospital. He told me you lot wasn't going to prosecute me. I thought it was all over."

The call had Simone's interest and she wished she could hear the caller. "What do you mean, a different matter? I ain't done nothing wrong, I ain't even stolen nothing, or anything." The two women stared at each other, one terrified, the other curious. "Ten tomorrow morning. Okay… I said okay, didn't I?" Julia cut the call and threw the mobile on the sofa, tears threatening and her brow furrowed.

"What's going on?" Simone was aching to get back to her husband and wished she had left five minutes before to avoid witnessing the distressing call.

Julia sank onto her place on the sofa and put her head in her hands, sobbing. "See, that's the thing, everybody promises this, that and the other, but it's always lies at the end of the day. That lot won't be fucking happy until they've banged me up and thrown away the key. I fucking hate my life."

Simone was too tired for dramatics. "Go on, who was it?"

"The coppers want to see me tomorrow. Said they're coming to see me at quarter to ten. They said it wasn't about Antony, but I haven't done anything else, I've been in bloody hospital."

Annoyed that the police weren't making her job any easier, Simone sighed deeply. "I'll be round at nine, we can make an appointment at the doctor's, then I be with you for support."

Despite the hour, the incident room was buzzing when Thirsk reached the fifth floor, with officers on phones, computers, hustling and bustling, all too anxious to sleep as long as Melissa Barton remained unfound. As soon as Thirsk strode through the door, three of his staff jumped him, all talking at the same time. "Give me a chance, boys. First things first: has the kid been found?"

"No." Three voices in unison, but at least they had said the same this time.

"Right, that's all I need to know for now. Someone get me a strong coffee; I need a few minutes before you all start bombarding me."

He closed his office door and slumped onto his seat, leaning under the desk to put the DVD into the computer. He listened without interest, fast-forwarding through the parts he had already seen. Every now and then he smiled at the two the rookies doing a fairly impressive job for their lack of experience, but throughout the interview, one sentence kept haunting him: *'They don't let you go, they hunt you down and either get you back like a prisoner, or kill you and your family, I've seen it all before.'* It was growled and seeping with heartfelt anger. The statement had been made early into the interview, and whereas he would have questioned it there and then, Ross and Fowler didn't have his observation skills just yet. It niggled him throughout the recording, which didn't reveal anything of interest, so once it ended, he restarted the DVD to listen again. Was he being silly out of tiredness? Was it a throwaway comment?

He drained the bitterly strong coffee that had been placed on his desk, deliberating the sentence until it tripped repeatedly through his exhausted mind. The magnitude of Melissa's disappearance was too great to leave the office and he wantonly eyed the makeshift camp bed in the corner of the room, wishing he were under the covers. When Gamboli called, explaining Maria Collins was kicking up because she wanted to go home, sleep was forgotten. "No, keep her there for a minute. Get her a coffee, or whatever, and tell her I want a word."

Thirsk ended the call and left his office. "Has the search of the Collins' house been finished yet?"

"I think they're just wrapping up now. I don't think much has been found though."

"So you're Maria Collins." She raised her head and regarded the man of a similar age to herself, before nodding. Thirsk introduced himself and sat opposite. "I've just listened to the recording of your interview with my two officers. I can see you've been through a lot over the years." She regarded him warily. "Tell me about the laptop. Jim tells me it's yours and that he never uses it."

"Oh, for heaven's sake, the lying git. I barely get a bleeding look in on that bleeding thing, he's the one who uses it."

His impromptu decision to speak to her was paying off. "He says he's a technophobe."

"Well, he ain't." Maria's confusion twisted her features. Jim had promised to protect her, so why was he pointing the finger at her?

"You know about the pornographic images on the computer. What's the story behind that?"

"They ain't nothing to do with me. He uses that thing for his reasons, I use it for mine. If there's dodgy pictures on there, it's not down to me."

"Do you trust your husband?"

She grinned lethargically, displaying rotting, broken teeth, and he grimaced. "About as far as I can throw him, and that's not far." The cliché grated on him, just as everything seemed to in the early hour. "He spends his life in the pub, my Jim, gets himself pissed up day in day out using money we haven't got, and when he gets home he can get a bit handy with me. But when he's finished with me, when I've gone up to bed, he sits on that bleeding thing for half the night, and Lord knows what he's up to."

"Looking at innocent little girls, Maria. How do you feel about that? Did you know he was into kids?"

Despite her tiredness, she could see the bait being thrown and she clammed up, searching for the right words. "I just thought he had another woman, I don't know. It's not up to me to question what he does, he makes sure about that."

"With violence, no doubt. On the tape you mentioned he would hunt you down and kill you if you left him, what did you mean by that?"

She splayed her hands, exasperated. "Nothing, I just know he wouldn't be happy. Your coppers were trying to get me to leave him and I don't want to."

"Don't want to, or you're too scared? What is it you've seen before, Maria?"

The walls came up instantly and he realised she wasn't going to buckle. Not yet, anyway. Any more time with her tonight would be wasted, and dawn would bring another day. "Thanks for your time, Maria. Look, we can't let you home tonight, the search is still in progress. Do you have anywhere else you could go? We can drop you off anywhere, as long as you stay in the area for now."

She laid her head on the table with a groan. "I'll have to stop at my brother's, I suppose." Thirsk opened the door to leave, but had an afterthought. "You know, Julia's recently become known to us, I think she could do with your support at the moment, as much as you could probably do with hers."

Maria sat straight again, vehement. "Look, I wish you lot would stop bringing her up. I ain't seen her since she was thirteen when they took her into care and I don't know nothing about her. I don't want to neither, it's bleeding good riddance to bad rubbish, that's what I say."

He was being rewarded for his perseverance and he faced her, smirking at his understatement. "It doesn't sound like you're very close."

"She was a bleeding ungrateful cow. I cooked and cleaned for her, brought her up as best I could, gave her whatever she wanted, I did, and she repaid me by begging the bleeding social to take her away. Don't you misjudge me, mister, I didn't send the bleeding tart away, she wanted to be re-homed. Ungrateful cow, she was."

Thirsk was shocked. "Why call her a tart, Maria, it's rather a strong word for your own daughter, don't you think? Especially one who was only a child when you last saw her. Was she promiscuous?"

Maria waggled her finger at him, impacting her view. "From the moment she turned two, I swear. Batting her bleeding eyelids at my husband, at my brother, my dad, at any man she could wind around her little finger, in fact. Little tart, she was, right from the word go."

Thirsk was uneasy, and now he couldn't wait to hear what Julia Collins had to say about her parents. He also realised there was something far more sordid about Maria Collins than they had previously thought, and he intended to find the truth. At this moment, though, he needed to sleep, and after arranging for Maria to be taken to her brother's house, and checking for news about Melissa, he asked the

100

overnighters to wake him if there were any developments and took to his camp bed for some well-earned shut-eye.

Chapter 10
The End of the Search

At just past three in the morning, Rob Bates managed to hack into the encrypted website that frequently came up in the search history of Jim and Maria's laptop. He had seen the photos that had been uploaded to the computer, Dave had copied them as soon as it had arrived in the technical department, so he was unsurprised that the website was devoted to child pornography, but his stomach lurched when he opened the first file. "Oh, my god."

Dave had been snoozing for a while, reluctant to go home until they had finished their part of the investigation, and the distressed exclamation reached his psyche. He lifted his head from the desk. "Are you in?"

"It's not good. It's definitely a child porn ring. There are dozens of video clips on there, poor kids. I only clicked on one, but I saw enough." Rob rang through to the incident room, repeating the news. "It gets worse. There must be seven or eight different girls, with several clips of each. I think someone had better come and see the footage."

Rob replaced the receiver and sat back, relieved that once he showed whichever detective was coming downstairs how to view the revolting site, his job was done for the night. He sipped the energy drink on his desk to keep himself awake for those few more minutes. Presently, Thirsk, dishevelled and yawing, his floppy, silvering hair mussed, strolled in. "I hear you have something for me."

Rob clicked on a file and a video-clip began to play on the screen. The first minute of sickening content had Thirsk reaching for a chair, his eyes not leaving the monitor for a second. "How much of this filth have you looked at?"

Rob had averted his eyes; he had a daughter of four and the images reminded him that she would never be safe from the perversity of the world. "Less than you, I couldn't handle it."

"You're going to have to, I'm afraid. We're going to have to analyse these videos, and right now."

Rob's eyes were reddened and watery from tiredness and he stared at Thirsk, almost pleading. "Right now?"

An hour of sleep that had only felt like ten minutes hadn't been enough, and Thirsk's volatile temper was threatening. "I don't give a shit about how fucking tired we all are. Somewhere out there," he gestured to the window, a slate sheet reflecting the fluorescent lights of the office, "is a terrified little girl. If we can work out from the videos where these atrocities took place, any clue at all, there's a chance we could find her alive."

The point hit and shamed the technicians instantly, and Dave mustered a calming voice. "Give me five minutes, I'll get it set up on the projector. Do you want anyone else in?"

Thirsk surveyed the screen and shook his head. "Just me, I don't want anyone seeing this filth unnecessarily, it's too degrading." He was resigned and unemotional to the job, but could see how pale Rob had become. He noticed a framed picture on the man's desk, grinning and proud, beside an attractive woman. They held a little girl jointly in their arms, a beaming, innocent child full of life and dreams. "That's your daughter?" Rob nodded woefully. "Go home, Rob. Dave, you're alright to stay, aren't you?"

Over an hour of sickening abuse flickered from the overhead projector screen. All the girls were young, very young, and all appeared to be either unconscious or dozy as they were assaulted. No attempt had been made to conceal their identities and periodically Thirsk took notes. Apart from their facial details, Thirsk avoided looking at the girls and the cruelty being inflicted on them, but he noted every detail of the room they were captured in. The camera always filmed from the same angle. In the bottom left corner of the screen was a pile of blankets with a blue-cased pillow, a yellow melamine-topped table stood in the centre, and a large, worn dining chair constructed from a dark wood, probably oak, was to the right. The victims, often the same girls more than once, were either on the chair or the table as the vile acts were carried out. No external light was visible, so either there was no window, or a set of very thick curtains. The walls were unpainted breezeblocks and the floor bare concrete. Over the course of the despicable screening, Thirsk realised they were still no closer to finding Melissa.

As the last video-clip closed, Thirsk and Dave were speechless as they digested the loathsome horrors. Dave packed away the projector screen, deeply troubled by the attacks, while Thirsk simply sat. Finally, he passed a slip of paper to Dave, his voice course. "Can you get stills of these bits?"

"I can, but you'll have to give me a while. How urgent is it?" Tiredness haunted Dave, he felt as if he were floating.

"We need to identify as many of those kids as possible, and that has to happen quickly, but that one," he pointed to one of his instructions on the slip of paper that had been double-underlined, "that's Melissa. I need to know when it was posted and from where, and I need you to find part of the clip that doesn't have her being abused, something we can show to my officers so they know what the room we're looking for is like. I don't want anything circulated that could possibly humiliate the girl or her family."

"I'll do it right away."

"Have you any way of finding out who else accesses those sites?"

"It's possible, but it won't happen quickly."

He nodded. "As soon as, okay? The sooner we round up the perverted bastards who get their rocks off to that revolting crap, the better."

It was four-thirty when Thirsk trudged back to his office, his opinion of the world sunken that little bit further after the harrowing screening. He returned to the warmth and discomfort of the camp bed that wasn't quite long enough to contain his tall frame if he stretched out, but too narrow to contain it if he didn't. Regardless, sleep took over without a fight in seconds.

Everyone who worked for Castle Street Police Station knew about Melissa's abduction, and DCI Nick Wainwright had half-expected the call that woke him at five in the morning telling him the body of a child had been found by a ranger patrolling Black Park half an hour before. At first, the ranger had thought it was some discarded clothing caught in the low branches of a tree that edged and dipped into the lake, but closer inspection had revealed a bloated human mass. "Has Thirsk been notified?"

"Not yet, sir, he's asleep."

"I'll bet he's been up most of the night. Don't wake him. I'll go there now and report to him when I've seen what's going on." Wainwright replaced the receiver, his heart heavy now the hope of finding the girl alive had been dashed, and dressed in yesterday's suit and shirt; he would shower and change later.

Soon after, he was picked up and driven to the nature reserve, normally a stunning haven, but today a sombre gravesite. Two constables guarded the main gates and they directed the car towards the crime scene. The dirt path that bordered the lake had evolved naturally, with only a smidgeon of help from the staff who lovingly tended the park, and was unsuitable for cars, which meant they had to park four hundred metres away and walk. Officers had cordoned off the area, but so far nobody had touched the body. A paramedic had been the first to arrive and had taken moments to confirm the child was dead, and probably had been a while. After, a photographer had taken images from every angle to accurately record the scene.

Wainwright greeted the officials already present, before studying the body. Head down in the water, with black rat tails of shoulder-length hair floating on the surface, the only thing at this stage that gave away her sex and probably identity was the clothes she had been dumped in: a pair of black trousers and the distinctive cobalt sweatshirt that was worn at Princes Street School. He could do nothing but wait for the rest of the officials to arrive, and because of the early hour, that was likely to take a while. He dialled his ex-boss and long-time mentor. "You sound rough, Guv."

Thirsk lay face down on the pokey makeshift bed, and he was bad-tempered and gravel-voiced with tiredness. "They've found Melissa, haven't they?" The silence on his mobile phone answered him. "Where are you?"

"Black Park Lake. The control room know the exact location, get someone to drive you down. I'm assuming you'll want to see her?" Thirsk agreed and cut the call, and after a wide yawn and relieving stretch, he began the day just over an hour after he had finished the last.

Wainwright made the most of the time before the various specialists arrived by surveying the area, careful not to tread or touch anywhere that may hold evidence to what had happened to the victim. The rising sun gently eased the night aside and the surrounding area became busy as scientists and officers arrived to carry out their individual tasks. Thirsk reached the car park at the same time as the duty pathologist, Hugh Smythe. They shook hands and Thirsk waited while Hugh took a white paper coverall, a pair of blue plastic booties and a cap from the boot of his car to wear once they reached the body.

Together, led by a constable, they traipsed along the pathway to where Wainwright waited for them, greeting them with a firm handshake. Hugh donned the outerwear to avoid contamination of evidence, while Wainwright briefed them with everything he knew, which wasn't much. The chilly breeze, exacerbated by the cool water, whipped around their shoulders as Hugh lifted the tape to enter the crime scene, and Thirsk dug his hands deeply into the pockets of his trench-coat. "You know we have a ponce in custody, don't you?"

"I heard something about it last night. Obviously I'll need all the details now." Before Thirsk had been promoted to his current position, he had been with the Major Investigation Team for fifteen years, and for ten of those had worked alongside Wainwright. They were friends as well as colleagues and respected one another. Thirsk had spotted the younger man's potential from the start and had deliberately given him a tough time to prepare him for the high places he had been sure to reach with continued dedication and thorough work. Only mid-thirties, Wainwright was a time-served and highly esteemed Detective Chief Inspector for the murder team, and he had learned most of his tricks from his former superior.

Hugh reached the bloated body, gently undulating as the wind caressed the water, the limbs tangled and trapped within the branches of the tree. He knelt beside the swollen heap, the bank of the lake muddy and cold, and his feet and knees settled into the swampy soil as he began his preliminary examination. He examined the muddied skin, pale blue and puffy in death. He checked the eyes, mouth, tongue and hair, relating the observations to his dictaphone as a reminder for his notes after the post-mortem, and after checking her fingernails, he bagged both hands. The two detectives watched, catching the odd word or two, but not enough to be sure of how the child had died, and finally he clicked the machine off and addressed them. "You can do the forensic testing now, but carefully, please." Wainwright nodded to a pair of crime scene investigators, who carefully took necessary samples of the area and body.

"Anything you can tell us yet?" Wainwright knew he wouldn't get a detailed answer until the post-mortem had been done, and Hugh's raised eyebrow mocking his impatience was heeded. "Even a rough time of death will do."

"Almost full rigor mortis, so she's been dead a while, and the lividity shows she died on her back, so she was dumped here. The rigor mortis may have been affected by being immersed in cold water, so I'm not suggesting a time of death without further investigation. I don't know the cause of death at this stage, but her eyes are bloodshot, which may indicate that she died from asphyxiation of some form or other."

"Drowning, right?" Wainwright suggested.

"I'll let you know when I have the facts."

"Is it definitely Melissa?"

"She's roughly six years old, maybe seven, that's all I can say for now."

"Can we rule out misadventure?" Wainwright received another sardonic expression from Hugh, and the exchange reminded Thirsk of how he had been years before when he had wanted all the answers immediately. He remembered hassling Hugh's predecessor in exactly the same way. Nowadays, he knew the constraints and had patience.

Two mortuary assistants bagged the body and strapped it to a trolley to wheel to a waiting ambulance a quarter of a mile away, and Hugh tore the soiled overalls from his daywear and placed them in a rubbish bag. He followed the trolley, his work in Black Park done, but a twang of guilt had him glancing over his shoulder at Wainwright and Thirsk. "Off the record, I'd say the child suffocated, and that he/she was dead before the body hit the water."

"He or she?"

"I can't confirm yet, not here. But it looks like a girl. Don't go telling the family though."

"I know that." Wainwright was sombre. "Hugh, do me a favour and do the post-mortem soon as possible, will you?" The pathologist walked away, followed by Thirsk and his former sidekick, who said, "I'll treat this case as if the body is Melissa unless I hear otherwise. Can you brief me back at the station, Guv?"

Thirsk smiled at the term; he hadn't been Wainwright's boss for the best part of a year.

Chapter 11
Crazy Demands

Having returned home from work in the early hours, Toni had set her alarm later than normal and forgone her exercise, which irritated her as her injured ankle had already hindered her usual activities. Her sleep had been heavy and refreshing, and she awoke with a smile on her face, which grew to a grin when she remembered Thirsk's instructions the night before to visit Julia Collins. A bubble of excitement flooded through her; she was actually going to be working for her dream boss for the first time.

As arranged before they had gone home the night before, Toni picked Sally up at nine, and they went directly to Albert Block on the Canal Estate, avoiding the extra mileage to and from the station. The journey was quicker than anticipated, arriving half an hour before they were due to meet Julia, and they sat in Toni's car to wait. Sally drew a packet of cigarettes and a lighter from her bag and Toni glared at her. "Outside with that filthy habit."

Reluctantly, Sally stepped into the cold morning air and leant against the car door, lighting and inhaling, coughing. Breathing deeply to control the wheezing, she ducked her head to the window. "Fancy going for a drink after work tonight?"

Toni shook her head. "Can't, I've still got to do some packing. I've been so busy at work I've only filled two boxes, and I move out in two days."

"Why don't I come back with you and help? We can pick up a couple of bottles of vino and some snacks on the way, have a laugh while we do it."

Toni considered the offer. She had never really had friends over, it had always seemed too girly, but the house she had grown up in wasn't home any more, the atmosphere thick from constant arguments between everybody except her dad, and Sally's bright company would dissuade her mother from creating another. She smiled. "Sounds like a plan."

Sally ground the cigarette butt on the tarmac with her foot and Toni hopped from the car, locking it securely. They were ten minutes early when Simone Lewis answered the door, letting them into the untidy flat. "Julia's just boiled the kettle, can I get you tea, or coffee if she's got any?" They shook their heads, and Simone leant close, whispering. "She's very nervous, she's been flitting from one room to the other, fretting and worrying. What's this all about?"

"We just need to see Julia, thanks. I'll tell you what, I will have a tea after all. White, no sugar, please."

Simone raised her voice. "Julia, can you..."

Toni held her hand up. "No, can you make it please, we need to see Julia alone."

"I'm her social worker, I don't know if you remember, but we've already met." She smiled, concern in her eyes. "Julia wants me with her. Is there anything I should know, she's been in a very low place the past few days and I'd hate to see her disturbed further."

The words 'nosy old busybody' sprung to Sally's mind, but she restrained herself from speaking aloud. "It's a matter between us and Julia, we'll have to ask her whether she wants you present or not." Sally pushed past Simone, who bristled, wondering why her profession was scorned by so many people; she only wanted to help people, what was so wrong with that? She tutted.

Toni and Sally regarded the familiar face as they entered the living room, each with differing opinions. Julia screwed her podgy face up, lips and nose disappearing into her cheeks. "Wasn't you two here last Friday night?" She was curled in her familiar spot on the sofa and she looked terrified.

Sally didn't smile. The young mother repelled her, the spawn of the man who had probably abducted innocent Melissa Barton. "Don't look so worried, Julia, we don't bite." Julia noticed the curtness and her concern grew.

"It's okay, you're not going to be prosecuted following last Friday, that's not what we're here for." Toni, the more sensitive of the two, reasoned that the woman would be more likely to talk freely if she wasn't scared. "I understand you're estranged from your parents, Jim and Maria Collins."

Instantly her fear turned to confusion. "Yeah, what about them? I ain't had nothing to do with either of them, ain't seen them since I was thirteen and glad about it."

"Your father is currently under arrest regarding pornographic images of a child found in his house, and it appears there's substantial evidence against him." Toni and Sally were ignorant to the developments overnight. "We need to know what your childhood was like, how he and your mother treated you." Julia hadn't expected the revelations and she hesitated, scared of saying something wrong and getting into trouble. "It would really help with our enquiries if you'd tell us as much as you can."

A knock on the door gave Julia time to digest the news, and Simone's sarcasm came from the hall. "May I bring your tea in? Is it an appropriate time?"

Toni and Sally smirked at each other. "Yes, thanks." Simone set a mug of extraordinarily pale tea on the table, wiped her hands on her skirt, and traipsed out, closing the door, and this time Julia smiled with the officers at the childish behaviour.

Sally grinned. "She thinks she's missing out, nosy old…"

"Sally!" Toni caught her friend in time, and turned back to Julia. "Do you mind if I sit?" The girl shrugged and both officers perched on the edge of the settee. "We can do this at the station if you want, you'd have more privacy there."

Julia wasn't used to being treated with respect, her esteem so low, but even though Simone was a busybody, she had shown her worth to Julia since the day before. "No, put her out of her misery, let her in. I'll only end up having to say it all again to her."

Once the four women were seated, the preliminaries done, Julia had prepared how much she was willing to reveal. "He's in for kiddie porno, you say?" Toni nodded. "And he won't find out about this?" The two constables shared an uncertain glance. "Will he be able to get me?"

111

"No. From the evidence we have, I think your father won't be going anywhere for a while."

The assurance was enough for Julia to relax and begin. "My childhood was shit. Mum and Dad are drunks and have been for as long as I can remember, and they both beat me if I even dared to breathe at the wrong time. I ran away more times than I can remember and I begged social services for help time after time," her eyes met Simone's, "but until I refused to go back home on my thirteenth birthday, said I'd slice my wrists if they made me go back, they kept sending me there."

"I'm sorry, but I have to ask the question: did your father ever touch you inappropriately?"

Julia wanted to tell the truth and was tempted to trust the kind officer, but the threats from years before taunted her from within and she knew she was too scared still. She looked away, focusing on the middle distance. Simone, as always, had something to add. "I've been suspecting the same thing, aspects of her behaviour have raised my suspicions." She moved from the wooden chair and sat beside Julia, her large frame forcing the two officers to squeeze up, and laid a bejewelled hand on the girl. "I've been encouraging her to talk to me, but it's obviously very painful for her."

Sally viewed the huge coloured woman, her tight black curls cut close to her head, the doe-like brown eyes full of concern, and she wanted to slap her. "If you don't mind, Miss…"

"Lewis, Simone Lewis, Child and Adolescent Support." She was proud of her job, regardless of what anybody else thought. "We *have* been introduced before."

"We'd like to speak to Julia without interruption." Sally moved to the wooden chair in order to see the girl more clearly. "Julia, it's really important that you tell us as much as you can. You could be responsible for other girls being molested if you don't speak up."

Toni gasped. "One minute." She grabbed her colleague's elbow and led her from the room like a naughty child.

"What?" Sally didn't understand and it showed in the tone of her voice.

"It's not her fucking fault her father's a fucking pervert, don't you dare lay the responsibility on her fucking shoulders. You're a fucking insensitive bitch, you know that? Now, just shut the fuck up and let me do the fucking talking."

"Hey, hold on a minute, young lady."

Toni took a deep breath, calming herself, but still whispered through gritted teeth. "I'm sorry, I just think I'm more of a people's person than you are. Just let me do the talking, right."

However, Sally's plain and unfair talking had done the trick, because Julia understood the point she had been making and was ready to open up when they returned to their seats. "He used to do things to me that I didn't like and now I'm older I can see that they were wrong, but he always told me that I'd be locked up if I ever told anyone about it." Toni and Simone exchanged a knowing glance, pleased she'd had the courage to finally admit that she had been abused. "I wanted Mum to help me, but she knew about it and never stopped him. I think she liked the peace and quiet when he came to my bed."

"Julia, what you're telling us is so brave, and you're absolutely right to speak out. Your evidence is crucial to our investigation, and I wonder if we could do a formal interview with you at the station?"

"This porn thing, the kiddies – what does he do to them?"

The two officers couldn't say too much and Sally, chastised into good behaviour, answered. "So far we've found explicit pictures on his computer of a young girl who was reported missing yesterday. That's all I can tell you, I'm afraid."

"Melissa?" Simone had seen the news the previous evening and was astounded. Sally silenced her with a glare.

"How old is she, the little girl? Is she still missing?"

Sally gave a shallow nod, if she didn't say yes aloud then she wasn't divulging too much – was she? "Young. That's all I can tell you."

"Not a baby, though?"

The question was odd and the two policewomen didn't reply. Concerned, Simone filled the silence, probably the most shocked person in the room at the hideous revelations. "Why do you ask?"

Julia hesitated, bulbous lips poised to spill her thoughts, but sifting her answer mentally to see how much she should reveal. Eventually the barriers that Simone had witnessed so many times returned. "I just wanted to see how much of a perv he is, that's all."

Toni was sure it wasn't the truth, that the age of the victims was important to her for some reason, but she was confident that Julia would tell them everything in her own time. Thirsk had told them to build a rapport with the girl, and that was going to take longer than one visit. "Do you remember the name of your social worker when you were young?"

"I had loads, they would come in and promise me the world, then they'd bugger off and I'd never see them again."

"Were there any that stood out, any that gave you just that little bit more?" Simone couldn't resist being an important part of the process.

"There was one called Janet something or other, she was with me for about two years or so, and she got me involved in a Girl's Group for a little while, which was good because it meant I had somewhere to go one evening a week. I had to stop going, though, because of the…" The silence was palpable, everybody on tenterhooks to find out why the pleasurable evenings that had obviously been important to her had ceased. "I just had to stop, I had no choice. And anyway, I think it was Mum and Dad who told Janet not to come back round."

"I'll tell you what, if a parent said that to me I'd be hotter on the case than ever. I can't believe that this Janet just tiptoed away without a backwards glance." Simone had been racking her brain to recall a social worker called Janet in the files she had seen, but nobody sprung to mind.

Julia was upset, the memory painful. "Well, she never came back to see me, that's all I know. But it was her who got me re-homed in the end. But I had to go and see her then."

"Julia, will you come to the station? It would be a great help."

Suddenly the old Julia was back in the room, the candour gone. "And what do I get out of it, eh? I've got better things to do. If you've got photos on him, you don't need to know what he was like when I was a kid. Give me a reason to come and I'll consider it."

Now Simone was in her element, she knew what funds were available for the families she helped and she was used to offering incentives to ensure they cooperated, it was commonplace. "Well, you look like you could do with some new clothes, how's that for a start?"

"Screw that. I'll tell you what I want. Baccy, weed, and a bottle of something strong. It's been a tough few days and I don't get my social for over a week."

"Julia, I can't get those things for you."

Sally laughed, impressed with the young mum for the first time, such barefaced cheek. "Dream on, Julia, this is real world, not lala-land."

"I guess I'm staying here then. Close the door on your way out."

Chapter 12
The Accomplice

Under the unusual circumstances, it made sense for Thirsk and Wainwright to join forces with the investigation into Melissa's death and Jim Collins' probable involvement. They had always worked comfortably together before, only scrapping once when alcohol had been heavily involved, and both were comfortable with the arrangement. Thirsk would concentrate on his inquiries into the porn ring, and Wainwright would focus on the child's murder. After the body had been removed, they returned to the station and Thirsk brought the consolidated team up to date with the latest events.

After a short discussion with his solicitor, Jim Collins was brought from his cell to Interview Room 2, and Thirsk and Wainwright took the lift to the first floor. "What's he like?"

Thirsk pictured the weasel-faced, vulgar man and shuddered. "Just what you'd expect and none too clever with it. Obviously he's denying all knowledge, but I wouldn't expect anything less."

The lift stopped at the third floor on the way down and Dave squeezed in when the doors opened. "Ah, Thirsk, just the man I was coming to see." He thrust a pile of printed pages into Thirsk's hand as the lift took them to the first floor. "The video of Melissa was posted to the internet yesterday, at about four in the afternoon."

"So he must have been lying about being at the pub then, not that I believed him anyway." The lift stopped and the doors opened, Thirsk stepped out, followed by his colleagues. "I'll have a gander the landlord's statement when I get back upstairs."

"I don't think it'll matter whether he was at the pub or not. Thing is, the video was posted from a different IP address. It was posted from a different computer."

Thirsk stopped, scratching his head. "Oh, right. So was the other computer found in the search?"

"I wish you were more computer savvy. It was posted from a different location."

"So Jim wasn't at the pub, he was wherever the other computer is."

Wainwright shrugged. "Or they've got an accomplice."

"That's a scary thought, Nick." Thirsk tugged through his hair again, debating what he didn't understand. "Is that possible, Dave?"

"Absolutely."

"So where do we go from here?"

"There are two different issues here: who was with Melissa when she died, and who posted the footage."

Thirsk glanced at the prisoner through the glass, dishevelled from the night in the cell. "So we need to know his exact movements for the day and the time Melissa died. You've not heard back from Hugh yet, I suppose."

Wainwright shook his head. "I say we treat the interview as if there's somebody else involved. He may be more willing to talk if we're not pointing the finger directly at him."

"Wing it, then. I suppose we've got another," Thirsk checked his watch, "twelve or so hours to keep him in custody." He looked at the technician. "Can you find out any more about who posted the footage, or where from?"

"I traced the IP address…"

"Come on, Dave, speak English."

Dave flicked his fringe back with a pen; he hadn't slept for over thirty hours and was exhausted. "We're trying to find out, it's a difficult process and we're relying on outside companies to assist us. All I can tell you for sure is that the footage was posted from a computer other than the one I have on my desk. I'll let you know as and when I find anything." He skulked back towards the lift, unappreciated.

Thirsk frowned. "I'm trying my best to understand. What I know is that he had photos of Melissa on his computer."

"Or her computer. Didn't you tell me it belonged to the wife?"

"It wouldn't surprise me for a second if she's involved, she's hideous, but I genuinely don't think a woman could perform those atrocities on a child."

"Myra Hindley? Rose West? Mary Ann Cotton?"

"Fuck you, smart arse."

"I still reckon we go down the accomplice route. We've got twelve hours. We've got the computer and IP address. What if we tell him we've found his accomplice?"

Thirsk shook his head. "He's insisting on his brief being there, we'd never get away with it if it came to court." He opened the door and, without acknowledging Jason Averill's presence, stormed towards Jim, hovering close to his face. "We've found her, Jim. That poor little girl, dead…"

"Inspector, may I remind you, firstly, that there's no confirmation that the body is Melissa Barton and, secondly, my client denies knowing the child."

"Who's the accomplice? Who are you working with, Jim?"

"Inspector, I must object to your heavy-handedness."

Thirsk slowly turned to the lawyer. "Really?" A tirade ensued, describing the hours spent at the freezing lake, the pitiful condition of the body, the gut-wrenching sorrow of the family that he could only imagine. Hammering into the man that the heartbreaking reality of a child's life cut short should not be followed by time-wasting. But as he ranted, his tiredness venting uncontrollably, he remembered Maria's words – *'I'll have to stop at my brother's, I suppose'* – and it dawned on him. "It's the brother. It's Maria's sodding brother, isn't it? What's his name, Jim? Give me his fucking name."

He nodded to Wainwright and they left the room. "You go to the post mortem and watch over the proceedings, I want the results as soon as they're ready. I'm going to pick the brother up. Terminate the interview, will you, Nick, I can deal with that scumbag later."

Toni and Sally arrived at the station at quarter to eleven, and it was clear there had been some developments since they had left the previous night. They struggled through a crowd of reporters camped by the main doors, all throwing questions about Melissa Barton at them. The atmosphere inside the station was buzzing, and in the comparative quiet of the lobby, Toni tugged Sally's sleeve. "Should we go straight up to see Inspector Thirsk, do you reckon?"

"I guess so, he said he was going to okay it with Andy Pervert Pandy." Sally pressed the button for the lift, but Toni directed her to the stairs, scornful of her colleague's laziness.

They had reached the mezzanine halfway between the second and third floors when Sergeant Feldman's unmistakable bark halted them instantly. "What the hell do you two think you're doing?" Toni tried to explain but he silenced her, his glare daring either woman to speak again. "Your shifts start at nine, and when your shifts start at nine, I expect you to be in, and at your desk, by nine. Get to work, you lazy bints, I don't want to hear a peep out of either of you for the rest of the day."

They slunk down the stairs to the general office on the second floor and sat, chastised, and angry with Thirsk for not informing their boss of the extra duties he had given them. But when they heard about the discovery of a child's body, they understood why Thirsk's memory had lapsed. Toni took the initiative, hoping she wasn't being out of line, and emailed Thirsk to let him know of their meeting with Julia, asking what he wanted them to do next. And while waiting for a reply, the two women dealt with the usual mundane matters that filled their days – burglaries, car accidents, shoplifting. Not child abuse and porn rings, and not murder, like they had hoped on waking that morning. Their cheerful moods disappeared swiftly.

Midday came and went with no reply, but then Feldman loomed over them, his strong aftershave permeating the air. He was fuming, a snarl underneath glaring, pinpoint eyes. "In the side office. Both of you. Now."

Worried, they trotted through, each with a notepad and pen. "You pair of fucking tarts. Who's been fucking the big boss then, eh? Which one of you, eh?" Neither answered the impertinent question. "Somehow you've both managed to wangle your way onto the fifth floor, while us mere plebs have to stay downstairs and work the boring shit."

"I'm not quite sure what you mean, Serge." Sally was sure it was a pathetic practical joke, a commonplace pastime of bored officers.

"You know exactly what I mean. You're to start right away. Enjoy playing with the big boys, you pair of slags." He made no attempt to disguise his jealousy. The two women stared at him, and then at each other, until Toni grinned, her relieved joy at the reprieve from their tormenting boss obvious. "If you say so, Serge. Can't wait, to be honest."

He handed them an A4 envelope each. "I was ordered to give you these. It's confirmation that you've been transferred until further notice." He marched haughtily away, and under his breath, but audible enough for the girls to hear, he said, "Bitches."

Rooted to the spot with surprise, Sally waited for Feldman to leave the room. "What do you reckon that's all about?"

"Maybe it's just for the day, but I can't say I'm unhappy about it. It can't be worse than working down here for that sexist prick." Toni hated Feldman, he made her skin crawl.

"You don't think he's lying, do you? Trying to get us in trouble for leaving our desks, or something. You know what an arse he is."

Toni tore open the envelope in her hand. "There's an easy way to find out." She withdrew the paperwork and scanned it briefly. "Fuck me. It says, 'because of your previous involvement with Julia Collins it has been requested that you assist the Child Abuse Investigation Unit under the direct command of DCI Thirsk'. And get this, it says, 'until further notice'. Wow, I can't believe this, we're going to be working for Thirsk." She prodded the letter with her finger. "It's signed by Chief Super Bradbury; this is no practical joke."

"Thirsk. God, I've heard allsorts about working with him. Apparently he's a right unconventional bugger and grumpy with it."

Toni chuckled. "He seemed like a pussycat last night, and anyway, he can't be any worse than that arse out there."

Snatching their belongings together, reluctant to waste time in case Feldman changed his mind, Sally and Toni bounded up the stairs to the coveted fifth floor, feeling freer and more successful than ever. They had run errands before to the upper floors, but to be working on such a high profile case was a dream coming true. Reaching the incident room, they were stunned by both the noise and hectic activity; a contrast to the environment they had become used to.

Steadman had been informed of the constables' temporary transfer and was grateful for the extra help. A clerk had emptied some desk space for them, a cramped area each amongst the copious paperwork, equipment and heaving bodies. Everything that was happening in the room, including the speech, was hurried and disjointed, with phones trilling constantly and printers spilling data. "I need both of you to look back over the files for the past couple of years for girls, say, age five to ten for now, reporting any form of sexual abuse. Concentrate on the Moor End area at this stage, print details out and collate them. You are self-starters, right?"

Steadman didn't wait for an answer, turning her back to address another detective, and the two, thrown from a cliff, were befuddled. "I guess we'll have to be." Toni tapped her password into the computer, trying to work out what was expected of her.

Thirsk rushed into the room, puffing and red-faced from the trot up the stairs. "Benson, get on to the front desk, see what address Maria Collins gave them last night when we released her." He glanced at the expectant faces watching him. "Steadman, Gamboli, Bridges, Hall, Squires, you're coming with me, take a partner each. As soon as we've got the address,

I want it covered, back, front, sides, the fucking roof if you can. Chippy, arrange a search warrant for the house. And Benson, get the name of the geezer who lives there. He's the accomplice, I'll bet my fucking life on it."

Within ten minutes the office had all but cleared, and Toni allowed herself an exhilarated grin at Sally. One day she wanted to be a proper part of that excitement.

The unmarked Audi, driven by Steadman, hurtled towards Moor End, and Thirsk listened keenly to the radio. The address they were heading for was close to Jim and Maria's house, but they didn't yet have a name for the man they were about to arrest. "What have you got on him, Guv?"

"A hunch. A bloody good hunch."

"Jesus, I hope you're right or you're going to get your arse kicked. Has he got any previous?"

"I don't even know his name yet, so how the fuck would I know that?"

A voice crackled over the radio and Thirsk listened carefully as the controller explained that Sean O'Connor was an all-round good guy with no arrests, complaints or disturbances, nothing at all that would suggest he could be involved in such a vile operation. Thirsk gulped quietly, his knuckles white with hope that he wasn't wrong.

The journey across town, sirens blaring and blue lights flashing, took just a few minutes and as they neared, Thirsk radioed the cars to turn them off. "I don't want to give him any warning."

The house was of average size, a neatly kept semi-detached, and the garden was still colourful despite the cold weather. A silver Fiat 500, economical and environmentally friendly, was parked in the drive, and a small, ornate plaque over the inset door stated 'Laus Deo' – *Praise be to God* – in calligraphic lettering, decorated with kaleidoscopic, enamel painted flowers and leaves. The setting gave no indication that Sean could be a child molester and possible murderer, and that made Thirsk suspect him more. Sometimes good was too good.

The officers surrounded the building, a couple heading through the wooden, slatted gate to the back of the house, and Thirsk hammered on the door. "Sean O'Connor, open up, it's the police."

"He won't hear you." He looked at Steadman derisively. "He's got music playing, can't you hear that shit?" Strains of choral boys floated through the door and Thirsk smacked the door in frustration, feeling stupid. He nodded to Squires, of equal height to his superior, but younger, fitter and bulkier, and moved aside for the man to ram the door, which burst open surprisingly easily. The team ran inside, with agile Steadman leading up the stairwell, followed by gasping Thirsk. The music was quieter by the time they reached the landing and Thirsk was relieved.

Steadman pushed a bedroom door open and was met with Maria's shocked face, her eyes widened and mouth agape, huddled in bed, seemingly naked, with a man of a similar age. Steadman dragged the man from the bed, thrusting his discarded pants at him. "Are you Sean O'Connor?"

The man, a little plump, deeply tanned still from the summer, with soulful blue eyes that begged trust, squeaked a shocked yes, and Steadman looked to her boss for guidance. He nodded, his skin paling, and she waited while Sean dressed, before snapping handcuffs over his wrist. She cautioned him and bundled him down the stairs and to the car.

Thirsk watched them leave, and returned his stunned gaze to Maria, who hurriedly tugged her clothes on. Her face was flushed, partly a hangover from lovemaking, and partly from embarrassment at the sudden intrusion. Soon the commotion died down and he was alone with the woman. He was bewildered. "What's going on?"

"I could ask you the same bleeding thing." She indignantly shrugged her faded green cardigan over her shoulders, its presence reducing her from semi-sexy siren to dowdy fifty-something.

"But he's your brother. Isn't he?"

"So bleeding what."

"Does your husband know about this?" His voice was cracking; he had seen a lot of things over the course of his career, but this – consenting incest – was a first.

"Of course he does. He ain't the kind of guy you lie to, my Jim."

Thirsk knew he had to pull himself together, he was losing his credibility fast, and he pulled his core string to bring him to his full, confident height, shoulders back and breathing controlled. "Melissa's been found, no doubt you heard, it's been all over the local radio."

She haughtily brushed past him and began descending the stairs, oblivious to the detective's shock. "I ain't heard nothing, I've been in bed all morning." She turned to him and smiled grotesquely as he followed her.

"I am *so* having you for incest, Maria Collins. I know you're part of this, abusing little girls, tormenting and torturing them. Killing them. You happily sit there and watch the two men in your life play out their perverse sexual fantasies on innocent children." They reached the bottom of the stairs and he followed her to the kitchen.

"If Sean had a little kiddie to play with, do you think he had be screwing me? He's not like that, he's only interested in me. He had nothing to do with what's going on."

There was no emotion in her voice and Thirsk wondered if she realised that what the three paedophiles had been doing was wrong. He didn't bother concealing the contempt in his voice. "You're nicked, Maria. Whatever the truth is, you know about it, and believe me, you'll have told me everything by the time I've finished with you." He looked her up and down, disgusted, and strode from the kitchen, nudging Gamboli as he passed. "Nick the slag in the kitchen, I'll interview her back at the station after I've had a look around the house."

"What shall I bring her in for?"

"Oh, I don't know. Suspicion of being a low-life slut? Sex with her brother? Abduction and murder? I don't know, take your pick."

Chapter 13
A United Stand

Once he had returned to the station, Thirsk gathered the team together to update them on the shocking developments. Sally and Toni stood by the wall, shy amongst the older, more confident, officers. Wainwright had attended the hastily arranged post mortem that morning and he informed Thirsk of the unofficial conclusion.

"Thanks, Nick. Right, first of all, I'm afraid it's not good news. As I think we all expected, the body found at Black Park Lake this morning has been identified as Melissa Barton by her mother." He indicated the photo Val Barton had given them, depicting a button-nosed, cheerful face with chubby cheeks, and brunette, shoulder-length hair, tied back with a pink hair band. It was a sad contrast to the other photos that showed the child in death. "The post mortem has shown that Melissa was already dead by the time she was dumped in the lake, and the report states that the cause of death was suffocation."

"What about the cuts and scratches on her hands and face?" Steadman was studying the photos of the crime scene.

"Defence wounds, she clearly put up a good struggle."

He took a pile of stills that Dave had printed from the website and attached them to the whiteboard, each showing the apparently drugged faces of young girls, whose only common attributes appeared to be their youth. "Unfortunately, we have also identified her as one of the girls who was filmed being sexually abused on the pornographic website we are investigating." Muttering rang around the room and Thirsk waited until the hubbub had died down before continuing. "In total, there are six other girls and forty-nine video-clips, and these vics need to be found."

Wainwright waved his hand to get attention. "For my team, we'll have no involvement with the website unless any of the girls match records of missing children."

"I stress, it's a priority to identify these girls." Thirsk stretched his arm high to attract the attention of Toni and Sally, who hid meekly against the wall. "You two newbies at the back." Neither responded, the attention unexpected.

Steadman had the benefit of knowing their names. "Fowler. Ross. The guv is talking to you."

Thirsk rolled his eyes as they stared at him eagerly. "Missing children. Last five years for now. Take the search from the city centre to a twenty-mile radius. There can't be that many, but get what you can." The constables grinned importantly and Thirsk sighed with irritation. "Well, go on then, get moving. Chop chop!" Both scurried to the minimal working spaces they had been allocated.

"Now, I worked through the night, last night..." A collective groan sounded from the detectives who knew he expected the same from them regardless of families and social lives. "Yes, yes, very funny. I spent the night watching each and every pornographic video-clip that is on the website, and..."

"You filthy bastard." It was said in jest, but Thirsk wasn't smiling.

"Shut the fuck up, Chippy, and get a fucking life." He took a deep breath, composing himself. "There was nothing tantalising about them. They're disgusting, the perpetrators are fucking animals, and I believe the two men we have in custody, Jim Collins and Sean O'Connor, are involved, but we have no proof yet. The techies are doing their thing, so if you need any explanation on that business, you'll have to ask them."

"Can't you explain it to us, Guv?"

There were a few snorts of amusement and Steadman felt protective. "Shut up, you lot, it's not his fault he doesn't understand computers."

Ashamed of having a woman defend his inadequacies, Thirsk shook his head. "Unnecessary, Steadman, let them think they're funny, they'll get bored in the end. Now, we also have Jim's wife, Maria Collins, in custody. What did you arrest her for, Gamboli?"

"Soliciting, sir."

Thirsk smacked his forehead with his palm, feeling as if he were in a monkey sanctuary. "Where the fuck did you get that one from? She was in bed with her fucking brother, did you not hear me when I said incest?"

His head bobbed down amongst the sniggers. "Sorry, Guv, I thought you were joking."

With a deep sigh, Thirsk continued. "We know that Melissa was abducted before school started as she was marked absent on the register. She was taken to this room," he indicated a still from the video-clip of Melissa, "probably drugged – her blood and stomach content samples are with toxicology at the moment – and then filmed being abused by at least one person, a person with no obvious marks – tattoos, scars, whatever – who wore yellow rubber gloves during the entire assault. She was subsequently suffocated – fibres that were found in her throat, mouth and nose are being analysed – and dumped in Black Park Lake in the early evening."

"No exact time?"

"At this stage we can narrow it down to between nine and ten. What have we got from the CCTV footage? Anything?"

Bridges raised his hand. "We've searched between eight thirty and ten in the morning, and they show Melissa arriving at and entering the school, but there's nothing that shows her coming out again."

"So some of the school premises aren't covered by the security cameras. Look in to that, Bridges." Thirsk scrolled through his notes. "Have we heard anything from forensics regarding the search of Jim and Maria's house?"

Squires raised his hand. "Not yet. No memory card or disc. Nothing untoward on the cups and glasses. Two hairs were found in a crack on the cellar floor, both from the same person, but the DNA doesn't match Melissa's."

"Didn't they find any traces of Rohypnol?"

"They said one of the glasses looked as if it had been wiped clean."

"Shit. So we've still got nothing that places Melissa in the house." He tapped the picture of the bare room. "We need to find where this place is. I understand that a laptop, a camera, and a cam, er, video camera…"

"Camcorder."

A couple of detectives sniggered and Thirsk silenced them with a glare. "Have we any news about them?"

"The camera and camcorder's memories have been wiped clean, but Rob and Dave are looking at the laptop right now."

"Okay, let me know when they get back to you." Thirsk leant against the table and gulped his coffee. "We have the animals who did this in custody, but now we've got our work cut out to prove it. We need to know everything about Jim Collins, Sean O'Connor and Maria Collins. Their lives, habits, who they know, what they do – whether they pay the milk bill or not, damn it – and we need it now."

Thirsk dismissed the officers and Squires approached him, finishing the call he had taken. "That was Rob on the phone. The IP of the laptop they took from Sean's house matches the one that posted the video of Melissa."

"What does that mean?"

"The footage was posted from Sean's computer."

"Right. What about the other videos?"

"They're looking into that now. But it's a start, Guv, it's a link, and enough to hold him on."

Thirsk headed for his office and Wainwright followed. "Next step is to interrogate the motley crew again. Are you sitting in?"

"Well, it's pretty much an open and shut case for me, really. Those two are definitely guilty; we just need to fit the pieces into the puzzle. The hard work's pretty much all yours now."

Thirsk realised his colleague was allowing him to take the lead with the investigation and he had no intention of taking all the glory. "Well, that depends on whether any of the girls on the video clips are matched with missing people, well, kids. If any of them do, you'll be looking for another body."

"You've got officers checking the missing persons register, so time will tell."

They had reached Thirsk's desk and he clicked on an email titled 'Julia Collins', recalling the morning visit he had asked the two rookies to make. Neither of their names had registered in his memory yet and he leant through the doorway, calling Steadman. "Those newbies that started today, send whichever one is called Fowler in."

"Will do."

"And get her to bring us coffee."

Steadman surveyed the girls as she approached, Ross with dark hair, chopped into a neat bob similar to her own, and blonde Fowler, who was far too pretty for her own good. A tang of jealousy surfaced, which annoyed her. "Fowler, the guv wants to see you, and take in a couple of mugs of tea, one white, no sugar, I don't know about the other. Just chuck some on the tray, or whatever."

Five minutes later, nervous, yet buzzing with excitement and disbelief, Toni brought a tray through, with two black teas, a small jug of milk and a few sachets of sugar. She laid it on the desk and stood, awkward. "Thanks." Thirsk sniffed. "Is that tea? I asked for coffee."

"Oh, sorry, but Stead..." Toni realised she had been deliberately misinformed and had no intention of being labelled a snitch. She would have to watch her back. "Sorry."

"You sent me an email. How did it go with the daughter?"

"We went over there, sir, but it didn't go quite to plan. She's not prepared to make a formal statement unless we supply her with booze, tobacco and marijuana."

She waited for him to chastise her, but instead he laughed, much to Toni's amazement. He had a reputation for being a miserable grouch and the uncommon sound silenced the incident room briefly. When he had caught his breath, he said, "Brilliant. Just brilliant. What did you say?"

"Well, no, of course. What else could I say?"

"I'd be tempted to give it to her just for giving me the best laugh in years."

"How much do you need her statement?" Wainwright had guessed how much and he knew Thirsk's unorthodox ways well. "Forget that, I don't want to know. I'll leave you two in peace."

Thirsk waited for Wainwright to close the door. "Do you have a transcript of the conversation?"

"No, sir."

He groaned, remembering how inexperienced she was. "Lesson one for the day, then: Write. Everything. Down."

Toni nodded shyly, figuring the man she had first met ten years before hadn't become any less scary over the decade. "Yes, sir."

"So apart from demands for illegal substances and a damn good night, did you get anything at all?"

"She did say that her father had abused her, though not in detail. Says she told her mum but she wasn't interested."

Lack of experience grated on Thirsk, things would be so much easier if everyone had his knowledge. "Forget it, I'll send someone who doesn't pussyfoot around to get her to spill. You carry on searching for missing kids. Go on then, get out of here." He turned his attention to the paperwork on his desk and she timidly crept out.

Simone had been furious with Julia Collins and her ridiculous request to the police that morning. She really wanted to help the girl exorcise her childhood trauma, to be in a position where she could be reunited with her son, but how could she help someone who wasn't willing to help herself? What a stupid thing to demand, especially in front of two officers of the law. Her head pounded, aching with frustration. The only productive thing she could do was to find the social worker Julia had mentioned, Janet, and as much background information on the girl, her parents and her childhood, as possible.

The search only served to intensify her headache. The filing system was incomplete, and a search of the Collins family file produced little. There was no mention of a Janet being involved in the scant information she uncovered. She was new to the job and desperate to impress; the promotion had been welcome both professionally and financially, but though racism wasn't supposed to exist in this day and age, she suffered the effects daily, especially from those higher up the ladder. She had to work twice as hard to prove herself, as prejudice was still rife in the workplace, especially when ambition was involved. Grace's behaviour the previous day had unnerved her, especially as she had been the one to employ her. Maybe she had recruited someone she considered wouldn't be a threat to her own job security, as so many managers tend to do. Simone knew from bitter experience to withhold her trust until it had been earned.

She knocked on the door and entered when instructed. "Grace, you've been here a lot longer than me, I wondered if you could help me with something?"

"Is this about the Julia Collins case?"

"Yes, I need the records from when she was a child. Did you know about her father being arrested?"

"The police have been in touch. In fact, I was about to ask you to find her file just before you turned up. They want everything."

"That doesn't surprise me, but the thing is, I can't find much for her." She dropped the single folder on the desk and opened it wide to expose a small pile of papers and handwritten notes. "There must be more than that. From what Julia's told me, social services were involved for much of her childhood, and she was taken into care when she was thirteen after refusing to return home. There's nothing at all about that in her file."

"Oh." Grace perched her reading glasses on her nose and flicked through the pages, muttering to herself as she scanned each piece. "How old is Julia, remind me?"

"Twenty-three."

"So let's just say she became known to us aged seven, seems a good place to start, that would have been nineteen, nineteen…" Her non-mathematical brain struggled.

"Ninety-seven, she was born in ninety."

Grace removed the spectacles and sat back. "I tell you, Simone, I've been here eight years now and they've changed the filing system three times, Lord knows how many times they've changed it since ninety-seven. All I can suggest is that you try the archives, maybe you'll find more in there, but don't hold out too much hope."

"Okay, it's in the basement isn't it, the storeroom?" Grace nodded and handed the insufficient file to Simone. "Look, one more thing, do you know of a social worker called Janet? She probably worked in these offices because Julia has lived in this area all her life."

"There was a Janet Dremill who left shortly after I came to work here, nice enough lady."

"Do you have any idea where she moved to, you know, what job?"

"She was retiring, I remember the cake and speeches. No gold watch, of course, we social workers don't get special treatment." Simone noted the despondency in her superior's voice, her words, and despite appearances, it was evident that Grace was unhappy in her job. Simone could empathise, it was tough work for low pay, and social workers were deemed by all to be interfering busybodies, if the way she was treated was anything to go by. She forced 'Dremill' into her memory, determined to find the woman. Surely that would impress the police; she needed the recognition.

Chapter 14
Two Opposite Accounts

Thirsk and Steadman had spoken to Sean's lawyer, a well-respected and expensive man, who had an excellent reputation in criminal defence across the county. He had spent some time with his client, and now sat with him in Interview Room 2. The two detectives entered and Thirsk set the camcorder to record. "So, Sean, you're clear why we've brought you in?"

His smile was wide and friendly, the blue eyes twinkling. "Yes, it's totally understandable that you need my help in this whole, revolting fracas."

Thirsk felt his stomach lurch; the man was a slug. "Would you please tell us, from the beginning, what happened yesterday."

"Of course. I got up at about ten, I'd had a lie-in because it was one of the rare days that I had no dealings planned with the church. I went to see Maz..."

"Maz?"

"My sister, I call her Maz. I went to see her just before lunchtime and we spent the afternoon together, pottering around, watching a bit of telly, not much really. Then I went back to my house at about three, did a bit of work in my study, and then the police came round saying that a child had gone missing from the school across the road. Obviously, I couldn't rest after that, I went out and tried to help as best I could on the streets, you know, handing out photos of the girl, that kind of thing. I helped search for her, there's a lot of people who can corroborate that. Then, at about eight-thirty I realised there was nothing more I could do, so I went back home. That's as exciting as it got for me." He flashed his winning smile and Thirsk wanted to punch him.

"I think not, Sean. We already know that footage of Melissa's abuse was posted from your laptop, and at about the time you were home. How do you explain that?"

"The thing is, Jim came round to my place in the afternoon, he's over all the time, what with him being my best friend and brother-in-law. He asked to use the computer, like he often does, and I had no reason to say no. I sent him upstairs and left him to it, thought nothing of it."

"Do you know what Jim had been doing all day? Did he tell you?"

"He said he had spent it at his lock-up, I didn't ask him what he had been doing, he's always down there."

Thirsk didn't trust the man before him, his raven hair peppered with grey and a confident, affable grin, and he suspected the story had been rehearsed. "We found a camera and a camcorder, along with your laptop, under your bed. If you had been doing some work in your study, how come the laptop was hidden in a different room?"

Sean faltered for a moment, his mind searching for a credible answer. "No, you see I didn't use my computer. I just did some filing, housework as I call it. Just mundane things. Remember, it was my day off. If you found the computer under the bed, then Jim must have put it there after he had used it."

"Come on, Sean, I don't think so. What really happened?"

"Honestly, it's the truth. I never put anything under my bed, nothing but clean linen, anyway. To be honest I didn't even notice the computer wasn't on my desk when I was in the study."

"A five-hundred pound machine and you didn't notice it was gone? This is all a bit far-fetched."

The solicitor leant forward with an air of authority. "You asked my client for his account of the day and that's what he's giving you. Please keep your personal opinions to yourself."

Thirsk bristled; the story fitted and he couldn't prove otherwise at this stage. "You mentioned that Jim was at his lock-up, what's that all about?"

"He rents a lock-up somewhere, or that's what he's told me. He's keen on model railways and…"

"Model railways, my arse. I can't see Jim being interested in anything like that."

"Do I have to remind you again, Inspector, that this isn't about your personal opinion?" The solicitor was beginning to irritate Thirsk.

"Do you know where the lock-up is? Or who he rents it from?"

Sean shrugged. "I'm sorry, but no. I think it's his equivalent of a garden shed, somewhere of his own that he can go to and do his own thing. He's told me and Maz that he's got a miniature railway set up, a Hornby one, and I've had no reason to doubt him. I have no idea where it is."

"Is it rented from the council, this lock-up?"

"I have no idea who he rents it from, I've never seen a reason to ask."

The smile returned and Thirsk's stomach churned. He asked Steadman to find someone to contact the council and she left the room. "You like little girls, don't you, Sean. Did you…"

"What an intolerable line of questioning. I will not have my client treated like this."

"Oh dear, if we must dodge around the obvious, then so be it." Thirsk was weary, his eyes smarting from lack of sleep. "You have a lot of involvement with the children in your community, don't you?"

Smile. "Yes, I do, I run a youth club for children aged seven to twelve and I help with the Sunday School. I think children are wonderful and I certainly wouldn't do anything to harm them. It's a tragic shame about Melissa Barton. She was a lovely young girl, so promising. Such a shame."

The interview continued in the same frame for a few more minutes, and Thirsk felt he was taking two steps back for every step forward. There was no point continuing until he had spoken with Maria and Jim, and he terminated the interview, sending Sean back to the cells.

Twenty minutes later he returned to the room to question Maria, who had refused legal representation. "Sean told us that Jim spent the day in his lock-up, what do you know about that?"

"A lock-up? I didn't know he had a lock-up. Where is it?"

"I was hoping you'd tell me that. According to Sean, Jim says that he plays with toy trains down there."

"Toy trains? No, don't know anything about that, he ain't said nothing to me about no lock-up or trains. I thought he was down the pub, like I told you last night."

Maria had a newfound confidence, which Thirsk found unnerving, and he was irritable. "Your brother – you know, the one you have sex with – says that he lent his laptop to Jim yesterday. What do you know about that?"

"Nothing, but if Sean says he did, then he did, my Sean's an honest bloke."

The worthless interview lasted only a few minutes longer, before Thirsk decided it was a waste of time. He terminated the second interview of the hour and returned to his desk to wait for Jason Averill to return, in order to interrogate Jim again.

"Jim, I've read this so-called Smacker's statement and he's confirmed that you were in the pub in the evening, but not during the day. We also have a signed statement from Sean saying that you spent the day in your lock-up. Where is this lock-up?"

"I don't have no lock-up, I don't know what he's on about."

"He says you play there with a Hornby train set."

Jim snorted. "Total and utter shit, that is. I ain't got no lock-up, and I ain't got no train set. Sean's talking out of his arse." He quietened as it dawned on him that Sean was laying the blame for Melissa's disappearance on him, that the well-planned story they had concocted was forgotten. He couldn't believe the treachery. His grin waned and he began to fidget. "What's Sean been saying, then?" He really needed to know.

137

"He told us you used his laptop yesterday afternoon and hid it under his bed alongside a camera and a camcorder. We've identified his computer as being the one the improper videos of Melissa were posted online from, and he says he didn't use it yesterday."

Jim paled and his voice became weak. "That's a lie. He posted them videos, not me, I wouldn't even know how to." And now he realised he had readily admitted his knowledge of the website, inadvertently pointing the finger at himself. Thirsk smiled knowingly and Jim shrank into the chair. "Okay, okay, I'm going to tell you everything. Me and Sean, we did take the girl, right. We took her and we played with her a bit. It was nothing serious, just a bit of playing about, and she was up for it, alright. It weren't just me, it was him too. He takes photos of the kiddies outside school and we picked her this time."

"So you admit you've done it before?"

Jason whispered to his client, but Jim shrugged him away. "Yes, a couple of times. We gave the girl some of that date rape drug they have in the nightclubs, just to calm her down, like, and then we played with her for a while."

"Where?"

"At Sean's house, he's got a cellar. We took her down there for a while. But when I'd had enough, I left and went to the pub, and I was there until you lot picked me up. I never killed that kid, she was perfectly alive when I left her, and I just thought he was going to steer her back to school when home time came around, like what we've done before. She was alive, and I ain't got no clue how she got dead and ended up dumped in that park."

"Do you think Sean would do that? Maybe abusing the girls wasn't enough for him any more, maybe…"

"Mere speculation, all these maybes. Have you finished with my client yet?"

"Butt out, Jason. Would you conceive it possible that Sean took the abduction a step further and killed the girl, dumping her body later?"

Jim shook his head. "No, he likes to play, but he's not a murderer, I'd swear that on my good mother's life if she weren't dead already. Maybe after he left her at the school someone else took her, she would have been pretty woozy, I reckon, an easy target for someone like that, you know, someone who kills. But it weren't me, and I'm pretty sure it weren't him neither."

Thirsk wasn't sure whom to believe, if any of them. Jim had admitted to abducting and abusing Melissa, and he had implicated Sean, but Sean and Maria's accounts opposed his. Who was telling the truth? Regardless, his line of investigation was the website, and he was comfortable that Wainwright's superb detective skills would uncover the truth behind the tragic, sordid events of her death. "You say that you've done this before, abducted girls to 'play with', as you call it." Jim visibly relaxed with the change of subject. "It's abuse in our language, by the way. How many times?"

There was no point hiding anything any longer, Jim knew that his days as a free man were either numbered or over. "Five, six maybe, I'm not sure. A few times."

"Do you have the names of any of the girls?"

He raised his hands with an exaggerated shrug. "I don't fucking know, do I? It ain't their names I'm interested in, if you know what I mean."

"Unfortunately I do know what you mean, having seen your despicable website. Let me get this straight then, you and Sean abduct girls, drug them, abuse them, and then take them back to the school, groggy, and with no reliable memory of what's happened to them."

"That's exactly it. It ain't harming nobody, and me and Sean get some kicks out of it. I can't see no problem with it, nobody gets hurt."

"Except Melissa, of course. She got hurt, didn't she."

"I don't know about that, I told you. She was alive when I left her."

"After the girls are returned to the school, you put images of the abuse onto a website and charge viewers to see the videos?"

Jim beamed with pride. "It's a nice little earner, that. It was Sean's idea; he's the computer bloke in our family. He does all that stuff, but he gives me half the dosh anyway. It's a neat set-up."

"See, this is where I'm getting confused, because Sean insisted you were the one who posted the footage yesterday."

"I told you, he's lying, I wouldn't even know how to. How many times do I have to tell you, it weren't me."

Although the obscene material had been published from Sean's laptop, the person who had uploaded it was still a mystery. Fingerprints found on Jim and Maria's computer were from all three suspects, and the other laptop had Jim and Sean's, but these only proved that they shared the machines. However, although it wasn't enough to charge either man, Chief Bradbury agreed to hold Jim Collins for a further twenty-four hours based on the evidence.

Chapter 15
Jack the Nark

Thirsk left the office at six in the evening, wishing he were going home to bed, but it would be hours before he would accomplish that luxury. However, he had heard the unsubtle hints that he could do with a wash and change of clothes, and stopped home for half an hour before the next visit.

One of Thirsk's informers lived in a bed-sit in Moor End, a happy-go-lucky type named Jack who'd had the foresight three years before to spill the beans on several criminals to save his own skin. He was clever, and knew how to work the seedy characters he associated with. Jack liked Thirsk, they had always had a good rapport, and he loved his plain speaking.

When Thirsk suggested they meet at Jim and Sean's local, The Nag's Head, Jack made him promise to wear clothes that would blend into the crowd rather than his usual old-man attire, as Jack insolently called it. He defended the request by reminding Thirsk he had a reputation to think about, and being seen with a copper was fatal in his line of 'work'.

Initially affronted, Thirsk surmised he was average enough, although tall at six foot four, to disappear into the background. He chose worn jeans, a vintage Whitesnake concert T-shirt and some greying, tatty trainers. He threw a battered leather jacket, a hangover from his motor-biking, headbanger years, on top for warmth and headed across town to Moor End, stopping at a convenience store on the way. He left his car in a cul-de-sac a few streets from the pub and walked the short distance to the house Jack's room was in. He knocked and waited.

Presently Jack opened the door, his jacket thrown casually over his shoulders ready for the trip to The Nag's Head, but Thirsk pushed him inside. "What are you doing, mate?"

"I'll tell you in your room." He followed Jack up two flights of stairs and they reached a narrow, unlit corridor with a low ceiling, the air heavy with stale cigarette smoke. Jack unlocked one of the four doors and let himself in, leaving the door ajar for Thirsk.

"You're out of order with this, mate, this isn't part of the agreement." The man had a dreadful lisp.

Thirsk shook his head, dismissive, moving to the tiny kitchen area. He opened the fridge and shut the door immediately with a grimace. "Lucky I brought some with me, isn't it?" He tugged a half-bottle of whisky from his pocket, unscrewing the lid, and took a long gulp, wincing at the cheapness. He passed it to Jack. "Mate, indeed. I'm not your mate. Call me by my name."

Concerned, Jack took a swig, unsure what Thirsk was up to. "I have a problem with my ethes; you try thaying your name when you can't pronounthe your ethes."

Thirsk turned away to conceal his smile, his shoulders shaking lightly while he controlled himself. "I know you do a bit of dealing from here, Jack. I want some."

Jack snorted, derisive. "As if I'd sell anything to a copper. What kind of idiot do you fucking take me for, mate?"

"Okay, let's try it a different way. You roll one, we'll share. Then you've got something on me. I have no intention of splitting on you, my normal dealer's out of green and I won't use resin."

"You're fucking having me on. Where are the wires? I thought I was safe with you, mate, and you're trying to set me up."

Thirsk had noticed the lisp before but, now it had been pinpointed aloud, everything Jack said made him want to chuckle. He was giddy from holding his breath long enough to restrain the laughter. He grabbed the bottle from Jack and took a deep slug, the liquid burning his throat. Slowly, he placed the drink on the table and glared at Jack, who shrank back, disconcerted. Suddenly, Thirsk's hand was on Jack's throat, clutching tight. Squeezing. "I've not had a smoke for three fucking days, arsehole, and I know you've got shed-fucking-loads in this fucking room. If I don't have a toot soon, I won't be responsible for what I do. Is that clear?"

"Fuck you, man." Jack angrily shrugged Thirsk's hand away, straightening his collar indignantly. "I don't believe you smoke, no fucking way. It's more than your fucking job's worth."

"So I won't think twice about giving you the once over now you know my destructive little secret. Roll me a fucking joint now, and get me twenty quid's worth out, is that fucking clear?"

Jack opened the wardrobe door and dragged out an old-fashioned, plastic, screw-topped sweet jar. "If there's any fallout on this, I'm not fucking covering for you."

Fifteen minutes later the atmosphere was calm once more. Both men were chilled and thoughtful, Jack lounging on the unmade bed, Thirsk slouched on a wooden chair. The detective took a mouthful of whisky and screwed on the lid, tossing the bottle to Jack. "So you don't really want to go for a drink then, that was just a ruse to get some weed."

"Yes, we are. You're going to introduce me as your Uncle Fred. Do you know Jim Collins and Sean O'Connor?"

"Jim practically lives at the pub. Sean goes sometimes, but he's not a big drinker."

"What do you know about them, apart from their drinking habits?"

"Jim's a bit of a hard nut, I try and keep away from him. I think his wife's called Maria. Sean? All round good guy, does his bit for the community, does stuff for the church, grins pompously at everybody he sees. You know the type; a regular smarmy bastard. I heard rumours he's knocking off Jim's wife, fuck knows why, but if it's true, they keep it pretty discreet."

"You should have been a detective, crime's wasted on you." Thirsk hadn't smoked pot since his teenage years, those heady nineteen-seventies before the risks were emblazoned on posters and brochures, and he was finding it difficult to keep up the ruse of 'junkie-cop'. But he couldn't deny it felt good, being so relaxed, it was welcome after the chaos and stress of the past couple of days. "Roll us another, then we'll go."

"Thieving bastard." Jack laughed, impressed.

Toni and Sally were exhilarated as they trotted down the station steps to the car park, neither could quite conceive they had actually spent the best part of a day working on the coveted fifth floor. The work had been hard, but they had produced a neatly collated file for the detectives, complete with a title page and index, which had been Toni's idea, for ease of use. It documented the details of seven missing girls, who had disappeared between the ages of ten and fifteen. They had passed the details to Steadman, who thanked them and sent them home.

"Are you still coming to help me pack?" The reality that she was leaving home in two days had never left her mind, regardless of the hectic day.

"Are you still planning to stop at an offy to pick up some plonk?"

Toni chuckled as she unlocked her car. "You're a bad influence on me, Sal." The journey was short, and soon they parked outside Toni's childhood home.

Carol Fowler heard a key in the front door and, as she had for the previous five days, wondered if tonight would be the night Toni realised something was missing from her wardrobe. Nursing a mug of tea at the table, with four cooling dinners on the side and a stack of pans in the sink, she watched Toni come in, the smile waning instantly on seeing her mother. Although she was still in a mood with her mum, she realised someone had to be the adult. "Alright."

It was the first word between them since the argument the weekend before and Carol hoped the tension would begin to dissipate. "Evening, love, your dinner's on the side."

"Thanks. I've brought a friend home to help me pack, so I'll have it later."

"A…" She was going to say friend – Toni never bought friends home – but stopped herself abruptly. "So you're still going ahead with the crazy idea of moving out? You'll be back in days, mark my words. Once you realise how much I do for you. Your cleaning, your cooking, washing. Cheap rent."

Toni rolled her eyes, wishing she hadn't bothered to instigate conversation, and turned, tagging Sally on the arm as she strode by. "Come on, let's go upstairs."

"What about glasses," whispered Sally, shy in front of the older woman. "You know, for the wine."

"Not worth the fucking hassle, we can have it out of the bottle." Toni led Sally up the stairs to her room, her temper subsiding, and was pleased her annoying sister wasn't at home. "Gray at the pub gave me a load of boxes," she pointed to the stack in the corner, "they're flat-packed, but the tape to rebuild them is there."

"Fair do's, but let's get this bottle started before we do anything, eh?" Sally lived for a drink in the evenings, a party girl, through and through. She unscrewed the cap and took a few gulps, grimacing a little. "Damn, it's a dry one." It didn't stop her drinking more.

Toni didn't have the same affection – need – for alcohol, and she took only a sip before assembling the first box. Opening her wardrobe to expose the boyish clothing and boxes of treasured memories, she began to stack them neatly in the box. Her friend relaxed on the bed, propped on one arm, and Toni realised Sally's concept of helping was the opposite to her own, but she didn't mind. At least she would know what was in each box at the other end, and having company for once was pleasant. Sally finished the first bottle of wine in the time it took Toni to pack three boxes, taping the lids and labelling them clearly. She assembled the fourth, but when she began packing the contents of the top shelf, she realised her mother had been snooping again. "I don't fucking believe it." She shouted, "Mother."

Furious, she stormed from the room, itching for an argument. She thundered down the stairs, while curious Sally

145

followed at a distance, gripped by the true-life soap opera that was unfolding. Toni screamed, "Mother," as she burst into the kitchen.

Carol knew she had been busted, and now she had to ride the storm. "Mmm."

"What have you done with my Baby Jane things? I want them back."

Sally moved close to the kitchen and leaned, out of sight, against the wall. She had no idea what 'Baby Jane things' were, but assumed they were items for a newborn in anticipation of a family. Carol muttered something about an unhealthy obsession.

"They are not unhealthy and I'm not obsessed. It's an interest, and I hope to work on the case one day. That poor baby deserves recognition, otherwise her short life was a waste." Sally dismissed her assumption instantly; Baby Jane things were clearly something far more intriguing.

"So you intend to make it your life's crusade, discovering the identity of a baby that nobody gave a monkey's about ten years ago. Nobody came forward, the mother was never found, there were no records of a baby going missing, no pregnant mothers who unaccountably lost their babies. Nobody wanted that child. Why can't you just let it go? Forget about it and move on."

"I move out in two days and I'm taking my collection with me. If you don't give it back now, I'm going to tear this place apart until I find it." Toni stormed past Sally, who followed her, less noisily, up the stairs. "Sorry you had to witness that, Sal, now you know why I'm getting the fuck out of here."

Sally closed the door and laid on the bed, taking a long swig of the wine. "Are you going to tell me what Baby Jane things are, or do I have to interrogate it from you?"

Toni sighed, her anger still rife, and chucked more belongings from her cupboard into the waiting box. "Just over ten years ago, the remains of a baby were found inside a tree in

146

Black Park. The mother never came forward and eventually the case went cold."

"I vaguely remember it; I was a paper girl at the time so got to read the headlines every morning. You must have been, what, ten? Why does it mean anything to you?"

"It was me who found the baby. It was me who called her Baby Jane. Over the years I've collected cuttings from newspapers, researched it a bit at the library, and it was the main reason I joined the police. I guess I hoped that one day we'd find the mother and find out how and why Jane died. I don't know, give some finality to the case. Someone, somewhere, had a baby, and either it died of natural causes, or it was killed, and they left the poor little body to rot as if it'd never existed. I just can't fathom that. I can't let it go."

"So your mum's right, it is an obsession."

The door burst open and Carol stood, relieved, on the landing. "I'm so glad I'm not the only one who thinks that. Thank you, whoever you are." She slammed the door and her footsteps echoed on the stairs.

Sally tittered. "Yep, I can see why you're leaving home."

Thirsk spent an hour in the pub with Jack, who had followed his instructions and introduced him as his Uncle Fred. Despite Thirsk's attempts to blend in, he was regarded with suspicion by the landlord, a man whose loud clothes and manner fitted his surroundings. He fished a little about Jim and Sean, but although large quantities of alcohol were being readily consumed, none of the regulars were willing to discuss the men. He tried again, saying he knew them of old and using the gossip that both had been arrested, but lips were tight and he came away with nothing.

He intended to leave Jack behind when he gave up, mumbling an irritated farewell, but the young man followed him, falling into step, and shiftily glanced around before whispering, "Look, mate, I know some stuff about both Jim and Sean. Is it worth anything?"

"Well, that depends on what you know."

They reached Jack's lodgings, but he continued to walk alongside Thirsk, past the house, heading towards the cul-de-sac where the car was parked. "I know that they like girls, and the younger the better." Thirsk instantly spun on his heels and strode up the pathway towards the front door of Jack's home, and Jack shrugged, rooting in his pocket for the key. Once they were inside and had climbed the bare wooden stairs to the top floor, Jack unlocked his door and they entered. Jack tapped his hand, begging. "Make it good and I'll tell you everything I know."

Thirsk withdrew his wallet and pulled out a two twenties and a ten, and he showed them to the man he had grown to like over the years. "Go on. I want everything."

"I think Sean's behind something, he's the smart one, and he's always talking to some kid or other. I had to go to his house a while ago, had to pick something up, and while he was upstairs getting whatever it was, he left me in the hallway. I had a look around, you know how you do, and I noticed he had a camera at the front window there, on a tripod. I reckon he takes photos of the kids as they pass his house going to and from school. I don't think he noticed me looking."

Jack snatched the twenty that Thirsk offered. The information could positively incriminate Sean, but there was no proof as the recording equipment had been found in the drawer under his divan bed. He would have to check the records to see if a tripod had been recovered. "Have you been in his cellar?" He knew that the cellar had revealed nothing but some old paint tins, some wood, and everyday tools and equipment, but he was testing Jack.

"I didn't know he had one. If there's a door from the hall, I didn't see it. I reckon that Smacker's part of it too."

"The landlord? Do you know his real name?"

"Don't think anybody does, I doubt he even know himself. Everyone round here knows him as Smacker."

"How much of a part in it is he? For example, would he have a room anywhere in the pub where children may be taken to." Thirsk passed him another twenty.

"I hardly ever go there, can't afford it nowadays." He grinned, fondling the note in his hand. "Well, maybe I can now. No, I only know the bar and the bog. What's going on then, is it something to do with that little girl?"

Thirsk held the final ten pound note up. "So, you know Sean takes photos, but do you know anything about touching children, even abducting them?"

"You think he might have something to do with that Melissa girl, don't you?" Thirsk coughed, dragging a packet of cigarettes and a lighter from his pocket. He offered one to Jack who grabbed it eagerly. "B and H. How the other half live, eh. No, I've never seen either with a kid in unusual circumstances and I've been here three years now."

Thirsk took a deep drag, the smoke filling his lungs, and coughed again. "No meetings on the street, you know, even if it looks perfectly normal. Any contact at all with any child, no matter how innocent it may have seemed."

Jack sagged onto the only armchair in the room. "I already told you, Sean has a lot to do with community events, he's always organising something or other, or raising money, that kind of thing. He has a lot of contact with the kids around here, but I've never seen anything that made me think anything susp… susp…" he gave into the lisp and changed the word, "weird was going on."

"So you'd say that Sean was innocent of anything indecent going on?"

Jack leaned forward. "Look, if I had a kid I wouldn't let it near the pair of them, that's for sure, but all I know about is the camera. I've heard rumours, well, not even rumours, just snippets, that you can get, let's say, unsavoury photos, and Smacker's always doing dodgy deals from behind the bar. If there's something going on it's very cloak and dagger, but I suppose it has to be, 'cos I doubt they'd survive long if the parents found out. That's all I know."

"I hardly think that's worth a nifty, is it? Stop messing me about, Jack."

Jack took a long, pleasurable drag on his cigarette. "Look, I know Melissa's mum, Val, we've shagged a few times, you know. So if I see Melissa I look out for her, you know what I mean." His face screwed a little and he tapped his lips subconsciously. "You know, come to think about it, I did notice Maria Collins with her on the day she went missing, but not Jim or Sean."

Thirsk was astonished and withheld the threatening cough. "And it didn't occur to you to tell the police? Even you should have some kind of conscience."

"It's only 'cos you're saying this now that I'm remembering."

"The fucking streets were littered with cops last night, and pictures of Melissa were everywhere. Surely even a thick shit like you must have tied the two together."

"I was tripping, off my head on California Sunshine. I saw blue lights flashing, alright, but I didn't think they were real, if you know what I mean."

Thirsk groaned, calming himself. "What time was it? Had school started or not?"

Jack sprawled back on the chair, his mind searching, trying to bring up the image in his head. "I was looking out of my window, the dustmen had woken me up and I was a bit pissed about it. Thinking back the school bell must have gone because the playground was empty. Maria was walking up her garden path, holding Melissa's hand. I thought nothing of it."

"Will you come in and make a formal statement?"

"Come on, mate, I don't want to be involved. I've told you everything I know."

Thirsk wasn't one to shout in anger, and he had no emotion for children, so his outburst shocked him as well as his company. "It's a fucking six-year old child we're talking about. I'm sending a fucking car to take you in."

Chapter 16
Cherry's Hell

Julia was fed up – bored of the television, bored of the loneliness, bored of the quiet – and was surprised to hear a knock at the door. She looked at the clock: it was just past nine. She momentarily wondered if it signalled trouble as it so often did on the Canal Estate, and then dared to consider it may be a friendly face, a thought she quickly dismissed. She trudged to the door, reasoning it was either the wishy-washy social worker or another policeman. Checking the chain was across the door, she pulled it ajar. Thirsk introduced himself, showing his identification, and she sighed audibly as she let him in, bolting the door behind him. "I just told you my name at the door, do you remember it?"

"I don't know, detective something or other."

"Good." Thirsk reached into the pocket of his black leather jacket and pulled out a small plastic zip-seal bag, and the smell that wafted from it was unmistakeable. He dangled it in front of her nose and she pushed his arm away. "You told my officer that you would tell us about your childhood if we got you some smoke, booze and tobacco. There's a half bottle of gin in my pocket and a pouch of Golden Virginia."

"Yeah, I've got you, I take it and then you arrest me for it, I ain't stupid. Anyway," she slouched onto her comfortable seat, "I hate Golden Virginia."

Thirsk sat on the other end of the beaten sofa and threw the three presents to her. "I have no intention of telling you my name again, because I don't want anybody knowing that I've brought these for you, but if anyone's about to get into trouble over it, it'll be me. You spill the beans and it could cost me my job. Now, roll yourself a smoke, have a G and T, and chill while you tell me your part of the bargain."

Julia couldn't fathom the bizarre guest and his welcome gifts, but she wasn't about to complain. She dragged some cigarette papers from underneath a pile of magazines and opened the bag, nimbly breaking the green with her stumpy fingers before adding tobacco and a roach torn from an envelope. "Get me a drink then while I do this. I ain't got no tonic though."

Thirsk stood and shrugged his jacket off, the room too hot to be wearing leather. He took the bottle from where it lay, untouched, beside Julia's feet on the settee. "What do you want with it then?"

"I don't know; just chuck in whatever you can find. I would have bought some cheap coke if I'd known you were coming."

Minutes later, they sat comfortably, Julia nursing a strong gin mixed with value blackcurrant cordial and water, and a burning joint, and Thirsk patiently waiting for the conversation to begin. She passed the roll-up to Thirsk, who didn't refuse, suspecting she would relax more if he joined in, maybe even trust him. Or at least that was the excuse he was giving himself. The two he had shared earlier with Jack had gone straight to his head, even to his nauseous stomach, but it had been the first weed he had had since his experimental college days. This one barely affected him and he was pleased, if not a little hungry. "You want me to tell you about my childhood then. I hear you've arrested my dad?"

"Yes, and your uncle, Sean. But first I want you to tell me about your mother."

"Mum? Okay then, where do I start? Right, here goes: she didn't want me, made it clear mine had been an unwanted pregnancy because her religion frowned on the pill. I don't know what she did to stop it happening again, but I was the only one. I don't ever remember a hug, not from her. My dad was always hugging me, even though I didn't want him to sometimes, but she wouldn't. Her nickname for me was 'the tart'."

"Yeah, yeah, you're touching my heartstrings and I can hear violins. So you had a bad childhood, most of us do." He tugged his cigarettes out, taking one and lighting it haughtily.

"I'm answering your bloody question, aren't I? What more do you bloody want?"

"A concise account," he noted her dazed expression and sighed, enjoying the nicotine kick, "just a quick version without the sob story. Bear in mind we're investigating child abuse, pornography and possibly murder."

"Murder?" Julia became small before his eyes and her reaction to the word intrigued him. "Who? What is...? I don't know anything about...."

"The little girl whose body was found in Black Park Lake yesterday, we have evidence to suggest that your father, possibly mother, and uncle were involved in her torture and death."

She visibly relaxed, which didn't go unnoticed. "Oh, I thought you meant, I mean, oh, that's terrible. What do you want from me?"

"What, exactly, did your parents used to do to you, anything you wouldn't do to your own child?"

The recollection that Julia had become known to the police by dangling her child from a third-floor balcony swept over him and he couldn't restrain himself from laughing at the irony. Julia's sense of humour was on the same wavelength and she joined in. "I'd never have dropped him you know, I just wanted someone to listen. Thing is, I don't want him because I'm scared of what he might do to him as he gets older. Girls in my family expect to be, well, the men do that to them, it's just the way it is. But I don't know what they do to the boys. I haven't seen Mum and Dad for what," she calculated for a while, "nine, ten years. I kept away from Moor End so they wouldn't find me, and once I had Antony I asked for a house over here. They hurt me for all those years, but I don't want them touching my boy." Julia, her eyelids showing the effects of the drugs, leant forward and began to roll another joint, having only just finished the last.

Thirsk was hopeless at suppressing his plain speech. "If I ask you some questions straight, do me a favour and just give me a yes or no, I haven't got time for all this emotional crap."

Julia laughed again; she liked the mysterious copper who didn't appear to give a toss and she topped up her glass with gin, not diluting it this time.

Thirsk spent over two hours with Julia and had to admit he found her compelling. She was damaged goods, no hint of a doubt, and she lacked education and manners, but she was a survivor, and remarkably strong, mentally, for what she'd had to endure in her younger years. He liked her, and oddly felt an affinity for her.

His own childhood hadn't been wonderful by any means. He had been brought into the world by two unemotional people who'd had no idea, in fact still had no idea, of how to bond or nurture, and the idea of hugging was alien to him. Money had never been an issue for Thirsk's immediate family, his parents both professionals, so he couldn't compare himself to Julia financially – the poor girl had lived in poverty all her life – but emotionally he'd always had to rely on himself, and the lesson he had learned from his parents was to not care, because if you did, you were at risk of pain. The warning had served him well in his line of work; he had seen so much horror over the years, but always remained detached. But now, somehow, he felt an affection for Julia, a responsibility. Over the course of his visit she had gone from angry at the world, snappy and confrontational, to utterly relaxed, eyes heavy, the mellow smile never waning. She had frankly told him of her upbringing, of the way her mother had beaten her regularly, of the abuse she had suffered at the hands of family members who should have loved and protected her, not used her body as they wished. However, despite the probability they would be sentenced suitably if she were to press charges, she wasn't interested, happy to leave the past where it belonged: in the past.

He was sure the disgraceful picture Julia had painted of the three main carers in her early life was truthful, and it would serve excellently to describe their characters in court but, because Julia hadn't been part of their lives for ten years, it bore no direct relevance to Melissa's abduction and probable

154

murder. Regardless, he was pleased he had visited and given her the company she so badly needed – that he had crossed a big line in bringing the illicit gifts.

He stood at the front door, ready to leave, and expected his final question to revolt her. "Did you know that your mother is having sex with her brother?"

Julia shrugged, her eyelids droopy and speech impeded. "Of course."

Thirsk left the graffiti covered building, hoping to find his car in one piece. He was exhausted, but Jack was at the station waiting to be interviewed. He nipped into the twenty-four seven shop on the ground floor and purchased his third half-bottle of spirits of the day, cognac this time, another packet of cigarettes and two energy drinks. He drained the first can in the car, closely followed by the second. A bit jittery, he was unsure if it was due to smoking pot or a glucose rush, but once the sensation passed he started the car and drove back to the station, stopping briefly for a kebab, loaded with hot chilli sauce, on the way.

Taking Jack's statement was a mere formality. He told Thirsk for the second time that he had seen Maria Collins holding Melissa Barton's hand after school had begun, and that they had walked up the path towards Maria's house. He had stopped watching after that so didn't see either enter. He had never noticed Melissa with Jim, Sean or Maria before. He mentioned again that he suspected the pub landlord of dodgy dealings, yet had nothing but supposition of what they may be. It took fifteen minutes, and Thirsk arranged for a patrol car to drive Jack home, before instigating an immediate search of The Nag's Head in Moor End.

It was eleven-thirty in the evening and Thirsk was shattered, eagerly anticipating a stiff drink and bed. He sloped through the drizzle to his car and was about to drive away when Wainwright knocked on the window, startling him. He let the window down, irritated. "Does it have to be tonight?"

"I thought I'd better let you know that they've found the one of the girls on the videos. She's thirteen and says it happened three years ago. Says Maria took her from school."

Thirsk thought back to his meeting with Jack. He had not told anybody that Jack had seen Melissa with Maria, so this was a second independent witness. "Just to clarify, we are talking Maria Collins here?"

"Yes, says she was," he looked at the black sky, the clouds bursting and drenching the trench-coat he had bought to emulate his former boss's style. "Does this have to be done out here?"

Thirsk rolled his eyes, wishing he had bought a case of energy drinks rather than two. "Fuck my life. Have you got a statement?"

"She's in there now."

Thirsk clambered from his car, dragging the black studded jacket half-heartedly over his head against the downpour, and they jogged through the rain to the rear entrance of the station. "I thought you said she was thirteen."

"Uh-huh."

Drenched, they entered the reception area and Thirsk grasped Wainwright's arm. "Then what the fuck is she doing in here at this hour then? Couldn't it wait until tomorrow?"

Wainwright summoned the lift and shook his head, grinning. "Nope, she's here now."

"Can't you do it? You're the one who brought her in."

"Hey, you old bastard, that side of the investigation's yours. Anyway, we didn't bring her in, her aunt did, and she kicked up a right fuss, screaming and shouting that she wanted it dealt with yesterday. Do you want me to sit in?"

"Let's get it over with. But if you give me anything else after this, I'll break your fucking neck." They had reached the first floor and Wainwright directed Thirsk to Interview Room 3, where Maria had been interviewed the previous night. Through the window, he saw an adolescent girl, who was a clone of every other adolescent girl he saw on the streets, with long straightened hair, an orange face that stopped at the jaw

156

line, blackened eyes and a sullen attitude. She sat at the table, arms defensively crossed and biting the nails of one hand, her back turned to a woman, who Thirsk assumed to be her aunt. "Not a happy customer, then?"

"Aren't they all like that?" The two men entered and closed the door behind them. "Cherry, this is Detective Chief Inspector Thirsk. He's going to be in charge of the investigation into the alleged abuse you have reported." They sat and the girl remained unmoved. "This is Mrs Robinson, she's Cherry's legal guardian."

"Her mother's no longer with us, she died last year. Breast cancer." Mrs Robinson stifled tears and Thirsk willed her not to cry, detesting emotional scenes. "She was only twenty-seven."

Thirsk glanced at the young girl, a child but only on the inside, and did the mental calculation, shuddering at the thought of becoming a parent at the age of fifteen. "Why come forward now?"

The girl shrugged and continued chewing her nails, leaving her aunt to answer for her. "She told me that she was taken from school once. We were talking about Melissa, God rest her soul, and she just came out with it. I asked her more but she kept clamming up."

"Would you rather speak to us alone, Cherry?" He hoped she would, everything about Mrs Robinson irritated him.

For the first time the girl looked to her guardian for guidance, and the woman smiled, enjoying being wanted. "Yes, I would, please." Affronted, her aunt was led from the room. "I don't know why she brought me down here, I ain't got much to tell you."

"Let me be the judge of that, Cherry. I'll be honest, I know nothing about why you're here, so why don't we just start from the beginning? You said you were taken from school once. Who by? Do you know?"

Cherry stopped biting her nails and turned to the detectives. "Well, she didn't take me from school, I kind of went. She…"

"She?"

"It was Mrs Collins. She called me over before school, she was outside the fence, I was in the playground. She said if I wanted a day off to bake cakes she wouldn't tell anybody. She said I could come back to hers for the day and nobody would know. I thought she seemed sound, I knew my mum knew her, so I didn't think anything of it."

"So, what happened?"

"When the bell went I hid in the bogs and waited until everyone went into assembly. Jenkins was…"

"Jenkins?"

"The caretaker, he was locking the gates, so I squeezed through a gap in the fence. Mrs Collins was waiting and she took me to her house."

"The gap in the fence, whereabouts was it?"

"Sort of to the side of the school, there's a path that goes around the outside of the school, and there was a gap in the fence."

Thirsk whispered to Wainwright, "Get someone to check out the area, see if it's still there, and if the security cameras cover it."

Wainwright nipped from the room to issue the instruction to an officer who stood outside, and was back in seconds. Thirsk waited a while to see if Cherry would continue, but she needed prompting. "And then what happened?"

Cherry shrugged, palms up. "That's all I remember. Next thing I remember I was in my bed, waking up. I thought it was a dream, to be honest."

Thirsk glared at Wainwright, who imagined he could read his thoughts: 'how dare you keep me back for that piece of shit'. He took over where Thirsk clearly wasn't going to, sulky and pedantic in his exhaustion. "So what made you think it might not be a dream?"

"Well, Melissa, of course. Everyone's saying that Val took her to school and then she wasn't at register. It made me think back and I wondered if the same had happened to her as what happened to me." She hungrily attacked the ends of her fingers with her teeth.

"Are you aware that we've found one or more video-clips of you held as a..."

"A word outside, Guv." Wainwright stood, tall and authoritative, and Thirsk squinted with confusion. "Now."

Mrs Robinson did her utmost to hear the whispered discussion between the two policemen, but the few words she strained to catch gave her nothing. "You can't just tell her something like that, she's thirteen, for fuck's sake."

"Well, what can I tell her? That she's been dragged down here at stupid o'clock so we can tell her we're interested in her accusation because somebody abducted her and sprinkled her with fucking fairy dusk? Get real, Nick, kids like to be treated with respect, and they like to know the truth"

"What do you fucking know about kids, you fucking hate them? I don't think she should be party," he calmed himself, his breathing slowing, "to that side of things until we've discussed if she should have a suitable adult with her."

Mrs Robinson caught the final four words and sprung from the seat enthusiastically. "I'm here, remember."

"No." They chorused together, breaking the tension, and returned to the room.

Wainwright started the conversation, not trusting his insensitive colleague. "So, you met with Mrs Collins, then what?"

"What was he going to say?" She jagged her reddened, wet finger at Thirsk.

"All we need for now is an account of everything you can remember about that day. Do you remember the date?"

"Not exactly, but I know it was just after the summer holidays three years ago, because I still had a tan from our holiday in Benidorm." She quietened, meek. "That was our last holiday before Mum got ill, she was okay then."

159

"I'm sorry your mother died." Thirsk's vain stab at compassion brought filthy looks from both sides of the table.

"Where did Maria take you?" Wainwright tried again.

"I think we might have gone back to her house, but I can't be sure, everything seems hazy.

"Close your eyes. Good. Tell me, did she hold your hand?" Wainwright was unsure what Thirsk was doing.

"She did, actually, yes, I remember. Her hands were hard and wrinkly, and I kind of wanted to go and scrub her off. It's getting clearer. We was in her kitchen, and she was kind. She gave me a choice of cakes to make, she had three boxes, and I said the chocolate ones. She gave me a drink of juice, I think. Then I don't remember any more."

Cherry's eyes sprang open and the officers glanced at each other. "You said the next thing you remember is being in bed, your own bed."

"Yep."

"Did you have any, um, pain? Anywhere?"

"My head was sore, I know that much, I felt rough all night, what I remember of it."

"So it was night when you woke up?" The girl nodded. "And you have no memory of the day at all?"

"No."

Wainwright checked they had Cherry's contact details down correctly, assuring the girl and her aunt they would be in touch soon, and Thirsk gratefully returned to his car, blearily focusing on the streets to find his way home. He checked the time before he closed his eyes: one a.m.

Chapter 17
Location, Location

Smacker furiously checked the locks on the outside doors of the pub that he had managed for the past five years, feeling like his home had been violated. Running The Nag's Head was a dream come true, his goal throughout his adult life, having first had a taster working behind the bar to help fund his days through university. He hadn't passed his degree, seemingly doomed before even starting. Growing up in Moor End had been hard, the final child and only boy of poor parents. He'd had ambition, but his seven sisters had accepted their place in life and chosen motherhood alongside lowly jobs that brought in just enough pennies. He had wanted more, some status and respect, and had worked his way up the ladder, first to head barman, then acting manager, and finally managing his own pub. He loved The Nag's Head.

The area was downtrodden, but he knew nothing different. He had chosen the nickname Smacker himself to sound tougher at school, and it was a useful deterrent when trouble was threatening. And he had realised early that trouble was an unavoidable side of the job – at least one drunken brawl could be guaranteed per weekend – but so far he had never felt out of his depth. However, this wasn't a weekly spat, a drunkard gone too far, or a loud lover's squabble. This was a police raid looking for evidence of porn – child porn. If the police had found anything, then he had been set up. The sheer thought that he could be, would be, involved with anything so vile, it made him sick to the stomach.

He had gone to the station voluntarily, concerned an arrest would endanger his career with the chain that owned The Nag's Head, and had answered all the questions succinctly and truthfully. He denied knowledge of any kind of porn ring, and swore that if such an activity was going on, he was not involved in any way. Faced with the accusation by an unnamed witness that he sold pictures of children in compromising positions from behind the bar, he was flabbergasted. He would never, ever do such a thing. He loved children – in the right way – and would never see harm come to them.

Finally, they took him back to the pub, now empty and tarnished, and he fixed a nightcap to take up to bed. He tossed and turned for an hour and gave up, thrashing his head back on the pillow with frustration. No names, no suspects, no details, nothing had been fed to him and he genuinely had no idea what was going on. In the lonely, dark hours of the night, he felt he had failed his task as landlord; surely he should know everything that was happening amongst his clientele. A loud rapping on the door stopped his lamenting, worried now that the police hadn't finished.

Smacker pulled his silky kimono over his naked, bulldog body, goosebumps springing up on his arms and calves, and tugged the curtain aside, scanning the street two floors down from his bedroom. On the pavement, expectantly looking up at him, was one of the not-so-regulars, Jack. He shrugged exaggeratedly in question, and in a stage whisper Jack told him he needed five minutes.

Snarling, he dragged on some boxers, jeans and a sweatshirt, and trotted down the stairs, unbolting the door to let Jack through. He locked it behind him. "What?"

"I saw they raided you, sorry, mate."

"Why are you sorry? Did you have anything to do with it?" He raised a fist. "If you did I'll…"

Jack flapped his arms, pacifying, a peacemaker, not a fighter. "No, mate, no, it's sound. It's just they had me in earlier too, I wondered if you knew what was going on?"

"They were asking questions about Jim Collins and Sean O'Connor, and that Melissa Barton kid, and said they had been told I was selling dodgy pictures from behind the bar. What do you know?"

"Probably less than you do, it's just I saw you get back from the station and thought you might want to swap notes."

Smacker led a lonely life, despite his bar being occupied for every opening hour of the day, and knowing sleep wasn't about to come easily, he relaxed. "I'll fix us a drink. Whisky okay?" Jack nodded and sat on a barstool. Smacker was about to fill a glass from the optic, but changed his mind and dragged out an unopened bottle of single malt. "Might as well enjoy it, seeing as neither of us are going to get to sleep without a good few in our bellies." They downed the first couple of drinks, slowing with the third, and Smacker lit a cigarette, offering one to Jack. The minutes ticked by, both lost in thought, but finally Smacker said, "Any idea who would say I've been selling porno photos of kids from behind the bar."

Jack lowered his head, his cheeks suddenly hot, and he sucked his cigarette, buying time. Okay, so he had told a white lie, but Smacker would never find out, and Thirsk had seemed impressed, which meant more snout money coming his way as and when. "They never said that to me. I wouldn't worry too much, mate, probably stringing you along to get you rattled."

"I don't like being accused of something I haven't done. Look, what do you know about the whole business, you know, a child porn ring. Isn't that a bit metropolitan for the likes of us?"

Jack was surprised at the terminology; he hadn't realised Smacker was capable of words longer than two syllables. "From their questions it's got to be something to do with Jim and his wife, and they asked a few questions about Sean. The copper I saw was very interested that I saw Maria with little Melissa Barton before she died. Dreadful tragedy." The final two words were added simply because they were expected, but the lack of warmth went unnoticed.

"What are they supposed to have done?"

"Sexy stuff with kiddies and possibly murder, apparently." Jack had been told nothing of the sort, but the line of questioning had made it easy enough to deduce. Jack finished his third shot and regarded Smacker quizzically. "You really know nothing about it?"

"No, but if I'd known what I know now when I was at the station, I would have had a whole lot more to say. Drink up and get out, I've got things to do."

"What? Come on, Smacker, it's three o'clock in the fucking morning. Let's have a couple more and get some sleep."

"I can't handle this, this whole child abuse thing, the thought I may have interacted with somebody who'd do something so disgusting. It makes me sick to the pit, and after what you've said I think I may have been inadvertently involved. I have to check it out, so if you don't mind leaving, I've got things to do."

"What kind of things? What if I help?" Jack was enjoying the free cigarettes and alcohol, and also the surprise of discovering that Smacker was miles smarter than he appeared.

"No, I've got to do this on my own. Anyway, I don't trust you as far as I can throw you, Jack. I'll be open again by eleven tomorrow, let's see what we hear on the grapevine then, eh? Now piss off."

Jack patiently waited outside, hidden from view by a wilting cerise hydrangea, the rusting petals caught in the glow from the streetlight, and although it was possible Smacker wouldn't come out of the pub again that night, something told him he would, and at three-thirty the side door opened a crack. Wearing a hoodie, Smacker searched the alley to ensure his solitude, before creeping out, locking the door and heading towards the blackness of the back road behind the pub car park, away from the main street. In the shadows and staying close to the walls, Jack tailed him. Smacker furtively trotted the short distance through the alleyways to a block of garages at the foot of a nearby tower block. He withdrew a key, checking for witnesses, and tried the padlock on the garage door, but it wouldn't open. The change of lock told him everything he needed to know. He pulled his mobile from the pocket of his hoodie and dialled the emergency services.

The duty Sergeant was unsure, as were most people, who was heading the case – Wainwright or Thirsk – so he tossed a coin and Thirsk lost. At the deadly hour of four forty-five in the morning, he was notified that they had found the room used for the videos, the place where Melissa Barton had been tortured, and probably killed too.

Thirsk knew he shouldn't be driving, his head heavy and tired body uncoordinated, but his desire to see the den of horrors was too great to wait for a driver. Forensic experts were already combing the dank, stark room, the rough breezeblocks grey and cold. In the back corner, a pale-blue fleece blanket was screwed in a heap. The yellow melamine-topped table they had seen in the clips was central and the dark oak chair against the wall. Apart from those, the room was empty, with none of the objects that had been used in the abuse of the girls. It had been wiped clean.

Photographs were taken from every angle to compare with the stills of the videos, and the dimensions measured, and while Thirsk was confident it was the room they had been searching for, it held no obvious evidence to incriminate the three prisoners. Thirsk scratched his head, wondering if it had been worth getting out of bed for.

Steadman, bright and bubbly for the unsociable hour, tapped him on the shoulder. "They told me I'd find you here. What do you make of it?"

"It's the room, alright, but that's about it. Unless there's microscopic evidence, it's not giving us anything we don't already know."

They strolled out to the road, hopeless still. "The guy who rang this in, what do they call him?"

"He's the landlord of The Nag's Head, goes by the name of Smacker."

Thirsk grunted. "Doesn't he have a proper name?"

"Yeah, but I can't remember it. He suits his nickname. Anyway, the garage is leased under his name and Jim has sub-let it for the past four years. He said he became suspicious in the early hours – said he couldn't sleep – and went down to have a look, but the padlock had been changed, and that's when he called us."

"Became suspicious in the early hours, what kind of crap is that? You don't…"

"He said someone tipped him off that it was Jim who was involved with Melissa's disappearance."

"Who?"

She glared at him, annoyed. "Guv!"

Thirsk raised his hands, shrugging. "Okay, I was only asking."

"So what did you make of the report of Sean's car?" When no reply came, she sighed. "Don't you ever read your sodding emails, Guv? I give up. There was a shopping trolley, you know, one of those old lady things, in the boot. They're testing it now; they think it may have been used to transport Melissa's body to the dumpsite."

His eyes lit up and he checked his watch. "I suppose if we have to be awake at such an ungodly hour, we may as well do something constructive." Steadman smiled coyly, blushing. "Have you got your car?"

"No, Higs gave me a lift in."

"Good, come with me." Barely refreshed from under four hours sleep, but sobering up quickly, Thirsk drove Steadman across the city centre to the university and left the car in the vast parking bay. The morning sun peeped from the edge of the horizon, bathing the buildings in a grey half-light, and they waited for someone to let them into the science block. Gordon greeted them with a warm handshake, not having seen either for a few weeks. "I'm guessing you're here about the Melissa Barton case." He showed them into the lab and began to detail the items that his skeleton staff was testing. "We've got hairs and fibres from the shopping trolley that was found in the boot of the car." He gestured to the silver Fiat 500 that had been taken in its entirety to be examined. "A few partials match Maria Collins's fingerprints."

"It's probably her trolley."

Gordon's smile was condescending, but he didn't mean it to be; it was just his way. "It probably is, but I'm not paid to make assumptions, I'm paid to find facts." He paused for an objection that didn't come. "Of course, all our findings so far have been emailed to you…"

Steadman winked. "You're best off mailing them to me, Gordon, that way you know they'll be seen."

"If you say so. Right, blanket found in lake, no direct link to Melissa, but it was waterlogged, which hasn't helped. The fibres have been compared to those found in her oral and nasal cavities and aren't a match. There were no hairs on it, probably by luck rather than design, the wool's harsh and would easily trap hair and fluff. Fingerprints on the car have been identified as Sean O'Connor's, nothing less than we'd expect considering it's his car, but it does seem that he's the only person to have driven it recently."

"Bare-handed. Our perpetrator was possibly wearing rubber gloves."

"There's no blood, no…"

"Gordon, the hair from the trolley is Melissa's." The technician passed a printed report to him. "I thought you'd want to know."

Thirsk felt like dancing. "Just to clarify, you have found one of Melissa's hairs inside a shopping trolley that was in the boot of Sean O'Connor's car?"

"That's what the lady said, sir."

"Bingo." Thirsk forced Steadman into a high-five, a beaming grin from ear to ear. "We've got enough to charge him." He grabbed the reluctant assistant, swinging her around, and Steadman tingled with an irrational jealousy.

Toni was missing her active lifestyle, keen for her ankle to mend so she could get back to normal. It was another cloudy, miserable day, the clouds threatening and gloomy, rain spitting in sporadic bursts, but nothing, especially the weather, was going to ruin her day. Tonight would be the last night she would spend at her parents' house as their child rather than guest.

Black Park was her favourite place in the world, a sanctuary of peace and tranquillity, somewhere to reflect on life without interruption, and it had a charming way of dusting away the cobwebs and giving clarity to thought. It was the perfect setting to spend the early hours of the monumental day. She parked her car and took a relaxed, yet brisk, stroll, heading for the embankment where Melissa's body had been found, where she intended to have a look around before retracing her steps.

Time was an issue now she was working on the once unattainable fifth floor, as she preferred to arrive earlier than she was paid for to show willing and dedication.

Nearing the area, she noticed a figure ahead, and she recognised the anorak, the hood fastened tight with the integral string. She put her own hood up immediately to avoid being seen, but it was too late. "Toni? Toni Fowler, is that you?"

"Shit." Toni forced a bright smile, with no choice, bar rudeness, but to greet the dreaded woman. She pushed her hood down and walked over. "Mrs Frobisher, I didn't expect to see you again. Are you walking your dogs?"

Joyce shook her head. "No, believe it or not. Ronny went down with a tummy bug last week, and now Pickering and Byker are doing their business everywhere. The vet told me to let them rest for a few days."

"Oh, dear. Well, I must be getting back, I've just been promoted so I want to show them I'm committed." She couldn't understand why she was boasting, trying to impress the woman she had hoped to never see again.

"Liar."

Toni halted mid-step and turned back. "I beg your pardon?"

Joyce laughed, her face transforming from stately and authoritative to welcoming and friendly. "You were leaving because you want to get away from me. Why is that? Did I scare you the other day?"

"No, no, of course not. No, you see, my ankle's still a bit dodgy so I thought I'd just to walk to this part and back, I decided that way before I saw you."

Reluctantly, Toni fell into step with the woman and they sauntered towards the car park. "Why were you walking to this spot, anyway?"

"What is this, twenty questions?" Toni was smiling, but not on the inside.

"Well, it's obviously to do with Melissa Barton, isn't it?"

Toni stopped. Joyce Frobisher knew too much about everything and was seriously beginning to irritate her. "What do you know about Melissa Barton?"

Joyce also stopped, shrugging. "The same as everybody else who watches the regional news, dear. But you're a policewoman and your station's heaving at the moment with the investigation; of course that's why you're here." She laughed again at the indignant stare from the annoyed woman. "Oh, Toni, you're funny. I have friends on the force, many of them. I did have a career once, you know, I wasn't born old."

"So you were a policewoman too? Now, that makes sense, I understand the other day at the hospital now. Wow, I bet you've got some stories to tell." It seemed a silly thing to say, but she couldn't think of anything else; small talk had never been her strong point.

"No, I wasn't, but I worked alongside the police on many occasions. I came this morning because *I* wanted to see where poor Melissa had been dumped, I wanted to see how it correlated with another dumped child ten or so years ago, see if there could be a link."

Now the older woman had Toni's full interest. "Baby Jane?"

"Good lord, I would have thought you were far too young to remember that, dear. Yes, I was talking about the Baby Jane case."

They continued walking, slow and lazy, now engrossed with their shared interest. "Well, Jane was found miles from here, and in completely different circumstances. I can assure you there aren't any similarities between the two." Toni felt she was the lord and master of the subject and allowed herself a contented smirk.

"I beg to differ, actually." Joyce grasped Toni's arm. "Come with me." Reticent, but compelled, Toni followed the deft footsteps of the older woman, away from the muddy path and into the wall of trees that surrounded the lake, unbroken. They stepped over the undergrowth, low ferns and foliage, their trousers soaking up the morning dew from the leaves. From the tremendous whooshing noise, Toni realised a heavy downpour had started, but the trees above protected the women from the drops. Lightning flashed across the sky, an instantaneous illumination between the branches, and was followed seconds later by a crashing roll of thunder. "What an ominous time for a storm to start, eh. Spooky, don't you think?"

Toni couldn't make Mrs Frobisher out. She half-liked her, but was dubious, and she felt guilty because the woman had shown her nothing but kindness. They clambered a few more steps, and it was as if a curtain had been pulled aside; before them was the clearing she had visited on that unforgettable day a decade before. And so was the old, lopped yew tree, now a mast of moss, ivy and fungus. "Oh my god, you're right. There must be only twenty metres between them. Fuck me. I mean, I'm sorry, my mum tells me I swear too much, I try not to."

"Then your mum's right, it's a dreadful habit for a young lady. My dogs have had me wandering through these woods on many an occasion, I know it like the back of my hand."

Without regard for the storm that raged in the tumultuous sky, Toni was compelled to head for the tree stump, unseen for many years, since her worried parents had stopped taking her to the park following her sombre find. She couldn't even remember which path from the main gates would lead to the tree. It was like stepping back in time.

She slowly circled the tree, soaked but not caring, and the memories flooded back as if it were yesterday. The excitement at finding the inviting hollow, her mother's warning, the snap of the tiny bones as her sandaled foot landed on them. Glancing to see what she had landed on and the sheer horror of seeing a decomposing baby. Of the scream that had echoed around the inside of the tree, which she had realised was coming from her. And then the amazing events that unfolded after she had clambered out, of the police, her now long-time friend, Pam MacAllister, of the terrifying man she was now working for. She could feel the memories, taste them, hear them, live them, as she ringed the tree yet again.

Eventually Toni awoke from her trance, and the intrigued woman who had shown her the shortcut stood watching her, astounded. She reddened. "I'm sorry, I got lost for a minute there."

"I noticed."

The moment had been magical, with Toni in wonderment at the body-blowing recollections, and she was reluctant to move. She was drenched, the water dripping from her ponytail to her jacket. Suddenly aware that her behaviour must seem peculiar, she sheepishly felt the need to justify herself. "I found her. I found Baby Jane."

"I guessed, my dear. I knew I'd heard your name before."

They retraced their steps through the undergrowth, the thick cover of trees and branches, back to the lakeside for the sodden journey to the car park, in silence. Both women felt an understanding had been reached between them and their partnership was amicable now, not awkward. They had a shared bond that could never be lost. It didn't occur to Toni to ask why Joyce was so interested in the location of the dumpsites until they reached the cars. "I was the coroner on the case. It was me who recorded the open verdict."

"You've got to be kidding me? No way." Toni chuckled heartily until she realised that Joyce was serious. "So what are you thinking about the distance between where the bodies were found?"

The rain pounded, the periodic rumbling deafening in its ferocity, but neither woman was perturbed. "Not distance, but location. And method. Melissa was suffocated before being placed in the lake, and it's my belief, and that of the pathologist who performed the post-mortem on Baby Jane, that she was also suffocated, although there wasn't enough evidence to record her death as unnatural. To dump a baby, dead or alive, is an incredibly emotional process for a person to go through, and whoever left Jane in that tree did so for personal, probably sentimental, reasons. I wonder if they had an affinity with the place, it could hold good, but possibly bad, memories. That type of emotion would usually come from a woman. With Melissa being abandoned so close by, I'm wondering if it could be more than coincidence."

"What, you mean the same person killed them both?" Toni was aghast, the thought wouldn't have occurred to her in a million years.

"It's just my theory, of course." Joyce opened the car door and shuffled onto the dry seat. "Probably just the musings of an old and bored woman, but at least it keeps my mind busy." With a wink she closed the door and drove away, leaving Toni rooted to the spot.

Chapter 18
Breaking Rules

Carol had feigned illness to her husband, Dan, that morning, groaning and writhing in bed with a non-existent headache, telling him she wouldn't be going to the factory with him, and she had patiently waited for him to leave.

Toni had blanked her mother when she returned from her early morning walk, fuelling Carol's decision to involve a third party with her concerns for her daughter. Eventually Toni had left for work, and Leon and Maisie had marched to the bus stop for college and school. The house now quiet, Carol went up the stairs to her room, tiptoeing for no reason, and dialled the familiar number to her daughter's workplace. "Can I speak to Sergeant Feldman please?"

Andy was amazed to hear Toni Fowler's mother on the line and he readily agreed to discuss the urgent concerns she had about her daughter, inferring they may affect her work. Intrigued, he listened intently.

Carol was nervous at first, timid about her exposé, but soon despair and raw emotion took over. "I don't think it's healthy, Sergeant, and she's admitted it's the only reason she joined the police force."

Andy smiled, knowing she would hear it in his voice. "You were absolutely right to bring this to my attention. I had no idea she was so closely involved in that case, she's never mentioned it at work, as far as I know. It does seem a trifle obsessive, I agree. You say the items are kept in a box, is it possible you could bring it to us so I can see how serious the situation is?"

She would have to take two buses to reach the station, but it was important and time was running out. "Of course, I'll get it to you as soon as I can, it'll take an hour or so on the bus."

"The bus," his patter was sickeningly slimy, "take the bus, indeed. Carol – may I call you Carol?"

"Of course." She was relieved he wasn't dismissing her concerns, as others, including her husband, would.

"I'll send the next patrol car in the area to pick it up, and then I'll look into it and let you know, is that okay?" Andy ended the call and phoned the front desk, asking to be informed when Thirsk arrived, and he rubbed his hands together gleefully. He had been fuming since the day before, when Ross and Fowler had been temporarily transferred to the fifth floor. Neither were time-served, and if anyone deserved the honour of working for the detectives on an ad-hoc basis, surely it should be him.

He had watched them excitedly trotting down the stairs the previous night, grinning at him smugly about their prestigious new positions. Jealousy had raged, but now he had the chance to impede Toni's career and he intended to enjoy it.

Ten minutes later, Thirsk groaned when Feldman, with his rat-face and beady eyes, opened his door. "What do you want?"

Feldman sidled to his desk with a twisted leer. "I thought you might want to reconsider one of those rookies you took on yesterday, a girl by the name of Fowler." Thirsk couldn't put a face to the name, but that was irrelevant; it was clear Andy was stirring for trouble.

"Really." Curt and bored. Andy voiced Carol's concerns with relish, detailing the newspaper cuttings, the scrapbook, the unhealthy obsession, but Thirsk waved his hand, dismissive. "Is that all? I knew of this when she joined the station. Be a good boy, go and crawl back into your hole." Embarrassed, Andy bustled from the room and Thirsk smiled.

So the newbie was *that* Toni Fowler. And she was interested in the unsolved case. Thirsk was intrigued.

Caught in rush-hour traffic, the drive to work had given Toni plenty of time to think about the finality of the day she was becoming a real adult. She was confident leaving home was the right thing to do, and it was the perfect time. It seemed such an adventure. But, despite the recent arguments, she would miss her family acutely. After twenty years of loving her, caring for her, of being her protectors, her guides, she was leaving her parents, and she dreaded how lonely she would feel tomorrow night. The situation at home was so sad, a family who loved each other, at each other's necks day in, day out, or not talking at all. It was crazy to live in such a gloomy atmosphere when they had so much to be grateful for. Others had to cope with plights such as illness, bereavement, homelessness, financial ruin; why couldn't they appreciate their solid stable home?

She had planned to speak to her mother at the table before leaving for work, a gentle, pleasant chat to smooth the tension – an opportunity to request the return of her collection without hostility – but she had seen sparks igniting between Carol and Maisie, so had left quietly, buying a healthy breakfast and lunch on the way instead.

Recalling the morning's brewing fight reminded Toni why she was escaping, and she had banished the slushy, unrealistic idealism to the back of her mind, turning the stereo loud and singing fervently until she reached the car park.

Toni trotted up the steps, beaming cheerful smiles to anybody who crossed her path, and she sat next to Sally and switched the computer on. Several courtesy-copied emails sat in her inbox, one of which confirmed that the room Melissa had been held in had been located, and another stated that one of the unidentified victims featured in the video-clips had come forward.

In his office, Thirsk organised stacks of paperwork to give the morning briefing a smidgeon of structure to help his team digest the developments that had happened overnight. Eventually, he gathered the team together to bring them up to date. Toni struggled to keep up with the succinct update, unable to garner much from the short snippets. An eyewitness had placed Maria Collins with Melissa on the day she was abducted. Maria Collins was in an incestuous relationship with her brother. A hair found in a shopping trolley in the boot of

175

Sean's car had been confirmed as Melissa's. Sean denied putting both the girl and trolley in his car. In fact, he swore he didn't drive the car on the night she was murdered, and confirmed his sister and her husband had a spare key.

The detectives absorbed the details and Toni wished she had that ability, the same self-assurance they all seemed to have. So many things had happened overnight, and in the time it had taken her to pack a couple of boxes and get a few hours of shuteye, the case was all but done and dusted. Did these crazy people ever sleep?

"Just to add a cheering thought in the midst of this vile investigation, Jim and Maria's estranged daughter has agreed to make a statement as a character witness. She's got a lot to say, so watch this space." Frustrated, Toni slammed her hand on the desk, an outsider on a case that had seemed so exciting, one she thought she'd had some responsibility in. Now the only task that had truly been hers had been cracked. She'd wanted that glory.

The team reverted to their busy days – at desks, in cars, on phones – but Toni simmered with irritation at being sidestepped. She angrily munched on her apple and banana, and sullenly devoured the cereal bar without chewing properly, wishing the disrespect didn't bother her so, but nothing calmed her mood. Thirsk had deliberately steamrollered her, taking her under his wing one day and wiping the case clean the next. Her spell in the department was all but over, so what did she have to lose?

She steeled herself, the resentment bubbling, and rapped on his door. He answered with an irritable grunt. "Sir, I want a word with you about Julia Collins."

Not an aggressive person by nature, Toni would fly off the handle now and then, but never for long. However, the Julia business had rattled her and she arrogantly held her head high as she glided into Thirsk's office. "You said that Julia had come up with the goods; that was my job."

The older man looked at the impertinent girl with disbelief. "For a start, I decide who has which job on this team, not you, and secondly, she had no goods to come up with." He returned to his work, indignant. "Piss off."

Damn the man. She tried to restrain herself, but couldn't. "You know what I mean, sir, that's why you brought me and Sally on this case, because of our prior involvement with Julia."

Thirsk shook his head, incredulous. "For fuck's sake, give me strength."

"No. You listen to me." She had nothing left to lose, it was inevitable he would send her back to the second floor now the ends of the investigation were tied and knotted. "You hardly gave me a chance before marching in and taking over. How am I supposed to learn if you steal my jobs away?"

Her insolence was intolerable and highlighted her youth. Thirsk had no time for upstarts and took such boorishness from nobody, especially after eight pitiful hours sleep in three days, but he had no intention of an argument with a rookie either. He glared at her, seething. "If I send you on a job, I expect to see it done. You didn't get results, I did. What's your fucking problem, newbie?"

Her mouth churned, mind whirring, but she couldn't deny he was right. She felt he was stamping 'failure' across her forehead. And then she realised her hot-headedness would have repercussions and she felt like a fool, whimpering, "Right, sir, okay," as she turned to leave.

Thirsk loved having the power to scare her, but she reminded him of his younger self, when he'd had hopes and dreams, before the reality of life had drowned him. He tipped his head to one side, intrigued by her feistiness. "What's your name?" He already had his suspicions.

She shrank, forlorn. "Toni Fowler, sir." Thirsk leaned back and drank in Toni's features, a contrast to the scrappy little thing he'd had no time for ten years before, and he remembered how she had eagerly watched the retrieval of Baby Jane's body. Hadn't she said then that she intended to become a policewoman? "Sir, I'm in trouble now anyway, so I may as well ask how you cracked her before you send me back to Andy Feldman and his lecherous ways."

It seemed she instinctively knew how to rub Thirsk the wrong way. "Look, newbie, you can be rude to whoever the fuck you like, but never to me. Have you got that? I cracked Julia because she trusted me. She has no reason to trust anybody, so I gave her reason and she let me in. In return I promised to keep the details she revealed as private as possible. She's prepared to stand in court and tell the truth but she wants to retain her anonymity as much as possible. We came to an agreement. Now, stop taking your own failings out on me, and remember your rank – or lack of it – before you ever talk to one of your superiors like that again. Because if I hear one more word from you I'll be putting you on report."

"You gave her the stuff she wanted, didn't you?"

Thirsk was gobsmacked; the girl didn't seem able to stop herself, and how dare she judge him. "That's it, young lady, I've fucking had enough of you and your cheek. I've been on the force for longer than you've been alive, I was arresting murderers when you were in nappies. If I had done my work using the goddamned rulebook, I wouldn't have bagged half the criminals I've put away. So you just trot along and do your own job your way, and leave me to do mine my way."

"Heard and understood, sir, but all I was going to say was, I like your style."

They locked eyes in silence, each oddly impressed with the other. She had made her mark on him and they both restrained a grin. "Sit down." Toni almost fell into the chair and waited for him to put her out of her misery, but he lounged back, regarding her. Every part of her wanted to run. "We've met before."

"I know."

"Did you disclose your part in the Baby Jane case when you applied for the job?"

She gulped, wondering how he knew, and realising she was in trouble. "No, it didn't seem important. I'm sorry if that's a problem."

She was petrified and he couldn't torture her any longer. A warm grin spread across his face and she relaxed tentatively. "It's not important, of course it's not. I just enjoy scaring people." His unlikely chuckle rang through the room. "Don't worry, I don't hate you any more, you're over twenty now. Anyway, you haven't changed a huge amount, a bit less gangly, maybe."

"Yes, sir."

"Toni," it seemed wrong to address her by surname or rank, having known her as a child, "I've never been satisfied that the Baby Jane case went cold, and it's one of the cases under consideration for a new investigation when time allows. You'd be perfect for the job with your first-hand knowledge." Music, merry melodies of jaunty fiddles with tweeting birds in the background – the sound of dreams coming true – flooded Toni's mind and her mouth opened and closed. "I want you permanently on my team. I don't know how, but I'll swing it somehow. You're good, you've got balls and you've got instinct. But if you're ever rude to me again, don't think you'll lose your job through it, because you won't. Instead, I'll make damned sure you stay right by my side where I'll make your life hell every step of the way. Is that clear?"

"No fucking way. Sir, are you for real?" Her eyes were popping, unbelieving.

"Quit the gushing, it's unbecoming." He grabbed a notebook and slipped a biro behind his ear. "I'm interviewing Maria Collins again in a minute, I'd like you to sit in with me."

She was woozy with excitement, her knees jelly, and she couldn't believe how the day was turning out. "You bet, sir."

Eventually he winked at her. "Piss off."

As soon as she had closed the door, Thirsk phoned Andy Feldman. "That box you were telling me about this morning, the one you're collecting from Carol Fowler, bring it to me as soon as it arrives."

Chapter 19
A Meeting of Minds

Maria couldn't believe how slowly time passed when incarcerated in a ridiculously tiny, stark cell. The four walls had become imprinted on her mind since she had been arrested the day before. Arrested! It was ludicrous; in her mind she had done nothing wrong. The police had thrown solicitation at her as their reason, which was crazy, because she would never be involved with something so appalling. She had screamed and shouted, raged and blasphemed, and when she had calmed down, she'd spoken to the detectives several times, giving them as much of the spiel she and Sean had concocted in their brief time together after Jim's arrest as fitted their questions.

Breakfast had come and gone, which meant they would have to let her go soon, and she was eager for some fresh air, a few cigarettes, a few glasses of something strong. She hoped Sean would be able to join her; if he had stuck to their story, there was no reason why he wouldn't be.

Although the circumstances were unpleasant, she had used the time wisely to think things through, what they had done, what they were going to do, to say. Free of domineering Jim, the lengthy discussion with her brother, her lover, in the early hours of the night had given her infallible guidance. He had helped her to see that what she had thought was bad was actually great, that the future looked rosier than ever. She loved Sean; he was an amazing man.

Heavy footsteps approached and an officer unlocked the door, leading her from the basement cells and up the back staircase to the interview room she had been in two nights before. "Ain't it time for me to go home yet, I must have been here twenty-four hours by now?"

"Fuck off."

"Hey, there ain't no need for that kind of talk."

He pushed her roughly into the seat and was about to leave when his revulsion got the better of him. "Shagging your

180

fucking brother, you fucking slut. You're disgusting. Pure filth." Maria bristled. Her relationship with Sean was so much more than sex, it was a meeting of minds.

Toni and Thirsk entered, and he wasted no time on pleasantries. "Why do you sleep with your brother?" He slipped a memory card into the static camcorder and pressed record, while she hung her head, silent. Having watched the footage of her interviews, the account she had given in her previous interviews was plausible, and fitted the evidence, but it niggled him. They could wrap the case up now, have Jim sent down for the rest of his life and all go home for a good night's sleep. But it was too easy. Sean may live up to his reputation for being genuinely nice, and Maria may be a damaged victim of circumstance, but Thirsk had an ominous sense about the pair. Something was wrong, and if the other detectives hadn't found the problem, then he intended to.

Attempting to justify what she deemed as normal, she explained that she had heard it was wrong, against the law, but incest in some form or another was all Maria had ever known. Starting when she was a toddler, she was unsure how old she had been, she couldn't remember a time when it wasn't happening. Her father had initiated her, as was his right, and he had been followed by her grandfathers on both sides, her uncles and brothers.

Her mother had died shortly after her birth – she had never known her – and her grandparents a few years later. Her father died of liver cancer five years ago, months before one of her brothers had an untimely heart attack caused by an undiagnosed congenital defect, and the other was stabbed in a drunken brawl.

Sean had always been the closest to her emotionally and if she'd had to choose a member of the family to survive the cull, it would have been him. Not only did she not see a problem with their lovemaking, she enjoyed it now it was only with Sean. She loved him dearly and was proud to say it aloud.

Toni didn't know whether to be pleased the woman was so open and honest, or to give in to the repulsion and run to the loo to be sick. Her dad had never been anything but fatherly in a caring and sensitive way, and she couldn't even begin to imagine Leon as anything but annoying and brotherly. She knew Maisie hadn't been touched either; the men in her family weren't capable of such hideous atrocities.

Thirsk, however, was emotionless, having heard the revelations from Julia the night before. "I spoke to your daughter at length yesterday. She told me everything."

"What do you mean, everything?"

Thirsk thought the cagey response was odd, but couldn't put his finger on why, and she clearly wanted her question answered before continuing. "Feel free to add to the list if you have anything more, by all means. She's cited violence and beatings, rape, drug use, alcoholism, to name a few."

"She deserved a good beating, that girl, always in bleeding trouble for summat or other. Yes, the men in the family had their way with her, it was their right, but they never raped her, she always let them."

Toni couldn't believe what she was hearing. She looked to her boss, admiring his unflappable composure. "She told me it started when she was two or three. How can you possibly conceive that a child that age can have consensual intercourse?"

Now Maria was annoyed. "Come on. She sat on their knees, batted her bleeding eyes at them, that cute little grin just to let them know she's theirs when they want her. She wanted it as much as they bleeding did."

"Not from what she tells me. Unsurprisingly, she's pretty scarred from it, and that's why she begged social services to take her away ten years ago."

"I can tell you, God's honest truth, that she used to love it. Jim used to sleep in her bed more often than he did mine. If she's saying different now, it's just to get some attention. She always was a bleeding attention seeking tart, that one."

"So you were jealous of sharing your husband with your daughter then?"

Maria's face twisted and she snarled bitterly. "She should never have been born, I didn't want kids, never had a maternal bone in my body. I'm a strict Catholic, but I bent the rules, kept my little pills hidden in a drawer, and I don't know how it happened with Jules, but it did, and after that her bleeding father was all over her, not me. It's just lucky I had Sean by my side, he picked up the pieces when Jim stopped wanting me."

"Tell me about Melissa Barton."

"There's nothing to tell. She was a kid who lived down the road, I know her mum to say 'hi' to, but that's about it."

Thirsk leant towards Maria until she winced under his glare. "Oh, there is something to tell, though. Like why, after school had started for the day, you were seen not only holding her hand, but bringing her to your house. You see, I've been speaking to both Sean and Jim, and they tell me it was all your idea."

Toni's jaw dropped, sure she would have heard it on the grapevine if they had said such a thing. Maria shook her head, eyes squeezed tightly shut. "You're lying, you bastard."

"I'm sorry, Maria, but that's what they said, and they've both signed the statements. Sean told us you devised the whole plan."

"Like Hell I did. Double bleeding crossing gits. Jim asked me to get her." She stopped, forcing the conversation with Sean to her mind. He would never betray her. She was sure Thirsk was lying. She must stick to what they had discussed. She chose her words carefully. "It was Jim. He had taken a few pics of her and he liked what he saw. I'm getting over the hill a bit, I can't always service them, and since Jules left home he's mostly had to find it elsewhere. I give them what I can, but I get tired."

She had lost track and Thirsk prompted, "I want to know about Melissa, not your sex drive."

Her eyes flashed, angry. "I saw her outside the school and told her that if she hid in the toilets until the bell went, she could have the day off, come over to mine and bake some cakes. I know Julia's had a baby, and sometimes I just want to be a gran."

Thirsk stood and began to pace, incredulous. "Oh, you do know how to talk out of your arse, don't you? I just want to be a gran. Bollocks. Two minutes ago you were telling me you didn't have a maternal bone in your body. You took Melissa because your husband and brother wanted to mess with her. Just remember that – they wanted to mess with *her*, not you. Not tired, old you, with your saggy belly and rotten teeth, scruffy hair and wrinkles. They wanted something fresh and beautiful. Did you get jealous again and take it out on her? That's what both of them are telling me."

Fuming, Maria stood, but Thirsk pushed her back onto the seat. "I didn't kill her. I had nothing to do with it."

"Nobody told you Melissa was dead, what makes you think she has been killed?"

Maria had gone too far and was scared. She shrank into the seat, her temper gone, and sighed, defeated. "I brought her home for Jim, that was it. He said he'd beat the living daylights out of me if I didn't. I had no choice. I never had a choice, not with any of them. He took her away somewhere and I never saw her again after that. God's honest truth." Tears had started, her fleshy face scrunched and grotesque. "I asked for a solicitor, where is he? They told me he had be here soon."

Thirsk grinned as he switched the recorder off, removing the card, and he tugged the door open. "Oh, so you did. Sorry, love, I forgot about him. It's a bit late now though, isn't it? Ho hum."

Toni grabbed the door as it was closing and trotted to catch up with him, grasping his arm. "I just don't believe you. She had asked for legal consult and you interviewed her alone. You can't do that."

He stopped by the lift, irritated. "Oh, enough of the judgement, you silly little girl. I invited you to the interview because I thought you might learn from it, and you have; you've learned how *not* to do it. I'm over fifty and jaded, and if the powers that be don't like the way I do things, then they can sack me and I won't give a shit. You, however, have your life and career ahead. That woman in there," he jabbed his finger, "is a victim, she just has no idea of that. But the men in her life have moulded her into somebody who shouts how high if they tell her to jump, and with her jealousy raging I think she's capable of anything."

"Murder?"

"My money's on Jim Collins abusing the kid, then killing and dumping her, and that's what he's been charged with, but I don't think that creature in there is as innocent as she makes out. Now before you get on your pathetic high horse again, get back to the office to see if there's any news from the lab that would confirm Melissa was in that lock-up." He'd had an email from Wainwright that morning stating they had found evidence placing Jim and Melissa in the garage, but he couldn't think of another task to give the inexperienced woman on the spur of the moment.

Neither spoke as the lift took them to the fifth floor. Toni wondered if she should mention the strange conversation that morning with Joyce Frobisher, but worried he would belittle her. She had steeled herself by the time the doors opened. "Have you ever considered that whoever murdered Melissa was also the person who killed Baby Jane." He was about to bark at her so she quickly added, "I bumped into the woman who was the coroner on Jane's case this morning, Joyce Frobisher, and she said…"

"Oh, for heaven's sake, not that bloody woman. I thought she had retired and gone to live in some coven somewhere. And to think I thought highly of you." He stormed into his office and closed the door.

Forgetting the vast difference in rank, Toni burst through, slamming the door behind her, leaving every person in the incident room staring.

"What's going on?" Steadman glanced at Sally, who shrugged her reply. "Is there something going on between those two? He can't seem to get enough of her and we're left doing the shitty jobs. Why did she get to sit in on an interview, anyway, she's only a bloody rookie?"

Wainwright had been passing when the commotion started and he chuckled. "Got the hots for the guv, Steadman?"

"Give over, he's probably old enough to be my father." Her cheeks reddened, exposing her lie, and Steadman knew that within an hour or so the news of her schoolgirl crush would have travelled through the station.

"Whatever." Wainwright laughed, winking.

Joining in, Sally added, "I heard he's only keen on Toni at the moment because she's the one who found the body of a baby in one of his cold cases. She told me about it last night, and according to Andy Pervert Pandy, he told Thirsk about it this morning."

"Well, I don't care what she found, I still think she's out of order." Steadman watched from under her fringe as the office door opened, hoping her nemesis would be thrown out for bad behaviour, but Thirsk strolled out with smiling Toni by his side and they headed for the lift.

Despite Toni having no idea she had annoyed anyone, Steadman declared war.

Tears tumbled down Maria's cheeks as the officer locked her cell door, and she sat on the floor in the corner, weeping woefully. Two cells away, Sean tried to pacify her, gentle, soothing, encouraging. "Come on, Maz, it'll all be okay in the end, I promise."

She was too embarrassed to admit she had said too much, worried about Jim's reaction, but anger at being involved against her will surfaced. "I don't get it, why have they got me? I ain't done nothing wrong and I can't stand being locked up here on my own."

"Oh, for fuck's sake, shut the fuck up, woman. I can't even get no sodding peace from you in a sodding police cell." Jim wasn't as patient as Sean. "You'd better have kept your mouth shut."

"What, like you bleeding did last night, eh?" Neither man spoke. "They told me you told them it was me who got the girl."

"Shut the fuck up, Maria." Walls have ears, and Jim realised she was breaking. He couldn't afford that, not with the charges looming over him like a thick blanket. The panic was evident in his voice. "Don't say another word, Maria Collins, I'm warning you. The pigs will be listening to every word you say."

"You can't do anything to me now, Jim, we're past all that. I'm just going to come clean and…"

"Shut the fuck up, woman. You say another word and I'll hunt you down and kill you."

Chapter 20
A New Angle

Thirsk and Joyce Frobisher had met twenty years earlier when she had been appointed as a consultant psychiatrist for the police. He considered her profession to be mumbo-jumbo and had purposely avoided her, but occasionally she had assisted on unusual or difficult cases when he had been outranked. He thought her patronising and arrogant, unable to admit to being wrong, and she found him impertinent and coarse, with sloppy work practices. Nobody had been surprised by their frequent clashes. They had never screamed and shouted, that wasn't their style, simply hurling churlish quips and digs, insults. Sometimes they ignored each other, which their colleagues preferred. Thirsk had been pleased when she had accepted the prestigious position of County Coroner, as he wouldn't have to work with her again. Then came the Baby Jane case.

The pathologist had recorded no injuries to the skeleton, except the clean break where Toni Fowler had landed when she had found the body, and he had been unable to determine if the child had been killed, or had died of natural causes. He had assumed from the clothes that the child was female, but the rotting dress had not revealed any hairs or DNA that may lead to either a parent and/or the killer.

The area surrounding the tree in Black Park had been scoured by officers, but nothing could ascertain her identity, let alone what her story was. Finally, the Coroner – Dr Joyce Frobisher – had called an inquest and concluded that the baby, now officially dubbed Baby Jane as a nod to the girl who found her, remained unidentified and the cause of death unknown.

Unable to accept his failure in finding justice for the child, Thirsk had bristled throughout the inquest, frequently objecting to experts as they presented their hard facts and educated views, but when he'd tried to heckle Joyce, she had brutally reminded him of her superiority and the respect he

188

should have for her position. She had informed his superior, insisting he be disciplined, and the process had tainted his career and chances of promotion for several years. Ironically, they both believed Baby Jane had been murdered and were desperate to put her killer behind bars, but without knowing her identity, or her mother's, they'd had no choice but to accept an open verdict.

The savage humiliation of being openly reproved, both at the inquest and in the office, had nixed any possibility of burying the hatchet. They hated each other.

But now Toni Fowler was back on the scene, a ghost from the past who forced Jane into their minds once more, and her suggestion that the two meet again had good reason.

Under the murkiness of threatening rain, Thirsk drove to the address Toni had given and pulled into the crescent-shaped driveway of a modest, detached house. It was stone built and quaint, with late-flowering roses, peach coloured and resplendent, framing the dated oak door. Built over a century before, according to the inset stone in the gable end, it was unusually stunning, and the mature, landscaped garden was delightful. For a while, Thirsk and Toni stared wantonly through the window, enviously coveting the comfortable lifestyle they wished they could live. Eventually, Toni clicked the door open. "I still reckon you should have let her know we were coming."

"Change the track, will you? I told you, if she knew I was coming she would have made sure she was out. There's no love lost between us."

"Why though? I mean, what's your history? You didn't have a fling, did you?" Toni shuddered, wishing her words back; the resulting image in her mind was nauseating.

He glared at her, repulsed. "Me and miss high and mighty. Get bloody out of here." He now also had an unpleasant picture in his head. "We just don't like each other, nothing more or less than that. And I strongly doubt we ever will." He omitted the embarrassing castigation nine years before. They dashed through the downpour to the shelter of the porch and rang the bell.

Presently, Joyce Frobisher opened the door, a tea towel in her hands, and her face soured when she saw her old enemy. "Oh, it's you," she said politely, managing a fleeting smile for Toni. "You didn't tell me you were working with *him*."

"Nice to see you too, Frobisher. We need to speak to you."

She crossed her arms. "I can think of a thousand things I'd rather do than speak to you."

His head fell and he mumbled, "I might not like you as a person, but I've always had respect for the way you carried out your job." Crushed.

She laughed, mocking. "I can't retaliate the sentiment; the way you operate is shoddy."

Toni held her hand out, grimacing. "Oh come on, you two, it's pissing down… sorry, Mum says…"

"You swear too much, we know. I guess you'd better come in." Joyce reluctantly moved aside and led them to the living room. "If it were just you, Dick, I wouldn't bother, but seeing as there's a lady present."

"How many times, it's Richard, not Dick, and I prefer Thirsk from those I dislike."

She chuckled, gesturing to the sofa as she leant against an armchair. "Would you like a drink, and by drink I mean non-alcoholic, Richard?"

"No. Thanks. Sarcastic bloody cow." She smiled, patronising. "I want to know what this rubbish you've been spouting about Melissa Barton and Baby Jane being killed by the same person is all about?"

"Oh, I see, I'll remember to be more careful about what I say to you, Toni."

"I'm sorry, but I really thought you had a good point, and we've all got something in common with Baby Jane."

Her childish innocence was enticing and Joyce patted her hand. "Truce for now, Dick, because of the young lady. Tell me what's going on."

"You probably know that we have a man in custody whom we've charged with Melissa's murder. He's a paedophile, and he's been active for a long time. Toni tells me you think he could be linked to Baby Jane, and to solve that case would close doors for all of us. So, in your professional opinion, do you think it's possible that Jane could have been killed by him?"

"I didn't say *killed* by the same person, I said dumped. It was an offhand comment with no evidential base. I merely suggested the possibility that the dumping sites were chosen because of an emotional tie to that area of the park. That's all."

"No it's not, Frobisher, you're too thorough for that. You're a psychiatrist, and a fine one at that, much as I hate to admit it, and I'm interested in your theory."

"*Was* a psychiatrist, Richard, I've been retired a long time now. I found Melissa's case interesting and I have too much time on my hands. I was thinking out loud when I linked the two cases. It was irresponsible and I shouldn't have said anything."

The way Joyce was backing down confused Toni, as if Thirsk's presence stifled her, and she couldn't contain her exasperation. "Just tell him like you told me this morning, about it being a woman."

Cornered and defensive, she stood. "How many times do I have to repeat myself? It was speculation on my part, nothing more. Maybe I miss the intellectual stimulation of being in the workplace, but really, apart from the name of the victim and a few details gleaned in conversation with Hugh, I know nothing about this business."

Thirsk hadn't considered a link between the young girl and the baby; when he had witnessed Melissa's retrieval from the lake, the proximity to the old tree had gone unnoticed. But the suggestion seemed plausible. Jim Collins had killed the girl either for, or because of, his warped desires, and it was absolutely possible he had killed other children over the years. And while Wainwright was merrily preparing to prosecute him for murder, he wasn't actively considering there may be prior victims.

With none of the previous antipathy, Thirsk detailed the recent events, what the accused man was like, the porn ring and the vile videos of young girls being molested and raped. It was confidential information, but he trusted her. "It makes a big difference to my investigation. We only know of six, but if he's been doing this for at least ten years, heaven knows how many more victims could be out there. Alive or dead."

"You're being paranoid, Richard. When children go missing the world goes crazy, there can't be many young girls on the missing person's register."

"Countrywide, there were seven in the age bracket we've looked into, two of whom have been ruled out. One from Leicestershire, one in Scotland, two from Wales, and the other is London."

She held her hand up. "It's irrelevant where they're from. I assume you've questioned the men about Baby Jane." He shook his head, ashamed. "Well, I'd say that's a good place to start, wouldn't you, rather than wasting your time here with a daft old woman?"

"I suppose so. You know, according to Jim's daughter, both he and her maternal uncle assaulted, abused and raped her until she demanded they take her into state care, threatened suicide otherwise. She would have been at home still when Baby Jane was found, and I suspect she knows something about it. Don't ask me why, it's a gut. But while she readily describes the atrocities she suffered, she blames her mother rather than father or uncle. And the mother is equally shocking when describing her daughter. Her pet name for her is the tart, and she says her daughter invited the abuse, even at the age of two. I see mothers and daughters who don't get on all the time, but there's a deep hatred between those two, and I'm sure they both know more than they're telling."

Joyce smiled, regarding the man she had no respect for. "Well, well, well, I never thought you'd come to me for help. That is what you want, isn't it?"

The antique clock on the mantelpiece ticked loudly, filling the silence. Toni had a coal of excitement burning in her belly, imagining the irascible characters working together. Working with her. Eventually Joyce chuckled, and Thirsk didn't miss the supercilious tone. "Frobisher, I fucking hate your guts, you know that, and it really pains me to request your opinion, but the truth needs to come out. It's so important, we need to know how many more kids we're looking for, either dead, or if not, severely traumatised." He lowered his head, speaking quietly. "So yes, I'd appreciate your help."

"Pardon, I didn't quite hear that." Joyce was relishing the moment.

His expression was thunderous. "Yes, you did."

Toni witnessed a fleeting glimpse between Joyce's sparkling olive eyes and Thirsk's pools of chocolate brown, and it dawned on her that their personal attacks and derisive comments were merely banter that they both enjoyed. She relaxed, ready to enjoy the ride.

Despite being wasted already, Julia rolled her third joint of the day. She hated to admit it, but she missed Antony. The noise he created, the work involved in his care, the bursts of chuckling that she couldn't help but smile at. Without him she saw nobody. Apart from the police, of course. She took a deep drag, savouring the taste, smell and effect, but a tapping at the door startled her and she stubbed it out. Tentatively opening the door, she moved aside to let Simone enter, closing the door behind her. The social worker wafted her hand. "Is that what I think it is, Julia?"

"Oh dear, mum of healthy toddler smokes weed. Big news. All the more reason for you to keep him then, ain't it?" Rebellious, she re-lit the joint and drew it in deeply, before blowing the smoke directly at the woman, who leant back and wrinkled her nose.

Beaten, Simone sat down and sighed. "I was calling to see how things are going, but I can see you've not moved on from the other night." She glanced at the spliff with a sneer. "I thought you couldn't get any." And suddenly she recalled Julia's cheeky request to the policewoman. "No, they didn't. No, they wouldn't, surely."

"Of course they bloody didn't. My child benefit came in so I bought a twenty bit. Big deal." She couldn't believe she was covering for a bent copper.

Simone sighed again. "I came here to see if you wanted to visit Antony today, but I'm not sure that you can if you've been taking drugs, I'd have to ask my superior."

Julia sucked the relaxing smoke, eyelids heavy, and regarded the irritating woman who wouldn't leave her be. "I don't want to see him anyway. I wouldn't care if I never saw him again." She felt a physical pain in her chest and it shocked her. She missed Antony. Maybe that was love. But she was doing the right thing for him.

"Have the police been in touch about your parents? What's happening with that business?"

"As far as I know they nicked them both, and my uncle too."

"Does it surprise you? I know you were mistreated as a child, but would you have thought them capable of the things they've been accused of?" Julia laughed, a high-pitched, animal-like noise, and the image of a hyena sprung into Simone's mind. "What's so funny?"

"You trying to analyse me. I just ain't seeing what it's got to do with you. Why do you keep coming round anyway? I ain't got a kid here, you've no reason to keep coming by."

"Your child is under social services care and I want to see you reunited. That seems reason enough to me. Have you been to the doctor yet, like you promised?"

"Are you serious? Like I'm going to go to the quack and fill myself up with stupid Prozac or whatever. I don't need bloody tablets, I need a bit of cash, a bit of practical help." Her mobile chimed conveniently and Julia answered, listening intently to the caller. Her challenging sneer waned, becoming frightened, shocked. "But what do you need me for? I ain't even seen them for ten years, I'm nothing to do with this." She dropped the phone and unwanted tears tumbled from her eyes.

Instinctively, Simone grasped Julia's hand, while snatching the mobile from the floor and putting it to her ear. "Hello, are you still there? My name is Simone Lewis, I'm Julia's social worker. Who is this, please?"

When the call ended, Simone threw Julia's shoes towards her, fishing her car keys from her pocket. "Hurry up, I'll take you."

Twenty minutes later, they sat on hard plastic chairs in Castle Street Police Station. Simone had never seen Julia – normally emotionless, cold, uncaring – in such a state. Howling, sobbing, sniffing. Face red and shiny, eyes bulging, swollen. Presently, Toni arrived and guided them to the lift, sharing concerned glances with the black woman. She couldn't understand why the girl was upset, they simply wanted a quick interview with her. Then she realised – Thirsk, insensitive and boorish, had made the call. "Do you know what you're here for?" She really wanted an answer, because Julia was terrified and she suspected Thirsk had threatened her with something to ensure she attended.

"I ain't done nothing, I promise, they're lying. All of them."

The girl was too emotional to be coherent and Toni gave up, leaving Simone to mother her, mopping the tears. "There, there."

They knocked on the door and Toni led them into Thirsk's office. "What the bloody hell is that racket for, I could hear you halfway down the stairs."

"I ain't done nothing. I don't want to go to prison."

Thirsk shrugged, questioning Toni, who shrugged back. "Stop behaving so childishly, you silly girl. Shut that bloody noise up and calm down. Jesus H Christ. Women." Bemused, he gestured for his guests to sit. "I take it you're Simone Lewis, whom I spoke to on the phone." She nodded. "As I'm sure you'll understand, I'll need to see Julia in private, so can you please wait outside. My officers will get you a cup of tea."

Simone grasped Julia's hand, disguising her nosiness with concern. "I think she needs someone by her side at the moment, don't you?"

Unnoticed by Simone and Julia, Joyce was watching the debacle from where she stood by the window, and she moved confidently forward. "I'll be by her side, don't you worry."

"Who are you?"

"Dr Frobisher, I'm here to attend to Julia's welfare."

"Oh my god, like a solicitor?" Julia's tears restarted and she said breathlessly, "I swear on my life, I never did nothing to that girl, they're lying. I ain't even seen them for ten years." She had never been so frightened.

"For god's sake, shut up woman."

Simone glared at Thirsk, who waved his hand dismissively, and Toni led her from the office, motioning to Sally to make the woman a mug of tea. Unaware of the snide comments bandied by envious colleagues, she closed the door and sat on the sofa, out of the way. Thirsk regarded Julia, ungraciously heaving as she wept. "I know it's lies, Julia, we all do. But I thought it best to hear things from you. You're not in trouble, I simply want to talk to you."

She relaxed, controlling her sobs. "What's she said, my mother?"

"It wasn't just her, I'm afraid, it was all three of them. They've all said that you were with them at the house when your mum took Melissa from the school. They've told me that it was you who killed her."

Toni's jaw dropped, stunned at the deceitful rubbish he was spouting. Maria, Jim and Sean had said no such thing, she was sure. Thirsk was relaxed and smiling, and she looked to Joyce, hoping the older woman would stop his cruelty. But her composed expression suggested she was part of the fabrication. Once again, the thought that she may be in the wrong job crossed Toni's mind; she had always believed the police were about honesty. About protecting people, not destroying them. All she could do was hope there was a solid reason to distress the poor girl so horribly.

"The only chance you have of keeping yourself out of prison, Julia, is to tell me everything."

"But I told you everything last night."

"No, you didn't, and now your freedom could depend on you telling me the bits you conveniently left out. Your mother says you used to enjoy having sex with your uncle and father."

"What fucking planet are you on, of course I didn't. That's disgusting to even say it."

"What's to say you didn't keep in touch over the years. That when your father secured another victim, you went to help finish her off?"

Her eyes brightened and she caught her breath. "I couldn't have done it, though, I was in hospital on Tuesday." Giddy with relief. "Simone will tell you, she took me home."

The news that Melissa's body had been found had made the local press almost immediately and was now in the tabloids, but Thirsk couldn't imagine Julia being interested in current affairs. "How do you know Melissa was killed on Tuesday."

"If your old man was arrested for running a child sex ring, wouldn't you read up about it?"

"You were released from hospital Tuesday tea-time and the girl was killed in the evening." Toni had received a memo stating time of death was early afternoon and she wanted to scream at his inhumanity. "Remember, Julia, your parents, your uncle, people who you should be able to trust, people who should protect you, they're all pointing the finger at you. I don't believe them, but you need to tell me why I'm right not to."

"So if I can't prove I haven't been in touch with them, and that I didn't go out of my flat all night, you're going to nick me for the kid's murder?" She had forgotten Simone had been with her until the early hours.

"I'll throw the whole fucking book at you."

Julia's sobs returned, and Thirsk rolled his eyes unkindly. She took some deep breaths, building courage, preparing to spill. "They never had another girl as far as I know, not as long as I was at home. I think that between me and Mum, we was enough for them. When I left home, I can't say after that. I didn't keep in touch, I wanted nothing more to do with any of them." She clutched her chest, anguished. "They took something from me, stole something that I'll never get back, and they said it was my fault. It was a relief to be in a kid's home because, even though there was no love and we was treated like dogs, I was safe. There weren't no more beatings from my mum, and no more visits from Dad and Uncle Sean. Why would I go back to that? I wouldn't, and I didn't." The tears streamed, coursing down her ruddy cheeks to the end of her chin and dripping to her knee.

"Have you ever heard about the Baby Jane case? You would have been about twelve, thirteen, thereabouts."

Julia hesitated, staring at Thirsk, her lips trembling from the emotional outburst. Guarded, she said, "I remember it a bit, I know everyone was talking about it. Why?"

She sounded like her mother, querying his line of interrogation, and it grated on him. "We think they may have been involved with her death."

"Have they said anything?"

Thirsk was unprepared for a retaliating question. "I asked them and they denied it. But they would, wouldn't they. Do you know anything about it? Did they ever have a baby staying that disappeared? Did you have a sister who suddenly disappeared?"

"I don't know nothing about the baby apart from what I heard back then. Mum never had any more kids after me."

"You know you'll be put in prison if you're lying to me, it's imperative for your own wellbeing that you tell me the truth."

Her jaw set and she stared directly at him. "I know nothing about a baby."

Her finality was resolute and he changed tack. "We have your father for Melissa's murder, but we can't tie in Sean, and although your mother's an accomplice, I doubt she'll ever see the inside of a prison for it, what with the circumstances and the fact she's suffered years of violence and abuse from your dad. We're going to have to let them both go. In your opinion, is Sean capable of murder? Is your mum?"

"No way, with Sean. I know he used to screw me, and all, but he never hurt me and he was always kind. Mum, I don't know, I really don't. But I wasn't there."

"Did your dad kill Baby Jane?"

"I told you already, I don't know nothing about no baby or nothing."

Joyce signalled to Thirsk and mouthed, "I've got enough."

"Okay, Julia, you've been really helpful. You know, if you were to press charges for the abuse and sexual attacks you suffered…"

"No. That was ten years ago, I've moved on."

"You know where I am if you change your mind. You're free to go."

"What? So you're not arresting me for killing that girl? I thought you said they said I'd done it?"

"I'm satisfied for now that your alibi covers you for the time that Melissa was killed."

After Julia had left the room, Thirsk was about to ask Joyce for her professional opinion of the young mother when Toni raged in, furious. "That was uncalled for. You know damn well that her father used to threaten her with prison if she dared say a word to anybody about what he was doing. That must have been the worst threat in the world for her."

"And so the most likely to get a response. Now shut up and sit down. Frobisher, what did you make of that?"

Joyce was adamant. "She knows something about Baby Jane, I have no doubt of that."

199

"Do you have any basis for that conclusion, or do you just always have to be right."

"I am always right, you know that as well as I do." Her smugness irked him. "Her barriers went up as soon as you mentioned the baby, but I suspect she's scared of saying something, rather than deliberately perverting the course of justice. Have you got records of her childhood, you know, social worker reports, school details, doctor's notes?"

Thirsk knew his team had requested them, but was unsure if it had been followed up. He nodded to Toni. "Run after Julia and see if she's still with that social worker. We'll cut the middleman out and get the notes directly from her. Find out what school she went to, and they should have the details of her doctor somewhere."

The whole time Toni had been working on the fifth floor, she had felt on the outside looking in, but now she had a proper job to do. She dashed out of the office with an excited salute of thanks. Shaking her head and smiling at her eagerness, Joyce continued, "You also need to contact the lab and see what they still have of Jane. If they kept any DNA they might be able to match a family member. I'm not sure how all that works, it progresses so fast nowadays, but it's a thread worth trying."

"Family member? As in the baby was either Maria's or... Shit, I see where you're going with that."

"Now you know why I asked for Julia's medical records. If she'd had a child it would be documented. The biggest problem you would have then is justifying the cost of investigating an old case to your bosses."

"Don't think I'd let a small detail like that get in the way."

Both were lost in thought and the minutes drifted by. Finally, Joyce eyed him, questioning. "You like Toni, and yet you despise Jim Collins and Sean O'Connor for liking young girls. Where's the boundary in your mind?"

Thirsk was exasperated by her directness and indignant at the suggestion, but more than anything he detested the comparison. "Uncalled for, Frobisher, and another reason to deplore you, you scathing cow."

She loved to get a reaction and her mocking smile returned as he squirmed. "Nubile, pretty, sexy – bear in mind I'm describing Toni's attributes in the order and description you would think of her, not me – smart, charming. What is there not to like? And I'm sure you must still be single, I doubt there's a woman out there who would put up with your tedious droning and slovenly ways."

"I see a brilliant detective in the making, yes, and her presence makes me remember a time when I was still hopeful, she takes me back ten years. But relationship material? Never, ever would that happen. And nor would I want it to."

"The point I'm making is still valid. Wealthy men commonly take younger wives whose main interest is the money. Men with younger women on their arms are revered by their contemporaries, seen as successes, sly dogs. What difference does a few years make in the age of the women? So those two have a preference for young girls, but those girls will be adults soon."

"Those men don't have a preference; they have a perversion. I don't have a penchant for younger girls, adult or child. I simply don't have a desire for a relationship at all, and, as you cuttingly reminded me, there doesn't seem to be a woman who would put up with me, even if I wanted to."

"Then you need to make that clear to Toni, because she's naturally looking up to you. She sees you as a success, a role model, and often women can confuse that with love, especially at such a young age. I'm surprised that even somebody as emotionally cold as you could miss the signals, Dick. It's obvious."

Thirsk was taken aback; he hadn't noticed a thing. But, then again, he hadn't been looking. "I fucking hate you, Joyce Frobisher. And stop calling me Dick."

She basked in the glory of winning again. Thirsk only reacted rudely when she had hit the spot, and now she would drive the nail in. "And I have no love lost for you either. Dick."

Chapter 21
Cut and Dried

Sprinting down the stairs two at a time, Toni caught up with Simone and Julia as they climbed into Simone's car, huddling into their jackets, which gave lame protection against the latest downpour. She said they wanted to see the social services case notes from their childhood dealings with Julia, and Simone shuddered as she recalled the scant file.

"I've already tried, actually, but I'm sure there's got to be more." She explained she had searched the records in the archives, mainly the section labelled 'C', where she had found another file. But she had felt there was more information somewhere and had ploughed through the boxes for hours. The intense and monotonous search had gone on well into the night, but had produced only a few more pieces to the jigsaw. She agreed to scan the details to her computer and email them to Toni as soon as she got back to the office.

"There are just a couple of other things I need from you, Julia."

"Look, it's pissing down out here, can't we do this somewhere else?" Julia's inadequate clothes were drenched, rain dripping from her ungainly features.

"I'll buy you a coffee from the canteen. Come on."

Toni led them, three drowned rats, through the building to the canteen. Several officers glared at her, sneering; they didn't appreciate civilians in their dining hall. Having seated her guests at a table and taken orders, she collected the drinks, throwing a couple of portion-sized packs of biscuits onto the tray. When they were settled, Toni took her notepad and pen from her jacket pocket. "What school did you go to, or schools?"

Julia saw no threat in the question. "I started at Princes Street, just down the road from home, then there was Moor End Secondary, but I never really went there, I bunked most of the time. They kicked me out after a year."

203

"Was there another school after that?"

"I never went to one, and they all stopped bugging me after a while, especially after I left home. They never got on at me then and the staff never made me go."

"Right." Toni scribbled the details on her pad. "The other thing is, do you know who your doctor was, or medical practice."

Julia's awkward features scrunched, thinking back. "That's a toughie. I only remember seeing a quack once when I had a shitty cold, but I was just a kid. They gave me some yellow medicine."

"Any idea where the practice was?"

"Not really, but it wasn't far from home, I don't think."

Simone's previous job had dealt with the same region but in a different capacity, and as a high percentage of the families were known to the social services, she knew the area well. "If you were in the catchment area for Princes Street, then it was probably the one on North Street."

"That rings a bell. They ain't going to have nothing about me though, my mum kept me away from quacks."

They finished the biscuits, supping the dregs of their warming drinks. Simone would take Julia home, before starting the arduous task of scanning the documentation she had on the girl. It was her husband's last night in England for another month, and she would have to work late, but at least she would have the chance to read through the file as she scanned the paperwork. It was a poor second to a night of good loving, but her career was important too.

Toni returned to the fifth floor and entered the minimal details into the computer's search engine. She jotted the addresses of the surgery and school on her notebook, wondering whether to take the initiative and visit them herself, without bothering her boss, or let him decide the next step. His office was empty and his absence sealed her decision. She motioned to Sally. "I've got to go and visit a couple of places, do you want to come with me?"

Steadman overheard, furious at the girl for forgetting her lowly rank. "Under whose orders?"

Baffled, Toni held the addresses up for Steadman to see. "Thirsk asked me to find these out and I thought I'd go and see them to get the details he needs for something."

"Police Constable Fowler, and I repeat the constable just in case you'd forgotten that you're not in charge, you don't think, you do what you're told, and if the guv hasn't given orders for you to visit those places, then you don't do it. Tear the page out and give it to me. Come on, Ross, we'll take this one."

Sally felt like piggy in the middle. She had grown fairly close to Toni recently and liked her, even if she could be a little boring. She had a good sense of humour and her quick wit made Sally laugh. But, then again, she could understand Steadman's annoyance. The whole department had noticed Thirsk's favouritism towards the new recruit, that her presence in his office was highly irregular, and nobody thought it fair. Also, Steadman clearly had a crush on her boss, and jealousy never made for a comfortable working atmosphere. When Steadman turned her back, Sally shrugged and mouthed sorry to Toni.

"So, what do we need from," Steadman scanned the paper, "Princes Street School and North Street Medical Practice."

"He wants as much background on Julia Collins's childhood as he can get." Toni couldn't understand the antipathy, why the older woman was so curt.

Steadman scribbled Julia's name above the addresses and turned to Toni with curiosity. "She's Jim Collins's daughter, isn't she? Threatened to chuck her kid off the balcony the other night."

Sally's shoulders drooped as she remembered where she had heard the name before. "Oh no, she's loopy, that one. What's he investigating her for?"

Toni was caught between a rock and a hard place. If she told them, Thirsk would probably go crazy, but if she didn't,

Steadman would no doubt make her life hell. "I don't know. He hasn't told me."

Thirsk had heard Joyce's concern that Toni may be enamoured with him, not that he understood why, and when Joyce had frostily bid him goodbye, he'd gone into hiding to work out how to handle the circumstances. His solution was to keep Toni at a distance and be less friendly; it was for her own good.

He found Wainwright in the canteen nursing a steaming mug of coffee and half a chicken sandwich. "How's it going on your side, Nick?"

"It's just Jim, of that I'm sure."

"Really, what about Sean?"

"The proof is all pointing to Jim. I don't think Sean's involved with Melissa's abduction and killing at all. That's not to say he wasn't part of the porn ring, but that's down to you to work that one out."

Thirsk had no reason to not trust his colleague's conclusion, but his ears pricked up when Wainwright mentioned his suspicions about Maria Collins. He had interviewed her at length regarding the sighting of her with Melissa on the fateful day of her murder, a discussion that had annoyed the woman greatly, having already related the story to Thirsk. "Says she arranged to collect Melissa after the school bell had rung, and brought her back at Jim's request. She knew he intended to abuse the child, but was scared of him following years of violence. Says she did what she was told."

"Same as what she's told me, so far. What else did she say?"

"She took Melissa to the kitchen and gave her a choice of three boxes of cake mix to make, and she gave her a drink of cordial, before letting Jim know that the girl was ready. She was adamant she hadn't laced the child's drink to knock her out, though. She seemed believable to me."

"So you've ruled her out for murder?"

"Yes, unless you know anything more."

"No, that's exactly what she told me. Are you done with that sandwich?" Wainwright pushed the plate over and Thirsk hungrily took a bite. "Thing is, Jim is equally adamant he didn't drug Melissa, so one of them has to be lying."

"He told me he bought the Rohypnol from the street dealer who supplied him with resin – refused to give names or addresses – but insists that Maria drugged Melissa before he saw her."

They continued to compare notes and the two accounts almost matched: Jim had been at the lock-up, Maria thought he was at the pub, although she admitted to lying when she told them Jim had woken at lunchtime and gone straight to the pub. She agreed he had been up since eight, saying he had drugged and taken the girl, in the shopping trolley, from the house. She hadn't known about the garage.

And now only Jim could retrace Melissa's final journey. She had been groggy, but awake, when he bundled her into the trolley and zipped it closed, but she was floppy and dazed enough for him to do so without a sound or a fight. Within half an hour any noise from the bag had stopped and he supposed she was unconscious.

Jim told them Sean had picked him and the trolley up and driven to the garage he rented from Smacker. They locked the door and opened the trolley to reveal the sleeping girl, curled tightly in a ball at the bottom, and lifted her onto the table. Sean set up both the camera and camcorder, while Jim placed the sexual aids beside her. Jim said they had taken turns to assault her, and Wainwright had balked at the catalogue of horrors the child had been subjected to.

However, Jim remained firm that he hadn't killed her. He said that when they had finished their abuse, they left her on a rug at the back of the garage, a grey woollen blanket draped over her for warmth, intending to set her free, near the school, later that day when she had recovered enough to walk, but not to remember.

He swore she had been alive when they left, and had no idea what happened to her after he had gone to the pub in the early afternoon. This didn't correlate with the landlord's statement; he was certain Jim hadn't been in The Nag's Head all day, but had arrived at about nine-thirty in the evening.

Sean hotly denied any involvement.

Wainwright elaborated on the forensic reports he had received, details Thirsk already knew from his visit to the lab that morning; the grey blanket she had been wrapped in had been recovered from the lake, not too far from where Melissa's body had been found, but, cleaned effectively by the fresh water, it held little evidence. The post-mortem confirmed she had consumed enough Rohypnol that, had she not been suffocated, it was probable she would have died anyway. The post-mortem also revealed some fine fibres around and inside her mouth, nose and throat, and analysis showed they were a blend of polyester and cotton, 4-ply, pale blue, and probably came from the object used to suffocate her. In a second search of Jim and Maria's home, a pillow in a Wedgwood blue case was found in the spare bedroom, and the fibres matched those found on Melissa, confirming it was the murder weapon.

Numerous pieces of evidence built an almost complete picture of Jim's guilt, and as far as Wainwright was concerned, his investigation was cut and dried.

Thirsk detailed his short visits to the prisoners, stating Maria had strenuously denied abducting other girls, despite the accusation from Cherry the previous night and the other girls caught on tape and camera. However, Jim had admitted his part in a previous interview, and the attack on Melissa had been so organised, it was nigh impossible that it was the first kidnapping they had carried out. Also, Cherry's account of her abduction was so similar to Maria's description of Melissa's, it couldn't be left to coincidence.

Thirsk believed he would soon have enough evidence on both men to prosecute them for their involvement with the website and the previous assaults, but something about Jim's unwavering denial of killing Melissa niggled him. He wanted to agree with Wainwright, seal Jim's fate and slam him behind bars where scum like him – a revolting, depraved pervert – deserved to be. Should be. But that tiny doubt wouldn't leave.

Having collected another coffee each, Thirsk related the latest spin-off from the investigation: that Jim, and possibly Sean and Maria too, may have also been involved in the Baby Jane case ten years before. The revelation came as a shock to Wainwright. "What on earth made you link those two?"

He knew he shouldn't take the credit, but Joyce Frobisher was his enemy, and Wainwright would never find out. "Actually, it was the location where Melissa was dumped. It's so close to Baby Jane's tree that I wondered if they were dumped in that area for sentimental reasons."

"I think that's a bit far-fetched, really, don't you? I mean, one dumped inside a tree, the other in the water, completely different dumping grounds. That's not an MO."

"The whole tree doesn't exist now, it's just an open stump, so…"

"That would make it easier for the old killer to leave the new body in it, then, wouldn't it?"

"Maybe there wasn't an opportunity." Thirsk shrugged. "Perhaps there were other people around that made it too dangerous to go back to the original spot. And, of course, you've got to consider that it would be unlikely for the killer to want the crimes linked."

Wainwright missed the intense debates they had enjoyed when working together, and conceded that the avenue was worth exploring. "So where do you go from here?"

"I've subpoenaed Maria's medical records, they should be here this afternoon, and I'm looking into their daughter's childhood paperwork to see if there's any indication of her witnessing anything that could help. She's like a closed door, their daughter, and I know she's holding back on something. I also want to ask Jim about Black Park, whether it holds anything for him. Maybe they used to go there for family days out, or something."

"Have you been back to the records on Baby Jane, see if there are matching fibres found on her or her clothes."

Thirsk looked at him in disbelief. "She was a rotten bag of bones, remember. They found nothing on her."

"It might be worth doing anyway, see if there was something you missed at the time." It was said without accusation, but still bothered Thirsk.

He sat, peeved, sulkily reasoning that the suggestion was a valid one. He hated having his work criticised and changed the subject. "Did you know that Toni Fowler was the girl who found Baby Jane. I'd never have worked it out without being told, she's changed a huge deal."

Wainwright smiled enigmatically, staring into space. "Well, I'll be damned."

The conversation had come to a natural end and they drained their mugs and took the lift back to the fifth floor, each going to their own departments on opposite sides of the corridor.

Over the course of the lengthy conversation, Thirsk had forgotten the suggestion that Toni had a crush on him, but it returned instantly when he saw her at her desk. He had no choice but to speak to her, needing to know what she had found about Julia's younger years, and he grudgingly approached her. "What have you got?" His voice was harsh and Toni worried she may have slipped up somewhere.

"I've printed all the attachments that Simone emailed and I've forwarded it all to you as well." She tapped a folder on her desk. "I've sorted them into chronological order."

He took the file and flicked through. "I'll study this lot in a minute. What about the doctor and school?"

"Umm," she hesitated, wondering if he was being terse with her because he had found out Sally and Steadman had gone instead of her, "DI Steadman told me to stay here, said she would do it." *Damned if you do, damned if you don't.*

It gave him the excuse he needed to get tough with her, to make it blatantly clear that she would be safer hating him, alongside everyone else, and the relief he felt was immense. It didn't matter to him, Steadman was more than capable of doing the job effectively, but he wanted to hurt Toni, get her off his back. He raised his voice. "I gave you that job to do, it was my specific orders that you do it, not delegate it." She cowered, publicly shamed, and he knew his target had been reached, but to make sure, he shouted louder. "From this moment on, you are off the case. I shall arrange for you to go back to Sergeant Feldman's charge."

As soon as he had yelled the words he regretted it. He liked having her on the team, she was detective inspector material in the making, but he supposed it was the only solution to the distasteful situation. Maybe she could come back in a couple of years when she had more experience, when she had forgotten her silly crush. He marched away, slamming his office door, and Toni kept her head down, desperately controlling her tears to not lose face.

"You see, the thing is, if you'd called beforehand and told me what you needed I could have got it all ready for you but, seeing as you didn't, you'll just have to wait while I traipse through all the records."

Sally and Steadman couldn't understand the woman's hostility and felt admonished. They sat on the low sofa in the school's reception area, watching small children flit from one place to another, and waited, trying to ignore the huffing from behind the desk as the woman tapped on her computer, printing documents as and when, scribbling notes to herself occasionally. Twenty minutes later she waddled from the desk and presented them with an impeccably neat folder, each printed page hole-punched in exactly the same place and clipped together. "That's all we've got. I haven't looked at the documents in detail, obviously, because of the pressure you put me under, but I did notice that she was absent a great deal. Now, can I help you with anything else or can I get on with my day?"

They thanked her for her time and left. The health centre was only a short distance from the school, but the rain was pelting, as it had been for days, and the wind bitter, so Sally drove.

The surgery was heaving with waiting patients, coughing, sniffling, sneezing germs into the over-warm air, only to be recycled and fed back into the building by the air conditioning system. Sally wished she could pull her shirt over her mouth to protect herself from the floating virus's and bacterium, but instead breathed normally and prayed they wouldn't be long. The young man behind the reception desk smiled pleasantly, his manners impeccable, as he typed Julia's name into his computer. "Nothing's coming up. How long has she been a patient for?"

Steadman looked to Sally for an answer, but neither knew. "Toni said she was looking for childhood records. I know she's in her early twenties, but I can't remember exactly how old."

"Am I right in thinking that this isn't a current patient?" His smile remained, and Sally wondered if his cheeks hurt from spending so much of his day grinning.

"She lived around here when she was a kid, so I guess if you look back twenty years she should be there somewhere."

He shook his head. "It doesn't work like that. Our computerised system's been up and running for a few years, but before ninety-six, ninety-seven, thereabouts, if the girl wasn't a current patient her records would either have been sent to her new doctor, or filed in the storeroom. Do you have the details of the doctor she sees now?"

"No, but I'm sure we can find out."

"It might be worth giving them a call to see what they've got before you banish me to the archives for hours." His ever-present grin was intact and he chuckled lightly to ensure they knew he was joking. They smiled their agreement and headed back to the station.

When they entered the office, they immediately noticed the icy atmosphere, and Steadman inched towards a colleague. "What's going on?" He nodded towards Toni and gave a thumbs-down.

Chapter 22
The Box

Thirsk sat behind his desk, feeling dreadfully guilty. The best thing to do would be to knuckle down to work, read through the social service's records, bury himself in details to avoid firstly having to leave his office and, secondly, bumping into Toni. He opened the file and the first page was dated nineteen ninety-five. Julia had become known to the child protection team when her school contacted them, suggesting she may be having trouble at home.

Subsequent notes depicted Maria and Jim as reasonable parents, albeit not likeable. Their alcohol and illegal drug intake had been a concern, but the girl had been allowed to remain in their care. Despite Julia having told him that she was beaten repeatedly as a child, not a single document mentioned bruising, or the typical behaviour a child subjected to violence can display. By all accounts she had been a pleasant girl, small for her age, but healthy and well nourished.

Julia seemed to go off the rails after her eleventh birthday. She would frequently 'leave home' only to be brought back by the police or her social worker. She had refused to attend school, her attitude became surly, and she refused to cooperate with anybody who tried to help her. A year later, she became more withdrawn and a social worker named Janet Dremill suggested she had calmed down, banished the teenage angst ready to fit in with society. Janet had been shocked when, on her thirteenth birthday, Julia turned up at the office and threatened to kill herself if they made her return home. Janet had found a place for her in a children's home, regardless that she believed it to be the wrong decision.

Thirsk mentally calculated the dates, noticing that Julia had stopped behaving waywardly when she was twelve. Had she been pregnant? He double-checked the paperwork, taking in every single word, not wanting to miss anything. There was no mention of a pregnancy or baby with either mother or daughter. So if Baby Jane had been killed by the family, she hadn't been a close relation. Thirsk slammed the file shut with frustration.

He sat for a minute, Toni forgotten once more, and debated everything he had read. Then, from nowhere, he recalled the box that Andy had brought to him, the one he had meant to return to Toni after he'd had a quick nosy into the contents, and he pulled it from his filing cabinet, setting it on the desk. The items were mainly stuck into a neat A5 scrapbook, newspaper cuttings and hand-written notes depicting dates and names, and he woefully took in the black and white pictures of the man he had once been, a man with hope and ambition. He had achieved those ambitions, but at a price, because he had lost the hope on the journey.

He had been reminiscing gloomily for a short while when the door burst open and Toni sauntered in, her head high and expression terse. He hurriedly covered the scrapbook with some paperwork and knocked the box to the floor with his elbow. She closed the door and threw an envelope on the desk. "My resignation." A few moments passed. "Sir." It was dripping with contempt.

"Oh, for god's sake, you bloody women and your bloody drama." He took the envelope and tore it in half before chucking it in the bin.

She was unperturbed. "I have some copies, obviously, and if you won't accept yours, I'll send one directly to human resources."

"Human bloody who? Don't be so bloody stupid, woman. So I ticked you off today, well, if you can't handle that, then you'll be no good in the police force anyway." She infuriated him and he knew it was because he had an affinity for her; he had been a hothead himself in his younger days.

"I joined the force because I was determined to get to the bottom of Baby Jane's mystery. By some miracle I got put on that case, and now you've taken me off it. I've lost my inspiration. The police force holds nothing for me now."

"Don't think I'm going to let you blackmail me, Toni Fowler."

She shrugged and turned to the door. "Who's blackmailing? I'm simply saying it how it is."

He was fuming but indignant. If she wanted to throw away a promising career over something so trivial, so be it. He wasn't responsible for her or her actions. Let the silly cow go. What was the saying? Act in haste, repent at leisure. Something like that. "Close the door on your way out."

She flounced through and slammed the door, the bang echoing through his office, and from under his steel-grey fringe he watched her grab her holdall and leave, not speaking to anybody. She had been gone five minutes by the time his anger abated, and he remembered the box. Thirsk swore to himself, wondering how such a promising day could have gone so bad. It was all Joyce Frobisher's fault. If she hadn't said anything about Toni having a crush on him, things would have been so different. He collected the clippings and notes together, shoving them untidily into the box, and resolved to take them back to her house when the air had cleared.

Steadman had seen the bizarre altercation and restrained a smile as Toni packed her belongings into her bag and stormed out. She didn't like her. From her unprecedented and outrageous promotion to the fifth floor, which had annoyed the whole team, to her innocently cute attractiveness, and the icing on the cake was Thirsk's affection for her. Steadman had always remained professional with her colleague, but they had a long history and she couldn't help the way she felt about him. It was unlikely, but a tiny part of her hoped that one day…

Steadman shook the thought away for the umpteenth time, ashamed of her irrational dislike for the girl, and she knocked on Thirsk's door. "Guv, I've got print-outs of the school records here, the ones for Julia Collins."

He invited her in, pleased to see a friendly face but still in a foul mood, and she sat across the desk, passing him the neat folder the aloof receptionist had given her. "I've had a look through to see if anything stood out."

"And what would stand out to you?"

"Guv?"

"Did Toni tell you what I was looking for when you stole the job from her?"

"Stole? Guv, I don't know…"

"You had no place to demand that job, I never gave you permission to order my staff around?"

Steadman was equally rattled now. "She's a sodding rookie, damn it. I outrank her by miles."

"Maybe so, but I had a good reason for letting her investigate, not that I should have to justify my orders to you. Now I'm going to have to brief you and that other kid from downstairs, and that's a bloody waste of my time."

"Guv, you're being unfair. You know I have no trouble picking things up, I'm a self-starter. Direct me where to find the information, I'll find it and make sure I know everything there is to know."

Not knowing Toni's link to the Baby Jane case, she completely missed the point of what he was saying. Fed up, he stood abruptly, grasping his trench-coat from the hook on the wall. "I'll tell you where the information is." He clenched his fist and hammered his chest. "In there. Toni had it all in her heart, she really cared. You: you see a dead baby, a waste of a mother, a case that could do with being solved. You don't give a shit about the people involved, about their feelings or reasons, you don't care that Baby Jane needs her real name to her grave, that it's about emotional closure."

He was as surprised as Steadman at his outburst, that he was spouting sentimental piffle. "I've had enough of this." Disgruntled and shamefaced, he grabbed Toni's box and stormed out.

Toni made it to her car before letting the tears flow, coursing down her cheeks, and she dabbed her eyes with toilet paper from the roll she kept in the glove compartment. Her ten-year dream had been shattered. She had achieved so much, so quickly, but her hopes had been dashed in an instant. She hated Thirsk more than she had ever hated anyone before. What right did he have to destroy her life? And why? They had been getting along so well.

Her mobile started ringing and she hesitated, wiping her eyes and nose before answering. "It's me. Are you okay?" Sally's concern was whispered and Toni guessed she must be calling from the office. Unable to restrain them, the tears restarted and she couldn't speak through her sobs. "Where are you?"

Using all her strength, she controlled the embarrassing outburst, concentrating on breathing deeply. "I'm going home."

"Good idea. Get yourself home, have a hot bath and relax, and I'll come round later. I'll bring a bottle or two of something with me."

"No, no, you don't have to do that." She didn't want company, just to wallow in her misery.

"I insist."

Toni reluctantly accepted and cut the call, starting the car and driving away. What was she going to do now? She had impetuously typed the letter without thinking of the ramifications, and the reality of being unemployed, and possibly unemployable after her hot-headedness, loomed. She had just paid a deposit on a flat, how would she pay the bills?

The traffic was dire and the stop-start journey gave her plenty of time to digest how irrational – how unprofessional – she had been. Thirsk had torn up her resignation, but she had stormed out anyway, and now she wished he would beg her to come back, tell her she was essential to the investigation. But of course she wasn't indispensable. In reality, she was simply an inexperienced beginner who could easily be replaced by the next eager rookie.

By the time she arrived home, she regretted her childishness bitterly, the flouncing and prima donna behaviour. The resignation. Her tears had long gone, a deep sorrow replacing them. At least her mum, warm and caring, never complaining, was in the kitchen; she could get things off her chest.

"You look glum, have you had a bad day?" Carol was on tenterhooks, worried Toni may blow up at her again.

"I've lost my job." She didn't want to admit to her petulant behaviour; her mother didn't need to know the details. She simply wanted sympathy, and maybe a cuddle. But Carol didn't hug her, as she normally would, remaining seated at the table, gazing into her steaming drink. "Mum? Did you hear me?"

"It'll be because I took your box of Baby Jane things to your boss. They were as concerned as I am about it, and if they've..."

Incredulous, Toni took a second to digest the admission. "You did what?"

"I spoke to Andy Feldman about it and he said I'd done the right thing. See, you need to understand..."

"Understand! Understand! What am I supposed to understand? That my own mother has gone behind my back and fucking lost me my fucking job. I don't fucking believe this." It had been her decision to walk out, but at this moment, using her mum as a target, shouting her anger at her and apportioning the blame... It took the responsibility from her own shoulders. Plus, she was miffed that her personal, harmless collection of clippings had been laid bare for all to see. She couldn't understand what the fuss was about and resented the intrusion to her privacy.

Carol was too tired to argue. The constant bickering or rowing that echoed through the house, the home she desperately wanted to be harmonious, was pointless, a futile waste of energy. Toni slammed around the kitchen, swearing angrily while she prepared a hot drink, and, eventually, she stormed from the kitchen, stomping up the stairs to her room.

Defeated, Carol sat, stilled, the hot chocolate now cold and unappetising. When someone knocked on the front door, she didn't move, listening to Maisie's feet thudding down the staircase. She heard muffled voices, then her youngest child retracing her steps to the room she shared with Toni, and assumed the visitor was a friend of the girls. So when the door opened and the tall man, older and greyer now, still badly dressed but ruggedly handsome, came in, apologising and embarrassed, she was stunned. He smiled, tentatively holding his hand out for her to shake. "Carol, it's been a long time."

Bewildered, she stood, needlessly wiping her hands on a tea towel before greeting him. "Richard. Ten years, it must be. What a surprise. I mean, gosh," she patted her hair, "Dan will be…"

"I'm here about Toni." Thirsk removed the box from the carrier bag in his hand. "I've brought this back."

"That damned thing, I hoped I'd never see it again."

He immediately returned the box to the bag, worried she would throw it away if he left it in her care. "Has she told you what happened?" Carol was instantly coy, guilt swamping her, and she nodded. "It's all so silly, it's a shame it's come to this, because she's a promising officer."

Carol smiled, relieved, and gestured to a seat, returning to her chair. "I know, and I'm so pleased you can see the dangers in her obsession."

Thirsk remained standing and scratched his head, confused. "Carol, why do you think Toni has come home?"

Now she was equally perplexed. "Andy sacked her. Andy Feldman."

"She told you that?"

"Yes, just now. Why, is there a problem?"

"Where is she? Is she here?"

"She's upstairs…" She stopped when he marched out, and listened as he plodded up the stairs. Intrigued, she followed and was halfway up when Maisie shrieked indignantly, drowning out Toni's maddening curses.

Thirsk was embarrassed, his face reddening. "I'm sorry girls, I should have knocked. Toni, we need to talk." He glanced at Carol, who was listening intently. "I'll take you for a drink."

"As if I'm going to go for a fucking drink with you. You're not my boss any more, so fuck off and leave me alone."

"Your boss? I thought Andy Feldman was your boss." Clueless, Carol wished she had gone to bed early, eradicated the tiresome day with a vague ray of hope that tomorrow would be better.

"It doesn't matter who my boss *was*, it's all irrelevant now. Piss off, Richard, you've ruined my fucking life."

A rookie using his first name smacked him hard and overwhelming relief that he had never had children of his own flooded him. He grabbed Toni's wrist and dragged her from the room, past her mother and down the stairs. "Young lady, you are coming for a fucking drink with me whether you like it or not, and don't ever call me Richard again. We need to sort things out, they can't be left like this. Bloody little upstart." His barking continued as he hauled her to his car, leaving Maisie and Carol with their jaws hanging, gobsmacked.

"Well I never. What was that all about?"

Watching through the window now, Maisie rolled her eyes dramatically, pulling a face. "Der! They're obviously shagging. No wonder she's leaving home tomorrow, she's bagged herself a boyfriend, well, an old-wrinkly-granddad-friend."

"You have got to be joking." Carol shook her head, disgusted by the thought, and sank onto Maisie's bed. "No, that's horrible, it can't be." Recalling the affair they had started after Baby Jane had been found, of how he had taken advantage of her vulnerability and boredom – of how she had wanted him to. How could he be sleeping with her daughter? It sickened her. She stood slowly and, using the wall for support, staggered from the room, heading for her own.

"God knows what she sees in him, 'cos he sure doesn't look rich." Maisie smiled, enjoying, but not understanding, her mother's discomfort.

Carol closed the door and slumped onto her bed. "I give up." She stripped off and tugged on her pyjamas, willing the revulsion to melt away, and poured a large glass of red wine from the bottle she had opened the night before. Slipping into bed, she dragged the covers over her head. Dan would have to sort out his own dinner tonight; she was officially on strike.

They had been sitting opposite each other at the pub table for nearly an hour with barely a word exchanged between them. He had tried to catch her eye a few times, but she had sulkily glanced elsewhere. He gave up, taking the empty glasses to the bar for a refill, and the break from the prickly atmosphere was welcome. Ready to give up and go home if it didn't work, he gave it one more chance. "Toni, this is ridiculous, it doesn't have to be like this. And for a start, you can't just resign like that. You'll be disciplined for your behaviour, and I'm guessing your contract states that you need to give at least one-month notice. You can't just flounce out like a fucking diva and not expect repercussions."

She didn't answer, sitting in silence, picking at the skin on her fingers. Never before had a woman aggravated him so much; he wanted to lean over and shake her, make her respond. Instead, he waited patiently, restraining himself, gulping beer to while away the time, but eventually he snapped. "For fuck's sake, Toni, you're so bloody infuriating. Can't you see that you're behaving like a little child."

"You started it."

"See what I mean?" He was tempted to sacrifice his pint and tip it over her head, he was so rattled.

"You shouldn't have blasted my arse for something that was out of my control. You know as well as I do that I had no choice but to follow Steadman's orders, bitchy cow that she is. If you had told her you wanted me on the job specifically, this would never have happened. In fact, it would have been thoughtful if you'd told me too. You're a fucking arse. Sir."

Her bitterness was grating and he'd had enough of the pathetic messing around. "Well, you shouldn't have gone and got a crush on me, should you, and then I wouldn't have had to make you hate me just to get you off my fucking back."

Her eyes boggled, unable to comprehend what he had said. Struggling to find a retort, or a reason, she gasped, "A crush? On you?" Her face crinkled and she laughed, clutching her belly. Every time she tried to speak, she burst into a fit of hysterics again at the ridiculous thought. Thirsk, aged probably ninety, garish, unfashionable, obscure penchant for music recorded before she was even a twinkle in her father's eye. Battered, craggy, wrinkled, old man. Tears of hilarity ran down her cheeks and she struggled to catch her breath.

Meanwhile, Thirsk sat silently, his expression sardonic, failing to see the joke that seemed to have delighted her so greatly. He crossed his arms, eyebrow raised.

Finally, once the giggling had died down, he felt the need to justify his remark and told her what Joyce had suggested. Still breaking into sporadic laughter, Toni assured him that she was way off the mark, questioning her credibility as a psychiatrist for even having dreamt such an outrageous idea.

Now the air had cleared they were able to talk through the events of the tumultuous day. When he dropped her home at ten o'clock, they had decided to forget the resignation, on the understanding she was not to forget her rank again.

She was about to close the car door when he called her back, his voice nervous. "Just out of interest, why is it so laughable, the idea of you and me?" Her uncontrollable giggling restarted and he gave up, revving the engine to signal his desire to leave. It wasn't until he reached his apartment that he realised he still had the box, and he cursed.

Simone had spent the afternoon tediously scanning each and every page from the folder on Julia Collins to her computer and sending them in endless emails to the policewoman, and she was more than ready to return to her husband for a final night of passion before he flew back to Jamaica the next morning. She hastily tidied her desk, slipping her shoes back on with a grimace as they pinched her chubby feet, and hurried home.

Before she had gone to work that morning, she had thrown some diced braising steak and vegetables into the slow cooker, mixing up a hot pepper sauce for it to simmer in over the course of the day. She had wanted to have a relaxing bath, pamper herself to bring out her dusky beauty, and slip into a sexy dress that accentuated her womanly curves to welcome her husband home from his day at the office, but the extra hours spent fulfilling the police's request had ruined her plans, forcing her to do unpaid overtime yet again.

The pleasant smell of dinner had seeped through the house to greet her when she opened the door. She dumped her bag in the hall and slipped the uncomfortable shoes off, darting to the kitchen to stir the stew, before hastily setting the table for two, complete with cotton napkins and centrepiece candles. Stepping back to admire the flickering scene, romantic and sensual, she heard Ian's key in the door and her heart flipped with excitement. Finally, she could relax.

Ian sweetly offered to defer dinner, and he drew a tempting, bubbly bath for her to soak in, and afterwards they tucked into the delicious dish, sumptuously rounded off with a bottle of Champagne he had bought to celebrate their final night together for the next four weeks. Satisfied and chilled, they retired to the lounge, playing some gentle background music, and soon they made their way to bed for an early night.

Hours later the two were sleeping when the bedside phone began to ring. They groaned and ignored it, waiting for the answerphone to kick in. The call ended and they snuggled back down, but the phone began to ring again. Now they were wide-awake. Annoyed yet curious, Simone grabbed the receiver. "What?" She listened for a moment. "Oh my God, that's awful. What do you want me to do?"

Ian watched his wife with concern, wondering which aging relation was ill this time. "I'll be there as quick as I can." She cut the call and jumped out of bed, throwing some clothes on. "It's work. I've got to go out." As an afterthought she leaned over and kissed him. "You get back to sleep, honey, I'll be home as soon as I can."

Simone sped through the dark, quiet streets to Albert Block on the Canal Estate. She locked the car and traipsed up three flights of stairs, stopping occasionally to catch her breath, and rapped on the door to Julia's flat. When no answer came she dialled Julia's number on her mobile. Dishevelled and sleepy, Julia answered, but was wide awake when she let Simone in, worriedly dressing so they could set off for the hospital.

The journey was hurried and silent, and they hastened to the accident and emergency department, asking the receptionist where to find Antony. But when a sympathetic nurse led them to a private room, Simone realised they had arrived too late. Antony was dead.

Chapter 23
Rumours

Steadman was perkier than she had been for a few days, more comfortable now Toni, whom she considered a rival, had gone. Every now and then she glanced surreptitiously through the window into Thirsk's office. He had snapped at her the day before, but having worked with him for years, she knew of his tendency to do so when stressed. She had thought long and hard about her boss the previous night and realised that if she wanted him, she would have to be more obvious, because subtlety didn't appear to register with him. She planned to suggest lunch when she next saw him. Waiting patiently for an opportunity, she used the time to try and locate Julia's doctor, and the third call she made, to Givens Lane Medical Centre, hit the jackpot. And now she had a reason to see him. She knocked on the door and entered when he beckoned.

"Morning, Guv." He grunted unintelligibly. "I've found Julia's current medical practice, would you like me to go and see them?"

He shook his head, which surprised her. "No."

"I thought you wanted..."

"I do, but last night I asked Fowler to call in and see Julia this morning, get the details, then she's going straight there."

Steadman's entire world fell at her feet as she digested the words, the cruel realisation that, not only had Toni somehow retained her job despite her ridiculous and unprofessional performance the day before, but she had also been with Thirsk the previous evening. Her heart felt as if would break in two. Unable to continue with her misjudged plan, she left the room and headed straight for the ladies for some solace.

Thirsk had no inkling that he had just destroyed his colleague, it had never occurred to him that the woman may have feelings for him. He returned to the folder he had been given that morning containing Maria's health records. He didn't understand much of the technical terminology, but was sure he would recognise something if she had been pregnant in two thousand and three, the year Baby Jane lost her life. The scant file showed that Maria was not a fan of the NHS; he had expected, having seen the frail and unhealthy woman – pallid in colour, almost grey, with an alarming smoker's cough – the file to be full of notes taken during copious consultations, but in the past five years she had only visited once, receiving a prescription for antibiotics to treat a chest infection. Her pregnancy with Julia was detailed, but no subsequent pregnancies had been recorded and, even so, she had been forty-five ten years before, which made it not impossible, but unlikely that she would have been able to conceive a viable foetus. Sighing, he ruled her out as a possible mother to the dead child.

His eyes tired and watery from concentration, Thirsk was grateful when his phone rang and he answered to hear Toni's voice, telling him breathlessly that she was at Julia's flat and had some shocking news. She was clearly shaken, and he understood why when she related the dreadful details. "Dead? But how? Why?"

"No one knows until the PM is done."

"I want a copy of the report as soon as…" He hesitated for a moment. "Sod that. I'll let Hugh know that I want to attend."

"Do I stay with her?" Toni's voice cracked; she was finding the situation difficult, unused to such terrible circumstances.

"Is anyone else there?"

"Her social worker has been with her through the night, she took her to the hospital, in fact. She says she's cancelled her appointments for the day and can stay until five."

"Then come back here, she doesn't need two people with her, it's not our job. Have you managed to get the name of her doctor yet?"

"I don't believe you! How can I ask her something like that at a time like this?"

"It's bad timing, yes, but we have an ongoing investigation and I need those records." He recalled the conversation with Steadman and relaxed. "Actually, no, you're right. Forget that. Just come back to the station, we'll go from there."

Thirsk ended the call and left his office to find Steadman, but she wasn't at her desk so he called Sally over. She gave him a disgusted look, which confused him, and he knew he would never understand women if he lived to be a million. "Any idea where Steadman is?"

"In the toilets crying her eyes out," she spat, blunt and accusing.

"Oh dear." He attempted to be more sensitive. "I suppose it must be her time of the month."

Sally stared after him in disbelief as he sat at Steadman's desk and scribbled the name and address that was still on the screen onto a scrap of paper. He was about to call Toni, but remembered he only had one cigarette left and decided to go himself so he could pick up a couple of packets from the newsagent on the way. "Sally, call this number, tell them I'm on the way and need to see Julia's doctor. Tell them it's urgent, I've got no intention of sitting there waiting for god knows how long."

The surgery was fitting with the area it served. Although recently built, it had suffered from the contagions of the poverty filled Canal Estate and was graffiti covered, the attempt to provide a pleasant garden to brighten the neighbourhood destroyed by bored youths and street roaming dogs. Metal grates had been fixed over the windows to stop them being smashed for mindless fun, and the clientele who were arriving and leaving were downtrodden and badly dressed. He watched from his car for a while, steeling himself to enter the germ-ridden building.

The doctor agreed to see him for five minutes at the cost of his already-late patients, but when Thirsk asked him to bring up Julia's details he refused, stating that, for confidentiality reasons, he couldn't divulge any information. Something inside Thirsk snapped; he'd had enough of Julia Collins, of her solemn life and mental craziness. The case was bringing him down, and all that lay between him having nothing more to do with her was to be assured that she hadn't given birth at the age of thirteen. He explained that her child had died the previous night and he needed to know if she'd had any other pregnancies 'to assist the Coroner'. "If I were to ask you if she had a baby, say, up to ten years ago, would you at least be able to say no. In fact, you don't even have to say a word, just shake your head."

The doctor was about to object, but his patients were waiting and he wanted to get home on time for once, so didn't need to further the backlog this early in the day. "I'm making it clear that this is unofficial." He turned the screen away from Thirsk and brought up Julia's details, reading. "Are you aware that ten years ago she was only thirteen?"

"Yes, but just so I can cross the t's and dot the i's, can you go back that far?"

"I have." And he shook his head, relieving Thirsk of ever having to have contact with the girl again, apart from when she testified in court. He thanked the doctor warmly and left the gloomy building with a spring in his step.

Her eldest daughter, first borne and dearly loved, was due to fly the nest in the evening and Carol was desperate to change her mind. She made a strong coffee on her return from the factory and nursed it at the kitchen table, wretchedly weaving through ideas. Then, and it wasn't properly thought out, but she didn't have time to waste either, she dialled Castle Street Police Station. "Can I speak to Toni Fowler please?"

The call was redirected to the fifth floor and, in Toni's absence, Steadman answered. "Fowler's not here. Is there anything I can help with?"

"Oh, I don't know. She's my daughter. I just wanted to speak with her." Steadman was silent and Carol felt daft for having called in the first place. "It's just, she's leaving home tonight, she's moving in with Ri... um, her boy... man friend." Her skin crawled at the thought. Disgusting.

Carol had Steadman's complete attention. "A boyfriend? Well, that's good. Isn't it?"

"No, he's in his fifties, damn it. She's only twenty." Carol wanted to scream.

And so did Steadman, who had arrived at five from two plus two, and her hope evaporated. She had thought the day couldn't get any worse, but this revelation made her blood boil and suddenly she hated Thirsk intensely. The filthy pervert obviously only went for youngsters. In fact they all did. She was thirty-five and already over the hill.

"Are you still there?"

Steadman struggled to find something to say. She wanted to know everything about their sordid liaison, but also wanted to clamp her hands over her ears and shout so she couldn't hear that it was really happening. She wished she could rip her heart out to stop the pain. Steadying herself, she spoke through gritted teeth. "I didn't know anything about that. Would you like me to get her to call you?"

"Gosh, I've forgotten my manners, I'm sorry, I didn't mean to snap. It's just it's all been quite a strain." Calm now, Carol felt stupid and was quiet. "I just wanted to try and persuade her not to move in with him, that's all. It's a big mistake and I can't just sit back and watch it happen." She sobbed lightly, only the slightest sniffle audible to Steadman, who detested Thirsk and Toni now with more passion than she had realised she was capable of. "I mean, isn't it inappropriate, you know, with him being her boss? I know they don't tolerate same department relationships at the factory. I don't think it's right."

Steadman wanted revenge on the man she had admired – coveted – for so long. Didn't she? Was it worth it? But watching them play out their tempestuous relationship under her nose was agonising. "Well, same department romances are frowned upon. I must say it's been a bit of a concern for us too." She wasn't sure where the conversation was heading and was playing it by ear.

Carol, however, was pleased to have a confidante. "I already voiced my concerns to Sergeant Feldman, but then she was transferred to your department, which I just couldn't believe when I heard."

"So he knows about their affair?" She doodled Andy's name on her pad unnecessarily.

"Well, no, I complained about something else, but it was to do with Richard, so I can't believe she was posted to work alongside him. It's all wrong, he's got to be nearly three times her age, it's disgusting. And now she's leaving home to set up a love nest with him, and I just can't let her make a mistake that she may regret for the rest of her life."

"Yes, I can see it must be very distressing." Toni, big, blue eyes and manipulating cutesy smile, came through the door and hovered beside her, and she wanted to scream *smug cow*, but she quietly assured Carol that her complaint had been registered and would be dealt with effectively. They ended the call, both depressed in their own individual trauma.

"Who was that? Was it for me?" Toni couldn't understand why Steadman was scowling at her.

"No, it was Andy Feldman. For me." In a foul mood, Steadman's tone was bitter, confusing Toni further. The older woman stood and 'accidentally' shoved her nemesis as she passed, leaving the room. She summoned the lift, but was too wound up to wait and took the stairs, two at a time, to the second floor, where she found Andy. He smiled at her lecherously and her skin crawled. "Have you had dealings with Toni Fowler's mother?"

"Depends what sort of dealings you're talking about." He grinned lewdly and winked. "Why?"

"Did you have any idea that Toni and Thirsk were dating?"

"You're kidding me." He hadn't managed to get into the girl's pants and he was only thirty-seven, so how on earth had the sly old dog managed that little beauty? Scandalous!

"How does that stand with the powers that be? Are there any rules about having a relationship with a colleague?" She was ignorant to the hypocrisy, having wanted Thirsk herself for so long.

"Come on, Diane. Everyone's shagging everyone else at Castle Street. If it was a sackable offence we'd have no officers left."

Steadman lowered her voice. "Look, I've got an axe to grind with Thirsk, so what can I do that will make him uncomfortable."

"Gossip. Best way to make them both squirm. Spread something around like you saw them having sex on his desk, or something. I can get it round the second floor in no time."

Julia hadn't spoken since she had heard the dreadful news and Simone was concerned. There had been no tears, no outbursts, no screaming, just a zombie with dull eyes that hid her inexplicable pain. She had asked no questions, nor answered any, hadn't made any calls, and had shaken her head when Simone offered to let friends or family know. The social worker had considered calling a doctor, but reasoned that everybody dealt with grief in individual ways. She was sure the tears would come eventually, and felt the most productive thing she could do was to supply tea aplenty, food and sympathy.

She called her manager from the privacy of the kitchen, uncomfortable discussing Antony in front of his bereaved mother. "Hi Grace, I was wondering if you'd spoken to Mr and Mrs Coleman about what happened to Antony Collins?"

"Yes, I went to see them as soon as I'd called you this morning, they were distraught, poor loves. They said Antony had been under the weather over the past few days, and they were going to take him to the doctor today if he was still poorly. They said they put him to bed at eight last night and he went straight to sleep, but when Mrs Coleman went to check on him later, nine o'clock, or thereabouts, he wasn't breathing. They called an ambulance and Mr Coleman tried to resuscitate the boy, but he didn't respond. The paramedics got him going as soon as they got there, but they lost him in the hospital."

"So there's nothing untoward about it?"

"Why on earth would there be?" The thought had never occurred to her. "Of course there isn't, the Colemans have been some of our best foster carers for years now. Anyway, the police are attending the post mortem, but they said it's standard practice for sudden deaths in children. I don't think there's any blame on the Coleman's shoulders, but I think it may be questioned why they didn't take him to the doctor sooner. How is Julia coping? Are you still with her?"

"I am. Unsurprisingly, she's completely numb, doesn't speak, or eat, or cry, nothing. I don't really know what to do. That young policewoman was here again this morning and Julia didn't even acknowledge her."

"Can you get hold of a relative to come and stay with her?"

Simone laughed sardonically. "Her parents and uncle are all under arrest, I believe, and they seem to be estranged anyway. She's never spoken of anyone else, friend or family. I'm staying here for the rest of the day, but after that, well, I don't know. Without a child involved I have no reason to come here any more."

Antony's post mortem had been put to the head of the queue and Hugh Smythe wasn't looking forward to it; children were always hard to do. His father had also been a pathologist and had often spoken about his work at home, so Hugh's interest in cadavers and what they can reveal had started at an early age. He had an analytical mind, and the bodies he worked on were never people with loves, hobbies, and characters, they were simply jigsaws to undo to see which piece had been put in the wrong place. Curious, he always had to find the cause of death, and would dwell on an unusual case endlessly until he found answers. As a result, his work was accurate, which had boosted his reputation of being one of the best pathologists in the area, despite his young age.

He found the cause of Antony's death almost immediately on analysing his heart. He'd had a congenital condition, complete atrial septal defect, a treatable abnormality that should have been spotted on the routine ultrasound scans, or even after his birth. Antony had died needlessly. An early operation would have given him a normal life. Instead, he must have suffered during his three short years; he would have struggled with his breathing, felt lethargic and dizzy, unwell without understanding why. Hugh explained the details to Thirsk, and added, "Some parents shouldn't be allowed to have children. This poor mite shouldn't be in here."

"Are you saying there's neglect to consider?"

"Very much so."

"But he died of natural causes though, so we're not looking at abuse?"

"Not abuse, no, but neglect, definitely. You need to speak to doctors, social workers, see if any concerns had been raised about his health."

"Not again, I've only just been to one of those germ-ridden hothouses. I think I'll delegate on this one."

"Eh?"

"Doctor's surgeries. I hate the bloody places. I know the family had social workers involved, so I'll get one of my officers to follow up on that." So much for ending all contact with Julia Collins, now there was a potential for manslaughter through neglect.

Thirsk made his way through the afternoon traffic to Castle Street, parked his car and strode through the building towards the lift, oblivious to the tittering and finger pointing of the malicious gossip that was rife at the station. He called Toni to his office when he reached the fifth floor and Steadman began her offensive. "I hope they're not going to have sex in there again." Ears pricked up, intrigued, yet she remained nonchalant. "I heard on the grapevine that they were caught at it, that's all."

Wainwright, who had come across the corridor to see Thirsk, knocked on the door and entered, immediately

233

repeating the scandalous accusation. Toni and her boss were dumbstruck. "You heard what?" The vicious dig explained the dodgy glares Steadman had been giving Toni since she arrived. The detective clearly had a crush on Thirsk and must have been mortified to hear such rubbish.

"I thought I'd better warn you, because it'll get to the sixth floor in no time. It's not true, is it?"

"Don't be so fucking ridiculous, I mean, I'm sorry, I mean ridiculous, Mum tells me…"

"You swear too much, we know." Thirsk shook his head, aghast. "Of course it's not true, and I don't have the slightest idea where it's come from. I'd better have a word with the Chief. As if I need this crap today. What are you here for, anyway?"

"I thought you'd want to know that Jim Collins is in court Monday afternoon and we expect him to be remanded until his trial. We've dismissed his allegations that Sean was involved, there's nothing to place him at the garage or the dumpsite, so he's off the hook. Oh, and we've formally charged Maria with Melissa's abduction, but we're expecting her to be bailed." Wainwright tugged a chair next to Toni, opposite Thirsk, and sat languidly. "So it should be easy from here, they'll throw away the key."

The news was good, but Thirsk still felt too many pieces were missing, and Jim's denial of the murder had been convincing. "Have you found out how he dumped the body?"

"He won't admit to killing her, or taking her body to Black Park."

"I've been meaning to ask him about the park. Damn. Is he still downstairs?"

Wainwright glanced at his watch. "Yes, for another hour or so."

"I'll pop down and see him in a minute. I won't bother with an interview room, it's not for the record anyway."

Standing, Wainwright strolled to the door, and turned back. "I remember you, Toni. You've turned out pretty fine."

She reddened, unsure of what he meant, and after he had closed the door Thirsk explained he had assisted with the Baby Jane case. "He was a youngster at the time, but I could see promise in him, like I can with you. Now," he passed a scribbled note to Toni and she read it, grimacing, "that's the name of the condition Antony Collins died of, it's a congenital heart defect that should have been picked up in pregnancy. I want you to speak to that social worker about the suggestion of negligence."

"Whose?"

"Everybody. Hers, doctors, hospital, Julia. Just find the truth."

Thirsk headed to the sixth floor to nip the rumours in the bud, sure they would have caused no harm at this early stage, but the Chief Superintendent had already heard, and despite disbelieving them, he felt it ethical for Toni to return to Andy Feldman's charge on the second floor.

Chapter 24
A Few too Many

The atmosphere in Julia's flat had been dreadful that morning and Toni was reluctant to return, doubting it would have changed much over the course of the day. Simone sombrely opened the door to let her in. "I need to ask you some questions about Social Service's involvement with Julia since Antony was born."

Simone led Toni to the kitchen and re-filled the kettle. "She's only been known to us for a couple of weeks. Why?"

Toni had briefly researched the condition on the net before leaving the office and explained it should have been diagnosed before it became fatal. "Did you notice any signs that he was unhealthy?"

"Well, he was small for his age and he was very quiet, but I put that down to Julia not having much to do with him, she wasn't a very hands-on mother. He was a bit breathless sometimes, I suppose."

"We'll need copies of any records you have since you've been involved with the family. I need to speak to her, do you think she'll be up to it?"

Simone shrugged, squeezing the flavour from a teabag before dropping it in the bin. "You can try and get through to her, but don't expect too much, I can't seem to get anything from her, poor thing."

Toni found Julia sitting on the edge of her bed, her expression blank and shoulders sagging. She didn't acknowledge Toni, nor answer when the officer spoke to her. Toni sat beside her, patting her hand. "Julia, it's PC Fowler, do you remember me?" There was no response. "I need to ask you about Antony's health. You know that they've had to perform a post mortem on him, don't you?" Julia was deaf, dumb and blind. "They found that he had a heart defect, and the symptoms would have been apparent since birth. Have you had him regularly checked at the Health Centre?"

No response. Toni hadn't experienced a similar situation and had no clue how to persevere with someone so vacant. Should she give up and try again later? Offer sympathy and hope the girl would open up? Maybe she should be nasty to anger her into talking. Her mobile rang and she answered enthusiastically, pleased for the diversion.

"I've been to see the Chief Super about those rumours, Toni."

She noticed the glumness in his voice and answered tentatively. "All dead and buried, I hope."

Toni was hot-headed in anger and devoted to the Baby Jane case, and Thirsk feared that as the messenger, she was likely to shoot him down. "Toni, you can't work for me any longer, you're being transferred back to the second floor with immediate effect."

"You fucking what? Why? I haven't done anything wrong."

"The Chief thought it was the only solution, he thinks if you continue to work…"

"But the rumours aren't true, you know that. Why does my career get stamped on just because some people can't keep their filthy minds to themselves? You know how much Baby Jane means to me and…"

Why did she always have to answer back? Toni Fowler exasperated him sometimes. "I don't care, your instructions are to go home for the day, and when you return on Monday you'll be back with Feldman. End of."

On hearing the dial tone, Toni swore under her breath, embarrassingly aware she had exploded in front of the bereaved mother. She turned to apologise, but Julia was staring at her, boring into her soul, and she was unnerved. Faltering under the glare, she tried to speak, but Julia demanded, "What's Baby Jane to you?"

"Oh, sorry about that, it's just a case I've been working on. It's nothing to do with why I'm here. Oh no," she realised that saying baby was insensitive, "I'm sorry, I shouldn't have said baby, I'm sorry Julia."

"Didn't you say your name was Fowler? What's your first name?"

She frowned, unsure what relevance that had to anything. "Toni."

There had been a minute of coherence but Julia drew the drawbridge up again, retreating to her own world. The world where her child had died and nothing else mattered. Toni shook her head and gave up, wishing she hadn't bothered to get out of bed that morning. In front of her was a traumatised mother of a child who shouldn't have died, she had been sacked from the case that had enwrapped her life for the past decade, and rumours were rife of her bonking a grumpy old man. It was humiliating that people even believed she would stoop so low. She jumped to her feet, thoroughly fed up. If they were demanding she go home, then that's what she was going to do. She stormed from Albert Block, intending to pack the final items and start moving her belongings to her new flat. At least that was something to look forward to.

Colin had received the developer's keys to Toni's new flat in the morning, and closed his shop after the schools closed for the week, picking Pam and their children up as arranged. They drove to St Martin's Place and took a dozen or so bags filled with goodies to make the place homely as a surprise for when Toni arrived. It was a big day for her and they wanted to make it special. They had some bits and pieces – an old kettle and toaster, a few utensils – to spare, and had bought essential groceries to help their friend out.

Pam hadn't seen the flat before and wandered from room to room expressing approval, while Colin ensured the gas and electric were on, setting the central-heating timer and warming the cool rooms. In the kitchen, Pat switched the fridge on and set up the kettle. From the bags she retrieved a jar of coffee, a bag of sugar, some teabags and a box of Toni's favourite elderberry tea. She placed two bottles of pre-chilled wine in the fridge door and unpacked the cheap glasses she had bought, rinsing them under the tap. "Col, the water's cold, can you sort it out, please."

"I'm onto it." The excitable shrieks of their four daughters almost drowned his voice out.

"What time will Toni be over? Do you know?"

"I think she was going to try and get off work early, but she might fill her car before she comes. I don't think she was too organised, to be honest, her mind was on other things. She was very vague on the phone."

Pam dried her hands on one of the new tea towels she had bought and found her husband inside the airing cupboard in the bedroom, tinkering with the combi-boiler. "I spoke to her yesterday lunchtime, she told me that she's been living her dream; it seems they're re-investigating the Baby Jane case."

Colin pressed a button, grinning when a green light with a tap symbol glowed, and closed the door. "All done, she can have a nice hot shower now, if she wants." He paced the empty room. "I don't know where she's going to sleep. Did she say anything about a bed?"

"I think she was going to bring hers from home. Did you hear me?"

"Yes, Baby Jane. That's how you met her, wasn't it?" They traipsed back to the kitchen and continued unpacking bags, a well-oiled machine together, moving as one.

She chuckled. "Yes, back in those wondrous days before I became tied to the sink with a hundred kids around my ankles. It's personal to her, it's always been her ambition to discover the truth behind the case, so I'm really pleased for her, and she's so happy."

Neither had heard Toni come in. "Not any more, I'm done with it. I'm done with the force. I fucking hate today."

Pam nudged her arm, issuing a chastising look. "Watch your language in front of the children."

In a filthy mood, Toni was intolerant. "Talking of your kids, are they going to be here long? You said you'd take them to your mother's."

"At five, I said." Pam had never known Toni to be irritated by her children, they doted on her and she adored them. Usually. She glanced at her watch. "It's not my fault you came home early from work."

Toni flounced out and Colin shrugged at Pam. "I'll tell you what. You stay here and keep setting up the house, I'll take her back to her mum's in my car and help her load up her stuff, maybe she'll tell me what's wrong."

Simone was exhausted, regardless that she had done little else but prepare endless mugs of tea over the course of the day. The raw emotion in the flat was unbearable and the cause unapproachable. It was nearly five o'clock, and she was relieved there were only ten minutes more before she could issue her sympathies for the billionth time and get away from the claustrophobic atmosphere. Too late for her husband, though; he would be at Heathrow Airport by now, checking in for his flight back to Kingston. She ached to be with him, reminding him of what he was going to miss over the next four weeks, but instead, she took the latest in a long line of teas to the bedroom and sat beside Julia on the bed.

"They think I killed him, don't they?" They were the first words Simone had heard her say all day.

"He had a heart defect, how can that be your fault? I think the hospital's more to blame, they should have picked it up on the ultrasound."

Julia's head was down, toes fidgeting in her socks. "Then it is my fault because I didn't have a scan. So it's definitely my fault, isn't it?"

Simone was astonished that anybody would refuse a scan, but she didn't want to hurt the grieving woman further. "So you didn't have one, but still you'd have thought they would have noticed something after he was born. They check for things like that."

"I discharged myself from hospital, I hate the places. I hate quacks."

"They must have looked him over, though. And even so, you'll have taken him to the health visitor, the doctor." She was struggling to make the woman feel better, feeling guilt herself for not having spotted the tell-tale blue tinge to Antony's skin that she now realised was a sign of his heart trouble.

"I've killed my baby. Nothing's safe around me, whatever I touch turns to shit. If only he had never found me, Antony wouldn't have gone away, and I'd have known something was wrong. My little boy would still be alive now."

"If only who had never found you? What are you talking about?"

"My dad. He found out where I was and said he was going to take Antony away. Well, he has now, hasn't he?"

Suddenly all the anomalies about Julia's behaviour made sense to Simone, she understood Julia's urgency to have her son taken into care, taken somewhere safe. It wasn't that she had no feeling for him, it wasn't that she was depressed and needed a break and some practical help. She had feared for his safety at the hands of the man who had abused her throughout her childhood. "Did you tell the police this?"

"What's the point, what would they have done?"

Simone knew the answer was probably nothing, but then, what could they have done? There was no crime in a man contacting his daughter. "Did he threaten you when he called?"

"He didn't call. He doesn't know my number."

"Well, visit, then."

"He hasn't visited, well, hasn't seen me, anyway. He posted a note through the door, it said 'Your boy next'."

"If your father has threatened you in a manner that led you to having your child placed in care, I really think you need to speak to the police about it, especially as they're investigating the situation as a possible manslaughter due to negligence."

Julia's eyes implored Simone, flooding with fresh tears. "Negligence? They *are* saying I killed him. I ain't the best mum, I never was, but I'd never kill him."

Simone gently patted her arm, a substitute mother to the bereft mum. "There's nothing to worry about, Julia, Antony wasn't even in your care the week before he died, all of us could have spotted he was ill." Even me, she wanted to add. Especially me. She controlled her guilt with a deep breath. "Look, that policewoman who just came round, you seem to get on well with her. Contact her again, let her know everything. Just to safeguard yourself, if nothing else. I've got to get home now, I've got plans for this evening, but if I were you, I'd give her a call."

A flicked switch and Julia was emotionless again, the tears drying on her cheeks and expression blank. Simone grabbed her bag and wearily waddled from the flat with a promise to return soon.

Once she was alone, Julia debated Simone's words. Negligence? She had always ensured that Antony had clean clothes and food, that he had a decent bed and plenty of children's television to watch. Was this really her fault?

Colin and Toni arrived at her childhood home after a silent journey, Toni's temper close to boiling. She stomped from the car and along the path, fishing her keys from her pocket, and he followed obediently. She led him to the bedroom and pointed to the packed boxes. "What about the bed? Pam said you were bringing this one."

"No, she is not. I bought that. If she's stupid enough to leave home on a whim, then she can buy her own bed." Carol stood at the door, an almost empty wine bottle in her hand, and wobbled against the doorframe.

"Mum, you're drunk."

"What do you expect, you ungrateful cow?"

Colin grasped Carol gently by the shoulders and tried to lead her away. "Come on, Mrs Fowler, emotions are running high at the moment, this can all wait until another time. I'll tell you what, Toni, we can stop at Argos on the way back and pick up an airbed for now. Or, if you want, we can lend you the money for a cheap bed. Let's just get the boxes packed into the car."

He was the voice of reason, but the two women had locked horns. "You won't let me take my bed? Fine fucking mother you are. I'm so fucking lucky to be getting out of this hole. And talking about your selfish and underhand ways, where's my box of Baby Jane things?"

Carol laughed, guttural and pissed. "Your lover boy had them." She swayed into the room, staggering waywardly until she managed to flump onto the bed, claiming it elaborately with her outstretched arms. "I mean, what's that all about, you and Richard. How did that happen? Do you talk about dead babies while you're doing it? Is that what gets you both going?"

Maisie arrived at the door, homework forgotten, eager to hear the next episode in the family drama. She chuckled with joy at her mother's ungainly display, but Toni wasn't amused. "What are you talking about, Mum?"

"You and my Richard. Yeah, that's right, he was mine first. While you kids were at school we shagged until we dropped. That's right. And now he's shagging my daughter. I think it's sick," she turned to Colin, her eyelids drooping and words slurred, "don't you, Colin?" He hastily grasped a box and heaved it through the door, sensible enough to know when he shouldn't be involved. Maisie, however, was thoroughly enjoying the show, especially having noticed her father come through the door, and she chuckled with glee. Carol stood again and drained the bottle. "Mother and daughter, eh? He shags the mother, then shags the daughter. It's poetic, don't you think?"

Colin passed Dan at the bottom of the stairs. "What's going on?"

"I'm, er, just helping Toni move her things to her new place. I think you might want to get your wife to bed, I think she's finding the situation difficult."

Carol's too loud words floated down the stairs. "He wanted me to leave Dan, you know that, but I wouldn't. And you know why I wouldn't? Because of you kids, that's why. I sacrificed my own happiness for the welfare of you ungrateful brats, and this is how you thank me; move out at the first sign of trouble."

Having run up the stairs, Dan stood beside his youngest child, face pale and bottom lip trembling. "Who wanted you to leave me, Carol? Who made you happy?"

"Her fancy man, get that, Dan. I wasn't enough for him, because he had his eyes set on a ten-year old girl. I always wondered why he dumped me, you know, and now I know I never had a chance. I spent years pining after him, I did."

"Dad, she doesn't know what she's saying. There's nothing between me and Thirsk, he's my, well, was my boss, and now he's not. Nothing ever happened like that."

His watering, sorrowful eyes settled on his wife, heart thundering. "Maybe not with you. I'll be in the greenhouse if anyone wants me." Dan thundered down the stairs, unable to digest the agonising revelation.

Carol was intent on clearing her conscience, exposing the years of lies and adultery. "See, that's why I wanted someone else, because he spends more time with his fucking tomatoes than he does with me, and does anyone care? No, as long as I get your washing and cleaning and dinner done, that's all you need me for."

Toni grabbed a box, her heart sunken, desperate to get away and start her new life. She trotted down the stairs awkwardly, the box threatening to slip, and passed it to Colin at the front door. "Get me out of here, Col, I'm not sure I can take any more today."

Julia had collected the few photos she had of Antony from a drawer in the sideboard. A couple were of his bright face on his third birthday, a cupcake bought from the bakery heralding three glowing candles that left an ugly glare on the image. Her child, her son who had died, despite her efforts to protect him. She had nothing, now she had lost her angel. She had chosen not to have contact with her family, for good reason, and had deliberately made no effort since moving to the flat to make friends in the new area. Completely, achingly alone. Now there was nothing left to lose, she needed to hear the truth, and she needed to hear it now. Castle Street Police Station was a few hundred meters away through a maze of back street alleyways, but she took the longer walk along the main road, under the streetlights, the noise of the car engines company and the chilly air bracing.

It was six o'clock when she climbed the stairs to the reception area and asked for Toni Fowler. The desk sergeant checked the computer. "Her shift's ended and she's not due in this weekend. Can somebody else help?"

Julia was disconcerted, not having prepared for Toni's absence, but as she faltered another officer she recognised came through the doorway. "Excuse me, miss, do you remember me?" Sally groaned inwardly. "You were at my place last week. I need to talk to somebody. Can I have a word?"

It was Friday night and Sally had an appointment with the pub; being disturbed by the odious girl was the last thing she needed. "What about?"

"I think my dad might have killed my son. They told me you've got him here and I want to speak to him."

Sally relaxed instantly, because anything to do with Jim Collins wasn't something she could deal with alone. Happy to pass the buck, she smiled. "Clive, can you let either Inspector Thirsk or Inspector Wainwright know that Julia Collins is here to see them." She indicated a chair, almost tasting the vodka and coke that was waiting for her down the road. "Someone will be down in a minute."

Ten minutes later, Julia had, for convenience, been taken to an interview room on the first floor, and presently Wainwright arrived, clueless to the girl and her reason for meeting him. She explained she was Jim's daughter, that she suspected he might have had something to do with her son's

245

death, and that she needed to talk with him. "It doesn't work like that, Miss Collins. I'm afraid your father has been charged with some serious crimes and we can't allow him to talk to just anybody."

"I ain't just anybody, I'm his daughter. This is important. My son's dead and my dad had something to do with it. That big, old fella that works here, the scruffy geezer, he knows all about it, I told him everything the other day."

"You've already spoken to somebody, good." He meant it; now he could pass the buck too. "Do you have the officer's name?"

"No, but he came to see me Wednesday night and spent a couple of hours there. He gave me some booze and some…"

Wainwright instantly held his hand up, stopping her. "Do me a favour, love, don't ever mention that again, okay? I know which officer you're looking for." An hour later Thirsk had arranged for Julia to meet her father, off the record and under the supervision of both himself and Wainwright.

Jim wasn't given any indication as to why he was to be interviewed again and he waxed lyrical about his solicitor being present, but Jason Averill wasn't called. As he was led into the room, he gasped. "Jules."

"Why did you hurt my Antony? He was just a baby."

"I ain't hurt nobody, I told you." He stretched out his arms, incredulous. "What is it with you people?"

"You sent that message for me, I saw it, the one that said that he was next."

"Message? What message? I ain't sent no message."

Thirsk, who had been leaning against the wall, stepped forward, concerned. "Julia, you never told me about this."

"I was too scared, and I thought that as long as Antony was with the social he was safe. But he's not, he got him somehow, and I want to know how."

"Julia, concentrate. What message, and where?"

"I ain't sent no message, I told you, I swear. Why are you doing this to me, Jules?"

Julia stared into her father's eyes, challenging and angry, and Thirsk noticed Jim's face transform from bewildered and innocent, to harsh and commanding. He held Julia's gaze, but she didn't waver. "No, Dad, you can't bully me no more. They say you killed that girl and that you're going down for it, so you can't bully me now. And anyway, you've taken everything I ever loved already so I've got nothing to lose."

"I didn't kill that kid, Jules, I ain't never killed no one, I swear."

Was he furious or defensive? Thirsk couldn't be sure. It bothered him that he felt there was some truth in Jim's unshakeable insistence that he had had nothing to do with Melissa's murder. He had read Wainwright's notes on the charges against Jim and the case seemed watertight, but he had to acknowledge there was no solid evidence that Jim actually held the pillow over Melissa's face, nor that he had been to the dumpsite. "Julia, what exactly happened, what is this message you're talking about?" He spoke softly, coaxing her to pull herself together.

"He dropped it through my letterbox last week, it said 'your boy next'. I know it was him, and I never left no trail so I don't know how he found me. But Robbie wasn't safe and nor was Antony. I thought I'd got Antony somewhere safe, but he got him all the same."

"I don't know where you live, Jules, I never looked for you. Your mum did, but I didn't."

"Mum? Why would *she* want to know where I was?"

And the truth hit Thirsk immediately, the whole mental torture aspect matched Maria's bitterness perfectly. After ten years she still had the maliciousness to try and undermine her daughter, play with her mind and self-esteem. "Who is Robbie, Julia? You mentioned that he wasn't safe."

Gasping, Julia and her father focused on the table between them, silent, and Thirsk and Wainwright frowned at each other. Eventually, Jim looked at his daughter. "Jules, I swear, I never killed Melissa, and I never hurt your boy." The question had been neatly avoided.

Julia's resolve was weakening, reduced to a ten-year old through an inbuilt fear of her father, and she rounded her shoulders with a deep sigh. "You did, Dad, you killed my Antony."

He was astounded. "Killed? I didn't even know your boy was dead, for fuck's sake, and I've been locked in this shit hole since Tuesday night, how the fuck could I have killed anyone. What am I, a fucking ghost who can fly through walls? Jesus."

"That's why I have to know how you did it."

Although the altercation held a wealth of information, Thirsk felt the thread had become worn. "Julia, Antony died yesterday evening, he was at a house ten miles from here, and was taken to hospital. The post mortem shows that he died of a congenital heart defect. Jim was in here, in the cells, he simply can't have killed Antony. Antony wasn't killed, he died."

Her head bobbed down, beaten, and she willed away the tears that threatened. Moments passed before she had steeled herself to continue. "That's that, then, but before I go, I want to know why you hurt me all those years, why you made me do things to you, all those things I didn't want to do. Why were you always in my bed, not with Mum?"

"Because I love you, for fuck's sake."

Julia stood and headed for the door, confusing the three men. Turning back, but unseeing, she said, "That's all I needed to hear. My job's over. Dad, when all this stuff goes to court, promise me you'll tell the truth. About everything. If you love me like you say you do, then show it by telling the truth. And don't cover for Mum no more, 'cos she don't deserve it."

Jim bowed his head as his daughter left, and Thirsk glanced at Wainwright, before trotting from the room to follow Julia. "Julia, please, what is it you know that you haven't told me? You said you'd told me everything the other night, we had an agreement."

"I need some more stuff, especially the booze."

"Shhhh." He glanced around to see if she had been overheard. "For god's sake, that's blackmail. Just tell me what you know. Look, I'll give you a lift home, make sure you're okay, but I want you to tell me everything now, and I mean everything. But don't think you're getting anything else out of me, you cost me over thirty quid the other day."

Half an hour later they reached Julia's flat, and he took the goods he had bought from the convenience store on the ground floor of Albert Block to the kitchen, pushing dishes and clutter aside to make room for them on the worktop. He retrieved the bottles of gin and tonic water from the bag and poured a drink for Julia, adding an extra dash of spirits to relax her, and took it through, along with the bottles. She downed the drink and poured another, adding just a drop of tonic, and drained the glass again. "Go easy, you said you'd make it last all week if I got you a big bottle."

"It'll last until the end of my week." He had no idea what she meant, but the amount of alcohol she was consuming, and the speed with which she was devouring it, made him want to glean everything he could from her while she was still conscious.

"So, are you going to tell me the bits you left out now you've got your booze?"

"I ain't normally a drinker, you know." She had poured, and started, her third tumbler full, and it already showed in her eyes, an opaqueness appearing and shrouding her mind. "Have you got a fag?"

Thirsk wasn't in the mood for games; he'd had enough of women and their manipulating ways today. He held out his packet to her, throwing a further two sticks at her after she had taken one, and offered his lighter. She lit and inhaled, returning it, and he did the same. "Julia, my patience is wearing out and I'm a busy man. Have you got anything to tell me, or not?"

"I was looking at some pictures earlier, photos of my boy, I keep them all in here." She leant to the battered sideboard and tugged the drawer open. Taking a small handful of pictures, she dropped them carefully on the table. "Beautiful, wasn't he?"

He glanced through the small selection of images, but as with all children, he couldn't understand the attraction of the smelly, snotty things. He noticed that she took two pictures and tucked them into the pocket of her hoodie. "I'm sorry that he died, Julia, I really am, but Jim was in custody. He couldn't have done anything to harm him, that I can promise."

"What about Mum, though? Dad said she was looking for me, what if she found me? What if it was her who did the note? What if she went into hospital and pulled the plug or something?"

"She's out on bail, but only since this afternoon. Antony died of natural causes; he wasn't killed by anybody."

"What have you got on her? On my mum."

"She procured the girl for your dad. We're throwing the book at her, but after the way she's been treated by your father I don't think much will come of it."

Julia shook her head, her face reddening as the alcohol flowed through her. "She deserved every beating she got, she's a witch. She's the ringleader in this, I know she is."

She had downed the drink with a wince and was now pouring her fourth. The bottle was half empty already, and they hadn't been in the flat more than twenty minutes. Thirsk was tired, and he was miffed at throwing another ten pounds at the addictive woman in front of him. He snatched the bottle, screwed the lid on tightly, and put it out of her reach on the floor beside his chair. "Julia, you're talking in riddles. Either tell me what's going on, or I'm out of here."

Eyes watering, Julia grinned, her fleshy cheeks crumpling with unfamiliar laughter lines. "I've never told anyone this, Dad and Mum both said I'd be taken to prison and shot if I did. But Dad can't get me, and Mum won't have a chance. And if you lock me away for it, then it won't matter, and if you shoot me, it won't matter. I don't care about nobody, or nothing no more. My Ant's gone, and my Robbie's gone, so nothing matters no more."

Now she was opening up, Thirsk leant forward, enwrapped. He had a good idea of what she was about to reveal. "Robbie was your baby, wasn't he?" Julia nodded, her smile pensive. "Was he Jim's baby?"

She nodded again. "They said I killed him, but if I did, then I don't remember it. He was the most beautiful thing I'd ever seen, my Robbie. He was tiny, with tiny little fingers and tiny little toes, and a cute little button nose. It hurt when I had him, it was mental, but he was worth it, he was my little doll. I had him for three days, then one night I went to sleep and when I woke up he was gone, and I never saw him again.

"Well, when they told me I'd killed him and they had taken him away to protect me, I was scared, and they said that if I ever said a word about him the police would take me away and shoot me. So I didn't. Not until now, and you're the police so I'm telling you myself."

She drained the glass, and he was becoming concerned. "Julia, stop drinking, it's no good for you in the mood you're in."

She grinned ironically. "Then I saw it in the paper. It was my birthday; I was thirteen that day. I saw that Toni Fowler had found a baby's body in a tree in Black Park. There was a picture of her next to the tree."

The revelation eclipsed Thirsk's expectations of the conversation. Julia Collins, the mother they had been seeking for over a decade, was sitting in front of him and filling in the missing parts of the jigsaw that had haunted him for so long. "Baby Jane, I was the investigating officer."

Julia snorted derisively. "Fat lot of good you are then."

"So you guessed that your Robbie was the baby they had found, what happened then?"

"Pour me some more out and I'll tell you."

Thirsk growled as he retrieved the bottle and tipped a small amount into her glass, topping it up with a long measure of tonic water. "Bloody blackmail, this is. That's your last one. And drink it slowly, no more knocking it back or I'll leave. With the bottle."

Julia took a sip, savouring it sarcastically, her eyes provocative. "The thing is, it wasn't because it was my

251

birthday that upset me, it was because of where they'd put him. Mum knew that was my favourite place in the whole world, she used to tease me about it. I used to cycle down there when I bunked off school, leave my bike by the tree and climb in. It was nice and dark, and so quiet, and nobody else could fit in, so it was my place where I could get away from everybody."

"So you think they took him there to spite you, a direct dig at you?"

She was firm. "Yes, I do. It was the nastiest thing I'd ever known. I went straight to the social services and told them I'd kill myself if they ever took me back."

"Why didn't you just go to the police? You knew we were looking for the mother."

"Because they said you lot would shoot me," she said meekly.

"Do you think you killed Robbie, like they told you?"

"No, I mean, I don't know. I'd never have done it deliberately, I loved him so much. It broke my heart when I found him gone. He was mine, my little doll."

"Do you think they killed him?"

"I don't know. All I know is that I'm glad I told you, it's a relief." She grinned, her eyes watering as tears began to spill, and he felt an ominous chill. She stood, shaky for a second, and grabbed the bottle from beside the chair before he could stop her. "Come with me, I've got something to show you." Uncomfortable, he followed her lead to the front door, watching as she unlocked it and stepped into the icy air that chilled the balcony. Suddenly she was hurtling away from him, along the ledge towards the stairs. Trotting after her, he was annoyed.

Instead of heading downstairs as he had expected, Julia nimbly climbed the stairs, and he quickened his pace, adrenaline fuelling the overwhelming suspicion that something dreadful was about to happen. Although she was a chubby girl and had sampled too much alcohol in such a short time, she swiftly outran him, up the final staircase and bursting through

252

the fire door. She climbed the metal steps onto the roof and ran towards the edge, stopping to taunt her pursuer as he puffed after her. As he reached the top she threw the bottle to her lips and swigged, gulping, the clear liquid spilling from the sides of her mouth and down her cheeks onto her hoodie. "I don't believe in God, mister. They hammered it into me, told me I'd go to Hell, but there ain't no Heaven and there ain't no Hell, and I'm just going to be with my two boys. That's my heaven."

His intuition had been right, the situation was precarious, and he was desperate to close on her, near enough to grab her if she were to do anything silly. Julia teetered by the wall that shielded her from the six-floor drop, hungrily draining the bottle. He crept stealthily towards her. "Nor do I, I think it's all a far-fetched fairy tale."

"Everything when I was a kid, it was all about Him, and that if I wasn't good enough, it'd make Mother Mary sad. She said that every day I made Mother Mary sad, and I really tried to be good, I really did. They wouldn't let me go, but then when all the pains started, and I felt like I was breaking in two, and then he was gone, and I loved him, he was mine."

"Come on, Julia, let's get you back inside where it's warm. Come on, love," he couldn't believe he had just called her that, "it's the drink talking."

"They told me that if I ever said anything to anybody, ever, they said I'd go to jail because I murdered him. I didn't think I had, but they told me never to say a word."

His heart pumped wildly as he skulked closer, feeling far too old for such dramatic scenes. "Come on, Julia, you can tell me all this indoors, it's cold up here."

"So there it is, my big secret. You've got what you want from me. Promise me you'll dig him up and bury him with me and Antony, he belongs with his mum."

"Nobody's being buried, Julia, just come here and stop being daft." With a hefty gulp, she finished the bottle, staggering haphazardly, and he inched closer. "You don't need to do this." Thirsk dived forward, "Julia, no," grasping desperately to catch something – anything – that might hold her back, but he was too far away. And she was gone.

Chapter 25
A New Home

After the embarrassing altercation with her mother, Toni had left Colin and her brother, Leon, to bring the rest of the boxes from her old bedroom, sitting in the front of the car with a face like thunder. Meanwhile, in St Martin's Place, Pam had prepared a meal and it smelt delicious. Her mother had taken the children for the night to give the hassled couple a chance to spend time together, so there was no hurry to get home; they could even camp overnight on the floor if need be, not that either intended to.

Finally, at quarter past ten, Colin followed Toni up the stairs with the last box and they sagged to the floor of the living room, exhausted. "Are you two ready for some grub?" Pam checked the pan, turning it low, and gave the homely kitchen a once over, fridge and cupboards no longer bare. She took the chilled wine to the living room. "I've done bolognaise, let me know when you're ready and I'll serve it. Here." She passed the bottle to Toni and indicated the glasses on the windowsill. "I think we all could do with a glass of this, don't you? Happy housewarming."

Toni hugged her, patting her back. "You're too good to me, Pam. You pour it though, I'm bushed. And I'm bloody pleased as punch to be out of that place."

Pam laughed. "I take it your mum wasn't too happy?"

Toni raised an eyebrow to Colin. "You didn't tell her everything, did you?"

"Moi?" He feigned offence. "As if I'd do such a thing."

Toni relayed the excruciating display to her closest friend, and Pam gasped. She couldn't, however, contain a giggle at the news of her former boss in a love triangle with Toni's mother. "What could she possibly have seen in him?"

"I know, and then she has the audacity to suggest that I'm at it with him too. I'm so pleased to be away, I don't think I could have coped with it there any longer, it was driving me nuts." Her mobile, still in her workbag, trilled and she retrieved it, checking the display. "Talk of the devil, it's him now." She dropped the mobile on the floor and took the bottle to the window, loosening the top.

"Aren't you going to answer it?"

"Fuck off, am I. He's not my boss any more, he can call all he likes, but I'm not picking up. Stupid old man." Toni poured three drinks and handed two out, raising the third to the air. "To my new flat, to my new life, and to peace and quiet." They laughed and toasted her sincerely.

Ten minutes later, drinks half supped, they were tiring of Thirsk's repeated calls, and Toni turned her mobile off to avoid further interruption. Colin un-tucked the flaps of a box, grinning widely. "Come on, let's get the stereo set up. No kids, a few drinks – I can feel a party coming on."

Thirsk had sat in his car for an hour, chain-smoking. He couldn't clear his head, buzzing with truths, wishes and should haves. If onlys. Unusually, he was flummoxed. Did she do it because of the drink? Was it his fault? He had nearly caught the edge of her hoodie as she went, scrabbling over the wall, clambering over the edge to nothing, but his fingers had brushed the material and hadn't managed to grasp. He hadn't looked down after, he'd not needed to. But on hearing the echoing, crunching thud he had come to his senses, hurling himself down the six flights of stairs in the vain hope he may find her clutching to life. But when he saw her head, bloodied against the hard concrete, broken, her body distorted and spent, he had known it was futile. Julia Collins was dead.

He had heard the sirens in the distance as his colleagues responded to his call for help, but he didn't give further details as they would see for themselves soon enough. Without forethought, Thirsk reached into the pocket of the hoodie and withdrew the two snaps she had taken from the collection she had shown him, shoving them in his pocket without looking.

He had waited on the pavement, shaken, as paramedics checked for vitals, an ambulance took the body, officers took statements from anybody who had seen anything, and he had issued a concise statement himself, but the senselessness of her death was too much for him to struggle with alone. There was only one person in the world he could imagine would understand, and she wasn't answering her phone.

Having run out of cigarettes, and in need of a strong drink, Thirsk mooched to the shop where he had bought the gin for Julia earlier. A huddle of women gossiped eagerly at the counter and he didn't need to guess what the subject would be. He ordered forty cigarettes and a bottle of whisky. The cashier, her eyes glinting with excitement, mentioned the suicide, and he chucked the items into a bag without a word. As he left the store, Steadman, who had heard of his call for help on the radio, fell into step with him and laid a soothing hand on his shoulder. "Are you okay, Guv?"

He nodded, anguished. "I'll have a good drink tonight, I think. The report can wait until tomorrow morning." He stopped and tore the cellophane from a packet of cigarettes, lighting one, inhaling deeply. "I tried to grab her, you know. My hand was right there, right by her, but I missed. I could have stopped her, but I missed."

"Do you want me to drive you home, you look pretty shaken."

He shook his head. "No, thanks, but there is something you could do for me. Can you try Toni's number for me on your phone, she's not answering my calls? I need to see her."

Steadman withdrew her hand as if she had been burned. "You really are one insensitive bloody bastard, aren't you, Richard Thirsk? You haven't seen what's been in front of your eyes for years, and now you bloody flaunt her right underneath my eyes. Go to your bloody little girl, I've had it with you."

She strode away and Thirsk's brow furrowed with confusion. "What?" He shook his head; he had never, and would never, understand women, and he wasn't even sure if he wanted to any more. Slowly, aimlessly, he sauntered to his car and sat once more in the driver's seat, trying Toni's number again without success. Nothing.

257

The drink was tempting but he still had to drive. He remembered the photos he had taken from Julia's body and took them from his pocket. One was of Antony, all smiles and copious dribble, and the other was a baby who could have been Antony, but the image was dated, crumpled and ragged at the edges from over-handling. The child must be Robbie, the baby he had known as Jane, and now he could put a face to the corpse that had plagued him over the years.

Minutes passed as Thirsk gazed at the treasured picture, imprinting the crinkled, newborn features into his memory. Eventually he tried Toni's number again with the same result, and cursed as he slammed the door and put the key in the ignition. But before turning it, he noticed some writing on the back of the photo: *Toni Fowler* was scribbled at the top, and *Tony* underneath, scored out in thick pen, and at the bottom was *Antony* followed by a tick. Had she chosen her son's name in honour of the girl who had found her first borne? Toni needed to know the unfathomable developments and he tried her number, again without a result. Why wasn't she answering?

Thirsk started the car and manoeuvred through the estate and was about to head for his apartment when he gave Toni's number a final try. This time, the message told him the mobile he was trying to reach was unavailable, and he guessed she had turned it off. How dare she, the arrogant upstart. Something inside him flipped and he turned right instead, aiming for her parents' house.

Toni's teenage sister opened the door and informed him Toni had moved out. It was becoming a farce and he was fed up. "For god's sake. Where has she gone? What's her new address?"

"I don't know, she never told me. Dad might know. Dad." Dan had come in from the garden when the light failed and was in the kitchen, preparing himself a sandwich in the absence of the dinner his wife – his adulterous and drunken wife – would normally have prepared had she not taken to the bottle. He shouted that he would be through in a minute. "So, what's it like having both a mother and daughter? Bit weird, don't you think?" Maisie's sole purpose in life was to stir up trouble and she tittered at his discomfort.

Then came a flash, and intense pain. Thirsk didn't know what had happened. First there had been the face of a man he vaguely recognised, then something had been shouted, and then a dazzling bright light. The next thing he knew, he was flailing on the path, grasping the eye that throbbed as if it had been stabbed. Suddenly the man towered over him, fists clenched and waving wildly. "If you ever so much as come near my wife again, I'll kill you."

"What? What's going on? All I want is to know Toni's new address?"

Another blow rained on him, knocking him flat on his back, and Leon, watching from the hallway, winced, full of admiration for his father's hidden talents. As Dan stormed inside, dusting his hands, Leon stepped outside and knelt beside Thirsk, helping him to raise his shoulders from the ground. "Are you okay?" Frowning, his jaw and eye smarting, Thirsk nodded. "It might be a good idea if you go. Dad found out you had an affair with Mum, so I don't really think you're welcome round here."

"I need to see Toni."

Maisie had collected her pumps and joined them in the front garden, waving excitedly at the neighbours who were peeping through their curtains. "Mate, if she hasn't given you her address, then it doesn't look like she wants to see you either. Not your day, really, is it?"

Thirsk had managed to sit up, his hand clenching his aching cheek, his eye throbbing and reddening. "I really need to see her. It's important, please. It's about the Baby Jane case."

Maisie sighed elaborately with a pantomime roll of her eyes. "Is that what you crazy oldies are calling it nowadays? I don't know! Leon, have you got her new address? I know she'll have given it to you."

Leon nodded, checking the door to ensure they weren't being watched. "Don't tell Mum. Or Dad, I don't fancy a shiner like that." He dragged his mobile from his pocket and tapped on the keypad, before showing the display to Thirsk, whose thudding head memorised it. "Don't come back, I don't like seeing Mum and Dad arguing."

Toni kissed her friends on their cheeks, thanking them for the wonderful welcome to her new home, and gratefully closed the door behind them. She had enjoyed a couple of drinks and the meal was delicious, but it was definitely time for bed. She traipsed into the bedroom, the un-curtained window allowing the cold moonlight to bathe the room in an eerie hue, and switched on the light, shuddering a little at the spookiness of the arched, ancient windows against the blackness of the sky.

Colin had bought a cheap, single airbed from a supermarket, which came with its own pump, and set it up for her, with Pam fussing over the covers in her motherly way, and Toni was relieved that they had. It looked so welcoming. She stripped off and took some pyjamas from the small suitcase her parents had bought her before she had gone on a school exchange trip to France, dragging them on. She switched off the light and settled down, closing her eyes to wait for sleep. Moments later the buzzer to her flat sounded and she swore. "Bloody hell, Pam, what have you left behind this time?"

Pressing the intercom, she tried a weak smile to brighten her fatigued voice. "Are you coming up or shall I bring whatever it is down to you?" In the absence of a reply, she pressed the button to unlock the main door. Two minutes later Thirsk was at the door and she was furious. "What the fuck do you think you're doing here? Fuck off."

"Toni, don't. It's Julia, she's dead. She killed herself."

She gasped, stunned, and without a word moved aside to let him pass. He followed her to the furniture-less living room and they stood in silence. Eventually she took the bottle of whisky from his hand and, surprised to note it was unopened considering the state of him, set it on the stone windowsill.

She pointed to the floor and trotted into the kitchen. "Go and sit down, it'll have to be on the floor. I'll get you a glass."

Knees creaking, Thirsk sat awkwardly on the carpet. "Bring two, you're going to need it." He lay back on his elbows, head aching and sore.

"What happened to you, anyway, your face is black and blue?"

"That's a long story. Hurry up, you really need to hear what I've got to say." She came through with a glass and poured Thirsk a drink, before sitting across the room from him. "Julia was Baby Jane's mother. Antony was named after you."

"You're fucking joking, right? I mean, sorry, my…"

"Mum, yeah, I know." Taking a gulp, he ploughed into the story of how Julia had come to throw herself from her block of flats, ready and eager to face her death, to be laid to rest with the sons she adored in her arms. Taking the two pictures, stolen from the dead woman, he tossed them across the room to Toni, who was speechless. "I think the older photo is Baby Jane, except he was really Baby Robbie. The other must be Antony."

"Yes, that's Antony. But Jane was a girl."

"That was never formal, it was a nod to you, as that's what you'd called her when you found her. The post mortem didn't reveal the sex of the baby."

"She was in a Broderie Anglaise dress, though."

"Think about it, Jim and Maria never told anyone she was expecting, she was kept indoors, no doctors, no hospital, nothing. They're hardly going to go out and buy blue baby clothes, are they. They must have used the stuff they had left over from when Julia was a newborn."

"Fuck me, this is weird. All those years I wanted to find Jane's mum, and then I've been talking to her without knowing. Did Julia kill Jane, well, Robbie?"

"I'm pretty certain she didn't, but they'll never fund an investigation now Julia's dead, there would be no point."

"Sir, that's just bollocks and you know it. If she didn't kill him, then you know who probably did, and he could stand trial for it, Julia could get some justice."

Thirsk reached for the bottle of whisky and poured himself a large measure, before offering it to Toni, who refused. He dragged his cigarettes from his pocket. "Not in here, you don't. My place is non-smoking."

"Fuck you." He put them back inside his coat. "Can I be honest with you, Toni?"

"That sounds ominous."

"I believe Jim Collins. I don't think he murdered Melissa."

When Sean had been released from the cells the day before, he had set the wheels in motion for his relocation to the town he had never visited, but his family originated from. He had decided years before that should his and Jim's illegal activities be busted, he would not keep to their agreement, would deny any involvement and see his brother-in-law sent down, taking all the blame with him. His impeccable reputation and affable personality would ensure there was no doubt to his story, but he realised there would always be a smidgeon of suspicion to some. He had no intention of stopping his hobby; he enjoyed it too much. So if relocating to another area was what he had to do, that was what he would do.

An organised man, he had taken notes over the years, a manual of everything that would need doing to see the move run smoothly should this day ever come, and now it had, he had followed the instructions. Every waking moment from his return home had been spent packing, arranging, buying tickets, checking timetables, and he had even shown an estate agent around the house, taking photos, for it to be placed on the market immediately. He had also paid Maria's bail and collected her from the magistrate's court.

It had been a hectic twenty-four hours, but the excitement of the new life he was about to discover made the mayhem worthwhile. The flight was booked and was due to leave in the early hours. A fellow churchgoer, whom he trusted implicitly, had agreed to pick his car up from the airport within the next couple of days to sell, and would forward the proceeds to his bank account. A house-clearance firm would take the belongings he didn't want to sell in their second-hand shop.

He had a final cup of tea in the home he had lived in for twenty-three years and, after rinsing the cup under the cold tap, took the three suitcases from the hallway to his car and loaded them in the boot. With a deep sigh, he closed the door, unhooking the sign that heralded 'Laus Deo' in vibrant colours and tucking it into the side pocket of a suitcase, before settling into the driver's seat to begin the long drive to Birmingham Airport for the last minute flight to Dublin.

Losing sight of the house when he rounded the corner, Sean was free of the recent stress and fear, and he relished the wonderful adventure he had begun.

Joyce Frobisher was having a rare night out, a black tie event at an opulent hotel hosted by the Mayor, yet was desperate to make her excuses and go home, snuggle under the covers of her warm bed with a good book. It was a prominent occasion, however, and to be the first to leave would be regarded as a slight.

But when a frighteningly young-looking waiter notified her of a phone call, the tiresome evening became intriguing. She excused herself from the group, grateful to leave the mindless small talk, and hurried to the reception desk. "Doctor Frobisher, can I help you?" Her shoulders sagged when she heard the voice. "Oh, it's you. What do you want, Richard?"

"Joyce, we need to call a truce for one night. There have been some massive developments and I could really," his teeth grated and he grimaced, "do with your help. Can you make it down to the station?"

"How did you know where I was? And have you any idea how late it is? I'm at a function, for heaven's sake."

"I knew you were invited because I was invited too, I just chose not to attend such pompous crap." *If he had, would Julia still be alive?* "Anyway, you know damn well you're hating it. Now I'm giving you an escape route."

"Actually, I was having a wild time, seeing as you ask." She was aching to go, leave the drab people in luxurious surroundings to their meaningless, self-important chat, but making Thirsk squirm gave her pleasure.

"Joyce, please, not tonight."

Joyce mouthed 'work' to her curious husband, who had sidled beside her. "Wow, this must be serious." The concern in her voice was genuine. "Okay, tell me what it's about."

"Baby Jane. I think I know who her killer was, but I need you to tell me if I'm being ridiculous."

She was about to fall into the expected 'you're always ridiculous' trap, but stopped herself. There was something about his tone that she had not heard before, a vulnerability, a child begging for a protective cuddle. She had never known him to be emotionally affected by a case and it came as a surprise. "Where are you? I'll come and meet you."

"No, I'm at Toni's and she's asleep, can you meet me at the station?"

'It's not my business to judge him' – she mentally repeated the mantra to stop herself speaking, annoyed that he had taken advantage of Toni's crush on him. "Right," she said tersely, "I'll be as quick as I can."

Joyce ended the call and briefly explained the developments to her husband, who was also grateful for the get-out clause. He grinned and leant across the reception desk, flicking his fingers. "Please, would you arrange for a taxi for my wife." And to Joyce, "I'll take the car home. Get Thirsk to bring you home when he's finished with you. Enjoy yourself."

Shocked and disheartened by the news, Toni had gone to bed, needing to cry but not wanting to show weakness. Thirsk's head was in a mess, thoughts buzzing, and although he had tried to blot them out with alcohol, he wanted company, and

Joyce was the only person other than Toni who would understand the frustration. He left a note on the worktop of the state-of-the-art kitchen telling her he would call tomorrow and headed back to Castle Street, despite three glasses of whisky leaving him over the limit to drive.

The reception area was heaving with the usual Friday night mayhem, with drunken and bloodied revellers shouting, abusing, complaining, but the offices upstairs were peaceful graveyards. Thirsk busied himself by organising the notes on Baby Jane, Julia, Maria, Jim and Sean on his desk while he waited for Joyce to arrive.

Just past midnight, she let herself into his room without knocking. Thirsk glanced up briefly, then did a double take. "Frobisher. You scrub up well. You look," he was going to say fantastic but controlled himself, "alright."

She strode over, statuesque and stunning in the dress that had been masterfully tailored by her housekeeper, whose dressmaking skills were in high demand. "Have you been doing a few rounds with Mike Tyson? Your face is in a dreadful state." She wrinkled her nose and waggled her hand. "And how much have you had to drink, it smells like a brewery in here? Did you drive?"

Thirsk raised a scabbed eyebrow. "Then get me a coffee if you want me to sober up."

She snorted with derision. "You should be ashamed of yourself, you silly man. So, are you going to tell me what is so important that it can't wait for tomorrow morning?"

"You'd better sit down and I'll start at the beginning."

He told her of the suicide, of Julia's painfully young, incestuous pregnancy, and of the baby's disappearance from the family, and she listened without interruption, intrigued. When he had finished, she asked, "So was baby Robbie murdered and dumped, or was he dumped alive and died subsequently? Or did he die of natural causes and they dumped him?"

"If we can find out who dumped him, we may get an answer to that."

"And you think the father would be too simple?"

"I think it was Maria, Julia's mother."

"Interesting. Tell me why."

Thirsk leant forward to stress the point. "Julia told me that the old yew tree was her favourite spot in the world, it was her bolt-hole, her safe haven. If she had dumped him there, it would have been an act of love and kindness. But she didn't, so whoever dumped her beloved baby there did so out of maliciousness – revenge – and that can only exist in a female mind. Men just don't think like that," he remembered her high qualifications in psychiatry and added, "in my opinion." He brought an energy drink from his drawer and hungrily glugged it.

"Yes, I think you're right." Thirsk choked on his mouthful, fully expecting an argument. "And Melissa? Is there a link?"

"I'm asking you that, that's why you're here. Maria's just been bailed, and I've nothing but gut instinct to go on. The murder is another inspector's case so I'll be strung up if I go hassling her on a hunch. I need you to tell me what you think. Here," he chucked Maria's notes across the table, which included the details of the investigation and the transcripts of her interviews, "read those. Tell me I'm not crazy."

Again, the opening for a lame joke was ignored, and she immersed herself in the files, analysing every word. Eventually she closed the cover and put the notes on the desk, regarding her enemy. "You don't think Jim Collins killed Melissa either, do you? You think Maria killed the child and dumped her."

"The evidence they have on Jim is circumstantial, and backed up – or cemented by – statements from his adulterous wife and her brother, the man she's knocking off. It's an ideal way to get Jim out of the picture. Isn't it?" Thirsk shook his head, fuddled, uncharacteristically needing reassurance that he wasn't insane.

"Maria obviously has a deep hatred, a destructive jealousy, for her daughter. She resents that she became pregnant with her, and has seen her as a sexual threat from an early age. Then her daughter does the unthinkable: she dares to get pregnant with her father."

"Come on, that wasn't her fault, damn it."

"Shut up, Richard, I'm trying to stress it from Maria's point of view. So when the baby is born, she hates the latest rival for her affections, and she wants to seek vengeance on the daughter too. How better than killing the child and dumping it in the place that would hurt Julia the most? It's a masterstroke, a double whammy."

Thirsk never thought this moment would happen and his eyes were wide. "You agree with me?"

"Yes, I do. Strongly."

"Enough to warrant arresting her on suspicion?"

He wanted somebody's permission and she laughed at the attempt to defer responsibility. "I've never been a police officer, it's not for me to say, but the one thing I will say is that I think you need to get some sleep, you'll feel more rational in the morning. Julia's death has obviously had a huge impact on you, and unsurprisingly so. Look," Joyce wasn't used to treating Thirsk kindly, and he was equally uncomfortable with the conversation, "if you do decide to bring her in, I'll be happy to sit in on the interview and give my opinion, if you think that would help."

"Now?" He was eager again, the tiredness forgotten.

She scooped her shawl over her shoulders, chuckling as she stood. "Don't be so ridiculous, I'm off home to bed. Goodnight, Richard."

"Joyce, please don't go. I need to know that I'm on the right track and you're the only person who can help me. Really, all things aside."

She sighed and sat back down, surprised at his honesty. "Why is this so important to you?" He shrugged. "You never tie yourself to anything emotionally, what's so different here?" He shrugged again. "It's like drawing blood out of a stone with you. Right, I'll tell you why. You didn't care about Julia, may have been sorry for her, yes, but realistically she was just another troubled mother that you've become used to meeting through your work. You didn't care so much about the Baby Jane case, you had no qualms about it being left unsolved. Until you met Toni and realised who she was."

"Bollocks, you're seeing something that isn't there."

"No, what I thought I was seeing wasn't there, but something else has come into play here, hasn't it? You have an affinity for Toni, but not as a lover. She's like the daughter you never had. You want to solve this case because you want to please her, you know it's her dream to see the baby identified and buried with dignity."

"Total and utter shit, that is." The statement had slapped him on both cheeks, and he realised her incredible deduction was right. "Total bollocks."

"So, now we've established that, let's work together to give her the answers she's seeking." She rested back in the chair, making herself comfortable, and he glared at the table, annoyed with her perception. "We can start by placing ourselves in Maria's shoes. Let's go back to over ten years ago when she realised her daughter was expecting her husband's child. She's horrified, but realises she should have expected it; the girl is menstruating, a child in a woman's body, and she knows she can only blame herself for not ensuring her daughter was protected."

He held his finger up to stop her. "No, she despised Julia, she wouldn't want to protect her."

"I don't mean like that. She would have berated herself for not having put Julia on the pill, or suchlike. So, in her own best interests, Maria has ensured that nobody knows her daughter is pregnant, she's shunned the social services, the doctors, concealed the impending birth from everybody."

"Does Jim know?"

Joyce shook her head. "I don't know but, more importantly, would he care? For Maria this is deeply emotional, her ideas are warped, and she sees the newborn child as a threat. Does she murder it? Let's see how we feel when we've acted this out. So, it's late at night, and she takes the baby from her daughter's room while she's asleep – we have no idea if he's dead or alive – and drives to Black Park. She takes the child to the tree and dumps him inside, sure that if he was ever found her daughter would know exactly who the child was. It's a vicious attempt to hurt Julia, an act of revenge."

"That all seems believable, but we can't prove it without an admission and she won't do that. With Julia dead, the case is nothing. What I need to know is if she could be involved in Melissa's death. Jim swears blind that he left her alive, and that he has no idea how she ended up in Black Park."

"This Jim, has he abducted girls before?"

"If each one was documented on the website, then Melissa was the sixth. We've had another girl give a statement saying something similar happened to her three years ago."

"Okay, so this horribly jealous woman knows that her husband has replaced his daughter in his affections with young girls, and if she raises any objections she's beaten for the pleasure. So her anger is now directed at the girls, just as it had been with Julia."

"That makes sense."

"Of course it does. She abducts Melissa, as she's admitted doing, and waits for her husband to abuse the girl. It's too much for her, something has triggered her, and she smothers the girl and drives the body to Black Park. This time she leaves it in the lake – to spite Jim, maybe? I'll bet anything that he has an affection for the lake."

"There's a problem with that, though, because Maria can't drive."

"Can't or won't? If she can't then she had help, and I'd look to the brother there, and if she won't, it doesn't mean she didn't."

"So I'll get someone to check with the DVLA tomorrow to see if she holds a licence."

"She might not even hold a licence, she's still capable of driving a car, exam passed or not."

They sat for a while, mulling over the scenario, and Thirsk, with his knowledge of the woman and her bitterness, felt sure they were on to something, that the missing pieces he had not been able to find had appeared and slotted into place. "You believe this is the way it happened, don't you?"

"Yes, I do. Are you going to follow this through?"

"If I do then I'm undermining Nick Wainwright; he's the officer who has investigated and charged Jim."

"Then it's his problem for not doing his job thoroughly enough. I know I'm old and retired, but if you want my help I'm here, and I'll bet Toni will be too. I think the three of us need this final push to find justice for Baby Jane."

"Baby Robbie."

"I've known the case as Baby Jane for ten years, Richard, I'm not about to rename it now. Anyway," she checked her watch and grimaced, "I'm off home, it's far too late for me to be up. Let me know if I can do any more of your job for you, won't you?"

"Piss off, Frobisher."

Chapter 26
Persistence

Toni awoke, snuggled warmly in her covers, and the morning light, dry and crisp, beamed through the arched window. She sat up, stretching, with a wide yawn, and the dreadful news Thirsk had brought to her late the previous night came flooding back. She rubbed her eyes, recalling the details of the few words he had managed between gulps of whisky. She wondered if he was still on the carpet, sleeping where he had fallen in a drunken stupor, and steeled herself to leave the room, hoping he hadn't. She sighed with relief on finding him gone and went to the kitchen, filling the kettle for her morning mug of elderberry tea.

The intercom sounded and she groaned. "Damn you, Thirsk, how the fuck did you get my address anyway." She pressed the button on the box, not intending to let him in this time. "What?"

"It's me."

"Yeah, I knew it would be, you're like a bloody stalker. Anyway, it's the weekend and it's too early for visitors. Oh, plus the minor detail that I don't work for you any more, remember?"

"Toni, you can't work for me officially and that wasn't my decision, but as far I'm concerned you're the only person with the heart for this job. I know you'll understand when I say that I can't be happy just knowing Julia was the baby's mother and leaving it at that. I want to know if the baby was murdered, and if so, I want to see that person behind bars. I know it was Maria, and I want you to come with me to pick her up."

"Maria? Have I missed something?"

"I can fill you in with the developments on the way to her house."

"You're arresting her?"

271

"I'll talk to her and make the decision from there. Are you up for it?"

Toni's flat was littered with packed boxes, a multitude of jobs to do. "Give me a second to get dressed, I'll be down in a minute."

Toni ran into her bedroom and threw on a tracksuit and trainers that she found in the suitcase. She dragged a brush through her hair without finding a mirror and resolved to shower later. Ten years had been a long time to wait, and she wasn't about to miss the conclusion of Baby Jane's story. And it was more exciting than unpacking. She locked the door behind her and trotted down the stairs, through the communal entrance, and clambered into Thirsk's car. She gasped. "Mrs Frobisher, what are you doing here?"

"It sounded fun to me too, dear."

Quarter of an hour later they drew up beside Jim and Maria's house in Moor End, and walked along the untidy drive to the front door. Thirsk knocked and they waited. He rapped again, this time a little concerned. "Could she be at her brother's house?"

Thirsk nodded to Toni. "Go and see, we'll stay here and keep trying."

A feeling of doom was descending over him; the house was too quiet, too still. He hammered again, harder and louder, while Toni trotted along the street towards Sean's house. She turned back before she got there and shouted. "Did you know he's put the house for sale?"

"You're fucking joking." Thirsk was already running towards the car, followed by the slower Doctor Frobisher. "They've only done a fucking runner. Get in the car, we've got to find them."

The atmosphere in the Fowler household was dour following the previous night's mind-blowing revelations. Dan had slept on the sofa, unwilling to join his adulterous wife in bed, regardless that it had been ten years since she had strayed. He woke early and prepared a mug of tea, taking it to the haven of his greenhouse to drink while the air was still fresh and invigorating. Hungover and dishevelled, Carol entered the kitchen as the back door closed, and through the window she watched her husband trudge along the path. Why had Thirsk had to reappear in their lives and cause trouble? Even a decade before, she had realised the man was a walking time bomb, that doom and drama followed him like snarling dogs.

She filled the kettle and dropped a teabag into a mug, busying herself with everything and nothing. Her life was empty to the point of non-existence, a loveless marriage and kids with no respect for her. And her husband would be sulking for days, despite his part in the failing relationship. Dan wasn't a bad man and she loved him in a caring way, but the staleness of their union was numbing. Would there be something else if she ran away to search for it, or was she seeking greener grass that didn't exist. She wasn't sure.

Carol nursed the tea, wishing she were on a ship somewhere, mid ocean, away from life, struggles, arguments. Away from monotony. Was this really it? A childhood spent dreaming of marriage, children, of a two-point-four family that was respectable but not remarkable. She had wanted it all, and had got it from an early age, but the reality of the perfect family was so different to the dream. There was lead, not gold, at the end of her rainbow.

And now Toni was gone, her bed made but her belongings taken. And the circumstances of her departure were dire. And she realised she was in danger of losing her first borne altogether; the mere thought broke her heart.

She glanced at the clock and picked up the phone, hoping her daughter's friend, whom she knew to have young children, would be awake. "Pam, it's Carol, Toni's mum, I wondered if we could talk?"

Later, she sat neatly on the edge of the sofa in Pam and Colin's homely but messy living room, her head pounding from the screaming and whooping children, whose grandmother had gratefully returned them. Pam handed her a cup of tea and sat opposite. The two women had met on a few occasions over the past ten years and had always found each other likeable, but Pam was Toni's friend, and her allegiance was with her. She was sympathetic to the depressed mother, imagining how desolate she herself would feel when her own lively brood left home, but she was confident Toni had made the right decision. It was her turn to fly.

Pam diplomatically explained how necessary it was for Carol to allow Toni to grow into the adult she was, and how proud she should be to have raised such a generous and free spirit. The different perspective helped the older woman greatly and the discussion was pleasant and constructive. After a further cup of tea, Pam saw no harm in passing Toni's address to her mother, who assured her she would not cause trouble.

The conversation was coming to a natural conclusion when the local news caught the attention of both women. "A young mother has jumped to her death from the sixth floor roof of the block of flats where she lived, in Canal Estate, Kendrick. She is believed to be the daughter of a man who is currently in custody regarding the murder of six-year old Melissa Barton, whose body was found in the lake of local nature reserve, Black Park. Jim Collins, aged fifty-five, of Moor End, and…"

An image of Jim's face filled the screen, the first time it had been televised, and Carol gasped. "Dim Jim Collins, never."

"You know him?"

"I did once. He was the floor assistant at the factory before I started, a right old so and so, he was. I don't mind admitting that it doesn't surprise me if he was involved in Melissa's death, he was always a funny sort. So his daughter has killed herself."

"That's what they said; suicide, poor thing."

"Unless he's got more than one daughter, I knew her too. She used to hang about the factory when it was his home time, scruffy little thing, quiet. Wouldn't say boo to a goose. What a dreadful shame."

"Your Toni's part of the investigation into Melissa's murder, did she tell you? That's why she was brought up to work with Thirsk."

Carol's face filled with indignation, her lips pursed. "Is that the excuse he gave?"

"What, Thirsk? What do you mean?"

"I'll have you know that that disgusting old pervert is having relations with my daughter. He's old enough to be her grandfather."

Pam laughed. "Don't be so daft, of course he's not. If there's anyone who's got the hots for our Toni, it's Nick."

"You what? You mean there's nothing going on between her and *him*?"

"Of course not. As far as I've ever known Thirsk lost the love of his life, and nobody knows how, and vowed never to replace her. He's off limits to everybody. Nick says he gets his fair share of admirers and he doesn't notice it a bit. Anyway, Toni's tastes are a little, shall we say, younger."

Suddenly Carol could cope with everything, the blip in her marriage, her daughter's exodus, the poor treatment she received from her children. The weight fell from her shoulders and she could breathe again. "I'm so relieved."

"I can't imagine why you ever thought such a thing."

"Go on then, tell me about this Nick, is marriage on the cards? What's he like? Are they going out?"

Pam chuckled, amazed at the about turn. "Nick Wainwright, we used to be colleagues before I left to have kids, but we've kept in touch. He's, what, must be about mid-thirties, and pretty handsome, in a classic sense. Not my type, I must add." She winked, nodding at the photo of her black bear of a husband. "Nick has burned a candle for Toni since day one."

"Is he moving in with her?"

"No, I don't think she's even noticed him. She's living alone and I think that's how she wants it. Why don't you pop by later? Perhaps you two can kiss and make up, I'm sure she would like that. Tell her you used to know that girl, the one who committed suicide, it might interest her, and I know that she's always wanted you to have more interest in her work. I also know she's really into this case she's working on."

They said their goodbyes and Carol headed for the main road, hoping to catch the next bus home. As an afterthought she turned back, catching Pam just before she closed the door. "Richard Thirsk?"

"Ha ha, I never knew he was called Richard. What about him?"

"Do you know when he lost the love of his life?"

"I don't know. I've known him twelve years and I've never seen him chasing candy."

Carol could have wept, but instead she strode away, head high, knowing she had a marriage to fix in the absence of anything remotely more exciting.

Maria and Sean checked their luggage in as soon as they arrived at the airport. They had some fast-food and a nerve-settling drink in the bar, and made their way through customs – a regular couple of a certain age taking a jaunt to the Emerald Isle, be it for pleasure, work or family visit. They blended into the crowd without a hitch.

They wasted time browsing the shops, looking at the alcohol, the tobacco, sniffing the perfumes and aftershaves with no intention of purchasing anything, and soon the boarding gate appeared on the screen. Hand in hand, they strolled to the waiting aeroplane, another step towards their freedom to live as a couple, without prejudice, and without police intervention. Along the concertina corridor, they showed their boarding passes and were directed to their seats over the left wing. Patiently, they waited for the plane to move.

Take-off was seamless and Sean slept easily for most of the journey, but Maria was a nervous traveller and worried unreasonably, despite Sean's reassuring words and cuddles. After landing in Ireland, they caught a train to Cork, and took a bus south to Summer Cove where a childhood friend of

Sean's, who had moved there with his family sixteen years before, was expecting them.

Ennis drove them the short distance to his home, welcoming them, with his wife, into the quaint stone cottage that overlooked the bay. After the long, busy night, Sean and Maria melted gratefully into the sofa, cuddling together like needy children. "So, are you going to tell me what's going on, Sean?"

"There's nothing to tell, really there isn't. Myself and my lovely wife decided we needed a holiday, and here we are." Ennis smiled, pleased that his friend had finally found love. "Are you sure you're okay to put us up for a couple of weeks if need be?" It would take time to find somewhere for them to live, not that he could tell his friend that.

"Of course, anything for you Sean, you know that."

Thirsk parked the car and jumped out, rushing into the station, his passengers forgotten and the car unlocked. He took the steps two at a time, his urgency too great to wait for the lift, and was gasping for breath by the time he reached the fifth floor. Wainwright had been waiting for him and blocked his way. "What's this I've heard about you going after Maria? If you doubted my case then you should have talked to me, not..."

"Not now." Thirsk had inadvertently shouted and was ashamed. "Nick, I need your help on this one, I'll explain later."

"Thirsk, I'm not your deputy any more, you..."

"I'll fucking explain later. Right now, Maria Collins is gallivanting about to god knows where and I want everybody available searching for her. Airports, ports, bus stations – wherever she's gone, I want her found. Set up a meeting with Jim, I want to see him as soon as possible."

The lift doors opened and Joyce alighted, just as Toni came up the stairs. Wainwright was in no mood to have his case doubted, especially as nobody had thought to tell him why, but he didn't want to cause a scene in front of the women and restrained the bubbling outburst. "Look, Guv, even you must understand that I need to know what's going on."

"Get on the blower, sort out a meeting with Jim, and I'll explain on the way. Frobisher, will you come in with us?"

"I'd be glad to."

"Do I get to come?" Toni was so excited with the unfolding drama and urgency; it was everything she had dreamed police work would be.

"No, you start checking the airports, see if you can find anyone who's had either Sean or Maria on board." Her face fell, but her presence at the interview with Jim was pointless.

The meeting with Jim was arranged quickly, but he refused to speak without Jason Averill's presence, and the delay frustrated impatient Thirsk. He used the time to explain the situation to Wainwright, who grudgingly accepted that his former boss had acted fairly. Eventually, they were informed Jim and Jason were in Interview Room 2.

"So, what do you fuckwits want this time? Ain't keeping me banged up for something I ain't done enough for you?"

Thirsk took a seat and leaned forward. "That's why we're here. Jim, do you think it's possible that Maria killed Melissa?"

Stunned, Jim stared at the table. "What's she been saying?"

"Did you know that she and Sean have done a moonlight flit?"

"Eh, what do you mean?"

"I believe they had a lot more to do with Melissa's death than they've told me. If you know something Jim, if you're protecting them, they don't deserve it, they've left you high and dry."

"But she's on bail, Mr Averill told me, didn't you?" His lawyer nodded.

"Where would they go?" Jim didn't answer, frowning with confusion. "Jim, you've sworn time and again that you didn't kill Melissa, that she was alive when you finished with her. I think Maria went in after you and killed her, and that she dumped the body at Black Park, possibly with Sean's help. Stop protecting them. They've both been instrumental in putting you inside, leaving every scrap of blame on your shoulders. Why would you still want to cover their arses, it doesn't make sense?" Still nothing came. "Jim, your wife has left you, she's not by your side any more, she has set off somewhere for a new life, she's turned her nose up at you as if you're a bad smell."

"She's really gone and left me?"

"Yes, we're searching for her now."

"What difference will it make to my sentence if I tell you everything?"

Thirsk relaxed, he had broken the prisoner. "I don't think you'll get life if you tell the truth now." It was a lie – Jim's crimes were vile – but he was a desperate man.

Jim breathed deeply, steeling himself. "Everything I told you was true." Thirsk sighed, shoulders sagging despondently. "No, wait, just hear me out. Maria got the girl like we planned, and when she got her in the kitchen, she gave her a drink with Rohypnol in it, I've told you all that. You know that me and Sean took the kid to the lock-up and did stuff to her."

"Up until now we've not believed you that Sean was present, there's no evidence to place him there. Are you telling us the absolute truth?"

"I always have. Sean and me have done this a few times before and he was the one who got me in to it, not the other way around like you fuckers probably think. Anyway, we knew how much of the drug to give the kid, enough to keep her out of it while we did our thing, just enough that she had be waking up when it came to home time, and at ten to three we went back ready to drop her back at the school, like we'd always done. But when we got back she was dead."

"So you left Melissa asleep in the lock-up and when you returned she was dead?"

"What are you? A fucking parrot?" Jim bristled for a moment before continuing. "Well, as I was saying, we goes back to my place and we ask Maria, and at first she was saying that the girl must have got out somehow, but then I smacked her a couple of times and she told the truth. She told me she had gone in there and drugged her more, then put a pillow over her head and killed her. Well, we had to get rid of the kid, but then all hell broke loose on the street because they had reported her missing. Sean went back to his house, we was all going to stay at home, do our normal thing, until all the fuss died down. So, later, Sean goes back, and him and Maria went off with the kid's body. I didn't know where they was taking it, I didn't ask 'cos I didn't want to know, figured the less I knew the better. Anyway, you lot found the kid and here we are now."

The room was quiet. Jim had said his piece, Jason was in a state of shock, Wainwright and Joyce digested Jim's revelations, and Thirsk couldn't be sure they were true. He mouthed to Joyce: "Truth?" She nodded earnestly. "You'll still be on remand, Jim, you've committed a serious crime, but if your story checks out, we'll obviously see that the murder charges are dropped. But we need to find Maria. Does she have a favourite place, or family anywhere, anywhere you can think of that she had go to?"

He shook his head. "Can't think of nowhere. We ain't got family, we ain't hardly got no friends, no real friends, anyway. It was always just the three of us."

"Okay, let us know if you think of anything. Jim, I've got a couple more questions. First of all, has Maria ever learned to drive?" He asked merely out of curiosity now he knew that Sean had helped her to dump the body.

"Nah, she was too scared to learn. Why?"

"This might seem a little odd, but I want to know if you ever spent time at Black Park?"

Jim snickered, confused. "Well, yeah, but not for years. When I was still working, when I had a job, well, me and Maria used to take the little 'un down there for days out, and for a couple of months, before I lost my job, that is, I was going to the canoe club. It was something I always wanted to do, but then I lost my job and we didn't have the money no more, so I had to give up. Best days of my fucking life, they was." Joyce caught Thirsk's eyes and gave him an impertinent, gloating smile, and he rolled his eyes before smiling at her, mocking a bow. "Well? Is that it?"

"For now. We'll need you to make a formal statement about what you've told us, but just one more thing. We know that a baby found in Black Park ten years ago was Julia's child…"

"No, that's rubbish."

"Did Maria kill the baby?"

"I ain't got no clue what you're on about."

"No more lies, Jim, we're past that. We know that the body we found, the one we've always known as Baby Jane, was your son and your grandchild. I want you to tell me everything about what happened."

"Want away. I ain't saying nothing, there's nothing to say."

"Here we go again." Thirsk rose from the chair opposite Jim and began to pace; he had to stir his emotions somehow, catch him off guard. "Not only did Julia tell us that the child was yours, we have confirmed it using DNA comparisons." Another lie, but Jim wasn't to know that. "Julia said she woke up one morning and the baby was gone. What happened to him? What happened to little Robbie?"

"All I know is what Julia said, one morning he was gone. I always wondered when that baby was found if it was Robbie, but I never knew how he got there."

"You were the child's father, his grandfather, surely you wanted to know what had happened to him. You don't just have a baby one day and then think nothing of it when it disappears."

"Ask Julia, or Maria, they'll tell you I didn't give two shits about the noisy little brat, always wailing and howling and screaming. They could have made sure she didn't get pregnant in the first place, but, oh no, God forbid in Maria's fucking world that she give her daughter the fucking pill."

"But he was your child, that must have meant something."

"Jules is a slag, always has been. That kid could have been anybody's."

Joyce had been leaning on the wall and she stepped towards Jim, hands behind her back. "Tell me about the baby, was he healthy? Did you name him?"

"I didn't call him nothing, he was nothing to me. She shags around and gets herself up the duff. Have you any idea how difficult that time was? You know, when I realised she had a bun in the oven, shit, what was I supposed to do? I wouldn't have minded so much if she'd had a girl."

Thirsk couldn't stop himself. "I'll bet you wouldn't, you filthy bastard."

Joyce silenced him with a glare. "Jim, we've got Julia's childhood medical records and there's no mention of a pregnancy anywhere."

"We wasn't going to fucking tell anyone, was we? Social bloody services were over us like a rash because of Jules's attention seeking, and I didn't want them asking who the father was, did I? Anyway, Maria said she didn't need no doctor, she said she was fine."

Thirsk stood, memories hounding him – Julia's last words, reaching for her body as she fell, her smashed head on the pavement, blood everywhere – and he roared. "I'd say that a child of twelve, pregnant by her father and hated by her mother, was absolutely not *fine*. And I'd say that the fact she killed herself so violently last night is a good indication that she was never *fine* afterwards, either. How and where was the baby born, I want to know everything?"

Jim was silent, jaw hanging and eyes wide. He attempted to speak but uttered nonsense. Joyce glared sternly at Thirsk, who quietened, in control again. "You didn't know, did you?"

"Jules is dead?"

"That's why we need justice and truth for her child, it's a final gift to her."

Jim hung his head, clutching his chest with a fist, shoulders shaking. "She come to see me last night. She was okay last night. I saw her. She was fine."

"Would you like us to give you a minute, Jim? Perhaps we can get you a hot drink, or something?"

Jim raised his head, forlorn and broken. "She was fine."

Nobody spoke for several minutes. The resurging memories had disturbed Thirsk and the urgency seemed redundant now.

Eventually Jim stopped shaking, the pain easing from his face. "Let me get this straight. My wife and her brother have disappeared, leaving me to take the rap for something we was all involved in?"

"Yes."

"And now you want to pin the baby on me too." He was quiet for a moment. "We didn't call him nothing, at least I didn't, there was no time. If Jules said she called him Robbie, she never told me. Me and Maria was there when she had the kid, it was terrifying, she screamed and shouted in a way that Maria never did when she was having Jules. I thought she was going to die."

Thirsk would never experience the pain of childbirth, but he'd heard enough stories to be grateful he had never bestowed that pain on somebody he loved. However, a child in an adolescent body giving birth to a full-size baby must have been not only excruciating physically, but petrifying mentally. "Did she know she was having a baby?"

"She used to talk to it, tell it she loved it. I reckon she thought it was going to be a bloody teddy bear when it came out. We covered it up, Maria got her baggy clothes from jumble sales and her mates, and we stopped her going to school. Stopped that bloody social worker coming over too, nosy bitch."

"So Julia wanted the baby?"

"She couldn't keep it, we was struggling already, what with me being out of work and Maria having her panic attacks and all that. And I didn't want no brat in the house, screaming

283

and wailing, keeping us up all night. Anyway, he died three days after he was born, so the problem was over."

"How, Jim? How did the baby die?"

Jim, a bereft man, lonely in the knowledge that his wife and best friend had left him to shoulder the blame – and the prison sentence – was centre stage. His audience was silent, anticipating his mind-blowing performance, blackened against the glare of the spotlights that circled him. He willed tears from nowhere to emphasise his innocence. "Maria did it."

Chapter 27
Repent at Leisure

It had taken some courage, and maybe a degree of stupidity, but Carol somehow found herself on the bus taking her in the opposite direction of her home – and troubled marriage. The town centre was throbbing with Saturday shoppers, the repetitive chimes of canned music blaring through shop doors, plentiful displays of fireworks and Halloween costumes and props.

She had no idea what had come over her, but her life was a mess, a lonely journey of tedium, mediocrity and repetition, with no passion, excitement or change. If she had gone home, made a nice lunch to share with her husband while they had a sensible, adult conversation, they would have jumped the first hurdle of getting their marriage back on track. But today she was reckless and normality wasn't an option.

She rounded the corner into Castle Street, away from the city centre, and the police station loomed ahead. Her pace quickened.

Her husband. Dan was a good man. He had always supported them financially, never rich, but never wanting either. He was a brilliant father and had been from the start. The bulk of the childrearing had been on Carol's shoulders, but that had been her choice, and the fun times he had shared with the children in his kind and gentle manner had been a joy to watch. Carol hesitated when she reached the steps, but, throwing caution to the wind, she trotted up them, resolute, and asked at the desk for Thirsk.

She sat on a seat to wait and drifted back into her lonely world. Looking back, things had started to go stale after Maisie was born. They hadn't planned another child – Toni and Leon, one of each, had been perfect – but her contraception failed and she had been five months pregnant when a routine blood test revealed she was expecting. After Maisie's birth she had been too scared to have relations with Dan for fear of another baby, and after a couple of years, once the sparks of passion had disappeared, Toni had found the skeleton. And she had met Richard.

Carol shifted, the hard plastic seat as uncomfortable as the surroundings. Richard. He had been so handsome in a quirky way, and his job, his life – so exciting. Massively tall, with broad shoulders and a huggable paunch, and the wickedest eyes she had ever seen. She had thrown herself at him, finding any excuse possible to visit and entrap him under her womanly spell. He had not been easy to break, but a month after meeting, they began a torrid affair. It was wrong, but for the first time in years she had felt attractive, wanted, desired.

It hadn't taken long for things to sour. Carol had three young children and the factory job she still had, working for her husband, who had been climbing the management ladder at the time. She had realised quickly that Thirsk lived in a vortex, surrounded by the horrors he saw in his work, untouchable through the barriers that shielded him from emotion. In the week running up to Christmas, she had shamed herself by telling him she loved him. It hadn't been planned, and she hadn't known if it was true, she had simply wanted a reaction, good or bad. It had been bad; he had stopped phoning and avoided her calls. She had ploughed through the festivities, making exciting and joyous memories for the kids, and the kind love of her unwitting husband had dragged her back to the sanctity, safety, and security of their union.

Could she tolerate another thirty years or more of this banality? Thirsk came through the main doors, flanked by Wainwright and Joyce, and was surprised to see her. "Carol Fowler, what are you doing here?"

"We need to talk."

"I'm actually quite busy today."

"Not too busy for what I have to say. I need to see you in private, Richard."

He squirmed; why did these bloody women keep calling him that? And why was his past suddenly haunting him? "My office, I'll give you five minutes, but that's it."

Thirsk led Carol to the lift and pressed the button to the fifth floor before Joyce and Wainwright could join them, conscious of his privacy. "You know your husband thumped me last night, don't you?"

"He found out about you and me."

"Yes, I get that, but how did he…"

"I told him." Carol followed Thirsk into his office and sat where he indicated. He sat behind his desk, opposite. "Who was she, Richard? Was I really just nothing to you?"

"Who? What are you talking about? Carol, I haven't got time for this."

"The love you lost, that's who. You used me, you were never emotionally involved."

"Carol, it's been ten years. I know things are tough at home, god knows why you said anything to Dan, you should have let things stay in the past."

"It's been hard seeing you again, after all these years, and when I thought you… It doesn't matter. It just stirred everything up and made me realise how unhappy I am. Look, I know you hate kids, but mine are growing up now, they're not a problem any more."

"Carol, you've got to stop this. It's gone; there's nothing. Sort your marriage out and keep me out of it. What is it with you bloody women and your games?"

Carol stood, irate. She had a million truths she wanted to shove down his throat, how insular he was, how emotionless, how his job had destroyed any inkling of compassion he may once have had. Using the extent of her self-control, she took a deep breath, held her shoulders back and head high and walked with dignity from the room.

Thirsk wasn't, had never been, and never would be the man she had invented, the ruggedly handsome hero who cleaned the streets of crime, the passionate lover who adored every inch of her body and mind. That man didn't exist. He

287

was a figment of her imagination, the one that kept insisting that the grass was greener on the other side of wherever. She couldn't love him, because he wasn't really there. The truth was, with his annoying raised eyebrow and distasteful sneer, Thirsk was a sad and lonely man, overweight and unfit, scruffy and drab.

Thirsk had no time to dwell on the unpleasant exchange and was grateful Carol had gone, because he had plenty to do without worrying about a silly woman caught in a mid-life crisis. He peered through the window to find Joyce, and was about to call her in when his phone rang.

Outside his office, Joyce had been discreetly watching the exchange with interest, and when Toni ran after the distressed woman who had exited, she smiled.

"Mum, what are you doing here?" Carol had shown so little interest in her career, Toni didn't think she even knew where the police station was. She trotted into step as her mother, jaw tensed and watery eyed, neared the lift, jabbing at the button vigorously to summons it. "Mum, why are you crying?"

Carol stepped inside and Toni jumped in before the keen doors closed. "Mum. Talk to me. You've been to see Th…" It dawned on her and she shuddered. "Oh my god, I thought it was the drink talking last night, but it's true, isn't it? You had an affair with Thirsk."

Joyce waited for Thirsk to end his call and sauntered into his office, closing the door. "So that's who she was, Toni's mother. No wonder you showed affection for Toni, because you're in love with her mother."

"Keep your nose out of my business, it's nothing to do with you."

"I know it's not. Why don't you go after her?"

"Fuck off and butt out."

"Does Toni know?"

A sharp rapping on the door startled them both, as did a furious Toni bursting in with the answer. "You disgust me, Richard Thirsk. You knew she was married. You knew she had a family. Why did you do it? Was she just a neat shag while you waited for the next gullible housewife to come along? That's my fucking mother, you know?"

He took it on the chin, with not a word in his defence, yet his silence infuriated her more. "My parents have been together for over twenty years and you were willing to risk their marriage for your own fucking carnal desires. You make me fucking sick, do you know that? And to think that all this time I've been desperate to work with you. Well, you can shove that up your arse and smoke it."

Toni had no idea what she was saying, her tirade out of control, and Joyce guided her from the room, pacifying her. "Come on, dear, do you fancy a spot of lunch? I know a lovely place just around the corner. *The Gallery*, I'm sure you know it. We can talk things through."

Toni raced down the stairs, determined to be left alone, but when Joyce reached the bottom she had calmed down. She realised she needed to get the dreadful situation off her chest, and she had heard the restaurant was splendid, so she accepted Joyce's offer. They strolled through the icy wind, clutching their jackets close against the cold, and soon reached the tiny, elegant eatery. The maître d' recognised Joyce, welcoming her into the warmth with a beaming smile, and led them to a private back room, each of the four tables unoccupied. Toni and Joyce sat on the chairs he politely pulled out for them. "Can I get you something to drink, ladies?"

"I'll have a pint of cider." Toni never drank cider, she hated the taste, but she was feeling rebellious.

The waiter was flustered and stepped from foot to foot, imploring Joyce to remedy the situation, and she smiled at him, winking. "She's not quite herself today. Could we just have a jug of water at the table for now please, ice but no lemon. Could you give us a couple of minutes to choose our meals?"

He was relieved, the idea of a woman drinking from a pint glass in his restaurant was terrible. "Of course, Doctor Frobisher."

"I heard Toni found out about your fling with Carol." Wainwright let himself into the office without knocking and Thirsk was annoyed. "Not a good day, eh?"

"How do you even know that? This place is like Chinese fucking whispers." Thirsk had had enough of the day already and was itching to go home and bury himself in a stiff drink.

"I've, er, got Cherry Adams outside, with her aunt. They want to see you."

"For fuck's sake, how many more bloody women do I have to endure today?"

"I'll sit in with you." Wainwright showed the girl and Mrs Robinson in and pulled up an extra chair.

Cherry sat, more enthusiastic than before, and began. "After my aunt brought me to see you, it was like something unlocked inside me, and I started to have bad dreams, waking up screaming and sweating. Well, yesterday afternoon Aunty Lynn took me to the doctor."

The all-knowing woman took the story. "I couldn't settle her afterwards, she had tears, the works, and I thought she was beginning to remember what happened to her that day she was drugged."

"And were you, Cherry?"

"It was horrid, just horrid. I remember drinking the drink, it tasted funny, so I put the glass on the table, next to the cake mixes, and I felt a bit funny, so Maria helped me onto a seat. She told me to drink more and I said no, but she forced the glass to my mouth, tipping it inside, and I tried not to swallow, but it was hard. Then Jim came into the room and he said 'Is she ready?' Maria said yes and I remember being carried somewhere. My eyes were closing; I couldn't help it. I was pushed into something tight and dark, and I heard a zip and a click, but then there's nothing after that."

"So you're saying that Maria abducted and drugged you. I thought we already knew that?"

"No, I haven't finished yet. I began to wake up later and I felt like shit. I don't know what time it was, it was dark in the room, wherever I was, but there was a stream of light coming through the bottom of what seemed to be a big, double door."

"Like a garage door?"

"Yes. I was on something warm, but it was a bit prickly on my skin, it made me itch. I couldn't hear anybody, there wasn't any noise, and I didn't know where I was. My head felt fuzzy. I got up and sort of felt my way to the wall, then towards the light, the door, and I could just about make out a table with lots of things on it, and a chair. I went to the door and shouted a few times, but nobody came. My…"

She sobbed, hanging her head, leaving Aunt Lynn to continue. "She says that she felt a lot of pain, you know, down below."

"What sort of pain? Can you describe it?"

"It was sort of inside, and outside, it was stabbing pains, but aching too. It really hurt. I still felt woozy, quite sick, and I made my way back to the prickly thing, I was scared. Then I heard voices, so I got as close to the corner as I could. A little door inside the big door opened and the light blinded me for a few seconds, I squeezed my eyes shut, but I could hear voices. There was a man and he said 'she's awake, you didn't give her enough'. I saw what looked like a woman come up and she forced me to drink something that tasted like the juice had, you know, bitter."

"Why did you think this was a woman?"

"She had long hair and she was short, and she was bony, I could feel her knuckles and arms as she made me drink that stuff. I kind of guessed it had something in it so I struggled, but then someone else was holding me down. He had a beard, I could feel it against my cheek when I was trying to get away."

Thirsk tried to imagine Jim with facial hair and somehow it didn't fit, but Maria's wiry frame did. And he thought of how she had managed to escape their grip, free herself into the big world without a trace. What would Sean look like with a beard? He prompted Cherry to continue. "Did you see the man's face?"

"I'm getting to that."

"She's getting to that." Lynn Robinson showed her support.

Cherry fiddled with her fingernails, her head down in both recollection and shame. "I could feel my head going again and I was forcing myself to stay awake, I knew it was important, but my body wouldn't fight back any more. I felt myself being carried and put on something hard, I guessed it was the table. Then I felt my legs…" She faltered, forcefully withholding tears at the repugnant memories. "I felt my legs being forced apart, I don't think I had any knickers on, and something hard went there, and it was agony, I was trying to scream but there was a hand over my mouth and it made it hard to breathe. I heard a man's voice say 'that'll teach her to wake up before I'm ready for her', then it goes blank again."

Thirsk sat, stilled, revolted by the account, but not letting it show. He tapped the desk with a finger, waiting in case she had any more to say. A minute later she had composed herself and began again. "I don't know how I ended up in my own bed, I don't remember walking there, or being carried, I just don't know. I woke up and I didn't feel well, I felt so sick and my head hurt, and Mum said I could go back to bed, and I did. I stayed there until the next day."

"Did your mother ever say anything about it? Was she concerned about you not feeling well?"

"Well, I was bleeding, you know, down there, and my friend had just started having periods and I thought that this was what it was like. I thought I'd started mine. I knew that Mum kept things for it, you know, pads, so I put some knickers on and used one of those."

"You put some knickers on? Are you certain that you didn't change them, but put some on?"

She hung her head again, thinking, the strain showing in her eyes as the distant and blurry memories taunted her, ebbing and flowing. "No, I didn't have any on. I put a new pair out of my drawer on."

"What were you wearing?"

"My school dress. And I still had my shoes on, even though I'd been in bed, I remember being annoyed with myself in case I'd trodden in dog shit or something and got it on my covers."

"The man and the woman, have you any idea who they were?"

"I thought the woman was Maria, and the bloke sounded just like Uncle Sean."

Thirsk balked at the pet name that the neighbourhood children in Moss End had given the likeable paedophile. "Sean O'Connor?"

"He used to help out with the scouts, and sometimes they did stuff with the guides, so I was quite used to him. I always thought he was nice, he was always giving us sweets, and quick hugs and stuff, he was like a big teddy bear, and he was always smiling. It sounded like him."

"Did Sean ever have a beard, do you know?"

"Up until a couple of years ago, wasn't it, Cherry?" Aunt Lynn leaned forward with importance.

"Yep, he had a beard back then."

"And you'd be prepared to stand in front of a court under oath and say this?"

"She damn well will, filthy bastard." The woman leant close to her charge, stroking her hand. "You've been really brave, Cherry, you've done the right thing. Is this going to be taken seriously?"

"We already have officers searching for them as we speak." And now they had a witness who cemented their suspicions that Maria and Sean had a lot more to do with the hideous activities than they had admitted to. He thanked Cherry enthusiastically for her information and ensured them that another officer would take a video statement later that day. As soon as the women left the room, Thirsk and Wainwright did a high-five. "Now all we need to do is find them."

After finishing a hearty lunch of homemade rabbit stew with fresh, crusty bread, Sean and Maria excused themselves and caught the bus to the train station. As far as Ennis was concerned his friend was merely taking in the area, familiarising himself with the local attractions in order to plan their holiday outings, but Sean and his new 'wife' had other plans. After a comfortable journey, they walked into the estate agency, clutching hands, a blissfully happy couple. "We're looking for somewhere to rent for a few months. It doesn't need to be big, it's just the two of us."

The agent was pleased to help and he showed them brochures of numerous properties, the recession having swayed the house market in favour of buyers and tenants. "Just rental? Because we can help with mortgages if you've ever thought of buying."

"Just rental for now." Sean took a brochure from the growing pile. "There are loads here, are any near schools?"

The man chuckled. "Of course, sir, I'll take all the ones near to schools out, you two lovebirds don't need the hassle of kids running up and down outside your house."

"On the contrary, we love children. My Maz has a wonderful way with youngsters, don't you Maz?" She beamed at him lovingly. "We're keen to foster, so close to an infant or junior school would be a benefit. And we want somewhere yesterday, if you know what I mean."

He smiled and sifted through the stack, pulling out the details of a semi-detached cottage in Norcross Street. "This place has just become empty, it's a decent place, two bedrooms, fairly new kitchen, gas central heating. And it's right opposite a primary school."

Maria snatched the pages and scanned them enthusiastically. "It's perfect, darling, just perfect. Can we see it?"

"I think we have the keys." He shouted over his shoulder. "Briony, do we have the keys to seventeen Norcross Street? I've got a couple here who'd like to see it as soon as."

Seconds later, she threw the keys to him and he grinned. "If you want I can take you there now."

The red-brick cottage was enchanting, built a hundred years before, with a postage stamp front garden behind a low wall. Sean stared at the empty playground across the road and knew it was the perfect place, and the tour of the property was irrelevant, apart from not sowing a seed of suspicion in the estate agent's mind. The couple searched the rooms, smiling and cooing, before declaring on their way out that they loved it. "How soon can we be in?"

The agent shook Sean's hand heartily, amazed to have rented the old and craggy property so quickly. "I'll contact the owner as soon as I get back, Mr?"

"O'Leary, Seamus and Marilyn O'Leary."

Steadman had worked hard to rationalise her feelings about her boss, not wanting to lose credibility through unprofessionalism, and sometimes she wondered what she had seen in him. There was a thin line between love and hate. However, she would have to speak to him eventually, and now seemed as good a time as any. She took the paperwork from her colleague and knocked on Thirsk's door, entering and waving the page. "We've found the flight they were on."

Wainwright and Thirsk stopped what they were doing and gave her their full attention. "They flew from Birmingham at about seven this morning on a flight bound for Dublin."

"They flew out, or just booked tickets for the flight?"

She cursed herself for not having checked, and the notes revealed nothing more. "I don't know, Guv. This is all I have."

"Okay, get somebody to fax their photos to airport security, I want everybody on the flight crew questioned. And the check in desk. Get it circulated and tell them it's urgent. And I want you to contact the police over there, get them the pictures too. I want everybody looking for them."

She was curt, full of contempt. "Do you mean fax, Guv, or email?"

"I don't fucking know, you can send it by fucking courier for all I care, just get them the fucking photos."

Wainwright winked his sympathy to Steadman, and she scowled.

Chapter 28
Hunting the Predators

Toni had done her best in the little time she'd had to straighten up her new home but, with no furniture to place her belongings in, only the most important, everyday items had been unpacked. Her first week as a fully-fledged adult had mostly been spent working, the search for Sean and Maria having taken precedence over everything else. Despite having returned to the second floor offices, the ripple of responsibility over the botched case had touched every person in Castle Street Police Station, and Toni's duties had reflected this.

They had learned a lot in the previous week. Sean and Maria had definitely been on the flight to Dublin, or at least two people who closely matched their descriptions and held passports in their names. But from there the trail went cold. The Irish Garda had deployed many officers to try and locate the runaways, and they had ruled out the possibility of the pair having booked and taken another flight from the country. All the evidence led to Sean and Maria being in Southern Ireland, but nobody knew where. To catch the Saturday night prime-time viewers, Chief Superintendent Bradbury was holding a televised press conference at six, which would also be broadcast in Ireland, to implore the public to help in the search for the two murderous paedophiles. All available officers, including Toni, had been roped in to man the phones, and they were due in the Town Hall at five.

Toni had sorted a healthy snack in place of dinner and was due to pick Sally up soon. She was brushing her hair in the bathroom when the intercom buzzed and she answered to hear her mother's voice, pleading and sad. "Push on the door when you hear the noise, I'm on the top floor, I'll wait at the door so you know where I am."

297

Two minutes later, the two women embraced stiffly and Toni directed her mother to the living room, suggesting she sat on a box. "Tea?"

Carol nodded, wanting to run away, but aware she had to address their problems if she wanted a relationship with her daughter in the future. Toni went to the kitchen, while Carol took in the exceptional view from the window. "Do you mind if I take a look around, see what your flat's like?"

"As long as you don't poke around in my things. And if you've got anything bad to say, keep it to yourself, because I love it here."

Carol stepped into the tiny hallway and chose the door opposite the living room, finding the unusual bedroom, clothes scattered everywhere, and imagining it with resplendent wardrobes and a chunky divan bed. "Nice bedroom. I'll get your father to bring your old bed over, though, you can't keep sleeping on that thing."

"Actually that airbed's very comfortable, and anyway, I've been down to that shop out of town, you know, that bed shop, and the bloke told me they've got a sale coming up, so I'll probably get a bargain on a double bed."

Carol's heart sank. Now she had come to terms with her daughter fleeing the nest, she wanted to help her in any way she could, but Toni's stubborn streak had always been a problem. "If you're sure." She glanced at the other side of Kendrick through the window, rolling Chilterns in the background. "You've got great views."

"I know. I feel like the all-seeing eye up here."

Carol tried the next door, which revealed a small and functional shower room. "No bath? How on earth do you manage?"

Toni sighed; her mother just couldn't help herself. "I prefer showers, they're cleaner than bathing in your own filth."

The next door was the kitchen, and Toni was filling the mugs with hot water when Carol walked in. "Wow, this is amazing." She gazed around, fingers running along the worktops, stroking the opulence. "It's big for a small flat, isn't it?"

The backhanded compliment slapped Toni's cheek and she restrained the brewing sarcasm. "It's very big, yes. It's my favourite room. Well, after the bedroom. Well, actually, I love it all, I love it here." She handed her mother a mug of tea and took her own, and they returned to the living room.

Carol sat on a sealed box and Toni sat cross legged on the floor. "We'll need to get you some furniture, we can have a look in Ikea, or maybe Argos…"

"Stop it." She breathed deeply to withhold her tongue. "Mum, you've got to stop this control thing, this trying to organise me thing. I'm a big girl now, I'm twenty and I've left home. This is my gaff and I'll decide what I want in here, and where from, not you. You can't keep doing this."

Affronted, Carol couldn't argue back, her hidden agenda was too important. "I'll try. It's just I've spent so many years having to run your lives, you, Leon, Maisie, organising everything for school, your extra tuition and clubs, what you're going to wear, eat, say even, sometimes. It's so hard to stop; it's all I know. But I'll try."

The commanding tone she had always used to justify herself when she didn't get her own way with Toni – with all three of her children – wasn't apparent, and Toni realised her mother was trying hard to make amends. "You know, Mum, I could really do with your help on colour schemes, and you're a dab hand at making curtains. If you'd like to, that is."

Carol smiled gratefully, and both women recognised that an important step had just been taken in the transformation of their relationship. They sipped their drinks in comfortable silence, until Carol recalled Pam's words from the week before. "Oh, I forgot, I've been meaning to tell you, it's about a case Pam says you're working on, about Jim Collins."

"I'm not on that case any more, I was transferred back down to the second floor. Anyway, what about him?"

"I used to know him, that's all, he worked for your father around the time you were born, maybe a couple of years after. I knew his daughter, you know, the one who killed herself. Not well, obviously."

"Yeah, that was pretty harsh. She wasn't the brightest of sparks and she was pretty messed up, but it's a shame it all ended like that. We were trying to get some help for her. Thirsk," her face crinkled with distaste, "was with her when she jumped, he took it pretty badly."

Carol snorted, also awkward at the mention of her former lover's name. "Richard with emotion? That'd be a first."

The ice was broken and both women were on unfamiliar territory. Toni regarded her once-pretty mother, whose deepening lines and unflattering eye-bags showed her tiredness. "Why did you do it, Mum? Dad's a good man, he doesn't deserve to be treated with such disrespect."

Carol shifted her feet, sipped her tea, fiddled with her hair, anything to avoid answering, but she knew she couldn't. "I could give you a hundred – a thousand – reasons, but I'm not going to make excuses. I did it, and it was wrong. I wish it had never happened, but it did, and I have to live with that and try to make the best of things."

"That's very, um, unlike you, I mean, a very adult way of looking at things." Toni hadn't meant to be rude and she tried to backtrack, but Carol held a hand up to quieten her.

"I've made lots of mistakes, Toni, I'm human, and we all make mistakes. Every day is a new experience, things will happen in that day that have never happened before and sometimes you make the wrong choices. I've made bad choices in all manner of things, but the only thing you can hope for with mistakes is that you learn from them."

Toni nodded slowly. "What did you learn from your affair with him?"

Their eyes mirrored each other's, before Carol broke the spell and bowed her head. "I've left your father."

"You've fucking done what?" Suddenly she was standing, looming over her mother's broken, humble frame.

Carol stared up, face crumpled with anxiety, imploring her daughter to understand. "Just for a short while to think things through, your dad's in total agreement, he says he needs space too. In fact, I was kind of wondering if you could put me up, just for a week or so." She waited for the explosion and it happened in a nanosecond.

"I don't fucking believe you. I can't take your fucking side; I love my dad. You should be right back there apologising until he forgives you, not fucking leaving him."

Now Carol was also standing. "He agrees it's the best thing right now."

"And who's going to cook his dinner, and clean the house, and keep up with the washing? Who's going to help Leon and Maisie with their homework? Who's going to keep the bathroom clean, hoover? What about packed lunches?"

"That's exactly it." The words rang through the building, bouncing from the walls, impacting over and over. "All those chores, all those boring, tedious, mundane jobs, the jobs that nobody else wants to do, that's what my life consists of. Picking up after people, tidying their mess, putting things away, cleaning, scrubbing, day in, day out. And the worst thing? You know what the worst thing is? Never, ever, do I get a thank you. Just once in a while, a thank you for the clean washing, or the dinner, or the clean house, or the empty bins. But none of you see me, I'm there, I'm right with you, but you can't see me."

Carol was spent, the words that had been teetering on her lips for months – years, maybe – had finally spilled and she had nothing left to give. She took her handbag and keys, walking to the door.

"No, Mum, don't go." There was no anger left in the room, just sadness and guilt. "I'm so sorry that you feel like this, I've never looked at it from your point of view. I never realised, but I can see it now. I'm so sorry." This time their embrace was overflowing with warmth and a new understanding, and the mother and her baby clung to each other, not wanting the moment to fade away.

The Town Hall heaved with people, civilians and police alike, all preparing for the grand event that was due to happen shortly. A conference room had been set up with a stage at one end, complete with a podium for Bradbury and a few chairs for his assistants, and rows of chairs for journalists and their crew covered the large room. Thirsk and Wainwright had been working in conjunction with the Garda in Southern Ireland, who had been helping tirelessly in their search for Sean and Maria, and had finally left their offices to join the hubbub, ready to offer backup to the Chief Superintendent should he need any further information when questioned by the media.

Another hall had been transformed into a makeshift incident room, with rows of desks, each with a headset, an A4 notepad and a couple of pens, and officers of all ranks floated around, gradually taking seats for the anticipated influx of calls, of which most would end up being disregarded. At quarter to six the final call was made over the Tannoy system for everybody in the building to take their places. "Please ensure that all mobile phones are turned off." Toni hurriedly took hers from her pocket to follow orders, but noted a text from her brother and checked it. *'Glad mum safe. Dad ok 2. Will luk afta him promis'.*

Remembering her mother's statement at the eleventh hour, she checked no one was looking and hastily typed out a reply before killing the phone. 'Tell Dad to watch the news. I might be on it. Mum says he knows Jim Collins.'

At five to six Bradbury took to the stage, stroking his hair self-consciously as a make-up artist powdered the shine on his face and a sound technician checked his microphone and earpiece. Behind him, Thirsk, Wainwright, and two other detectives sat on the panel, alongside the Mayor, John Rubbledump, and a prominent criminal psychologist, Jaswinder Kumar.

Cameras were already flashing in the audience and a low murmured humming blanketed the room. The countdown

302

began, with ten seconds until airtime – four, three, two, one – Chief Superintendent Bradbury swallowed his nerves. "We have called you together today to appeal to the public to help us find two people who we believe were involved with the murder of six-year old Melissa Barton on the eighth of October. We already have a man, Jim Collins, in custody, but new evidence has come to light that shows he didn't work alone, but was aided by his wife, Maria Collins, and her brother, Sean O'Connor, who are having an," he cleared his throat, "incestuous relationship." Behind him, the stage lights came on, highlighting the huge pictures of Sean and Maria that served as a backdrop.

He continued after the gasping subsided, explaining the website, the unidentified girls who had also suffered the abuse, the victim who had come forward, and finally the details of their journey to Ireland – the last time they had been seen. "After the flight to Dublin, the trail goes cold. From our investigations we are confident that they didn't take a further flight, which means they are currently in Ireland, but we need to know where. If you have seen either of them, it's imperative that you let us know, because we fully believe that they will continue with their abhorrent activities if we don't intercept them. And I stress, if you know of their whereabouts, please don't try to tackle them alone as they're unpredictable and dangerous."

The two-minute plea was succinct and informative, and the audience were invited to ask questions. In the incident room a couple of officers were already taking calls, scribbling details on their pads to be followed up if necessary. Sally's line buzzed and she grinned excitedly at Toni, who sat at the desk beside her. "Here we go." She clicked the button and began the given spiel. "Hello, can I take your name please?" She wrote the details swiftly. "And your phone number. Thanks. How can I help you?"

Sean and Maria lay in bed, having not left it, apart from when making drinks or food, since the night before, after finally picking up the keys from the estate agent. They were oblivious to the manhunt, and when they switched on the television, flicking through the channels, and saw their faces on the screen, both paled, their mouths falling open. "Oh no."

"Shhhh." Sean leant closer, turning up the volume with the remote control. When the piece had finished, the newsreader took over to detail the other news items of the day and Sean clicked the telly off. They sat in silence, gobsmacked.

Eventually Maria managed a squeak. "What now?"

Sean wrapped a protective arm around her shoulders, hugging her close. "It's okay, my beard's growing, and with the glasses I look totally different. We'll need to cut your hair, and I'll pick up a brown dye to colour it tomorrow. You'll have to stay inside until then, and perhaps if you start wearing your own glasses more, they make you look totally different. Nobody's going to find us, I promise, it's all going to be fine. They can't have anything on us, or else they wouldn't have had to appeal to the public. Come on, we'll be fine. Give it a week and all the fuss will have died down."

Seven miles away Ennis sat with his wife on their chintz sofa, the sofa that had recently seated two known sex-offenders, and they were speechless. Ennis picked up the phone and dialled the number on the screen. He gave his details and explained his unwitting involvement to the man on the other end of the line. "They left yesterday, said they were going back to England. They said it was a holiday, I had no idea they had been involved in anything like this."

Over three hundred miles away, Dan Fowler also picked up the phone, hoping he would find his daughter on the other end of the line, but unsurprised when he didn't. "Is there any chance of speaking to Toni Fowler, she's one of your team manning the phones?"

"I'm afraid not, sir, but I can make sure a message is passed on to her."

"No, thank you. I'll catch up with her later." Dan dropped the receiver in its holder and immediately tried Toni's mobile number, but the message told him she was unable to take the call. "Leon, Maisie." He turned the volume on the television down. "I'm going over to see Toni."

"Dad, you can't, Mum's there."

"N'ya ha, der! That's why he wants to go over, dumbo. He's missing the fireworks."

"Shut up, Maisie, you can be such a child."

Dan had his head in his hands. "No, those two sickos on the telly, I think I might know where they've gone, Jim used to talk about it a lot, said it was Maria's dream to live there."

"Well, why didn't you just tell the police that?" Leon asked.

"If you're going to Toni's, can I come and watch the argument?"

Dan stood, angry, confused, lost. "You know, I can understand why your mother needed time out; you two are bloody hard work. Leon, help me dismantle Toni's bed; I don't know what she's been sleeping on, but your mum's going to need a bed, we can't expect her to sleep on a sofa."

"Toni says she hasn't got a sofa; she was moaning about it earlier."

"All the more reason to bring the bed then."

Their assistance on stage no longer needed, Thirsk and Wainwright had offered to help in the incident room, and joined the rabble, taking phone calls, documenting leads, sifting out the prank calls. It was late and, so far, no real developments had come to light. The Garda had visited a couple who lived in a village on the southern Irish coast near Cork, and were confident that the guests they had hosted for the previous week were the two escapees, but without knowing where the couple had gone next, they were still no closer to finding them.

Garda activities around the area had been stepped up, with extensive house calls planned for the next day, and all sea and air ports, and also flight companies, were to be circulated with details and photos of Sean and Maria. The company they had hired a budget car from confirmed that the vehicle had been returned, as expected, the day before. There were no further sightings, as yet.

The late evening news showed a condensed version of the press conference, again showing the phone number for the incident room, and the number of incoming calls picked up again, but by midnight they began to peter out. Andy Feldman, who had also been part of the team answering calls, wheedled his way between the two desks where Toni and Sally sat, and leered at them in turn. "We're sending all but a skeleton staff home now, so you two can pack up and go. Fancy a drink before you head home?"

"In your fucking dreams. Serge." Toni was tired, and unwanted sexual advances were the last thing she needed.

"You're a bitch, Fowler. You'll pay for that on Monday." His rat eyes narrowed with contempt.

"Yeah, yeah, give it up. Come on, Sal, I'll give you a lift."

Thirsk caught up as they left the room and he blocked their exit with his huge frame. "Toni, I need to talk to you."

She'd had enough and glared at him with contempt. "I've got nothing to say to you, please excuse me."

"It's important, it's about Julia and Baby Robbie, I really need your help on this one." He glanced at Sally. "In private."

Toni rolled her eyes, following him to the corridor, where he pushed her into the relative privacy of a nook underneath the impressive staircase. She was angry, whispering, "Look, my search for the truth behind Baby Jane and all that caboodle is over. I know who the baby was, I know who the mother was, and I know why the baby was dumped. It's over for me, and you can't blackmail me with it any more."

"It's not about that, it's…"

"Then what is it about, then? You know, I just don't care now. I don't work for you and I never will again — by choice." She lowered her voice further, aware that ears were everywhere and gossip was rife in the force, and there was no way she wanted the news that her mother had succumbed to Thirsk's unapparent charms spread across the station for the

306

amusement of her colleagues. "You disgust me. The idea of you and my mother, it's just hideous. Your morals, or lack of them, stink. But I'll tell you what, my family — we're stronger than that. Your sordid affair, it may have caused ructions, but it won't split my parents up. But, and I mean every single word of this, I don't ever want to see your fucking face again, I don't ever want to hear your fucking voice again. You're nothing to me, a big, fat, scruffy ball of nothing. Now fuck off and leave me alone."

She marched out of the Town Hall, her point well and truly made, but Thirsk, shamed and downhearted from her harsh lashing, trotted after her. He tagged her shoulder and she turned, fire in her eyes. He meekly passed her a small envelope, which she snatched from his hand, and he shuffled away, beaten.

With Leon's help, Dan had unscrewed Toni's bed and loaded it into his estate car, along with the rolled and tied mattress. He bid his children goodnight and drove to his factory to pick up two folding seats, concerned that his daughter and wife had nowhere to sit in Toni's new flat, and finally found St. Martin's Place.

Carol had never operated an intercom before and became even more flustered when her husband's voice came through. She pressed a series of buttons, hoping one of them would unlock the main door. Smoothing her hair and straightening her clothes as her husband climbed the stairs, she opened the door to see the familiar — and welcome — face. "Dan. You found me."

"Yes." He held out the chairs, one in each hand. "Leon told me that Toni doesn't have a sofa so I picked these up for you to sit on."

She took them to the living room and called back as an afterthought, "You'd better come in. Unless that was all you wanted." She hoped that he would stay; she had only left that afternoon and it surprised her that she missed him.

They made small talk in the neutrality of Toni's flat, each skirting the underlying issue of their rocky marriage, and eventually Dan traipsed to the car a few times to pick up the pieces of the bed to build in Toni's absence. Both wanted to address their problems, lay them out and sort them for good, but neither dared. "Did you see that business earlier, on the telly?" Dan lifted the mattress onto the bed ready for Carol put the sheet, pillows and quilt on.

"The press conference? Yes, our Toni was one of the constables manning the phone lines."

"I know. I tried to get through to her because, well, that's not important, anyway. Do you remember Dim Jim Collins?"

"Yes, I remember him, he didn't have the kind of face you'd forget, really."

The atmosphere was awkward, but neither wanted Dan to leave. However, when they heard Toni's key in the door they were both relieved and went to greet her. "Dad, what are you doing here?" She dared to hope. "Are you two, you know, well..."

"No, love. It's okay, we're not fighting, but we do both need some space." Carol marvelled at the way her husband always instilled a calmness in people, with his gentle manner and common sense. "I came over for a couple of reasons, and the first is," he dragged Toni to her bedroom by the sleeve, "da da! What do you think?"

The well-loved bed suited the room perfectly and Toni threw her arms around his shoulders, grinning widely. "Dad, you're a star."

"I thought that if you had your bed, your mother would be able to sleep on the airbed. I also borrowed some cheap fold-up chairs from the factory so you've got somewhere to sit until you get yourself sorted out."

Carol smiled at his thoughtfulness, her love for him re-igniting with every word he uttered. "You look tired. How did it go this evening?" Toni and her father sat on the temporary seats in the living room, while Carol prepared hot drinks in the kitchen.

"It was okay, there have been a few sightings reported, and they found where they've been staying the past week, but they moved on yesterday so are still on the loose."

"That's the other reason I came tonight, you see, I phoned in, but they wouldn't let me speak to you. I wanted to tell you first, not get involved if it's all just inconsequential. It's just, well, Jim Collins used to work for me, we called him Dim Jim."

"Yeah, Mum mentioned it earlier."

"Well, the reason I thought it might be important was because Jim was always mentioning that it was Maria's dream to live in Southern Ireland in the place her family originated from. I just wondered if they could possibly have gone there."

"What was it called?" She hung to his words, hopeful.

"I don't know." He shook his head, willing his memory to work. "I can't remember the actual name of the place, it was years ago, all I recall is it was on the western coast and had a long name, started with a 'B', I think, Bally, Ballin something, maybe. Has anybody asked Jim, I'm sure he would know, and you've got him locked up, haven't you?"

"Yes, I believe he was remanded this week, but I've been off the case for a week, so I don't know any more than that. I'll tell you what, you do your best to remember, and I'll mention it to Th..." she halted herself quickly, "Wainwright, I'll mention it to Wainwright. Even if it's no good to them, at least we've given them the option, eh?" Toni leant across and held her father's hand, whispering. "Is everything okay with you and Mum?"

He beamed lovingly, reassuring. "Me and your mum are going to be fine. Just fine."

Chapter 29
A Family Reunited

The first four weeks in their new home had passed without a hitch, despite two house calls from the Garda, who failed to recognise them, making enquiries on their whereabouts. They had watched the news avidly to keep up with the investigation and, as Sean had promised, it hadn't stayed on the screens for long, the public bored with the lack of results.

The transformation in Maria had been unbelievable. Sean had shown hidden talents when masterfully chopping her wiry, grey locks into a neat, shoulder length, layered bob, with a fringe that took years from her face. The colour change, now a shiny brunette, had reduced her age further, and the glasses, rarely worn before through self-consciousness, gave her image an intelligent edge. Sean had been helping to tone her bad language down, and lose the Berkshire accent she had adopted regardless of her original soft Irish lilt.

Sean's short hair was growing rapidly, bushier and un-styled, and his beard was progressing nicely. Coupled with Maria's amazing metamorphosis, not only had the public been fooled on their expeditions to furniture and food stores, but the Garda hadn't batted an eyelid when stood on their doorstep.

They had been nervous at first, although the stronger Sean ensured he did his worrying in private to avoid Maria fretting further, but as they morphed into their new characters, Seamus and Marilyn O'Leary, their appearances greatly altered and her manners improved, their confidence had grown. Although they didn't socialise, they had met the neighbours without any suspicion arising.

Sean had been a hard-worker, and sensible with money, so purchasing new furniture hadn't been troublesome, and bit-by-bit the items were delivered to the tiny abode, squeezed through the low, wide doorframe with difficulty. Every day, the homeliness on the inside of the cottage edged closer to that of the outside.

Sean watched through the window of the front room, the winter clouds grey and gloomy. It was the first time he had dared to act on his hobby in the cottage, although it had been on his mind constantly – a tempting, provoking fantasy that intensified with each passing day. It was half-past eight in the morning, and he had left Maria in bed to have a lengthy lie-in. She knew what he was doing, they had no secrets from each other, and she had no objection to him looking at the children, nor with him pleasuring himself as he watched, but they had fervently agreed that there would be no more abductions. She had explained how unwanted it made her feel, and he had insisted it had been Jim's compulsion, not his.

Through the net curtain, soon to be replaced by a slatted blind that would enable him to photograph the children clearly, he drank in the features of the innocent girls, their faces podgy and cute, hair neat in pigtails and plaits, all wrapped up warmly against the chilly wind, and his mouth salivated, his penis eager. The fierceness of his excitement was intoxicating, and his orgasm became unstoppable, grunting and gasping as his imagination ran riot.

Spent, he knew he had touch their pretty little bodies with hidden pleasure pockets again. He would have to work on Maria, but manipulating her wasn't difficult. He had been doing it all his life.

Toni's heart was heavy as she drove through the gateway into the grounds of the cemetery, and it weighed further when she saw the three parked cars. Joyce Frobisher's caused no concern, and Simone's only a little, but she groaned at the thought of coming face-to-face with Thirsk again. Watching her beloved parents rebuilding their marriage over the past month, of counselling her mother despite hearing details she would prefer to have never known, of seeing her father broken, lonely and scared, her hatred for Thirsk had escalated.

311

It had been easy to avoid him at work, but here, at Julia's funeral, it would be impossible and disrespectful.

On the night of the press conference, believing the envelope Thirsk had given her would contain a pathetic note of apology, a grovelling, selfish explanation, she had stuffed it unopened into her pocket. But when she'd finally relented, she had been surprised to find an expensive invitation to Julia's burial on the nineteenth of November. She had opened it just in time.

It was a dull day, setting the perfect scene for the sombre occasion. Wrapping her anorak closely around her, the whipping wind biting her extremities, Toni steeled herself with a deep breath and strolled around the corner to the entrance of the building, and she cursed under her breath when she spotted Thirsk outside, having a cigarette. She nodded to him politely, saying nothing, and he did the same, before taking another drag.

She found Joyce in the lobby and smiled, greeting her with a friendly handshake, and Joyce nodded to an elderly man. "This is Toni Fowler, I was telling you about her."

Misshapen, bent and gnarled, leaning heavily on his walking stick, the man held out a bony hand, his skin littered with age spots. His voice was weak. "Ah, the girl who found Baby Jane. It's so lovely to meet you, Toni. My name is Bernard Lambert; I'm the pathologist who performed the post mortem on the remains."

Toni shook his hand, shocked at how old the man was, and assumed he must have continued working well into his retirement if he had still been an active pathologist ten years before. "Oh."

He chuckled, a light, bubbling cough rumbling from his chest. "You think I look too old? I can see your surprise."

She backtracked, her eyes darting anywhere but at the veteran. "No, no, not at all."

"I'm only seventy-two, but I have advanced lung cancer. Joyce told me about the funeral and I didn't want to miss it. The Baby Jane case was an enigma that kept us all guessing for a long time, and the least I can do for the poor woman who gave me all those years of intrigue is to say my goodbyes. It's such a sad story."

Toni was uncomfortable with the honesty and her tongue tripped over itself as she searched for something to say. Joyce set her free. "It's okay, Bernard has accepted his fate, and I think it's important that you two have finally had the chance to meet. Bernard was as intense with his work as you are, you're two of a kind."

Wainwright, who had been standing with Simone Lewis, approached the threesome and his eyes twinkled as he smiled at Toni. "I'm glad you came, Toni."

"I couldn't miss it. Julia was a difficult so-and-so, but she didn't deserve this."

"No, twenty-three is no age, and after all that pain too. It's a shame her short life was tinged with such horror."

Thirsk joined them, his breath thick with the smell of stale ashtrays. "The coffin's just arrived."

The party of six trundled into a large room, indicated by the funeral directors, and Thirsk hung his head; he knew what was coming next. At the back of the room, handcuffed on either side by two prison guards, was Jim Collins. "What the fuck is he doing here?" Toni's stage whisper wasn't missed and Jim turned, revealing his yellowed teeth as he grimaced at her.

Thirsk spoke quietly, wanting no further interaction with the disgusting man. "I couldn't stop it happening, believe me, I tried everything."

"Did you tell them he abused her?"

"Of course I did, but they reasoned that he had a right to be at his daughter's funeral."

"That fucking stinks."

Joyce leant back and discreetly suggested that Toni stop swearing, and she reddened, embarrassed. "It's a shame the other two didn't show up, then you could have nabbed them, Richard." The joke, as planned, took the attention from Toni and she was relieved.

They took their seats, belittled by the vast room, and presently a casket was wheeled in, highly polished walnut adorned with brass fittings, and the entourage gasped. "Did he pay for this?" Toni still had to learn when to keep quiet.

But she wasn't the only member of the tiny congregation to notice the splendour, and Jim's plaintiff voice piped up from the back. "Fuck me, you don't half get a lot from those state funeral grants. This is well posh."

"Really, this was paid for by a grant? I'm with him – fuck me!"

"Toni." Joyce's admonishment was stern. "Shut up, this isn't the place."

A minister took ten minutes to describe the woman he had never met, taking facets of her character, given to him like an instruction manual, to elaborate on and share with his audience. The people who had actually known Julia, albeit for such a short time, recognised that he had glossed over the bad parts and snatched the good to twist her life into something more exciting than it had been.

The subject then turned to her child, the son who had died just before she, and Antony's tiny coffin was carried in and set on a table beside his mother's. There were few words to say, and nobody offered anything further to the minister's brief speech.

"It was brought to my attention that Antony was not the only child Julia had borne in her short life, and I'm very pleased to tell you that the police force's request to the Home Office that Robbie's body be exhumed to be given a proper burial with his mother was granted."

A further, tinier coffin, white to match his brother's, and brass-work to match his mother's, was carried in and gasps rang through the building. "Did you know about this?" Toni directed the question at Thirsk, whose head hung sadly, and Joyce nudged her firmly – 'shhhh' – with her finger to her lips.

The memorial service ended, leaving the few mourners in contemplation as Jim was led through a back door to a waiting van. They solemnly followed the three caskets – a mother leading her sons on their final journey to the grave – through the cemetery, eventually stopping by a newly dug area. One by one the family were laid together in the depths of the ground, united in death as they should have been in life. When the minister had finished his internment speech, Toni stepped forward and threw a single white rose onto the coffins, and trailed after the disbanding congregation.

With no place to go, no après-funeral celebration of life to look forward to, Simone bid her farewell before driving away, back to the doldrums of her job. Joyce helped Bernard into her car, firmly yet kindly, aware that his funeral would probably be the next she would attend. Thirsk despondently climbed into his car, shoulders sagging, and shut the door without a word, but Wainwright hung back for Toni to catch up. "Do you fancy going for a drink?"

"I won't drink anywhere near that man." She jabbed her finger in Thirsk's direction.

"Then I'll come with you, if that's okay. We need to speak."

Thirsk had had the foresight to realise his need to wallow in his sadness after the funeral. Ten years of wondering, of questioning, had finally been concluded with a fitting reunion of a mother and her sons, but the void he felt was inexplicable. He opened a new bottle of single malt as soon as he entered his apartment, the first and only thing he wanted. Taking it to the spare bedroom that he used as an office, a resplendent mahogany desk, wide and deep, topped with an inbuilt green leather blotter, central to the room, he sat on the expensive, adjustable office chair and melted into it, sipping the whisky.

The funeral had been the last-but-one piece to the puzzle, and he grasped the computer printout of a headstone, sparkling white marble etched with charcoal lettering that stated the names and dates of birth and death of the family whose burial he had just attended. They were followed by a short verse: 'In life we were broken, in death we are mended'.

Having attended the funeral, he knew he had chosen the right one; the depth of the phrase was appropriate.

He sat at the desk for hours, the bottle of whisky slowly depleting as he poured one measure after another, sipping and savouring the taste. Food was of no importance, and the burial had provided closure, but the one thing he couldn't come to terms with was Toni's vitriolic dislike of him, which upset him more than he would ever admit.

The doorbell jarred him and he realised he had dozed off. The darkening sky through the tall window roused curiosity of how many hours he had lost and he glanced at his watch: quarter past seven. He wasn't expecting visitors and was tempted to ignore the bell in the hope that whoever it was would go away; he didn't want anyone seeing him inebriated and depressed. But the unwanted caller was persistent and eventually, with a deep sigh, he traipsed to the hallway and answered.

Moments later Toni was in his flat, pleasantly surprised at the elegant décor and ornate furniture, and positively stunned by the tidiness. "Have you come to give me another ear-bashing?"

She shook her head, ashamed. "Nick told me."

"I told him not to tell anyone, the bastard." He retraced his steps to the study and Toni followed without being asked. "I'm pissed, I'm halfway through a bottle of Glenfiddich and I intend to finish it. Would you like some?"

She shook her head again, sitting on the armchair opposite the desk, as indicated. "Why did you do it?"

"Who else was going to pay? She would have got a cardboard box for a coffin, a cheap cremation with no celebration of her life, and she deserved more than that after the horrific life she'd survived for so long."

"You cared about her, didn't you?"

"I thought she was funny. She had a quick wit, despite all her suffering."

She noticed the printout of the gravestone on the desk and took it as he drained another glass of drink. She scanned it, absorbing every word of the touching gesture. Without a word, she stood and moved beside Thirsk. She put her arm lightly around his shoulder and planted a tender, daughterly kiss on his forehead. "I forgive you. Will you forgive me?"

He swallowed hard, stifling the uncommon emotion threatening to break through, and his voice cracked. "There's nothing to forgive."

THE END

Biography

Ricki is a happily single mother of four, and now the elder two have left home she has more time to write and research. Her biggest interest is the study of true crime.

www.rickithomas.com

www.ingramcontent.com/pod-product-compliance
Lightning Source LLC
Chambersburg PA
CBHW030932260626
47169CB00002B/450